beautifully
DECADENT

beautifully DECADENT

L.A. FIORE

ISBN-13: 978-1530169672
ISBN-10: 1530169674

Cover design by Indie Solutions by Murphy Rae, www.murphyrae.net
Rafe's chapter heading sketch and title page sketch by Benjamin Cornelius
Typeset graphics and paperback formatting by Melissa Stevens, The Illustrated Author, www.theillustratedauthor.net

CHAPTER ONE

RAFE

The corridor was lit with fluorescent lights, several of which were flickering, the smell of urine and sweat permeated the air. Distant voices carried down the hall. Raised voices, though whether they were fueled by anger or just boredom, I didn't know.

It wasn't a walk I was particularly familiar with; I had made it often in the beginning, but those visits dwindled as I grew older... hope giving way to bitterness. I had only been nine when the cops showed up at our door and took my dad away in handcuffs. I remembered that day, if not much else from my childhood. Remembered Dad had spent a good portion of the morning on the phone, growing more and more upset with each phone call. He tried to sit me down and talk and yet no words would come. My big, strong dad broke down as he held me close and then the cops came and everything I knew changed. Social Services came for me, a prim woman in a black suit and pinched expression. She took me from my home to a sterile-looking building where I was processed, like *I* had done a crime. I had been allowed to pack some of my things from home before being dropped off at another building that to me felt like a prison for kids.

There I was told I'd be spending the foreseeable future. No one had explained to me what had happened, where my dad was, why I'd been taken from my home. I had been reduced to an item on a checklist to be dealt with accordingly. For weeks I lived in fear and confusion, missing my dad and not understanding why he wasn't coming for me.

Armed robbery, even now I still couldn't equate that violent act with the man I knew. I'd been very young and had few memories of Dad, but what I remembered he'd been a good man. I had to wonder about that now, since he'd also been a man who had walked into a bank with a loaded gun. I never knew my mother, only that she gave me up and never pressed for visitation.

The media circus that followed Dad's arrest and conviction had been crazy. People swarmed; family services, lawyers, churchgoers looking to do a good deed for the poor little boy who now found himself an orphan because of his father's criminal activities. There were the sympathizers that thought Dad's sentence was too harsh, and the protesters who thought it wasn't harsh enough. It didn't take long for the buzz to die down, for the swarm to latch on to a newer story, leaving the nine-year-old I had been to fend for myself. There had been a few, after the story went cold, who continued to send letters; one who, even to this day, still stayed in touch. He or she only ever referred to himself or herself as 'A Friend'. I got it; I was the kid of a felon.

The guard led the group of visitors into a room with tables and chairs arranged for quiet conversations between loved ones. Taking a spot near the door, I waited for the one on the far side of the room to open.

He was one of the first people out; even with the passing of a quarter of a century, he looked exactly the same. More startling, I looked just like him.

He settled across from me. The man obviously took advantage of the gym because he was huge.

"Rafe, how are you doing?"

It was weird sitting across from my dad not as the kid I'd been but a man. I never really put much thought into it, all the time we missed. What was the point? It's not like thinking about it was going to change anything. But there were moments when bitterness gnawed at my gut because life growing up had sucked, not all of it, but much of it. I suspected had Dad not acted so foolishly, life would have been a good deal better.

He studied me in that way he had, direct and intense, as he waited for a reply. "I'm good, but what about you? You're getting out." After twenty-five years, the man was going to be free. How the hell must that feel?

"Fucking can't wait. To no longer be at the mercy of the guards, to do and say as I please, to eat what I want, to sleep when I want, to taste and smell a woman. Yeah, I am seriously ready to get out of here."

"Do you have a place to stay?"

"Yeah, a buddy found something for me."

I'd offer the carriage house at my place, even had room in the main house, but being in close quarters with someone I really didn't know any more, particularly being my father, I think it'd be awkward on both sides—as awkward as it was sitting across from him now and seeing a stranger.

"Why did you do it? Walk into that bank with a gun? I don't remember much, but I do remember we were doing okay." A little late in asking that question, but I'd been too young at first and then too bitter.

I wasn't sure what fueled the expression on his face—irritation, shame, regret or a little of all three. He rubbed a hand over his head and leaned back in his chair. "Money was tight. I had lost my job. The money I was making at the gas station was minimum wage and not cutting it. Bills were piling up and I couldn't get ends to meet. When I was approached, I was desperate, had convinced myself no one would get hurt and I could climb out from under the growing debt. It was stupid, so fucking stupid. I had never held a gun before that day."

"How did you meet them, the ones you did the job with?"

"Lucas Steele, I'll never forget that fucker's name. He was the one who recruited me. He and Jackson approached me at the neighborhood bar. Chatted me up for months. Over beer, we commiserated over the economy and losing our jobs. And then one night Lucas proposed his plan. It seemed so simple, in and out."

"Who shot the guard?"

"Lucas. The plan had been to take money only from the tellers. I thought we were being smart about it, hitting the bank early when there would be minimal people. The guns were for show. Flash it, get a stash, and out. They weren't even loaded, or so I had been told. But the first thing Lucas did was head into the vault. We were there for money and yet he comes out with nothing. I mean what the fuck? Another fact I've come to accept, I'd been played. He'd done it before, robbed banks, I've no doubt about that."

"Any idea how they ended up dead?"

"No. I've often wondered if I hadn't turned myself in would I have shared their fate."

"Yeah. In light of the alternative, twenty-five years doesn't seem so bad."

"My thoughts exactly. I wasn't young, Rafe, but in a lot of ways I was. A single father trying to make ends meet and my desperation made me stupid."

"You've paid your debt and in three weeks you'll be out."

"Yeah, to a world that's significantly different than when I went in. But at this point, I don't care. I just want a view that doesn't have bars."

"What time are you being released?"

"I can get a cab."

"Dad, what time?"

"Ten in the morning."

"I'll be out front."

Sapphire was packed, not that it mattered when you knew the owner. Trace and the others were already at his table. I settled on the chair across from him and signaled the waitress for another round. Scanning the dance floor, I didn't see Ember or Darcy.

"Where are your wives?"

It was Trace who answered. "Girls night at my house."

Looking across the table at Trace, he was grinning into his beer. Probably thinking about his three-year-old, Faith, and her obsession with painting nails. She tried to paint mine during one of her visits. She has these doe-eyes that could tempt a person to do just about anything. I'd been spared, Ember took pity on me, but I suspected Trace didn't dodge that bullet as often as he'd like.

"Emily had a suitcase of nail polish, brushes and makeup. She's three. I don't understand why Darcy encourages that." Lucien sounded disgusted, but he was grinning like an idiot. The man was completely besotted with both his wife and daughter. Enough that Emily often brushed and braided her dad's hair. I don't know that he knows I know this, but Darcy was very forthcoming one night after one too many glasses of wine.

Taking a pull from my beer, my thoughts turned back to my dad. I never really talked about him. My friends knew; Trace and Lucien had both been around when I was in my teens and had started getting into fights, doing petty crimes. I was acting out. At thirty-four, I got it. At fourteen, I was just angry, really fucking angry.

"My dad's getting out soon."

All eyes turned to me. "I saw him today. It's kind of a mind fuck that the next time I see him we'll be standing outside Sing Sing and not in it. I asked him, for the first time ever, why he did it. The bills were piling up, he couldn't see a way around it, he'd lost his job and the temporary one he had wasn't paying enough. I can't imagine I'd walk into a bank with a gun, but then I don't have a kid to feed. I guess it's different when you have others depending on you."

"You think you'll reconnect with him now that he's getting out?" Trace asked the question I'd been rolling around my head since seeing Dad earlier. There was a part of me that was okay with leaving our relationship as is, but I had missed him. Besides, he was likely going to feel off-balance and would need familiar faces to help him acclimate. And I had Sister Margaret, the nun who had helped raise me at St. Agnes, to thank for that annoying—always do the right thing—conscience.

"I think so, if for no other reason than to help him adjust to life outside."

"And it will be an adjustment, shit, just technology alone has changed so drastically."

Lucien wasn't wrong.

"We talked about the case, how the two who did the job with him ended up dead. I wonder if the cops ever figured out what happened to them."

"You could always ask Josh to look into it, even Shawn since he's a licensed PI now." Trace suggested.

"Oh yeah? Good for him." Josh was Ember's uncle and Shawn was her dad who had moved from Philly to the Bronx to be closer to his daughter and granddaughter. "Maybe I'll give them a call. It might be nice to give Dad closure on what happened to those two. I'm not sure how much he was entitled to hear while in jail."

"Josh is working on a few things for me already. Do you want me to ask him the next time I talk to him?" Lucien asked.

"Yeah, thanks."

Trace signaled to the waitress before changing the subject, "I'm interviewing for a new pastry chef at Clover."

That's not something you hear every day. "How the hell do you interview for a chef?"

"They have to feed me."

chapter two

Avery

I had never seen one so big and so perfectly formed. I was ruined for all others, nothing could compare to the perfection before me. My fingers itched to touch it, feel it. I wanted it in my mouth, wanted to feel the texture on my tongue, the burst of flavor sliding down my throat would surely have my eyes rolling into the back of my head.

"Oh, Avery, your soufflé turned out perfectly."

Hunching down, getting eye level with the masterpiece, I couldn't help the grin because Mom was right; I totally rocked this.

"Is that what you're preparing for the interview?"

Interview, just thinking about it had my stomach quivering. Pastry chef, I was doing it, reaching for my dream, and even being deliriously excited, there was a healthy dose of fear too. After graduating high school, I'd worked at the local bakery and I enjoyed it. In the beginning, I liked the routine and the familiarity of what the customers wanted—vanilla and chocolate, cupcakes and birthday cakes, éclairs and donuts. After a while it got old. I wanted to do more, wanted to express myself through my desserts, so I made the move

I'd wanted to but feared I wasn't good enough for. At twenty-four, I enrolled in classes, four years studying baking and pastry arts at the Culinary Institute of America in Hyde Park, New York. I did well in school, really well, picking up on the techniques with ease. I graduated with honors and still I was floored when I had a few interviews lined up before the ink had dried on my diploma. The interview I was preparing for now was pastry chef for Clover—a posh restaurant in Manhattan. The executive chef went by the name of Chef but his real name was Francois Moree. He was a legend, anyone who was anyone in the culinary world knew of him. He studied at Le Cordon Bleu in Paris, most notable for his mastery in spice infusions. The fact that someone of his reputation would be sampling my desserts was surreal. In preparation for my interview, I did a bit of research on the owner of Clover, Trace Montgomery, since he too would be sitting in on the interview. I didn't know anything about him—thank God for the Internet—and discovered he was a self-taught chef who owned a cooking school called Everything. And with the possibility that he was a hands-on boss, a fair assumption since he planned to be present at the interview, my sister and I were enrolled in one of his classes so I could see firsthand how the man worked. In the meantime, I practiced for the upcoming interview in my mom's kitchen, reworking my recipes. I had to prepare three different desserts to wow their palettes.

"I'm practicing technique, but the soufflé is a bit cliché."

"With the chilies and cardamom, it's hardly cliché."

I could bake butter cookies and Mom would think they were the tastiest cookies ever made. The thought brought a smile. Looks were deceiving when it came to Anna Collins now Green. Petite and unassuming, she really was a force to be reckoned with. She was like the flour in a recipe, a staple. Mom and Dad divorced almost fifteen years ago and both had remarried. Dad to Dolly, her name now was Dolly Collins, no lie. Half my dad's age, Dolly had the IQ of a twig and the personality of an enraged badger. Now she was like the powdered sugar on top, without it the dessert may not look as pretty, but you'd likely not miss it. For whatever reason, she didn't like my sister or me. My fifty-year-old father married a twenty-four year old—one year older than my sister—who had more hair than sense, but *she* didn't like us. And it wasn't insecurity or low self-esteem that fed her nastiness. She was just a bitch. Twelve years later, they now lived in Manhattan. That was the one downside if I got the job at Clover, I'd likely see Dolly more often. She'd insist on it so she could look down her nose at me. She didn't work, and though Dad wasn't crazy loaded, he was very well off, enough that Dolly could dress in designer clothes and get her hair and nails done every week…huge life ambitions that one.

Mom married Harold Green, owner of one of the bigger car dealerships in our town. His job was his first marriage, had dedicated his life to it, and now he dedicated his retirement to my mom. They were getting ready for their big adventure: RVing across the country. Harold purchased the largest RV known to man, a small house on wheels. Mom decorated it and had spent the past few weeks stocking it with food.

"You have your hotel room booked?" Mom asked as she dipped her finger in the bowl of chocolate I had melted.

"Yes. You didn't have to pay for it."

"We did. It's just terrible that we aren't going to be around for moral support, the least we can do is make sure you've got a roof over your head."

"You've had this trip planned for almost a year, I only learned of the interview a few weeks ago."

Mom waved off my comment, "Doesn't matter. At least Nat will be around to be your cheering section."

Natalie was my sister; she was five years older than me but sometimes she acted about five years younger. She was scattered, flighty and to those who didn't know her, an airhead but in truth she was a genius. Literally. A brain surgeon. Nat was like the baking powder in a recipe, lots of air bubbles.

"What will you do about your living arrangements if you do get the job? I know staying with Nat is out. Has your Realtor found anything?"

It was true; Nat had offered me her sofa, but her apartment was the size of a closet and the kitchen was nonexistent. These are things I could have learned to adapt to, however her place was a pigsty. I guess working in the field she did, when she got home she let it all hang out. I wasn't going to change her, but I also knew I couldn't live with her.

While attending culinary school, I had lived in a small apartment near the school, but the landlords were catering to the students of the school. I had to move out when I graduated. Natalie had offered to subsidize my living, but no longer being a student it was a point of pride that I earn my own way and since I didn't have a job yet, my current residence was Mom's. I had someone looking for apartments, but so far no luck. "Not ones that are affordable. I didn't realize how much it cost to live in Manhattan when it wasn't being subsidized by the coolest landlords ever."

Something twisted Mom's expression, probably thinking about Dad living in Soho. Dolly insisted, even though they could have gotten a bigger place for the same money just across the river in New Jersey. She wanted the zip code.

"You could always commute from here, there are several lovely homes for sale that are very affordable."

Clearly Mom wanted me here, but our town in Pennsylvania was about two and a half hours from Manhattan by train. Commuting that long held no interest for me. "It's too far, Mom. I'll be spending almost five hours every day on the train." If I didn't land a pastry chef position, I'd be checking out those homes since I doubted I'd find a job at a bakery in New York where I made enough to live there too. "I'll cross the housing hurdle when I get to it."

She touched my hair, tucking it behind my ear—something she'd been doing since I was little. "You're going to get the job. I've no doubt and not just because I'm your biggest fan. You've a gift, Avery. I've known that since your first time in the kitchen when you added the dried blueberries to the chocolate chip cookies, but only after you reconstituted them. You were six."

"You're also my mom, so you're a bit biased."

"Yes, but I also love sweets and yours are my favorite."

"Mine too." Harold stepped into the kitchen wearing pink, plaid shorts and a yellow polo shirt. His gray hair was thick and long, falling to his shoulders. For a man in his sixties, he kept himself in really good shape. Fun, charming and slightly odd, he complemented Mom's more serious nature perfectly. He was the butter in a recipe, adding not just flavor but a welcomed lightness. His focus was on the soufflé on the counter. "Tell me we're eating that for dessert."

Squeezing Mom's hand, happy that she found her soul mate the second time around, I turned my attention to Harold. "I've got to fill you up now, since you won't be getting desserts like this on the road."

Harold flashed me a smile, "That is definitely a strike in the con column."

Standing outside Everything, Natalie was practically jumping up and down. Unlike my petite five foot two frame, Natalie was five foot ten, long and lean, with blond hair that hung past her shoulders and blue eyes that tended to change color depending on what she was wearing. Me, my hair was auburn and my eyes green; my coloring so different from the rest of my family that Nat often teased that I was the mailman's. My mom—knowing I used to have an issue with my figure when looking at my svelte sister—called my build hourglass, which was code for boobs one size bigger than I wanted and a perpetually fat ass. I was okay with that though because I enjoyed every calorie I ate to create the curves I had.

"Nat, if you don't stop acting like you've got fireworks going off in your pants, you aren't going in there with me."

"I am to. I paid."

"I am trying to be discreet, to learn a bit about the man I may be working for. I can't be discreet if you're jumping around like a deranged Jack in the box."

"Cute. I can be discreet."

"I have yet to see that in the twenty-nine years that I've known

17

you."

"I perform brain surgery for a living. I can be cool, calm and collected."

"Well pretend you're prepping for surgery. I mean it, Natalie. I don't want to freak Mr. Montgomery out, have him thinking I'm stalking him or something." The truth was, the reason I was being a bit of a stick-in-the-mud, I kind of *had* cyber-stalked Trace Montgomery. It started out innocently enough, wanting to learn more about my possible future boss, but the man was delicious—very easy on the eyes—so I may have been a little gung ho with my Google searches.

"Fine, I'll behave. Let's go."

"I'm going to regret this, I just know it."

Inside was really cool. Twelve workstations set up with granite counters, Viking ranges and top of the line pots and pans. It was like something you'd see on one of those competition food shows. Natalie wanted to be right up front, I grabbed her arm and led her to the back.

"Discreet remember?"

"Yeah, yeah, yeah."

She said that as she rolled her eyes at me. Ignoring her, I checked out the place; it was packed. Some workstations had four people at them and every single person in the room was female. Before I could comment on that observation, Trace Montgomery appeared from what looked like the office. The pictures on the Internet did not do him justice and he'd been smokin' hot in them. Holy shit, he was sexy. Tall, spiky black hair, steel-blue eyes that were cool and assessing and a body made for sin: thick shoulders and arms, wide chest and narrow hips. It really wasn't a surprise that the room was filled with women, all of whom were staring at him like he was a large—right out of the oven—chocolate chip cookie.

"Holy shit, he's hot." Nat's voice carried.

Even agreeing with Nat, I felt a blush creeping up my cheeks because the woman did not know how to be subtle. Giggles and several agreeing whispers followed Nat's observation. I had to give Trace

Montgomery credit; he didn't seem at all fazed by it.

"Today's class will focus on perfecting your knife skills. It may sound unnecessary, but learning to prep your vegetables in a uniform manner aids in a more even and consistent cooking. We're going to start with onions. I'll demonstrate and then Carlos and I will walk around to answer questions."

"I could listen to him talk all day, stare at him too. Is he married?" Nat asked, at least she whispered that.

I watched Mr. Montgomery, the effortless way he chopped the onion. It was almost hypnotic. When done, he gestured for the class to try on the basket of onions in each kitchen.

"Yeah, and happily. At least according to the tabloids."

"He's delicious. Oh, he's coming this way. Let me cut that onion."

"Given what you do for a living, it doesn't seem like you need this lesson."

Her gaze jerked to me. "Really, and you who bakes needs to learn how to perfect your knife skills?"

She had a point, but this was the only class that both of us were available for. "Fine, but don't show off."

Her grin could definitely be called a shit eating one.

And then she started chopping, the precision and the control. It really wasn't a wonder that Mr. Montgomery walked over to watch. I had my hair pulled up into a knot, but suddenly I wished it were down so I could hide behind it. Natalie finished the onion, the pieces were perfectly uniformed and so finely chopped they almost looked minced.

"It looks to me like you should be teaching this class."

Natalie smiled one of her Natalie smiles that looked as if her brain had dripped out of her ears before she said, "I've just got a knack for the knife, love the feel of it in my hand. You know, it's a rush to have such control over something so deadly."

Oh my God, did she just say that? I was tempted to nail her in the head with an onion, several in fact. I could only imagine what ran through Mr. Montgomery's head especially with the twisted smile she flashed him. What the hell was wrong with her? I was going to

19

kill her and then she said, "I'm kidding. I'm actually here for Avery. She's interviewing with you next week and wanted to get an idea of what you were like."

"Jesus, why don't you give the man my pin number too? What part of discreet did you miss?" I may have screeched that and then realized I did so in front of my possible future boss. My shoulders slumped as I dragged my eyes from my sister, who would be dead as soon as we left the building, and settled them on Mr. Montgomery.

"Avery Collins. I'm sorry about Natalie. We've tried to have her committed but no hospital wants to keep her that long."

He chuckled. It was a nice sound.

"She's actually a brain surgeon, the reason for the skill with the knife. I know that's hard to believe since she doesn't seem to have the sense to find her way out of a paper bag, but she's rather brilliant, especially when her mouth is closed."

"Sisters?"

"Can you tell?"

Another chuckle and then he leaned against the counter and crossed his very nice arms over his equally nice chest. I could see the part of a tattoo on his left arm under his long sleeve. "So how am I doing?"

My focus was on his arm, so I wasn't quite following his question. "I'm sorry?"

"You came to check me out. How am I doing?"

"You're doing very nicely, very, very nicely." Natalie said. I kicked her.

"She has Tourette's and doesn't even know what a filter is. I think maybe this backfired because now you realize I have mental illness in my family."

He laughed out loud in response. "I think I'm looking forward to your interview."

"You won't hold it against me that she and I share blood?"

"No."

"Well that's a relief."

He moved. "It was nice meeting you, Natalie."

"Likewise."

"See you next week, Avery."

"Thank you again for the opportunity."

"You earned it."

I waited until he was out of earshot. "You are so dead."

"Yeah, well now you've one foot up on the other interviewees, he's met you."

"You did it on purpose?"

"Of course I did it on purpose."

I couldn't lie; it was nice to have the introduction over. "Next time share your plans with me."

"And miss seeing you in misery, no way."

"You suck."

"I love you too."

"Let's talk about this, Aidan. You don't want to do that."

Two eyes, like chocolate drops, stared me down from across the counter. If it was a battle of wills he wanted, so be it. Narrowing my own eyes, I shook my head. "I'm telling you, you really don't want to do that."

And then he really did it, scooped up a ladle-full of batter and hurled it in my direction. My cat-like reflexes kept me from getting a face full of chocolate, and while I congratulated myself on my quick moves, he attacked again. This time, I was not so lucky. As chocolate batter dripped down my forehead toward my eyes, I studied my opponent. He was covered in almost as much chocolate as me, but his had been self-induced.

"We need to clean this up before Mommy comes home."

Aidan immediately started giggling.

And then I heard Jessica Brighton, my best friend from grade school, calling a greeting.

Busted.

I turned in time to see as she stepped into the kitchen and then stopped dead. Her eyes went from Aidan to me and back again.

I, being the mature adult, pointed at Aidan. "He started it."

Jessica's hands went to her hips "He's four."

"Are you sure because he's got a hell of an arm for a four-year-old and his strategic thinking is down-right diabolical."

"You were bested by a four-year-old?"

"Bested, no, that's too strong a word." But I totally had been, had my ass handed to me by a toddler.

Jessica breezed into the kitchen and scooped up her son. "Let's get you all cleaned up while Auntie Avery cleans my kitchen."

"Gween the kiwin, gween the kiwin" Aidan started chanting as Jessica gave me the stink eye.

"And there better be cake with all this batter everywhere."

I heard her laughing, Aidan too, as they disappeared up the stairs. They were probably even now talking about my lack of prowess on the battlefield.

The cake had just gone in the oven when I heard the sound of the garage door opening a few minutes before Kit walked into the kitchen. Jessica and Kit were high school sweethearts, married after college and as in love now as they had been then. His blond hair was cut short, his suit tailored around his muscular frame and he always had a smile on his face. I supposed when you were living your dream, you smiled…a lot. As branch manager for one of the larger banks in our town, Kit was known around town, trusted and liked. He was a good guy, like the brother I always wanted.

He flashed me his smile as he dropped his keys in the tray on the counter. "Smells good." Reaching my side, he kissed my cheek. "Where's Jess?"

"She's giving Aidan a bath. He and I sort of had a battle."

Kit's eyebrow rose, as he leaned against the counter and crossed his arms over his chest. "Battle?"

"With batter."

"Who won?"

Blowing a rogue lock of hair from my face, I tried to ignore the question and Kit caught on immediately. "Bested by a four-year-old.

Oh, Avery."

Bested, Kit and Jess even sounded alike. "I don't want to talk about it."

"I can understand why."

He wasn't even trying to control his laughter. It was instinct, lifting the whipped cream covered whisk. Kit moved, backing up from me, his hands up. If he was going for fear, his uncontrollable laughter kind of ruined the effect.

Kit was saved from getting his hair streaked with whipped cream when Jessica and Aidan returned. I'd seen it before, countless times, and every time I got that ache in the center of my chest. Kit's face softened, his eyes just soaking up his family. I envied them. I never had someone who made me feel that. I'd had dates, had lovers, but I never had what Jessica and Kit had.

Kit walked to Jessica and kissed her, long enough that I looked down at my shoes. He took Aidan, who squealed with laughter.

"Hey buddy."

"Dadwe."

"I'm going to get changed. I'll take little man with me."

"Okay. Want a drink?"

"Yeah, a beer. Thanks, babe. I'll be down in a few."

I watched Jessica as she watched Kit and Aidan. "You've got an awesome family, Jess."

"I really do." She turned to me. "Let's get dinner on."

After dinner, Aidan had a small slice of cake before Kit and Jessica put him to bed. I cleaned up the dinner dishes, put the coffee on and was serving the cake when they returned arm in arm, whispering like schoolgirls. Kit's attention shifted to me, well the cake I was cutting.

"That looks fantastic."

He pulled Jessica's chair out before he settled next to her.

"Chocolate raspberry cake with a whipped chocolate icing. It is good, if I do say so myself. Hey, I'm sorry about earlier, the kitchen, but Aidan did start it."

Two sets of eyes turned to me, both thinking exactly the same thing, a sentiment Jessica spoke out loud. "You're blaming a four-year-old."

"Yeah. A freaking military genius four-year-old, who distracted me with assault number one so he could nail me with assault number two."

"You're silly." Jessica said.

Followed quickly with Kit's reply, "That's my boy."

"The cake isn't the only overly sweet thing at this table." I muttered.

"Jealous?"

"You know very well that I am jealous of the two of you, Jessica."

Kit forked up nearly half of the slice I had cut for him and stuffed it into his mouth.

"Can you even taste it?"

He grinned, chewed, swallowed. "Oh, yeah, so fucking good. Are you ready for the interview?"

"Nervous, but ready. Even as crazy as Nat is, I'm glad I've met Trace Montgomery because some of the pressure is off."

"And if you get the job, what's the plan?" Jessica asked.

"I've got my Realtor looking for places in and around Manhattan as well as in New Jersey. Commuting from here is just too far."

"Agreed, I'm going to miss you. I just got you back and you're off again."

"I haven't gotten the job yet."

Kit slid his plate over to me for another slice. "If they don't hire you, they're idiots."

"Can I tell them you said that?"

"Hell, yeah."

chapter three

Avery

Standing outside of Clover, my stomach performed a gymnastic floor routine. Even having already met Mr. Montgomery—thanks to Nat being a nut—I was still racked with nerves. I had spent the better part of two weeks perfecting the dishes I planned to make today. The first was an olive oil and lavender cake with a citrus glaze. The oil olive added not just a unique flavor but also tons of moisture. The second was strawberry ice cream, but the secret was to macerate the strawberries—my preference was a liqueur made of elderflowers—before oven roasting them. The punch of flavor was unreal. And last my twist on a classic, jalapeno/chocolate torte with a ganache drizzle.

Making the desserts wasn't my concern, being good enough for the caliber of restaurant like Clover, I wasn't so sure. Francois Moree's sous chef, Terry, had contacted me asking for the supply list I'd need for the interview. I had my own pans, knife, offset spatula but I worked mostly with my hands, so I didn't need much.

Squaring my shoulders, I pulled open the door of Clover. The place was exquisite: walnut paneling, crystal chandeliers, hardwood floors and a stone fireplace. The kitchen was in the back, partially visible to diners. A man worked at the bar—tall, broad shoulders, messy dark hair and pale blue eyes that locked onto me as soon as I stepped inside. He moved from behind the bar to greet me.

"You must be Avery Collins."

"Yes."

"Kyle Donahue. Trace and Francois are in the back. I'll take you. Are you ready?"

"I think so, but my hands won't stop shaking."

"Francois looks fierce, but he's really a marshmallow and Trace, well, he isn't a marshmallow, but he's a good guy."

Stepping into the kitchen, my heart hammered in my chest. Francois Moree stood at one counter, studying something, and right in front of him—his back to me—was Mr. Montgomery. I worried that after having a week to ponder our odd meeting, and knowing I had a nut for a sister, that he may be having second thoughts. I gulped, I did that when nervous, and apparently loud enough that Kyle's eyes caught mine and he grinned.

"Trace, Francois, Avery's here."

When Mr. Montgomery turned, my legs went weak seeing that intense stare. And then he smiled and realizing he really wasn't going to hold Nat against me caused a relief so profound that when he stopped just in front of me and extended his hand, I just looked at it. I did; I stood for a minute staring at his hand like I didn't know what it was.

And then he said. "I won't bite you."

Jerking my head up, I was treated to the sight of Trace Montgomery grinning. In response, I probably looked like I'd had one too many sessions with electric shock.

Pulling myself together, I took his hand. "Sorry, Mr. Montgomery. It's very nice to see you again."

"Call me Trace. Nervous?"

"Can you tell?"

A chuckle. "How's your sister?"

"Still alive."

He knew I was referring to her behavior at Everything, which he confirmed when he said, "It was actually quite a good plan, leaving an impression to make you stand out. She certainly did that."

"Um." I really had nothing more to say about that since the impression she left him with was that we were both crazy. Was a bad impression better than no impression? I suspected no. Francois Moree approached and I noticed he held my recipes.

"I like what I see, Miss Collins, now let's see how these taste."

And that was it. For the next hour and a half I worked, the nerves fading since this was second nature to me. I couldn't tell, based on their expressions, what they thought. Both would be killer at poker.

"We have a few more interviews, but we'll be in touch within the week." Trace, like Chef Moree, had peppered me with questions while I worked.

The interview had gone longer than planned, since I discovered their ovens ran a little cool. While I packed up my things, a woman walked into the kitchen holding the hand of a little girl who was maybe two or three. It was uncanny how much they looked alike. I hadn't a doubt they were mother and daughter.

"Daddy!" The little girl hurled herself at Trace, but my attention was on the transformation from boss to adoring dad. He lifted the girl into his arms and held her at eye level as he smiled—changing him from handsome to gorgeous.

"Hey, baby girl."

"Mama took me shopping. I got a cake pop."

He looked past his daughter to his wife, his smile still firmly in place. "I bet Mama got one too."

"She did. She got you one too."

"She did?"

Moving his daughter to his hip, he reached for his wife and pulled her to him and right in front of Chef Moree and me, he kissed her like he'd die if he didn't. I felt a bit warm under my blouse watching because damn to be kissed like that by a man like him. I'd die a very happy woman.

Even after he kissed her, he looked at her as if she were the most fascinating person on the planet. A look similar to the one Kit and Jess always shared. I think I liked that even more than the kiss. And then realizing they weren't alone, his eyes shifted to me.

"Avery, my daughter Faith and my wife Ember. Avery is applying for the position of pastry chef."

Ember moved from her family, her smile contagious as she approached me. Reaching for my hand she said, "Hi Avery. It's nice to meet you."

"Likewise."

"What did you make?" Faith asked from the safety of her dad's arms.

"Lavender cake, strawberry ice cream and chocolate cake."

"Sounds yummy."

Trace touched his daughter's nose. "They were yummy."

They were yummy, my heart pounded again.

"Good luck, I hope to see more of you." Ember said before turning to Trace. "We were on our way home. Seth and Brandon are getting sick of dining hall food, so they're coming to dinner."

"Give me a minute and I'll come with you." Trace said, kissing Faith on the head before dropping her to her feet.

I finished packing up my things before Trace walked me to the door. "If you get the position, your day starts at two and we're closed on Sunday. You'd be responsible for not just the desserts but also all the baked goods. We have runners that hit the markets. You would be responsible for supplying the list of ingredients the day before on what you'd need for the following day's menu. I noticed on your resume you live in Pennsylvania. Will you be commuting from there?"

"No, I'd like to find a place closer." And then I blushed because it was kind of presumptuous of me to have someone looking for a place when I didn't even know if I had the job, but it also showed how much I wanted the job. "I have a Realtor looking for me just in case, but so far nothing is in my budget."

His only response was a nodding of his head. "All right, we'll be in touch."

"Thanks for the opportunity."

He smiled, not the devastating one he gave his wife, but nearly as good. Kyle called from the bar. "Hope to see you again, Avery."

With a quick wave, I headed outside, walked down the street a bit and then nearly kicked my feet in glee. Trace Montgomery thought my desserts were yummy. Maybe I had just pulled it off.

RAFE

Running my hand down the length of the walnut feeling for imperfections, I knew this piece was one of the best things I'd ever made. The walnut had cost a pretty penny, but it was worth every cent. Chunkier in design than my other pieces, the farm table had mortise and tenon joints, thick square legs and tongue and grove planked top. The colors in the walnut were so varied I didn't need to stain it, just a coat or two of polyurethane. Ahead of schedule by two weeks, the bride's parents were thrilled. They wanted to get the piece into the soon-to-be-newlyweds house, prior to the wedding, to surprise them. The chairs were simple ladder-back design, same walnut. I had even, at no extra cost, cut and beveled a hunk of glass for the top. Imagining little kids doing homework, I'd hate to see simple arithmetic carved forever into the wood.

Loki sauntered into my workshop, my reminder it was lunchtime. A mutt, but with Bernese mountain dog and shepherd in him, he could be a lot to handle. Luckily for me he was also the laziest dog alive. After his puppy years, where he had a tendency to take off, now it was considered an active day if I could get him to move from the bedroom to the living room. "All right, Loki, let's get some food."

Closing up the barn that served as my workshop, I headed for the house when I heard my cell that I'd left charging in the kitchen. Seeing it was Trace, I answered. "What's up?"

"Is your carriage house still available for rent?"

"Yeah."

"I interviewed someone for the pastry chef position. She lives in Pennsylvania, but she wants a place closer."

29

"And you want to hire her."

"Yeah, her shit was unreal."

"Shit? Really? The best description you've got for Clover-worthy desserts is shit."

"You're a funny guy. Are you inhaling too many chemicals?"

"Ha."

"How much to rent it?"

"A thousand a month."

"Anytime not work next week for me to bring her around?"

"No, if I'm not here I'll leave the key. You've already got the alarm codes. Her baking is really that good?"

"Yeah, Francois' eyes rolled into the back of his head."

"Shit, that is good."

"Maybe you could add a clause in her renter's agreement that she has to bake for you every week."

"Maybe."

"Ember's been on my ass to get you over for dinner."

"I'll check my calendar."

"All right. If this works out, it'll be good for both of us."

"You're not kidding, an extra thousand a month, I won't turn my nose up at that."

"I hear that. Catch ya later."

I glanced down at Loki as I returned my phone to the charger. He looked as if he wanted to eat my leg. "I'm getting it."

A thousand extra a month would go a long way toward the renovations. Riverdale was a small suburban-feel community in the Bronx. I purchased the big white elephant, liked the yard and more particularly the barn that could serve as my workshop; even for house flippers, it wasn't a sound investment because not only would the remodel cost serious dough, it wouldn't be a quick flip. I bought the place for a song but even five years later, I was still working on it. I had fixed up the barn and carriage house first, living in the latter until the kitchen, living room, master bedroom and bath were done. Recently I finished a guest bedroom, a second bath and currently my focus centered on the library. Ember had lots of ideas for that room, designing a book lover's paradise—her words. Custom making the bookcases took time and serious cash, but with the infusion of income from a renter I could move up my timeline. Plus, I had recently tapped into my savings to install an alarm system—I had a fortune worth of tools in the barn—with the added income I could replenish my stash. The carriage house probably needed a good cleaning; I'd get my housekeeper to spruce it up the next time she was here. A quiet, calm presence that baked like a goddess, yeah, I liked this idea.

chapter four

Avery

$\mathcal{F}$olding my homemade crème fraîche into the batter for the pear/ almond cheesecake, my cell rang which immediately kicked off the butterflies in my belly. I'd been waiting for Trace Montgomery's call—nervously awaiting his call—which had me baking nonstop because I tended to bake when nervous or upset. My hand actually shook when I reached for my phone.

"Hello."

"Avery?"

Please don't say something stupid; please don't say something stupid. I did that too, babbled nonsensically when nervous. "Hi Trace."

"The job is yours."

I'd thought about this phone call since the day I accepted the interview. I had even practiced how I'd handle the news regardless of which way it went. I'd be poised and collected. Grateful and excited if I got the job or disappointed, but appreciative if I didn't. Reality, though, was slightly different than my imaginings. My phone slipped from my numb hand to crash loudly on the counter, a sound eclipsed by my screaming—a scream worthy of fangirls at a One Direction concert. I might have even pulled a Kevin McAllister from *Home Alone* by running around my kitchen shaking my arms over my head. I wasn't sure since my body had a mind of its own and my brain seemed to have shut down. Of one thing I was sure, I was not acting poised or collected.

And then I realized Trace was still on the line. Grabbing my phone, I heard him chuckling. "I'm sorry, have I caused permanent damage to your ear."

"I'll live."

"I really got the job?"

"Your dishes were incredible. Francois is still talking about the lavender cake."

Oh my God.

"So I'm assuming you're accepting."

I hadn't accepted yet? Poise and collected, not even close. "Yes, of course."

"Have you found an apartment?"

Some of the glee faded since I hadn't yet found anything that was even remotely possible. "Not yet."

"I may have a solution for you. A friend lives in the Bronx and he has a carriage house available for rent. A thousand a month."

"I'm sorry, did you say the Bronx and carriage house in the same sentence?"

That question earned me a full out laugh. "Yeah, sounds strange, but it's a small community tucked in the Bronx. I'll take you. Can you come into the city sometime this week?"

"Any time at all."

"Okay, how about Thursday? We can meet at Clover."

The magnitude of this conversation was finally beginning to penetrate. My knees got wobbly even as my heart started to beat in a staccato rhythm in my chest. "I can't tell you what this means to me. It's a dream come true. Thank you for taking a chance on me."

"It's not a chance, you've earned this. We'll discuss when you start on Thursday."

"Thank you so much, Mr.... Trace."

"Nine in the morning at Clover on Thursday."

"I'll see you then."

The line went dead, but I hardly noticed because I got the job! I dialed my mom and didn't give her a chance to say hello. "I got it."

Her scream left me partially deaf in my right ear. I'd done similarly to Trace and he had brushed it off. Nice guy. "I knew it. Oh, Avery, congratulations."

"He may even have a solution for my living arrangements."

"Oh, that's wonderful. I wish we were there so we could celebrate."

"We can celebrate by you coming into Clover when your adventures bring you to New York. My treat."

"You're on, though Harold won't let you pay. Keep us posted on the apartment."

"I will. All right, I've got to call Nat and Jessica."

"Tell them both we said hi. Talk soon, Avery. Congratulations again, honey."

"Thanks, Mom."

I called Nat, but she was in surgery. We could celebrate in person. And then I called Jessica.

"You got it."

Her confidence in me never wavered. "I did, I got it."

"I knew it. I'm so happy for you. When do you start?"

"I'm not sure yet. My boss has an idea on where I can stay. I'm meeting him in the city on Thursday to check it out."

"This is big, huge."

"I know."

"I want to do something for you, but I don't know if I could get something coordinated in time."

"You don't have to do that, but I really would love for you and the family to visit. Let's work out some dates once I get settled."

"I'd love that. You know I love my life, Avery, but I'm a little envious because you're embarking on another adventure. You'll have to keep me posted, so I can live vicariously."

I was surprised to hear those words from Jessica. She had always wanted to get married and have kids; that had been *her* dream.

"I know what you're thinking and I'm very happy, but my life is here. My life has always been here and until Aidan and any other kids I have are eighteen, here is where it will stay. But the idea of seeing the world, it's very appealing. Savor this Avery. You're the intrepid one, going after what you want. Scary as hell and yet, I just know it's going to lead you to everything you ever wanted."

"Love you, Jessica."

"Love you."

I disconnected the call and wiped at my tears just as the timer for the cheesecake went off. After it cooled, I had two slices.

On Wednesday, I keyed into my sister's apartment in Chelsea and even being prepared for the mess she lived in, somehow she still managed to offend all of my senses. I wanted to turn around and find myself a hotel with room service and charge it all to Nat, but I wanted to be with my sister more. Since I couldn't live like this, even for just a night, it was cleaning time. Leaving my bags at the door, I spent the next two hours not just tidying up, but hard-core cleaning. There were freshly laundered clothes on her chair in the living room. Why not just put them away? Her refrigerator, I'm pretty sure an entirely new ecosystem was forming. I threw most of the stuff in her fridge away, and then cleaned the entire unit with Lysol. After, I dusted, mopped floors and headed to the local market for food. When Nat came home around eight that night, she had a clean house and a home-cooked meal waiting for her.

"Oh my God, I hardly recognize the place. Are you sure you don't want to stay here? I could get used to this."

"No. You're a pig."

"Is that meatloaf?"

"And mashed potatoes and string beans."

"My death row meal."

"Yep."

"Please stay here."

"You had eggs in your refrigerator that expired seven months ago. Seven months ago. I cannot live in your version of squalor. I'd kill you and then myself and my fabulous new job would go to someone else."

"I guess I could make an effort to be neater."

"It's amazing you haven't poisoned yourself."

"I order in most nights. I had the eggs from when Mom visited once."

"You're ridiculous."

"Anyway, tell me how excited are you. You did it, Avery, you're the pastry chef for Clover. I'm so proud of you."

"I'm still pinching myself."

"And as a bonus, you get to be in Trace Montgomery's sphere all day, every day."

"His wife is exquisite, his daughter is a little cherub and he is totally and completely hooked and happy to be so."

"Really, you met the wife?"

"Yeah, Ember. We only said hi, but she seemed very nice."

"I wish I were Ember."

"Your Trace is out there somewhere."

"He needs to make himself known. I want to find someone who looks like Trace and treats me how Harold treats Mom. I've never seen her so happy."

"Yeah, happy enough to sleep in an RV." Reaching for her hand I added. "Seriously, you've got it all going on. You'll find him."

"Brain surgery isn't as glamorous as people make it sound. Talking about gray matter is not stimulating conversation."

"Take up a hobby?"

"Like what?"

"I don't know, but you've got to have interests. Maybe you'll find your perfect man in a knitting circle."

She tossed a string bean at me. "Funny."

All teasing aside, I understood where Nat was coming from. It wasn't that we needed a man, our father was a terrible husband and I'd rather be alone than deal with what Mom had had to deal with.

But seeing the other side, how happy finding the right person can make you, yeah, I wanted that for both of us.

"I get it. I want that too. Watching Jess and Kit, I want us both to find that."

"I don't understand why it's so hard."

"Me neither. Maybe for you they're intimidated by your large brain."

"You are so not helpful." She reprimanded, even as her lips cracked into a smile.

"Bright side, we have each other. When we're older we can get a house together, combine our cats to create a herd and yell 'get off my lawn' to all the neighborhood kids."

"I'm scheduling a lobotomy for myself on Monday."

"A lobotomy, I doubt I'll even notice the difference."

That earned me a dinner roll in the face. "So, Trace is taking you to a place in the Bronx."

"Yeah, a carriage house his friend has for rent."

"In the Bronx?"

"My thoughts exactly."

"What do you suppose this friend is like?"

"Having a friend like Trace, my imagination is going wild but he's probably happily married to a supermodel."

"Why would you think that?"

"Because I've never had much luck when it comes to men."

"Well, the rent is ideal, so maybe your luck is changing."

"I can't believe we're in the Bronx." Thursday arrived; Trace and I met at Clover, stopped for coffee and now we were in his car heading to Rafe McKenzie's house. When Trace mentioned the name of his friend it kind of sealed it for me that the man was going to be hot. It was a great name, no, sexy as hell name. "How did Rafe find this?"

"He's a woodworker and needed a place that had a large enough yard for his workshop, which focused his search outside of Manhattan. He found a place that needed a hell of a lot of work, but what he's done to it is nothing short of a miracle. My wife adores it, has started putting a bug in my ear that she'd like to find a home in a similar community. Get Faith into a more suburban-like neighborhood with grass and trees."

"I love it already. Even if the carriage house is no more than a cardboard box in the backyard with an extension cord, I'm sold."

"Trust me, the carriage house is way more than that."

We pulled into a gated drive, one that required a code to access, my eyes landing on the house and instantly I fell in love. A soft, gray stone made up the house that had a pitched roof and a huge covered porch. Gardens were needed to soften the lines where the house met the grass, but the place was exquisite. Pulling into the back, the carriage house—a nice-sized building with the same gray stone of the house, and white trim work—sat off to the left of the detached garage. The one-time carriage doors had been removed and were replaced with exquisite rustic doors with large windows to bring more of the light inside. Just past the carriage house was a huge heather gray barn: the workshop.

Trace's question pulled me from my study. "What do you think?"

"It's wonderful."

"Rafe isn't here, he's making a delivery; I'll show you around."

I didn't need to see the inside. I loved it and the price was a steal especially seeing what I'd be getting for it. But to Trace, I said, "Okay."

We headed to the back door of the main house and as soon as Trace unlocked it, a huge dog appeared. He was the size of a small pony. I'd never had a dog—even wanting one—and had never been around a dog, so unconsciously I moved behind Trace.

Sensing my discomfort, Trace immediately sought to put me at ease. "He looks scary, but he's harmless. He's like a walking ottoman." And even with his criticism, he scratched the dog behind the ears smiling the entire time. "His name is Loki."

And while Trace went to handle the alarm that was buzzing at us threateningly, I greeted Loki by waving. Yep, I waved to the dog.

And in response, it looked as if Loki cocked his head at me thinking, *what the...*

Trace led me to the carriage house. "The furniture comes with the rental." He opened the door and stepped back.

Hardwood floors as far as I could see. A living area to the right of the door and even though the leather and pine furniture was masculine, it worked. It was perfect. The kitchen was to the left and just to right was the hall leading to what I imagined were the bedroom and bath. For a small kitchen, it was nicely stocked with top of the line stainless steel appliances, quartz countertops and a window over the sink. I'd always wanted a window over the sink so I could grow herbs.

I loved it, my only hesitation, especially after seeing the place, was I'd be in close quarters with someone I didn't know at all. What if we didn't hit if off? What if this Rafe guy was a nut and not a harmless one like Nat and me? Turning to Trace, who stood by the front door, I asked, "What's Rafe like?"

"He's a good guy, private and not big on wild parties and shit. He'll respect your privacy and will expect the same in return. You'll be safe here, Avery."

"I'm that easy to read?"

"It's a fair concern, but I've known Rafe since we were kids. You've nothing to worry about."

"Okay, I'll take it."

It was Trace who cocked his head at me as if saying, *what the...* "You don't want to see the bedroom?"

"I don't need to."

"All right. The renter's agreement is on the table. Take a look at it, sign and return it. There's a self-addressed envelope attached."

Walking over to the table, I reached for a pen in my purse. Scanned the document and signed it.

"Just like that?" Trace was fighting a grin.

"I trust you, so yeah."

"All right. Here are the keys. I'll give you a few weeks to get settled so how about October 1st as your start date."

"Sounds great."

"We'll deal with the paperwork on your first day. Welcome to the team, Avery."

chapter five

Avery

Three days after I toured Rafe's carriage house, I pulled my old
Subaru station wagon up Rafe's drive—the gate had been left
open for me—and parked next to a fancy black Ford F-150. Climbing
from the car and stretching, since the trip had been hell, I looked
around at the trees that were just beginning to turn colors. And to
think we were in the city. In the next minute, Loki appeared from the
barn. Instead of most dogs that run to visitors, jumping up on them,
looking to play, he meandered toward me as if he knew his duty
but his heart just wasn't into it. When he did finally reach me, I got
down on my knees and rubbed his head to let him know how much
I appreciated the effort.

Shifting my focus to the carriage house, I admired the place I'd be
calling home—the large doors that were reworked with an overhang,
the same gray stone of the house, the creamy-white trim around the
windows. And it was while I studied his work that I heard Rafe calling for Loki—a deep and very sexy voice. I reminded myself that he
was Trace Montgomery's friend and after my embarrassingly exten-
sive Internet search on Trace, outside of my employment at Clover,

I wouldn't be moving in the same social circles as them especially since I was just Rafe's tenant. But that didn't stop me from spending more time than I'd care to admit, in the past few days, imagining what Rafe looked like because he *was* a friend of Trace's. Hot was a foregone conclusion. I kind of saw him as a happy blend of Henry Cavill and Chris Hemsworth; yes, the bar was set really high. In the next minute, Rafe stepped from the barn and I literally lost my breath. Damn they made them fine here. That bar…he just stepped right over it. And as alluring as his face was, it was the sight of his thigh muscles straining the denim of his faded jeans that caught and held my attention. I was a sucker for a man in faded jeans. And then realizing that to Rafe it would seem as if I was checking out the area between his thighs, I jerked my eyes to his face.

There was just so much to take in from the long black hair that swept his shoulders, to his face that was made up of all angles softened only by his lips; his only feature that didn't look to be carved from stone. His bright green eyes and his body—like his face—was what women's fantasies were made of. Including my own. Wide shoulders, narrow hips, biceps that stretched the sleeves of his tee and even though he wore a t-shirt, I just knew he had a six-pack. He was ridiculously sexy and this man lived here. I'd have paid $5000 a month for the pleasure. I wasn't sure what magic fairy dust had been sprinkled on me that I'd landed both my job at Clover and this man as my landlord, but I hoped my uncharacteristic luck held out for awhile.

As he approached, I mentally pictured the sight that greeted him—faded black sweatpants, a tee stating bacon as the reason why you weren't a vegetarian—the fabric clinging to my overheated skin and not in a sexy way, in a 'I really need a shower because I reek' way. I'd twisted my auburn hair into a knot on the top of my head halfway through the trip. It was unseasonably warm and my car didn't have a working air conditioner. I could only imagine how well I managed that.

Belatedly, I realized I was gawking at my landlord. *Nice first impression, Avery.* Walking toward the not-to-be-believed sexy man, I offered my hand. "Hi. I'm Avery."

He studied my hand like it had just materialized from thin air. It took him a beat or two before his large, calloused hand curled around mine. Inappropriate, absolutely, but for just a second I wondered what those hands would feel like roaming over my body. "Rafe."

Yes, he was Rafe—the name turning into an adjective, one synonymous with hot, sexy, delicious. And that voice, it had places stirring to life that hadn't stirred in far too long.

"Did you have any trouble finding the place?"

Still daydreaming about his voice and my body's very pleasant reaction to it, I didn't immediately answer him. Seeming to understand what fueled my hesitation, he grinned—the sexiest curving of lips I had ever seen in my twenty-nine years.

Snapping myself out of it, I answered, "No, not at all." And then I grabbed onto the first sane thought that popped into my head. "It's even prettier than I remembered."

"Can I help you with your bags?"

"I don't have much. I think I can manage. Oh…" Going back to my car, I grabbed my purse for the envelope. "Before I forget, here's the first and last month plus security deposit."

He seemed to hesitate in taking the envelope. If he were having second thoughts about renting me the place, I'd be crushed and up a creek. He seemed to pick up on my panic and clarified. "You're my first renter."

Exhaling in relief, I assured him, "You won't even know I'm here."

He had a thought on that, but he didn't share. Tucking the envelope in his back pocket, he gestured to my car. "I'll help you with your bags."

My car was a piece of shit—looking even more so next to his sexy truck—but it was a reliable piece of shit and was one of the only outings with my dad I remembered. He had bought me the car; sure it probably only cost a few hundred bucks, but the memory of that day was priceless since my dad was usually about as warm as the Antarctic tundra. Rafe didn't hide his look of disbelief that something so old still worked.

I felt the need to defend my sorry excuse for wheels. "1984, it's a classic." And it was, technically.

Rafe pushed his hands into the front pockets of his jeans, his head turning slightly in my direction. "It's something."

"5-speed manual transmission, manual windows and locks, pleather and though I don't know the factory name, I think of the color as a buttercup-yellow."

He studied me for a minute; the intensity of that gaze did very pleasant things to my insides. I keyed into the trunk.

"No fob?" Humor laced through that question.

"People today, so spoiled. Nothing like a good old-fashioned lock and key."

"Mmm hum."

I didn't have much; it only took three trips to bring my stuff inside. Excitement moved through me, touring through the place had been one thing, but I'd be living here. "It really is beautiful."

"Thanks."

"Do you have pictures of what it looked like before?"

Again the stare, more intense this time, before he jerked his head in the direction of the front room. "Over there, in the living room are a few before pictures."

I hadn't noticed them when I toured the house, but seeing what Rafe had to start with, I agreed with Trace's comment about the changes being nothing short of a miracle. "Wow, you've been busy. I love this furniture too. My mom would kill for that coffee table."

"Thanks."

Twisting my head to him in disbelief or maybe awe, I asked, "You made that?"

"Yeah."

"Trace mentioned the barn was your workshop. That must be nice. You don't have far to go when inspiration strikes."

In reply, I got one of those chin lifts before he changed the subject. "I left a list on the counter: grocery stores, pharmacies, liquor stores…that sort of thing. The code for the gates and the alarm codes for here and the main house are also there. The washer and dryer are in the mudroom of the main house. When you're settled, I'll give you a tour so you know where everything is."

I didn't really want to invade his privacy and I couldn't imagine his wife or girlfriend would be super keen on having another woman traipsing around the house. Before I could offer an objection, a woman's voice drifted through the screen. "Rafe?"

He glanced in the direction of the voice before he turned and started for the door. "Welcome to Riverdale, Avery."

And then he was gone, the door closed quietly at his back, but I was already moving across the room to peek out the window. The sight of him walking away was almost as sexy as the one of him stepping from the barn earlier. I didn't see the woman; Rafe was already walking into the house after his lady friend. Leaning against the window, I took a moment because it wasn't every day you met a man like Rafe. Sexy as all hell, the kind of sexy that made you want to drop to your knees and worship. Thoughtful: leaving the list of stores for me, talented in his craft as evident by my surroundings and totally taken. Not a surprise.

I spent the next few hours unpacking before I took a much needed shower. Afterwards I cracked open a bottle of wine, toasted myself and then called my mom.

"Avery, please tell me it's fabulous."

"It is. I'll send you a few pictures."

"And your landlord? He's not going to be some overbearing, always peeking out of the window and taking unwanted pictures, landlord."

If anyone was going to be peeking out of the windows snapping pictures, it wasn't going to be Rafe. The idea of wallpapering the ceiling with pictures of his likeness was not a bad idea. I wasn't about to share that with my mom though. So instead, I hedged. "He's great." He was so much more than great; fantastic, swoon-worthy, edible were better descriptive words. And then realizing I was lusting after a man I didn't know while on the phone with my mom, I said again, "He's great."

"Two greats. He's either significantly more than great or he's quite a bit less."

My mom knew me so well. "He's significantly better than great."

"Um." She had more to say on that, but didn't and instead asked, "Are you all settled?"

"I am. I didn't bring much since the place is fully stocked. I can't believe this is my home for the foreseeable future. Wait until you see the pictures. The yard is private with a gate and a fence that wraps around the whole property. But it's the trees and shrubs that make it feel a lot like home. And the little town in the borough that I passed, quaint and charming with super cute shops."

"I'm so happy to hear that. I worried you'd be living somewhere that made you uncomfortable."

"I thought I'd feel a little of that too, especially having my land-lord living right there, but I don't. It's comfortable and homey." I hoped that Rafe saw this arrangement as long-term because there was no way I'd be able to find anything even remotely as awesome as this for the price I was paying. "What about you? Where are you now?"

"We stopped off in Annapolis. We're going to dinner this evening on a fifty-foot sailboat on the Chesapeake."

"That sounds like a blast. Eat some blue claws for me."

"You know I will. After, we're heading to Virginia Beach and then the Outer Banks."

"Keep me posted, I want to know where you are and what you're doing so I can live vicariously."

"Likewise and good luck with your first day. Call me, I don't care how late it is and send the pictures. Get one of your landlord too."

"Mom!" But she knew I would.

"Love you, Avery."

"Love you, Mom."

Calling Jessica, I heard little Aidan in the background as soon as she picked up the line.

"Is Aidan okay?"

"Yeah, just tired. So, you're in."

"Yep."

"Send pictures."

"I will. If I had been given the okay to decorate this place, I would have done it very similarly. And to think one time this structure stored the carriages. What he's done is amazing."

"I can't wait to see it."

"And the backyard, it's like a secret garden, secluded and magical. I know he has neighbors; I passed them when I drove here and yet you can't see anyone. It's like entering a secret world."

"And your landlord? What's he like?"

"My landlord looks like he just stepped out of the pages of GQ, carpenter edition."

"No way."

"He's gorgeous: long black hair, bright green eyes."

"Get his picture."

"Mom said the same thing."

"Your mom is very smart. Do you see yourself making a move on your hot new landlord?"

"Nope."

"Why not?"

"He's my landlord."

"So. Did you get goosebumps when you met him?"

"Lost my breath, but it doesn't matter. He is with someone."

"Married?"

"I don't know. He wasn't wearing a ring, but he also works with his hands."

"Find out. If he isn't married, he's fair game. You've never lost your breath for a man, ever. You should make a move. With him being your landlord, there are so many options available to you: you can't open a window, or the refrigerator is making a strange sound or, better yet, the water stopped working when you were in the middle of a shower."

"You're as deranged as Nat."

Jess laughed and Aidan cried louder. "I need to get this boy down."

A reprieve. I'd have to sneak the kid an extra cookie for unknowingly getting his mom off my landlord's scent.

Jess added, "Pictures. Oh, I can't wait to visit."

"Speaking of which, maybe we could do Christmas in the city."

"December, that should work. I'll check with Kit and get back to you."

"Kiss Aidan for me."

"Will do. Talk soon."

Hanging up, I dropped my phone on the table, sat back and just soaked it all in. I was the pastry chef for Clover. I'd done it. I was living the dream.

RAFE

I needed more peanut butter. Scraping the sides of the jar, I realized a man in his thirties eating his dinner from a jar was downright sad. I'd gotten a lot done today. Not as much as I'd planned, but I lost a few hours with my tenant moving in and Melody's surprise visit. Dropping the spoon in the sink, I couldn't help the thread of anger when I thought about Melody's stunt from earlier. She never came here, preferred meeting me when we went out. I knew she was curious about my tenant; she'd reacted oddly when I mentioned I had taken one on. For her to show up here, she was falling into a pattern that was becoming far too predictable.

We'd met a few months back at Sapphire. Sexy and beautiful, she'd also been fun. It wasn't as much fun anymore because there was a vein of jealousy that ran through her that annoyed the hell out of me. She was even jealous of my friends' wives. On the rare occasion she joined us, she acted like a bitch, which put me in the position of making excuses for her. I was growing really fucking tired of the whole scene.

And my tenant...I hadn't known what I expected when Trace mentioned his pastry chef. No, that wasn't true. I had pictured a grandmotherly-type: older, gray hair, wide from eating her creations. I hadn't expected Avery. Kneeling next to my dog rubbing him down like he was a long-lost friend. She got serious points for that, my own

48

damn girlfriend kept a wide-berth from Loki. And how refreshing, a beautiful woman who was comfortable enough in her own skin that she didn't need to hide behind makeup and designer clothes. Not that she needed them, her ass in those sweats…fucking fine. I can't remember a time my blood stirred as much as it had stepping out of the barn and seeing her. She was a fucking knockout, but she was like a jacked-up fairy—happy and bubbly while spewing bullshit like that nonsense about her car with its good lock and key. She was a nut, but a sexy one.

Turning toward the trash can, a movement outside the window grabbed my attention. It was Avery and she was pacing in front of the carriage house. Had she locked herself out already? In the next minute, she stopped pacing and stared down at Loki, apparently talking to him. Loki's head tilted to the side as he had a tendency of doing, studying her probably a lot like how I was. What the hell was she doing? And then she started pacing again, but this time she was talking to herself. I could see her lips moving. I wondered if Trace ran a background check on her. Her words popped into my head about how I wouldn't know she was there, I had a sneaking suspicion that wasn't going to be the case.

Walking out back, I called to her. "Are you okay?"

Her head snapped up and she looked both surprised and embarrassed if her cheeks turning pink were any indication.

"Sorry, I was just thinking."

"Were you just talking to Loki?"

"Will you call for a straitjacket if I say yes?"

"Admitting you have a problem is half of the battle."

A smile spread over her face, her eyes bright with suppressed laughter. Envy, sharp and raw, cut through me because I couldn't remember the last time I had felt that kind of unbridled good humor. "I'm working out recipes and I think better when I pace." I wasn't really sure how to answer that. Before I could she added, "I know it's weird and I probably look crazy, but I've always been that way. Ideas come to me when I'm using more than one sense."

"Okay."

"I'm harmless, really."

The laugh that came from me in response took us both by surprise. "I'll hold you to that, being harmless."

She crossed her heart; fuck I hadn't seen that since I was a kid. And then she held up her fingers. "Scout's honor."

"Were you ever a scout?"

Her smile was more a grin when she replied, "No."

I chuckled, couldn't help it, and damn but that felt good. "So you're okay?"

"Yep. I'm fine."

"Good night then."

"Sweet dreams."

That stopped me as I twisted my head to see that she had started pacing again. Sweet dreams. Practically unconsciously offered and yet for some reason that jarred me, not so much the words, but the casual nature in which they were delivered. My new tenant was odd, but I suspected I was going to like her brand of odd.

Avery

The light scent of the hibiscus extract combined with the rich vanilla fragrance of the pastry cream was divine. A vanilla bean sponge cake sat cooling on the counter. How to top the dessert? In my head, I could see the presentation: a delicate chunk of white chocolate, two slices of starfruit and a dusting of powdered sugar. Continuing to whip the cream, I moved to the oven to check on the almond crisps for the almond and sweet cream panna cotta I was concocting. I may have gone a bit overboard with testing my recipes. The counters in the kitchen were covered with dishes, some fully formed, others still in stages.

Setting the bowl of cream on the counter, I checked the crisps. The edges were slightly darker and the buttery aroma that wafted up to me was heavenly. Crisps were tricky because it took only seconds to go from perfect to burnt and burnt nuts were bitter, overpowering every other flavor. Pulling the crisps from the oven, I transferred them to the cooling rack so they wouldn't continue baking on the hot pan. I had just started on the presentation of the vanilla bean and hibiscus cake when someone knocked at the door.

"Come in."

I sliced the sponge cake in half; I preferred the foam method of preparing sponge cake, whipping the egg whites until they were the perfect consistency and the result was a firm cake that was light and airy, the nooks in the cake soaking up whatever filling was spread over them. And as I spread the pastry cream on the cake, I realized whoever had been at the door hadn't entered. Walking to it, the sound of a little kid's voice reached me as I stepped outside. The sight that greeted me was Loki playing with Trace's daughter, Trace standing just behind her grinning. As soon as I stepped up next to him, his focus shifted to me.

"Hey, Avery. I wanted to stop by and see how you were settling in. Faith insisted on coming. She loves Loki."

"Looks like the feeling is mutual."

"You all settled?"

"I am. I was just working on some recipes."

Faith's head turned at that. "Cake?"

"Yes, and some other sweets. Maybe if it's okay with daddy, you could sample some."

Faith turned the cutest doe-eyes on her dad. "Please Daddy."

I thought Trace's quick response, reaching down and swooping his daughter up over his shoulder, was due to those doe-eyes but then he added, "Only if I get some too."

Nervousness twisted in my belly. I was still working through the recipes and he was my boss, I wanted to impress him. On the other hand, getting his feedback would also be helpful. "There's plenty to go around."

Leading them inside, Faith let out the cutest gasp. "Look at all those yummy things, Daddy."

Trace settled Faith at the kitchen counter, standing behind her so she wouldn't fall, but his attention was on all the yummy things too.

"Damn, you've been busy."

In response, I grinned like a maniacal genius—a sight I knew well since my sister was one. "Okay, Faith. I have chocolate cake, vanilla cake, a berry pie…"

"What's that?" She pointed to the vanilla sponge cake I'd been in the middle of working on.

"Vanilla cake, with a vanilla cream flavored with an edible flower."

"I want that." She said.

"Me too." Trace added which for some reason brought a chuckle because looking at the man, he didn't seem the type to want a cake flavored with flowers.

"I'm still working out the presentation, so bear with me."

Using the spoon, I smeared some cream on the plate, sliced a wedge of the cake and placed it off-center on the cream. I'd already broken the white chocolate into the shapes I wanted, so I gently pushed the triangular hunk of white chocolate into the top of the cake, added the slices of starfruit and dusted it with powdered sugar. Wiping the excess from the plate with a towel, I presented it to Faith. Her eyes went wide.

Handing her a fork I said, "Please tell me what you think."

She didn't hesitate to dig in; the sight of her eyes rolling into the back of her head was a pretty good clue that she liked it. Trace said, "That's a definite thumbs up."

After both father and daughter devoured their cake, Trace trying the panna cotta and berry torte, I walked them to their car. "A group of us are heading to Allegro next weekend. It's a jazz club. You should come, let us show you a bit of our city."

Happily stunned mute, since I hadn't expected the invitation, I didn't immediately respond. And then realizing my hesitation could be misconstrued as disinterest, I said, "I'd really like that."

"We're meeting around 7:00pm. I'll text you the address."

"Thank you."

"Thanks for the desserts. Fuc—" Trace cleared his throat. "I mean delicious."

"Good catch."

In reply, he grinned before strapping Faith into her car seat. He climbed into his car and started her up. His window rolled down. "See you on Friday."

"Thanks for stopping by."

"If you have desserts like that waiting, we'll make a habit of stopping by."

I liked the idea of guests, especially being so far from everyone I knew. "I'll have desserts."

"See you next weekend, Avery."

Faith waved, I waved back. When the gates closed behind them, I headed back inside and fixed myself a slice of that cake and I agreed with Faith and Trace, it was delicious.

chapter six

Avery

I loved Riverdale. The community was lovely; downtown was charming—very reminiscent of some of the towns from home. I had even found a gourmet market, which was dangerous since gourmet markets for me were like the Louis Vuitton store for other women. Grabbing a cart, I took my time walking up and down the aisles, filling my cart with more items than I needed. Nat was coming for a visit, so I bought groceries for some of her favorite meals since I was sure the last home-cooked dinner she'd had was the one I had made.

I couldn't wait for her to see my place, loved that I could say it was my place. Not only was it visually perfect, but also being tucked in a community that felt so much like home helped me with the transition. And my landlord, dear God, the man was exquisite. I planned on setting up a chair right outside my front door, positioned so I could see him coming and going from his workshop. I honestly didn't even care if he knew what I was doing—he already thought I was a nut.

Trace had been right; Rafe was very private. Outside of the day I moved in, he kept to himself and left me to myself. I hadn't seen the mystery woman; she hadn't paid a visit since that first day. I was curious about her, the kind of woman who could catch a man like Rafe.

Reaching the tea aisle, I spotted the tea Nat preferred, but it was on the top shelf. At five foot two, top shelves in grocery stores might as well be hanging from the ceiling. Scanning up and down the aisle confirmed I was alone, no tall person in sight. And even stepping up on the bottom shelf, I was still too short to reach the tea. Maybe I was shrinking. I was only twenty-nine; I didn't think that evil twist of aging happened until menopause. Of course, I wasn't using my female parts, so maybe my body decided since I'd closed down the factory it might as well board up the windows and retire to Florida. What a horrible thought. Though I couldn't deny, recently those neglected parts were slowly waking, stretching after a long hibernation and I had Rafe to thank for that.

Looking around for something I could use to knock the tea off the shelf, I spied the celery in my basket. That would give me at least six more inches. The boxes were stocked very close together and the celery was bulky so it didn't come as a surprise that my attempt to retrieve the tea resulted in several boxes, not the brand I wanted, tumbling to the floor. As they hit the linoleum, the accompanying sound echoed.

"Son of a..."

"Do you need help?"

Like warm honey over ice cream. I'd know that voice anywhere, and then I realized that Rafe had witnessed my ridiculous attempt to retrieve tea. Tea I wasn't even going to drink. How embarrassing.

Turning, I was treated to the sight of Rafe McKenzie carrying a shopping basket. Only a truly remarkable man could make shopping for groceries look sexy.

My heart felt like a jackhammer, my limbs turned to noodles and to cover the fact that the man physically affected me, though anyone not physically affected by this man wasn't human, I opened my mouth before I engaged my brain.

"They make these shelves intentionally too high so that the wicked, tall people of the world can stand in the security offices all across the land laughing at the vertically challenged. It's wrong, very, very wrong."

It took me a minute to realize what I had just said and when I had, I wanted to stick my face in the boxes of tea on a shelf I could reach.

Chancing a glance at him, he was grinning.

"I don't really think there's a conspiracy against short people. I mean sure the designers all cater to tall, thin women and most amusement rides I'm barely at the height to actually ride even though I'm almost thirty and sure I've been carded because I'm on the short side so I naturally have to be young too." Cocking my hip, I realized maybe there really was a conspiracy. "On second thought…"

"Did you get the tea you wanted with your celery prosthesis?"

"Tea? I don't drink tea."

This earned me a smile with teeth visible and honest to God my knees buckled.

"Then why are you in the tea section knocking boxes off the shelf? Is this some kind of short person protest?"

Momentarily stunned by the sight of his smile, it took me a minute to remember that I was indeed in the tea section getting tea for Nat and he had just called me short.

"I'm not short. Five foot two is actually considered average for a female." I didn't really know if that statistic was true, but he probably didn't know either.

Clearly hotness adversely affected the working of my brain since I had my extremely hot landlord offering to help reach my tea and through this entire exchange my take away was objecting to him calling me short.

"My sister is visiting, she drinks tea. And no, I didn't get the one I wanted. These celery prostheses are just not made the way they used to be."

He stepped closer and the sight of all that moving closer had those slowly, stirring places jerking upright and taking notice. "Which one did you want?"

I kind of felt like Clark W. Griswold at the lingerie counter in *Christmas Vacation.* In my head, the one I wanted had nothing to do with tea. I felt the stupid grin—openly lascivious grin—and snapped myself out of it. "The Lady Grey in the black box."

Effortlessly, he retrieved the box, our fingers brushed when he handed it to me and just that slight contact and my body felt like it was on fire. "Thank you."

"Do you think you'll need my help retrieving other items outside of your reach?"

He was offering to shop with me, but that spelled disaster since I couldn't seem to form a thought in his presence. God only knew what I'd get myself into, walking and talking without my brain taking part.

"Ah, I think I'll be okay. I've got this." I said as I waved the celery. Mortifying. When I got home I needed to order 'Talking to Hot People for Dummies'.

"All right. See you later."

I watched him walk away, even turned so I could see his ass that looked so nice in those jeans. And once out of sight, I lowered my head and giggled because I was seriously a clown. Oh well, I wasn't going to see him again except for every time I left the carriage house, returned to it, walked around the yard, played with Loki. No big deal. I resisted the urge to bang my head on the mockingly tall shelves. I needed to buy an invisibility cloak too; I hope that Harry didn't have the only one.

I didn't want to get out of bed; the mattress and sheets were like heaven. It felt as if I was sleeping on a cloud. Even down to the details of bedding, Rafe was all over it. I didn't run into him again yesterday. He was probably hiding from me. If he and Trace exchanged stories, the truth would be out—the Collins chicks were nuts. Climbing from bed, the aroma of coffee drifted down the hall to me. Never had I had a programmable coffeemaker and I suspected I would never again be without one. What a luxury.

A cool breeze blew through the window, the temperatures more in line with the fall season. Pulling open the front door, to get the breeze through the screen, I yelped at the sight of the black, furry figure sprawled out on the front stoop. Loki.

His head lifted and his black eyes settled on me. His tail gave a thump, I assumed in joy at seeing me, but other than those minor movements he could have been a statue.

"Morning, Loki."

His tail thumped again.

"Have you had a walk today?"

In answer, he moved, looking much like an old man rising from his rocking chair, but his tail continued to wag so I took that to mean he liked the idea of a walk.

Slipping on my shoes, Loki and I walked around the property. It wasn't a huge property, maybe an acre or so, but with the trees and shrubs, it really did seem as if we were miles and miles from others. With the fenced-in yard and the gate usually closed, I understood why Rafe allowed Loki to walk around unleashed.

There was a bench under a tree at the far end of the property. Sitting down, Loki dropped at my feet and together we enjoyed the quiet of the early morning. About twenty minutes later, Rafe walked from the barn. I could honestly say in all of my twenty-nine years of living I had never seen a sight as beautiful as the one I stared at now. Rafe's hair was pulled back in a man bun—never thought I'd find that sexy, but it was ridiculously sexy—and he wore sweats that hung from his hips, but just barely so you were rooting on gravity. He'd draped his tee over his exquisitely sculpted shoulder affording me a view of his naked and sweaty chest. I had been wrong, he didn't have a six-pack; he had an eight-pack...an eight-pack. What was he doing in that barn? And could I do it with him? And he lived right there, right outside my front door. Man, did I score with this place.

The sound of the gates opening pulled my attention from Rafe in time to see as a station wagon, nearly as old as mine, came rattling up the drive. An older woman—reed-thin with white hair pulled into a bun—climbed from the car. Loki and I joined the woman on the drive.

"You must be the tenant." She said in way of greeting, but it came across more like an accusation.

"Yes, I'm Avery."

"Mrs. Milner, the housekeeper. Leave your linens in the basket in the mudroom and I'll launder them for you."

No way did my rent include housekeeping services, not that I wouldn't welcome it. I hated doing laundry. "Thanks, but I can manage."

"I'm not asking. I like the linens done just so."

Her attitude definitely grated, however the woman was offering to wash my towels and sheets; I wasn't about to argue the point with her. "Thank you, Mrs. Milner."

"I'm here every Friday, please have the linens in the mudroom by Thursday evening."

"Will do."

And then she turned and walked away without another word. And as I pondered why Rafe would have a woman working for him with her disposition, he walked outside and the change in her was immediate.

"Rafe, dear. How are you?"

"Mrs. Milner. I'm good. I'd be even better with another one of those chicken and dumpling casseroles. It was so good I nearly wept."

"Any time, you know that."

"You look particularly pretty today. Did you get your hair done?"

What? Her hair was in a bun. How the hell could he tell?

"I did, just yesterday."

"Mr. Milner has probably been chasing you around the house."

Oh my God. I wanted to laugh out loud because Rafe was now handling the woman who had just handled me and she was happy to be handled.

She blushed; I could see that from where I stood. Rafe was out and out flirting with his housekeeper, who had to be in her sixties, and the woman was eating it up. And I liked it, liked the mischievous look in his eyes.

"He doesn't run as well as he used to, but I let him catch me."

I nearly laughed out loud again, Rafe did. His head tilting back as that happy sound rang around the yard. A sound that hit me right in the chest, the smile dimming on my lips because I had a feeling there was a lot to Rafe McKenzie and I really wanted to get to know *all* of him and not just in the biblical sense. And it was then that another car pulled into the drive: a sassy red convertible. The driver was exquisite, like sell your soul kind of exquisite, and probably the owner of that voice. She climbed from her car and she was nothing but legs. Even I stared, it was hard not to. She moved as if she floated, her hips swaying, her long curly—from a bottle but exceedingly pretty—red hair moving seductively around her shoulders.

Mrs. Milner glanced at the newcomer, her smile morphed into a sneer, before she turned her back on the woman and walked into the house. Rafe's focus was on the woman, and maybe it was just wishful thinking, but he looked annoyed. That look didn't last long because the woman draped herself around him like an afghan and took his mouth for an open-mouth—heavy tongue action—kiss. I was feeling suddenly really warm, and, if I was being honest, jealous as I stood staring at my landlord and his woman engaging in foreplay.

"Come on, Loki." We didn't need to witness what was sure to become a four-alarm fire. Once inside, Loki climbed on the sofa while I headed for the kitchen to work on my recipes, but all the while my thoughts were on that kiss, slightly edited with me as the one to bestow it on Rafe.

Waiting for Nat at the curb in front of Rafe's house, I watched as her black Tesla sedan rolled down the street. It really was an exquisite car, but talk about flashy. Especially when you saw my blond-haired, blue-eyed sister behind the wheel. It wasn't a wonder that heads twisted to keep her in their sights. She pulled into the drive and stopped at the gates.

"Nice car, show off."

Her grin widened. "Nice neighborhood."

Entering the code for the gates, she pulled her car up the drive and parked it next to mine. Seeing my car next to hers, yeah, my car was pathetic.

Nat climbed out, her focus on me. "Seriously, when are you going to get rid of that thing?"

"You know why I have it."

Her normally exuberant personality dimmed. She, unlike me, had given up on our dad a long time ago. "The sooner you come to terms with the fact that that man isn't much of a father, the better off you'll be. I'll buy you any car you want right now."

"No."

She reached for my hand. "You always were the eternal optimist. Okay, show me this place." Before I could, she turned in a full circle to take it all in. "Wow. You weren't kidding, it's awesome."

"Let's get your stuff inside and then I'll give you the tour."

Grabbing her bags from the trunk, I led her into the carriage house. She stopped just inside the door and looked her fill. "You scored, sister mine."

"Check out those pictures of what it looked like before."

Her reaction was much like the one I had, her eyes bugged out of her skull. "Hot and good with his hands. I think you need to make a play for your landlord."

"He's with someone."

Nat's head jerked around so fast I was surprised it didn't snap right off her neck. "What?"

"Yeah, saw her the other day. Victoria Secret models would be jealous of her. She and Rafe practically had sex right in front of me."

"No way."

"I almost came from watching them and they were only kissing."

"You're kidding." Her eyes narrowed as she studied me. "You aren't kidding."

"I wish I were."

"Did you tell them to get a room?"

How funny would that have been, watching their startled expressions because I was sure they hadn't even noticed me. In fairness to Rafe, he had been flirting with Mrs. Milner, but the chick...she walked right by me and hadn't noticed me at all. "I don't think they would have heard me."

We passed the kitchen, where I had fresh-baked cookies cooling, Nat snagged one.

"I wonder if she's a fling or someone serious."

"I couldn't tell. Seemed new, the passion was hot, but Mrs. Milner, the housekeeper, wasn't a fan, so maybe the chick has been coming around for a while."

"Housekeeper?"

"Yeah, she's kind of scary. Rigid and no nonsense but she flirted like a schoolgirl with Rafe and he flirted right back. It was sweet. You could tell it was the highlight of the woman's week."

"The man sounds like a contradiction. I'm looking forward to meeting him."

"I'm sure you'll see him while you're here since he spends most days in his workshop. Let's go outside, you've got to see the rest of it. The main house is incredible, but in dire need of landscaping."

"I did notice the lack of landscaping, but the stone of the house is gorgeous. And that porch, I see rocking chairs and mint juleps."

"And outdoor ceiling fans to stir the air."

We walked to the front of the house and Nat whistled. "It's even prettier up close, the stones sparkle."

"Imagine gardens softening the lines around the house, filled with colorful flowering plants, some variegated evergreens. Maybe even some hanging pots off the porch."

"It'd be magnificent. I wonder what he paid for this?"

"According to Trace, he got it for a steal. You saw the before photos, the place was a mess."

"He's probably already doubled the value of the property."

"At least." We headed around back, passed the barn that was locked since Rafe wasn't home, before ending the tour at the carriage house.

"You're only paying a thousand a month? He could have made

triple that, easily. All this and a sexy landlord for the price you're paying. Seriously, if your landlord is as sexy as you claim and you get to live here, I'm going to kill you and steal your identity."

At that moment, Rafe's truck pulled up the drive. "You can decide for yourself how sexy he is."

As soon as Rafe climbed from his truck, Nat exhaled. "Sweet Jesus."

Rafe was eying Nat's car before he turned and saw us staring at him. His head nodded to Nat before he gestured to the Tesla. "Yours?"

"Yeah."

"Sweet."

"He hates my car." I muttered.

"I hate your car. I'm seriously going to kill you. He's…I'm speechless."

Rafe walked over to us, his focus on Nat and I noticed how he took in Nat's height, since in heels she was nearly as tall as him.

"I'm Natalie, Avery's sister. Some place you got here."

"Rafe. Thanks." Those green eyes shifted to me. "Hey, Avery."

"Rafe."

Even though his focus stayed on me, he asked Nat. "Did you come from Pennsylvania?"

"No, I'm in Chelsea. I love what you've done with the carriage house."

"I needed a place to stay while I restored the house. It was good practice."

"It doesn't look like practice, it's amazing."

He looked a bit uncomfortable, not a reaction I would have expected from him. I moved the conversation along. "I was wondering if you'd be willing to be my guinea pig. Tasting my creations and giving me honest feedback. I've been experimenting."

"So the pacing was a success?"

My cheeks burned and not so much from what he said, but how he said it. He was flirting, and after witnessing him doing the same with Mrs. Milner, he clearly had a penchant for it. "Yes."

He grinned, that slight lifting of his lips that was just so damn sexy. "Twist my arm."

In my head, we were no longer talking about my desserts and what I was twisting wasn't his—*Pull it together, Avery.*

My face was on fire because my thoughts were so uncharacteristic; my reply was short and sweet. "Thanks."

He studied me, his head tilted in much the way Loki's did when I spoke to him. That grin never faded when he said, "I've got to get to work. Nice meeting you, Natalie."

"Back at ya."

We watched him walk to his barn and a glance at Nat confirmed that her eyes were on his ass too. "I am so killing you in your sleep."

Settling at a table in Lunar Moon pub on Riverdale Avenue, Nat ordered two bottles of her favorite red wine before I had even removed my jacket.

"Dinner is my treat and don't argue, Avery."

"I'm not going to argue. You make the big bucks."

"Yes I do."

We scanned the menu, "I think we should get a bunch of appetizers." Nat declared.

"Sounds good."

Dropping her menu, her focus shifted to me. "I have news."

My attention was split between the menu and Nat. "What kind of news?"

"I've met someone."

That unexpected comment gained my full attention. "What? When did that happen?"

"At the conference in Seattle, the reason I couldn't help you move in. He lives in Manhattan and yet it takes me traveling across the country to meet him. He's a personal trainer, one that focuses on rehabilitation for sports-injury patients."

"And you were at a conference together? Doesn't seem like you practice the same kind of medicine."

"Yeah, well, sports injuries aren't just of the bone and muscle, head trauma and concussions are huge."

"True."

"Anyway, his name is Tyler."

"From the way you're grinning, I'm guessing his first impression was a good one."

"Yeah. He's so alpha and yet there's a tenderness to him that just turns my insides to goo. And you know how the men I've dated tend to shy away from talk about my job; Tyler is fascinated with what I do. Not intimidated or uncomfortable, outwardly interested. And the sex…I thought it was lies, the way romance novels depicted sex, exaggerating for the benefit of entertainment. Oh no, I've first-hand experience that a man can actually give you multiple orgasms in one night."

At this point, I spit out my water. Nat hardly noticed. "I want you to meet him. I could be in an orgasm-induced bubble, seeing more fabulousness than exists because the man can play my body like an instrument."

"Seriously, he's that good in bed?"

"Better."

I was jealous, absolutely, because my sexual experiences had been good, but not great. And certainly not an orgasm-induced bubble great. "Definitely, I want to meet him? Orgasm-induced bubble?"

She sighed; clearly even the memory was good. Then she said, "It's more than that. Sure it started as sex, but we've spent every night I've been free together. I enjoy his company."

"Man moves fast."

"Is that bad?"

"I don't think so. If he knows what he's found in you, he'll want to make it clear he's interested."

"That's what I think too."

"I definitely want to meet him."

"I'll find out his schedule and we'll arrange something."

"I'm happy for you, Nat."

L. A. Fiore

"I want you to find someone."

"Let me get my footing with my job first and then I'll think about a man."

"That's fair."

The waitress returned with our wine. "Do you want to sample it?"

"Not necessary."

After the wine was poured and the apps ordered, Nat's attention turned back to me. "So are you ready for your first day?"

"Some days I think yes and then some days I wonder what I've gotten myself into."

"Sounds normal."

"I've been baking like a crazy woman, but the sheer volume in addition to the caliber of the restaurant, and the expectation of excellence from the patrons, it's nerve racking."

"You can totally do this."

"I know, but it's still overwhelming. Trace stopped by the other day with his daughter. They sampled some of my creations."

"And?"

"He said he'd make a habit out of stopping by with Faith if I had desserts like that on hand."

"Smart man. There better be some left for me."

"Like you have to ask."

Nat lifted her glass. "To the start of your new adventure."

"And yours."

She knew I was referring to Tyler when she replied, "I'll drink to that."

66

chapter seven

Avery

Standing in the living room of Rafe's house, envy burned through me. It was a little over a week since he offered me the tour. Nat had returned home, but only after purchasing me high-powered binoculars and demanding a blood oath that I send pictures regularly of Rafe, even suggested poses she'd like.

Studying Rafe's home, I adored his taste. Not a surprise since I loved what he'd done with the carriage house. He kept his rooms simple, almost sparse, but the pieces in each room were amazing. And the house itself, the crown moldings, the wainscoting, the hardwood floors were original to the house and painstakingly restored. He'd painted his living room a deep mocha, the crown moldings a creamy-white. A large, chocolate-brown leather sofa, with the softest leather, took up the one wall near the fireplace. The stone of the fireplace matched the outside of the house; the floors were a wide-planked walnut and built-ins, crafted by Rafe, surrounded the fireplace. An exquisite clock made from exotic woods hung over the sofa. And as picture perfect as it all appeared, it felt kind of cold. Where were the photos of friends and family? The afghan over the back of the sofa for the nights it got cold? Where were the magazines to page through while snuggling up in front of the fire? Hell, where was the television remote? It was like he was creating a home, but not actually living in it. And as I stood there, I couldn't help but indulge my fantasies as I visualized Rafe and me curling up on his sofa or better yet lying in front of the fire, naked and sweaty. Maybe my thoughts were inappropriate, but Rafe was a sexy man and I was only human. My focus turned to the clock over the sofa. For a craftsman, it was the perfect clock.

"Did you make that?"

"No, a friend sent it."

He was leaning up against the wall, his hands in the front pockets of his jeans. He had given me the tour, spoke very few words during it, and now he studied me much in the way I studied his house. His phone had rung a few times during the tour. He hadn't answered it at first, but the caller was persistent and when he did finally take the call, he was not at all happy with whoever was on the other end.

"Mrs. Milner, she's a bit rough around the edges, but she's a good woman. I'm mentioning this because I know you've met and on first impression she has a tendency to irritate people."

And by people I suspected he meant his girlfriend. "She offered to wash my linens. I loathe doing laundry, so rough around the edges or not, she's okay in my book."

He offered a smile so slight I'd have missed it if I hadn't been staring at his mouth. "I understand why this is taking you so long. Your work is exquisite."

"I'm trying to stay as close to the original as possible."

"Are there any photos of the house during its heyday? I'd love to see the landscaping."

"Nothing that has good views of the yard and unlike the house, I haven't a clue where to start."

Excitement burned through me because I adored gardening and getting a chance to work some magic on this property, I'd love that. "I could help. I'd love to, actually. I love gardening, haven't had a canvas since perfecting my mom's yard."

His focus hadn't left me, but it changed slightly. "If you have ideas, I'd like to hear them."

"Okay. I'll draw some up and show you." As much as I wanted to linger, I didn't want to overstay my welcome, so I added as I started from the room. "Creating time. I'll stop by later with a sweet. Be honest, I need honesty."

"I'll be honest." I had just reached the door when Rafe called to me. "Hey, Avery."

"Yeah."

"I probably should have mentioned this before. My dad is being released from prison soon."

Shock hit me first; Rafe's dad was in jail? Shock was quickly followed with curiosity. "Your dad is in prison?"

"Yeah."

"For what?"

"Armed robbery."

Alarm rippled down my spine, but so did interest since this was a first for me. Knowing someone who knew someone in prison. "How long has he been in jail?"

He hesitated, even looked a bit uncomfortable, before saying, "Twenty-five years."

"Twenty-five years?" I sounded like a parrot but Jesus that was a long time.

"A guard died, someone had to go to jail. They made an example out of him."

My heart twisted for the boy he had been. I knew all too well about an absentee father, but to have your father taken from you had to be tough. "How old were you when he was sent away?"

"Nine."

He'd been old enough to understand and still young enough to miss out on so much. "That must have been hard on you and your mom."

"It was just me."

My heart dropped. "You had no other family?"

"No. I ended up in Foster care."

Tears burned the back of my eyes thinking of a young Rafe having his world turned upside down. "I'm sorry." I didn't know what else to say because he'd been dealt a crappy hand.

The creases around his eyes softened a bit before he said, "He wasn't the one to shoot the guard, in case you were wondering."

"It hadn't crossed my mind that he had been, but why did he get twenty-five years?"

"Like I said, someone had to do the time."

"Why not the one who actually shot the guard?"

"The other two who did the job with him were found dead a few days later. Dad turned himself in or he likely would have..."

"Oh my God."

"If you'd rather not stay here, I'll understand."

"Why wouldn't I want to stay here?"

"He's an ex-con, some people would have a problem with that."

That was nonsense; the man did his time, but before I could say as much, we were interrupted by the sound of the back door opening and closing, followed shortly after with a "Rafe, babe." Rafe's expression in response was a bit terrifying before he hissed so softly I almost didn't hear him, "You've got to be fucking kidding me."

His girlfriend came breezing into the living room, but she stopped short at the sight of Rafe and me. Her expression, before she wiped it, was annoyance or maybe anger.

"I'm sorry. I didn't realize you had company." She didn't sound sorry, quite the opposite actually. And with the way she studied me, scrutinized was a better word, I had a suspicion she knew very well that Rafe had company.

The room went quiet; the dark energy coming from Rafe was like a living being. There was clearly more going on here than I knew, but the fact that his girlfriend was oblivious to Rafe's mood bewildered me. For my part, I couldn't tear my eyes from him. He looked as if he wanted to commit murder, so the fact that he kept his temper in check to offer the introductions was a testament to the man's self-control. "Melody, this is Avery. She's renting the carriage house."

"It's nice to meet you, Melody."

Her eyes darted to me. "And you, Avery."

The words were barely out of her mouth before I was completely forgotten. And I knew this because she moved into Rafe, her fingers curling at the waistband of his jeans. "I thought we could go to dinner tonight and after you could stay at my place. I know there's Loki, but Avery's here now, she can check in on him."

That was presumptuous of her offering my services when she literally just met me, even though I'd be delighted to have Loki for company.

Rafe clearly was of the same mindset. "That's fucking rude, asking for a favor when you've only just met Avery."

"It's not a favor. She's here, why can't she walk across the yard and check on your dog?"

Melody certainly wasn't named for her personality.

A glance at Rafe and he was as incredulous as me, but how exactly did you follow logic like that? As much as I wanted to stay, curious as to where this conversation was heading, manners dictated that I leave, so I smiled and hurried out. The screen door had barely closed when I heard Rafe's very loud and succinct question. "What the fuck was that?"

The oatmeal cake felt moist, the spring back was good. Once it cooled, I added the maple icing: butter, confectioner sugar, maple syrup, a touch of vanilla. It looked good, but did it taste good? Cutting into it, the cake was surprisingly light considering the oatmeal. Plating a slice, I went in search of Rafe. His delightful girlfriend had pulled down the drive not long after I exited stage left. The way the stones kicked up in her wake, she'd been in a hurry to leave. I'd love to know what Rafe said to her. Power tools had been going on and off since. Standing at the open barn door, I waited for him to finish with the cut he was making on the table saw. Sensing me, his head turned in my direction, his gaze falling to the cake.

"Is that for me?"

"It is."

He wiped his hands on his jeans as he started over to me. "New recipe?"

"Yes. Oatmeal cake with maple icing."

His brow arched slightly. "Oatmeal?"

It was so easy to read him; he didn't think he was going to like it. The cake would no doubt be dense and heavy, an odd consistency. He eyed the cake warily.

"I suppose I did offer to be a taster."

"You did."

Before he reached for the cake he said, "I'm sorry about earlier."

"No reason for *you* to be sorry."

"She was in my house, you're my tenant, and she was rude to you. That shit is not cool."

He was right, it wasn't, but he handled it. So there really wasn't much more for me to say but "Thanks."

"Oatmeal cake." He said as he took the cake, holding it like it might reach out and bite him. The ease in which the fork cut into the cake had him looking up at me through his ridiculously long lashes. "It's very light."

"Not what you were expecting."

"No."

Watching as the fork slipped into his mouth, between those lips, for just a moment I wished it was me he tasted.

"This is incredible. Have you tried it?" he asked.

"No, not yet."

He lifted the fork to my mouth, the same fork that had just been in his mouth, and I had to consciously bite down on the moan. As soon as my lips closed over the cake, my drooling over Rafe took a backseat. The cake was light and extremely moist. The sweetness of the icing was cut by the earthiness of the cake.

"Oh, it is good."

He laughed, his eyes sparkling from it; the sound was glorious. "You thought I was just being nice."

"I did."

"I wouldn't have thought oatmeal would make a good cake, thought it'd be heavy, but it's not at all. And the icing complements it perfectly: smooth, rich and sweet."

"You're good at this."

"It's not hard, knowing what tastes you like and don't."

I'd like his taste; I had no doubt about that.

Moving the conversation onto something safe, I asked, "Do you have a leash and those bags for Loki? He's been outside the carriage house in the mornings, so I thought it'd be nice to walk him. It'd been good exercise for me too."

"Yeah, there's a leash on the hook in the coat closet in the carriage house. There's a plastic bone on the leash that has the bags. Are you sure you want to walk him? He'll probably go about five hundred feet before dropping on his stomach."

"How old is he?"

"Five."

"Why is he so—"

"Lazy? I don't know. It's a recent development. When he was younger, I couldn't keep him still."

"Well, I'll try taking him for a walk and see what happens."

"If you're up to it, that would be great. He isn't fat, but he's going to get so if he doesn't move around more."

"We'll go tomorrow and see how he does." Taking the dish back from him, I added, "I never had a dog, but I always wanted one. It'll be fun for me too. Anyway, thanks for being my guinea pig."

"Any time, seriously. That was unreal."

Stocking up on chef jackets and pants from the restaurant supply store in town, since I really did hate doing laundry, I dumped my purchases in my car and headed to Starbucks. My first day of work was in a few days and I was ready—nervous, like biting my fingernails to the quick, but I had fine-tuned my dishes and they were as good as they were going to get. Lost in thought, I didn't see Dolly, my stepmother, until after she had noticed me. She wasn't happy about seeing me, the scowl on her face was proof of that, but still she moved through the bodies toward me on her four-inch heels.

"What are you doing here, Avery?"

How hard was it to say hello? Seriously, it was a pet peeve of mine when someone didn't greet you and considering this woman was married to my father, a simple hello was not asking too much. And then her question registered, which only pissed me off more. Accusation dripped from her words, as if she had staked her claim for all of Manhattan so my presence was in violation of some unseen boundaries. I could have answered her question, which would have moved her along and away from me quicker, but I was feeling belligerent.

"Dolly, what a lovely surprise. How are you? You're looking well. Manhattan clearly agrees with you."

I almost laughed out loud because she hadn't been expecting that, had a retort on her tongue that she had to swallow.

"I'm fine, but you didn't answer my question."

"Are you just getting here? Maybe we could grab a cup of coffee and catch up?" I'd rather have rats eat my face, but since I knew she'd like the idea even less, I enjoyed watching the expression that rolled over her face—like a deer in the headlights, blinking her fake lashes as her brain desperately tried to understand the dynamic. Why hadn't I thought to do this before?

"Your father and I have dinner plans. I need to get home to get ready. Why are *you* so far from home?"

"I live here now. Well, not here but close to here. I got a job, pastry chef for a restaurant right here in Manhattan."

"Pastry chef? For what restaurant?"

I hadn't expected her to congratulate me and still it annoyed me that she hadn't offered one. And because of her rudeness, I was rude in return by hesitating in answering her. The pink that infused her cheeks as her temper simmered was a joy to see. Right when she looked about ready to shout at me, I said, "Clover. Have you heard of it?" I had no doubt she'd heard of it, she probably kept a folder of all the hot and trendy places to see and be seen and demanded visiting those places frequently. My dad would hate that, but I felt no sympathy. He'd made his bed.

"You're working at Clover?"

The genuine disbelief shouldn't have grated—I knew it was coming—and yet it still did. "Why do you sound so surprised by that?"

"I just thought they'd want someone with a bit more…" she gestured to my overall appearance, the implication clear—a person with more style—before saying, "experience."

Dolly Collins, previously Dolly Tucker, prior to meeting my dad was cutting hair at the local barber. What the hell did she know about style? "Well, experience or not, Trace Montgomery adored my desserts. Offered me the job personally, even helped me with securing a place to live nearby."

She didn't believe me; I could see that very easily from her expression. Not that I cared.

"Really? And where are you living?"

"Riverdale in the Bronx."

As far as zip codes went, mine totally kicked her zip codes ass and she knew it.

"Riverdale? That's an exceedingly expensive neighborhood."

"I know; you should see the place where I'm staying. Unbelievable. Well, this has been fun but like you said, you have to get home to dress for dinner and I've suddenly lost my appetite. See you later. Give Dad my love."

I turned my back on her and walked out, without my coffee, but the sight of her doing her impression of a guppy had my smile going from ear-to-ear.

Whenever I was conflicted, I baked and seeing Dolly had me feeling all kinds of things, so, as soon as I returned home, I whipped up some peanut butter cookies. But not your ordinary peanut butter cookies, I added a dash of curry; the smell was divine. If they tasted half as good as they smelled, I was in for a treat. The nerve of that woman, but what was worse was my dad being oblivious to her treatment of Nat and me or uninterested. As much as I wanted a relationship with him, he was making it very hard.

The sound of a powerful engine thankfully pulled me from my unpleasant thoughts and I walked to window to see as the sexiest black muscle car pulled into the drive—parking next to my buttercup-yellow station wagon. In the next minute, a man climbed from the car.

"Are you freaking kidding me?" My face was pressed up against the glass but honest to God, what was it with Rafe and his friends? It was like the fairy godmother that worked this area had gone overboard, hitting them a few extra times with her beauty wand. The newcomer shared a similar look with Rafe, though Rafe edged him out in my opinion. This man's long hair was brown with hints of auburn and he too was built as if he was compiled from every woman's wildest dream. And then Rafe appeared and it was almost too much male beauty for a mere mortal to take.

The man studied my car; I could see the look of disgust even from my distance. And then his face turned in the direction of the carriage house, and what a face. I ducked out of sight. And then I did something completely mental, I ran to the bedroom for my binoculars, at the same time I grabbed the house phone and called Nat.

"Hey little sis."

"There's another one."

"What?"

"Trace and Rafe, there's a third. He just pulled up in some sexy, black muscle car."

"No way. Get a picture."

"That's a little hard with the binoculars in my hand."

I heard the humor and the unspoken, I told you so. "You weren't going to use them, huh?"

"What is it with the air here?" I said, not wishing to hear Nat gloating.

"I don't know, but I'll be able to put my impressive brain to the task of figuring it out if I had a picture to study."

"Oh my God, you're ridiculous. Hold on, let me get my cell."

Retrieving my phone, I hunched down by the front window and managed a few shots. "I'm sending them. Looks like his car is a Charger, an old one."

"Sweet baby Jesus, he's delicious. Ah damn he's wearing a wedding ring."

"He is? I didn't see that."

"You're right, it's an anomaly, all that hotness in one place. Maybe you should move here and I'll stay there, just in case it's not safe."

"I really can't believe you operate on people's brains when you haven't one of your own."

"I'm brainless? Have you made your move on your sexy landlord? Cause I got to tell you, Avery, if it were me, I'd have tapped that repeatedly by now."

"I'll repeat, since you clearly are hard of hearing, he's seeing someone."

"Whatever."

Still hunching down at the front window, eying Rafe and the new guy through my high-powered binoculars, I nearly fell out of it when the timer for the cookies went off.

"What the hell was that?" Nat demanded in my ear.

"My cookies."

Jumping up, I ran to the kitchen, placed the binoculars on the counter, shut off the timer and pulled the trays from the oven and placed them on the cooling racks.

"What kind of cookies?"

"Peanut butter."

"Oh, I love your peanut butter cookies. I'd hop in my car, but I've got Mr. Daniels aneurysm in a few minutes."

"Be nice and maybe I'll overnight some to you."

"You do love me"

"Yeah, I love you."

"Send cookies and get Rafe naked and then I want details, leave nothing out."

I hung up on her. The knock at the door startled me, followed quickly with nerves since I knew it was Rafe and the sexy new guy. Unconsciously I glanced down at my faded jeans and burgundy sweater, a step up from the sweats I usually wore but not by much.

With about as much enthusiasm as Loki usually demonstrated, I moved to the door and pulled it open. The force of the collective stare coming from impossibly hot men nearly had my legs going weak. Before I could say hi, Rafe's friend inhaled, noticeably, before asking, "What is that?"

"Cookies. I just pulled some out."

He then flashed me a grin, a panty-dropping grin. "I like cookies."

I laughed, couldn't help it, because what a clown-like thing to say especially coming from a man who looked as he did. Deciding I liked this friend of Rafe's, I teased him.

"I don't share my cookies with people I don't know."

He smiled again; this one was slower to form and was somehow even more spectacular than the last one. His hand reached for mine, his hold firm but gentle. "Lucien Black."

"Avery Collins."

"Delighted."

"More with the smell of my cookies, but seeing as you have obvious taste, please come in."

"You see right through me." Lucien teased.

"Right now you're about as transparent as glass, so not a great accomplishment."

"Touché."

"Hi, Rafe." I couldn't help the assessing stare I gave him, objectifying, absolutely, but the sight of him naked from the waist up, sweaty and sexy, was permanently burned on my brain, so much so that I was contemplating a new house rule. Some people had a no shoe policy; I think I was going to adopt the no shirt policy for sexy, hot men only. Sexist, sure, but it was my home. I was legally renting it, so I could be as sexist as I wanted. Glancing over at Lucien, yeah I think no shirts in this house were a must. I wondered if they'd be suspicious if I mentioned that policy now?

My gaze collided with Rafe's when he asked, "You okay?"

"Me? Yeah. Why?"

"You look a little flushed."

I probably had drool at the corner of my mouth too. Best to move the subject on, but Rafe beat me to it when he said, "I want whatever you just baked. It smells incredible."

Entering the kitchen, Lucien asked, "Peanut butter?"

"With a secret ingredient. Try to guess what."

Both Rafe and Lucien took a cookie, my eyes darting between the two for their reactions and seeing the look that moved over Rafe's face, one I often experienced when tasting something so good words failed to do it justice, I felt almost giddy. And then he said, "These are incredible."

"Understatement." Lucien said and then added, "Curry."

"That's right. Peanuts can be both sweet and savory, so I thought adding a bit of savory to the sweetness of the cookie would add another dimension."

"It's fantastic." This came from Rafe. "Is this a recipe for Clover?"

"No, patrons of Clover expect something more sophisticated than a cookie. I was just experimenting."

"And you didn't come find me?" He said that as his lips turned up on the one side. He was teasing me, I really liked that he was teasing me.

"I just pulled them from the oven. I'd have hunted you down."

"What were you doing with the binoculars?" Lucien asked.

How the hell did I answer that? *I was spying and drooling at you two, wishing I were the meat to your hot, messy sandwich.* The lie slipped easily past my lips. "Bird watching, just watching those birds. There are some really rare species around here."

Lucien leaned up against the counter, his arms crossing over his chest. I could not, for the life of me, discern his expression. "Are you into bird watching?"

No, I mean outside of an *Ah* when I see the brilliant red of a cardinal I wouldn't know the various species of birds indigenous to the area let alone rare breeds. But I had already placed my foot in my mouth, so I had to tally on. "Yeah, a little. Just a way to pass the time."

"What species have you seen?"

Narrowing my eyes at Lucien, he actually narrowed his in return. Son of a bitch knew I was talking out of my ass. I could have done the mature thing, fessed up and moved on. I, apparently, was not mature. Game on. "I saw an eagle just the other day. Big, ass bird."

An arched brow from Lucien met that answer. Rafe sounded odd, maybe concerned for Loki when he asked, "An eagle, really?"

"It was probably just a hawk, I'm not used to seeing large birds of prey like that."

Lucien shifted and now he was grinning. "Aren't you from rural Pennsylvania?"

It was true that we had lots of hawks and turkey vultures back home, but how the hell would he know that? Rafe, seeming to have had enough of the conversation, changed the subject. Thank God. "Your first day is coming up. Are you ready?"

"I go back and forth between absolutely ready and not even close."

A smile was his only reply and if Lucien's smile was panty dropping, Rafe's was bone melting.

Rafe headed for the door, Lucien held back until Rafe was out of earshot. "You're a terrible liar, but a hell of a baker."

I was now as red as a cardinal.

"I have to give you credit though, you're tenacious, digging yourself deeper and deeper but doing so with attitude."

Did he just say that to me? "You are not acting in a manner that will garner you any more of my baked goods."

"You're right, I'll behave."

Lucien followed Rafe from the kitchen as I asked, "Are you this candid with everyone you meet?"

"No, only the ones I like."

Reaching the door, I held it for Rafe and Lucien who said, "Nice to meet you, Avery. I look forward to the next time."

"You and me both."

"Later, Avery." Rafe said before following after Lucien. Closing the door, I pressed my forehead up against it, but I was smiling one of Nat's deranged smiles.

My phone rang pulling me from my ridiculousness. Seeing it was Jessica, I answered, "Hey you."

"How does December 16-19 work for a visit?"

"Once I get my work schedule, I'll try to get those dates off."

"We'll check out hotels close to you."

"Sounds good. So get this, Rafe and his friend Lucien were just here and I have to say they make the people out here entirely too sexy."

"What do you mean?"

For the next half an hour I told her about that over-eager fairy godmother.

chapter eight

Avery

Returning home the following day after taking Loki for a walk, I noticed the silver car parked in front of Rafe's house and the two women and two little girls standing at the gate, one of which was Ember Montgomery. The woman with her was slightly taller with long black hair. Ember was holding Faith's hand and the other woman held the hand of a little girl who looked very much like her. Both the women and the girls had their heads together, which gave the impression that they were up to something.

Envy stabbed me at the sight and had me missing Jessica and my sister.

When I was close enough to call to them and not sound like a raging nut, I said. "Hi, Ember, Faith."

Four sets of eyes turned to me. The woman with the black hair had the brightest blue eyes, her daughter's looked more green than blue.

"Avery. Hi. This is Darcy and Emily. We were just in the neighborhood."

My brow rose at that obvious falsehood. "Really? How long did it take you to get into the neighborhood?"

"Busted. I told you she wouldn't buy that." That came from Darcy and it sounded so much like how Nat and I spoke to each other that it was clear Ember and Darcy were very close "Lucien mentioned he met you yesterday, we were curious."

Lucien, yep Emily looked just like him. I shouldn't be surprised; that overeager fairy godmother really should have her wand confiscated.

Ember hunched down next to Loki, who was standing just a little bit taller than he had been only minutes ago. Even he appreciated the overachieving godmother's efforts. "Hey, buddy." Ember's gaze met mine. "The first time I met Rafe, he was walking Loki in the park. Well, Loki was actually running through the park without a care in the world. We had a head-on collision."

Rafe had mentioned that Loki used to be way more active. "That's interesting. He acts like an old man now."

"Contentment, I guess. And seeing Rafe's place, how could he not be?"

"True. So what brings you here?"

"Darcy wanted to get a look at you."

"Ember!"

"Well you did. There's no point in beating around the bush."

"Ember wants you to feed her."

If Darcy thought that tidbit would embarrass Ember, she'd be disappointed. "I do. Trace raves about you. Trace does not rave."

Excitement had my heart fluttering like a hummingbird's wings. "Really? He raves?"

"Yes and I know he invited you to Allegro this Friday, so we wanted to make sure you were still coming."

"I'm looking forward to it."

Darcy added, "Rafe's coming too, so you can catch a ride with him."

"I'll likely drive in case Rafe wants to bring his girlfriend." I didn't miss the look that passed between the two and more curious than I was polite, I asked, "What am I missing?"

"Have you met the girlfriend?"

"Yeah."

Glancing down at the girls, Darcy whispered, "She's a b-i-t-c-h. She never comes out with us."

"She's not a b-i-t-c-h, she's just shy." Ember was clearly the diplomat. And talk about sharing freely, and for some crazy reason I had no problem with voicing exactly how I felt about Melody to these two.

"I'm with Darcy on this."

It was like I'd just screamed that Brad Pitt was across the street, I had their rapt attention. Ember asked, "Why?"

"She's rude and crass and despite being exquisite, she's ugly."

Darcy's smile held a bit of wickedness. "How many times has she been around?"

"She showed up the day I moved in, came a few days later and the last time Rafe was giving me the tour of his house, he introduced us."

"And that was your takeaway, rude, crass and ugly?"

"Her first visit she had to know I was moving in and yet she made no attempt to meet me. The second time, she walked right past me and yet didn't acknowledge me. The third time, I'm pretty sure she was the one who kept calling Rafe while he was giving me the tour. When he finally answered and she knew he was entertaining me, she arrived acting all surprised to be interrupting. She even went so far as to suggest I could watch Loki now so Rafe could spend nights at her place. So, yeah that was my takeaway, she is a b-i-t-c-h."

Darcy threw her head back and laughed. "We are going to get along just fine."

Glancing at my watch, it was half past ten. I was meeting Terry, Chef Moree's sous chef, in an hour and half to discuss the menu for my first week at Clover, but there was time enough for a cup of coffee. "I have to be at Clover for a meeting, but I've time to offer you some coffee. And I have freshly baked apple cinnamon scones."

"You are speaking our language." Darcy said.

Once the girls were settled in the living room playing with toys that Rafe had in the closet, Ember, Darcy and I moved to the kitchen.

"Can the girls have a scone?"

"They would love that, but maybe they should eat in here." Ember suggested.

"They're having fun and it's only crumbs." Plating them each a scone, the wide eyes that greeted me when I placed their dishes before them was adorable.

"Yummy." Faith said after her first bite.

Emily followed Faith's movements exactly, her expression sweet. "Apples."

"Yep."

Rejoining their moms, I pulled the mugs from the rack and poured us coffee. I settled across from them, but both were too busy eating, their mouths full of scone. The amount of *oh my* and *good God* that came from the pair of them did wonderful things for my ego. When their plates were clean, practically licked of crumbs, Ember's focus shifted to me. "That was amazing."

"The secret, baking powder and cream of tartar, extra fine flour and the butter has got to be icy cold when you cut it in."

"Delicious." Darcy reached for her cup. "So tell us what you think of Rafe."

I had just taken a sip of my coffee; the unexpected question had it going down the wrong pipe. After I coughed it clear, I managed to ask, "Excuse me?"

"Come on. All that hunky male beauty, you have got to have thoughts."

Not only were they all ridiculously beautiful, they were the most outspoken people I'd ever met. "Do any of you come with a filter?"

Ember's brown eyes widened in all innocence, but I saw the mischievousness lurking behind her expression. "Whatever do you mean?"

"When Lucien was here, he called me on a few things and not knowing me, it was a surprise."

"What few things?" Ember asked.

Following the pattern in the quartz countertop with my finger, I muttered. "I may have been checking Rafe and Lucien out with my binoculars. He saw the binoculars and called me on it."

"That was likely for Rafe's benefit." Darcy said.

Rafe's benefit...what did she mean by that? "How so?"

"Lucien is also not a big fan of Melody's. I knew I married a smart man."

Ember's head, that was nodding affirmatively, looked like a bobble head. "Yes, you did." And then her gaze sliced back to me. "So, what do you think of Rafe?"

"He's very nice. Extremely talented."

"Come on, we already know that. Everyone knows that. What do *you* think of him?" Darcy was now leaning so far over the counter she was practically in my coffee mug.

"He makes me catch my breath, my brain disengages whenever he's around which causes me to say the most ridiculous things and when I saw him coming from his barn with no tee, hot and sweaty, I thought I'd died and gone to heaven."

This earned me dropped jaws from both of them.

"What? You asked."

Unlike her husband, Ember would be terrible at poker. Her thoughts were very transparent and right now she wanted to play matchmaker.

I tried to derail whatever she was plotting when I asked, "How did you all meet?"

Ember rested her head on her hand. "Let's see. Lucien and Darcy met at an orphanage when they were younger. Trace too was there and so was Rafe. I met Trace a few years ago. I was at a bar, a drunk was being overly friendly, and Trace stepped in."

I was beginning to better understand the dynamic between Rafe, Lucien and Trace. They were like brothers, not of blood but I'd guess just as strong. The idea that the boy Rafe had been had them to help him through what had to be a very difficult time made me happy. And it was the depth of that happy that gave me pause because it wasn't at all in line with the fun, flirty banter I had convinced myself was all I felt for my landlord.

Rocked a bit by that revelation, I almost missed what Darcy said. "I applied for a job with Lucien a few years ago. He was the love of my life at fourteen, turns out he's still the love of my life and luckily for me, I'm his."

"A second chance love story, I love those." And I did. I didn't even have a first chance love story, but whatever.

"What about you? Are you seeing anyone?" Darcy asked.

"No."

"Why not?" Ember asked.

"I've never had much luck dating and I've kind of been conditioned to not bother working on a relationship if it isn't worth the effort."

Darcy's head cocked as she studied me. She was clearly intrigued. "Conditioned how?"

"My dad married a twenty-four-year old when I was eighteen. The lessons started in high school. There was a boy in my senior year I really liked and one day I brought him home and he met my stepmother. Now my stepmother is a total b-i-t-c-h. She didn't like that I had a boyfriend and so she went out of her way to make it so I wasn't comfortable bringing him home. I guess if it had been real I'd have fought harder, but the fact that I caved as easily as I did was a sign."

"What did she do?" Ember asked.

"One time she came out of the bathroom, soaking wet, wearing only a towel that did very little to cover her. She acted appropriately embarrassed and hurried back to her room, but it was intentional. The next time she strolled into the kitchen wearing her very sexy nightie and thin little robe. What teenage boy isn't going to drool over a woman with a size four figure and double D cup? She wasn't even subtle about her scheming because when I didn't have a boy over she didn't even acknowledge my existence let alone walk around barely clothed."

"She is the b-word." Ember said, chancing a glance at the girls as if they would somehow know the b-word really meant bitch.

"When I was at culinary school I was so focused on school that I didn't make any serious commitments."

"Are you a vir…" Darcy started to say; my bark of laughter cut her off.

"Seriously with the filter. But no, I had boyfriends I liked enough to explore s-e-x with." Glancing at the clock I almost fell off my stool. "Holy crap, I've got to go."

Immediately a chorus of, "Holy crap" came from the living room. "Oops."

Ember waved off my faux pas as she stood and started collecting the dishes. "I swear Faith can hear a bat belch three miles away. It's unreal. Trace soundproofed our bedroom, hand to God. He didn't want to traumatize Faith, but he wasn't going to curb his appetites, if you know what I mean."

I wanted to put my hands over my ears because talk about too much information. Jesus, now when I looked at Trace I was going to be thinking about the various appetites he didn't want to curb. "That is too much info to know about my boss."

Ember's wicked grin was an indication that she didn't agree.

Within a few minutes, my kitchen was spotless and the five of us were walking out the front door. "You hang here, Loki. I'll text your daddy and let him know where you are."

Since Loki made no attempt to move from the sofa, I knew he was very happy with this plan.

Both Ember and Darcy were staring at my car when I finished locking up.

"It's a classic." I said in way of explanation.

"It's a piece of sh—" Darcy caught herself; she even blushed. "I'm sorry, that was rude."

"Rude, but true." I acknowledged because it was a piece of shit.

"Does it hold a special meaning for you? Did you lose your virginity in the backseat or it came with a million dollars?"

Ember had unknowingly hit it on the head. "My dad bought it for me. He's usually pretty unapproachable, so the memory of us spending the day searching for a used car is a good memory."

"Well, now I feel like crust on dog poop."

"What? Crust on dog poop? How would you even know that dog

poop forms a crust?" I asked and then put my hand up to stop Darcy from replying. "You know what? I really don't want to know."

Darcy was grinning at me now and Emily was jumping up and down, giggling. "Mommy said poop."

To which Faith immediately replied, "Poop, poop, poop."

"They're like parrots."

"You've no idea." And with the way Ember said that, I suspected someone dropped a few words they shouldn't have in front of the little one. And after Trace's near slip the other day, I suspected he was the culprit.

"I do have to go though. I'll see you on Friday."

"Absolutely and thanks for feeding us, the unexpected and nosey women that we are."

"I enjoyed it."

"Us too." Darcy waved, as did Emily. Ember gave me a half hug before lifting Faith into her arms. Faith reached over and touched my cheek, her little fingers so soft and then she said, "Pretty."

My heart melted.

chapter nine

Avery

Resting against the tree at the back of Rafe's property, I pondered my wardrobe for my night out at Allegro. I couldn't wait to get out and socialize; I was feeling a bit stir-crazy and, if I was being honest, lonely. I had known it was going to be lonely coming here, but I didn't realize how lonely. Jess had been so close that we visited each other all the time and even being closer to Nat now, with her schedule I couldn't just pop over like I used to with Jessica.

I liked that Rafe's friends had been by to check out his new tenant, more for his benefit than mine—wouldn't want a crazy person living within reaching distance—but to be included…yeah, I was definitely looking forward to the evening. Loki and I had just taken our walk and after, we usually sat for a bit outside as I enjoyed the quiet and he the sun on his coat. And it was while we sat there, that I pondered Rafe's neighborhood. It was seriously swanky, and remembering that Trace had said Rafe had purchased the white elephant, a description that no longer applied, what did Rafe's neighbors' homes look like if this place was the white elephant? How often did an average Joe like me get to see multi-million dollar homes? It was hard to see the houses on our walks because they were all set back from the street and, like Rafe's, cleverly concealed. Maybe I could see through the foliage along the fence to the neighbor on the other side. But even peering through a section of the fence where the vegetation wasn't as dense I still couldn't see through to the neighbors. Glancing at the height of the fence, I was sure I could scale it. How hard could it be? I mean, who would know? A quick climb up, a look over and no one would be the wiser. Reaching through the plants to the metal fence they concealed, I was about to start up when Loki barked.

Looking back at him, he cocked his head at me but I hadn't a clue why he barked.

"I just want to see. I'll only be a second."

He barked again.

I put my finger to my mouth. "If you bark, you're going to draw attention. I don't want the neighbors knowing I'm sneaking a peek."

I wanted to believe that he understood me because when I turned back to the fence, he didn't bark. Unlike the front of the house where the fence was a fancy, black wrought iron, the back fence was chain link. Getting a good grip, I started up. It was far easier than I thought it would be, but I wasn't congratulating myself for long. I felt resistance as I attempted to move higher and twisted my head around to see that my sweats were caught on a broken tree branch. I wasn't just caught, the branch was digging into my flesh and at the angle it was stabbing me, if I dropped to the ground it'd likely go through skin. I tried moving horizontally with the hope that the branch would pull free, but my feet didn't have great purchase with the links as small as they were, so I attempted to wiggle my butt to loosen the hold the branch had on me, but it wouldn't budge.

Loki started barking again, which was totally okay with me since I was close to doing my own yelling. The metal started cutting into my fingers; the sharp branch was stabbing me in the ass and my arms were beginning to tremble from trying to hold myself up.

And then I heard the back door slam shut, the sound of heavy footsteps, as if someone was running. Of course, because why wouldn't Rafe witness this humiliation?

"What the hell are you doing?" For obvious reasons, he sounded annoyed.

It was clear what I was doing, I was spying on the neighbors, but since he asked a stupid question, I gave him a stupid answer.

Turning my head, I was greeted to the sight of Rafe standing with his hands on his hips. I said, "I'm doing my interpretation of a spider. Do you want to join me?"

Annoyance shifted to humor, his focus moving to my ass and then the smug bastard said. "That doesn't look very comfortable."

"You mean the branch impaling my right ass cheek? It feels delightful."

This got me his eyes, ones that were laughing. "Is this another short person protest?"

I was pissed and wanted to laugh at the same time. I felt his strong hands wrapping around my waist. He lifted me, but that branch was not letting go. When he pulled me back to him, he did so with too much force, breaking the branch and sending us backwards. We landed in a heap with his hard body cushioning my fall. I heard the sharp exhale as my body forced the air from his lungs, felt as my cheeks burned. I moved like I was on fire, scrambling off him. He just lay there, on his back, like he was dead.

And then his head turned, his stare freezing me in place, and even being in the submissive position, there was no question as to who was the alpha.

"First you lay siege to the tea aisle in the market and now you're picking fights with my trees. What else do I have to look forward to?"

"Are you hurt?"

"Bruised ego, but I'll live." His body moved fluidly as he regained his footing. And even with leaves in his hair, he looked hot.

His ego was bruised. What about my ego from the ridiculous show I'd just put on? Maybe he hadn't seen all of it. "How long were you watching?"

"When you put your finger to your lips to Loki."

Naturally, he saw all of it. Looking around, I wondered if there was a shovel handy so I could bury myself.

"I liked your little butt dance."

"It was not a dance, I was attempting to make that traitorous tree branch release me. Seriously, what kind of trees do you have here?"

He offered no comment on that. "You wouldn't have gotten stuck if you weren't spying on my neighbors."

"I wasn't spying, I was looking." And then I realized he saw me get stuck and he allowed me to do the butt wiggle instead of immediately coming to my aid.

"Why did you wait to offer help?"

"And miss the butt wiggle?"

"So you knew what I was doing, even before I so masterfully scaled the fence?"

"Yeah, I cottoned on when you tried peering through the bushes."

"Wait, I peered into the bushes before I encouraged Loki to stop barking."

In response, he grinned.

"Well, I've learned that lesson."

"Not to spy on the neighbors?"

"No, next time I need a ladder."

And in reply, he laughed out loud. "I need to run out and I would really like to come home to my house still being here, my barn still standing and no neighbors forming a lynch mob because my tenant is invading their privacy."

"Fine. Loki and I will have the bonfire that can be seen from space another night."

He strolled to his truck; I called to him, "Thanks for the rescue, but next time it'd be nice if you were a little more prompt. Damsels don't like to be kept waiting."

In reply, he laughed out loud again.

Stepping through the doors at Allegro, I'd never been to a club like it. During the day, the place probably looked just on the wrong side of weathered and worn, but at night it was electric. The blues band currently on stage rocked with their soulful, sexy sound, the people crowding the dance floor were proof of that.

Like magic, Ember appeared all smiles. "You made it. We're over here." She grabbed my hand and practically dragged me through the bodies to a table sitting prominently up front by the stage.

"You know everyone, right?" She asked, well really yelled to be heard over the other sounds.

"Yeah."

As soon as I settled, Lucien asked. "What are you drinking?"

"Cabernet."

He signaled for the waitress as Trace pulled Ember onto his lap and pressed a kiss on her neck. It was almost unconsciously done, that show of affection, and I felt my heart twist. How must that feel? Then he asked me, "Did you have any trouble finding it?"

"I took a cab."

"Yay, so you can join me in getting stupid." Darcy said, but it was the look Lucien was giving her that held my attention. He looked hungry. "I don't often indulge, but I am tonight."

"Um, okay. This place is great." My answer was totally lame, but the pheromone levels at the table were turning *me* on.

"It's my favorite of Lucien's clubs, which is good considering I work here."

"You work together?"

"Yeah. He's a decent enough boss. I guess."

Lucien pulled her close, his fingers wrapping around her neck. "I'll give you decent." The heat in those words burned me and I was across the table from them.

"I love the band." I sounded like a child with my simple and obvious comments, but trying to think with all the sexual tension swirling around was very difficult.

Lucien didn't seem to have a problem stringing more than a few words together when he said, "They played during open mic one night. I liked their sound, so offered them an ongoing gig."

"Nice."

"Kyle's band plays here too." Ember added.

"You're in a band?"

"Yeah."

"And not just a band, they're a few signatures away from being signed with a label." Ember's enthusiasm for her friend was contagious.

"Congratulations. What kind of music?"

"Mostly alternative rock like Dave Matthews."

"I'm in awe of musicians, the way they blend music and lyrics to create a short story with each song. Have you always wanted to be a musician?"

"When I was younger, I was kind of wild. Got into some trouble, hung with the wrong crowd. My grandmother raised me, told me I had better get my shit together or else. She played piano for the church choir, sat me at a piano and it was like I'd been doing it all of my life. I couldn't read music, but I could play it, instinctively knew the sounds that worked together. Later, the lyrics came. I love it, even if this deal doesn't go through, I've got the band, we have our gigs."

"Your grandmother sounds like a very smart woman."

"Don't tell her, she'll get a big head."

A movement out of the corner of my eye had my focus shifting to Rafe who appeared at my side and with him was Melody. Begrudgingly, I had to admit they looked really good together. Not that I liked them together, I didn't like it one bit. Rafe pulled a chair out for her before taking the seat at her side.

After greetings went around the table, Rafe settled those green eyes on me. "Avery, you remember Melody."

Her eyes were violet; I hadn't noticed that before, they were the most unusual color of blue. Exquisite actually, but the look I saw burning behind them had me curling my hand into a fist. Time had not made her heart grow fonder.

"Hi, Avery. You all settled?" Saccharine-sweet her voice—I felt a cavity coming on—and completely insincere.

I could be as phony as the next gal. "I am. I didn't need to do much. The place was already live-in ready."

"No doubt Mrs. Milner worked her magic."

It was slight, but I picked up on the hostility in that comment. And I just had to ask myself. What was this chick's deal? She walked in here with the hottest man in the place and yet she just oozed nastiness. And really, what the hell did Rafe see in her outside of her obvious attributes?

"What are you drinking, Melody?" Rafe asked.

"Patron, neat."

"We missed you at ladies' night." Darcy's expression wasn't one that bespoke missing; it was quite the opposite. Melody didn't seem to notice.

"Sorry. I was getting ready for an interview. I hope I can make the next one."

"How's the job search going?" Ember asked.

"Slow, but I'm ever hopeful."

"What are you interviewing for?" I asked, not out of interest but curiosity.

"I used to model, but I'd like to get into the marketing side of advertising. I'm having a bit of trouble though. People aren't keen on a former model wanting a desk job."

I suspected it wasn't that she was a former model that people weren't keen on. A glance at Darcy and Ember and I knew they shared my sentiment.

"If you're being discriminated against because you're beautiful, clearly you're interviewing at the wrong places." Why the hell did I just say that? It was a true statement, but not one she needed to hear especially seeing the smug look she had in reply. I needed a drink or food to keep my mouth occupied since clearly my pheromone-soaked brain was not up to conversing. Then I saw the look Rafe was giving me, one that had my heart skipping a few beats as yet another more pleasant way filled my thoughts on how I could keep my mouth occupied. I openly harbored inappropriate thoughts for someone who was staring right at me as I did. I was losing my mind. My drink arrived and reaching for it, I drank half the contents in one swallow—an action that, to my horror, earned me the attention of every other person at the table. Trying to change the subject, I blurted out the first thought that popped in my head. "My sister is seeing someone who puts her in an orgasm-induced bubble."

My brain caught up to my mouth a second later, the urge to bang my head on the table almost had me doing so.

"Been there, done that." That comment came from Darcy and I recognized a rescue when I heard one. I mouthed, "Thank you," and she winked.

"We need to try that, Trace." Ember added.

"Right now?" He was already beginning to stand.

"No!"

His laugh turned everyone's attention away from me, thank God. *My sister is seeing someone who puts her in an orgasm-induced bubble.* I had the social skills of a goat.

RAFE

"I want to go back to my place. You ready, baby?" Melody asked as she pulled me into a small alcove. I'd just seen her to the ladies room since she'd had one too many and was wobbling on her heels. I hadn't wanted her to come with me tonight; I'd actually contemplated ending it with her prior to meeting up with everyone, but I hadn't wanted to deal with the fallout. Instead she finagled an invite out of me.

"We just got here." I tried for patience, but this scene with her was becoming too fucking familiar.

"I know, but I'm bored. I thought we could party, just the two of us."

I believed a man should acquiesce to his woman on some things; however, I was also not a man to be led around by my dick. Melody's constant attempts to do just that, especially since I was already one foot out the door, were trying my fucking patience.

"I'm not ready to go."

She pouted. "Come on. Please." Her fingers moved to my zipper. "I'll blow you right now, remind you of what you've got in store for later."

My dick stirred, an instinctual response because the woman gave killer blowjobs. A fucking gold medalist at sucking cock, but that pretty much summed up our whole relationship. Not that that was a bad thing for what it was, but no blowjob, no matter how fantastic, was worth the shit she'd been dishing. "I'll call you a cab."

Her head snapped up, those eyes drilling me. "A cab?"

"I'm not ready to leave." It went against the grain for me not to show the woman on my arm home after an evening out, but she had intentionally boozed it up, even when I had suggested she take it easy. We hadn't even been here an hour. I was done.

"Are you serious?"

"Yeah. You shouldn't have drunk so many cosmos so quickly."

"I can't believe this."

"Yeah, I think you can. You knew exactly what you were doing."

"I want to go and you are my ride."

"I was your ride, but I'm staying so I'll get you a cab. I'll even pay for it."

Her hands moved to her hips and she stomped her foot like a spoiled child. I had to give her credit; she'd had me fooled for two solid months, concealing well this side of her personality. I wondered what caused the change in her. Or had I just been blinded, thunder-struck by that face and body and the aforementioned blowjobs?

"I'm walking away, you want that cab or not?"

"Fine. But you and I are going to have words about this."

Oh yeah we would be, just not the ones she was thinking.

Lucien appeared, I knew by the way he regarded me, he picked up on the dynamic, not that I imagined it was too hard to comprehend.

"There's a cab out front. I'll help you." And by that he meant help me with not climbing into the cab after Melody knowing how much sending her home in a cab didn't sit right with me.

"You told your friend to call a cab?"

"He didn't have to, Melody. Anyone with eyes can see you've had one too many."

"You're an asshole, Lucien."

Lucien laughed, which was good because woman or not, I was tempted to leave her ass and let her find her own way home.

At the curb, she tried again, draping her arms around me her mouth seeking mine, which she missed. "Come back with me."

"Sleep it off."

"See if I suck you off again." She snarled before glaring at Lucien and then she practically fell into the cab. I gave the cabbie the address, paid him and watched as it drove off.

"You good?"

"Yeah, and since you're being so insightful this evening, any ideas on how the hell I end that shit?"

His hand came down on my shoulder. "Sorry, pal. I haven't a fucking clue."

Trace, Lucien and I were talking when Avery appeared. She'd been with the others dancing. You could tell she had had a few drinks, her cheeks were rosy and her eyes slightly glassy, but she wasn't tripping over herself like Melody. Pulling out a chair, she sat down and reached for the pitcher of water.

"This place is great, Lucien."

"You look like you're having fun on the dance floor," he replied.

"Yeah, but Darcy and Ember are like machines. I can't keep up with them."

Trace had a thought on that, and knowing him as well as I did, I knew exactly where his thoughts took him in regards to Ember and her stamina. He apparently didn't think it was appropriate to share with his employee because he didn't voice it.

Avery checked her watch and then reached for her phone. "I'm punching out."

"I'll take you home."

That earned me her face. Her eyes didn't immediately adjust, I suspected she was seeing double. I couldn't help the grin; she was adorable when intoxicated. "What?"

"If you're ready, I'll take you."

She had the most expressive face, her every thought was on display. She actually licked her lips. My cock grew hard. I wondered what she tasted like. Was she as sweet as one of her desserts? Somehow I knew that she was, suspected her flavor would be habit-forming too. I needed to tone back those thoughts since we'd be in my truck together and there were several reasons I couldn't act on what my body demanded, namely she was my tenant and she worked for Trace.

"But you're with your friends. I'll catch a cab."

The irony was not lost on me. My girlfriend demanded I leave, my tenant insisted I stayed. It wasn't lost on Lucien either.

"Avery, we are going to the same place. I'll take you if you're ready. Besides Loki needs to be let out."

Mentioning Loki was the magic word. "Loki, right. Okay, if you don't mind."

Did I mind having her all to myself in my truck? It was going to be an uncomfortable ride home and I couldn't wait. "Do you want to say goodbye to Darcy and Ember first?"

"Oh yeah. I'll be right back."

I felt Lucien's stare as I watched Avery disappear into the bodies on the dance floor. "Do not say a word."

"I wasn't going to."

"Yeah, you were."

He laughed. "Yeah I was, but you already know what I'm thinking."

Yeah I did.

Avery returned, said her goodbyes to Trace and Lucien before waiting for me to do the same. It wasn't until we were in my truck when she remembered Melody.

"What happened to Melody?"

"She was drunk, I sent her home in a cab."

"I'm not surprised with the way she was pounding back those cosmos. I'm glad you decided to stay. Although next time you need to get out on the dance floor."

"I'd rather watch."

"Why?"

Because watching her shake her ass all night had been the finest form of foreplay I'd had in some time. Sure, I wasn't going to act on that, but the sight was definitely one I'd like to see repeated and often. "I'm not much of a dancer."

She snorted, the sound adorable and ridiculous. "Right. The way your body moves just from walking, if you ever got on the dance floor women would be dropping like flies. So damn sexy." Her head snapped to me, my fingers were gripping the steering wheel because the urge to pull her across my lap was strong. "Did I just say that out loud?"

"Yeah." That came out in a growl, but hell. I was only human and she was just too fucking tempting.

"Oops."

My cock jerked in my jeans. Fucking Christ. I needed to get this temptress home and then take a cold fucking shower.

Her voice was so soft, almost apologetic when she said, "Thanks for the ride, Rafe."

Thoughts of a different kind of ride flooded my head, so when I responded I sounded almost curt. "Anytime."

CHAPTER TEN

RAFE

Pulling down the drive, I thought about last night. I hadn't heard from Melody this morning, didn't think I would since she was playing the martyr. She'd avoid me, believing I'd eventually seek her out and apologize. I'd be seeking her out, but Hell would freeze over before I apologized. Once Dad was settled, I'd handle her. And Avery. I wasn't lying; the woman could tempt a priest to sin, but it would be best if I didn't indulge too much in those thoughts.

When I arrived at Sing Sing, I climbed from my truck and leaned up against it to wait. I couldn't quite define how it felt standing outside a prison waiting for my father to be released. This moment had been a long time coming for him. Dad couldn't have asked for a nicer day—the sun shining, mild, only in the sixties. The trees were all starting to turn colors and after seeing only shades of gray for so long, he might experience sensory overload. An alarm sounded seconds before the gates opened. Dad, carrying a duffel bag and being escorted by two guards, emerged from the shadows. He stopped, as soon as the sun hit his face, his head tilting back as he soaked up the rays. I couldn't imagine how that felt, feeling the sun on your skin while being a free man for the first time in twenty-five years. After a few minutes, his focus shifted to me, a smile spreading over his face as he continued toward me.

He dropped his duffel and before I could react, he pulled me in for a hug. It was quick, but I felt tightness in my chest all the same.

My voice was a bit thick when I said, "Welcome to the outside."

"I'd kill someone for a decent cup of coffee."

"I wouldn't talk like that here."

Laughing, he reached for his bag. "Thanks for picking me up."

"How about lunch?"

"Food not served on a plastic tray. Yes. Lead the way. I have to meet with my parole officer at three."

"We'll eat first and I'll take you. You're going to need to ease into the twenty-first century by getting a cell phone."

Dad laughed. "And Bluetooth and Wi-Fi. I mean shit it's like a foreign language."

"You'll settle in."

"Yeah I will."

"For lunch, what do you want?"

"Italian."

"I know the perfect little hole in the wall. Best Italian food in the city."

An hour later, Dad and I were settled at the small place Ember had told me about. The food was ridiculous and the line was usually around the corner but since it was early, we didn't have to wait.

I tried to put myself in his shoes, watching as Dad scanned the menu, but knew I'd never really appreciate what he was feeling.

"It all looks so good. I think I want the lasagna and garlic bread."

"Good choice." After the waitress took our order I asked him, "How's it feel?"

"A little weird, a lot weird."

"Can I ask you something?"

103

"Yeah."

"Why didn't your lawyer appeal? There were eyewitness accounts that you weren't the shooter, accounts that you were even surrendering. I just don't understand how you lost so much time for what amounts to a stupid mistake." Lately, I'd been thinking a lot about Dad's case. He'd made a mistake, absolutely, but to get the sentence he had seemed like the DA had been out for blood.

"Had the two I did the job with lived, I may have been able to cut a deal. But with them dead, they needed a fall guy because a man died."

"It's bullshit."

"Consequences, Rafe. I made the decision to cut corners, to attempt to solve my problems the easy way. That's on me. So yeah, I lost twenty-five years, lost that time with you, but the man who was killed, Jared Lincoln, he lost his life."

"You know his name."

"I'll never forget it. His wife lost her husband; his kids lost their father. That's something I have to live with. And even though I didn't pull the trigger, I'm still guilty."

That seemed harsh, but then in his shoes it was likely I'd feel the same.

"Anyway, I've been hearing some rumblings in regards to the job."

"What kind of rumblings?"

"Interest in what Lucas was after in that vault."

"Why would anyone care twenty-five years later?"

"I don't know."

"You're thinking he went into that vault for something specific."

"It's the only thing that makes sense. And he didn't get it. Whatever it is, it's still out there."

"That kind of sheds a different light on Lucas and the other one showing up dead."

"Exactly my thinking. Lucas and Jackson didn't have whatever it was they were supposed to. Whoever hired them didn't like that."

"Which means whoever wants to talk to you could be a killer."

"It's possible, but it could be nothing, it most likely is since the" statute of limitations on most crimes has long passed."

"Not murder."

"Yeah, but that doesn't make much sense. Covering a murder with murder. I think the person who took out Lucas and Jackson panicked. And having that hanging over their heads for twenty-five years, they aren't going to be so eager to add to their body count by offing me: a recently released ex-con with a link to their original crime. I'm not worried. I don't want you to be."

I wasn't so much worried as I was curious, but now was about Dad so I let the subject drop. Watching him as he looked around the restaurant, his expression one I couldn't appreciate without having been in his shoes. It was a bit jarring when it finally settled that he was home. My dad was home and we'd lost enough time. "Stop by my house. Anytime. I'd like to show you what I've created."

"I'd like that."

Our lunches arrived; my dad's eyes grew wide, as he visibly inhaled the incredible scents. "This looks amazing."

I watched him, the joy over something most take for granted. As soon as he took his first bite, his eyes closed on a moan. "Fucking unreal."

"Welcome home, Dad."

His attention shifted to me, the smile fueled by another emotion when he said, "Happy to be home, Rafe."

Avery

It was late, I needed sleep, but for some reason I couldn't find it. Climbing from bed, I grabbed my robe and headed outside. I settled in one of my new Adirondack chairs and stared up at the stars. Mom had taught me that, to take a break sometimes and look up.

I was thankful to have this time to get settled before work started, to take a breather before jumping in. At the time, I thought the three weeks Trace had offered me was too much, but I was finding I needed it. I didn't realize how stressed out I'd been until I started to decompress.

I had had a bit to drink last night, happily tipsy my mom would call it, but I remembered the ride home. It would be hard to forget since I had been in a simmering state of lust, enough that I blurted out how sexy I thought Rafe was…to Rafe. I should be embarrassed and a part of me was, but unavoidable since my IQ took a hit every time the man was near. And even lusting after my landlord, I couldn't deny the flirty banter between us was fun, even comfortable. I'd never had that before with a guy, liking him as much as I ached for him. Rafe was so much more than a pretty face and I was beginning to discover that 'the more' was equally appealing.

The sound of the gates opening turned my attention to the drive as Rafe pulled up and parked next to my car. Climbing out, he noticed me immediately.

"Avery? You okay?"

"Yeah. I couldn't sleep."

"I've got to get Loki. I'll be right back."

It was dark so he wouldn't see me staring and I did stare because I had a pulse. Melody was a fool. She wouldn't keep Rafe, not acting the way she did. And how nearsighted of her, trying so hard to hold him close and yet behaving in a manner that would push him away. Loki came from the house, right to me and in a gait that could almost be called a run.

"He likes you." Rafe said as he followed behind him.

"I like him too. You know if you're going to be out, he can stay with me. Melody was wrong to offer for me, but I'd enjoy having Loki for company."

"Really?"

"Yeah, it doesn't make sense for him to be in there alone and me to be here alone."

"He'd like that." Rafe settled on the chair next to me and stretched his long legs out in front of him. We sat in comfortable silence for a while and then he said, "My dad got out of jail today."

I didn't immediately appreciate the significance of his statement since it was said in such a matter-of-fact tone. When it did click, I

almost snapped my neck with how fast my head jerked in his direction. "You say that like you're sharing what you had for lunch. That
had to be weird for both of you. How did it go?"

Meeting my gaze, he didn't answer right away and I'd have given
Nat's life to know what he was thinking because the expression on
his face could definitely be described as tender. "It was good, strange.
All day I tried to put myself in his shoes, free after twenty-five years,
no longer looking through bars. He was a little uncomfortable I
think, but there's so much he wants to do. Overwhelmed too, all the
possibilities and now being free to pursue them. And being around
him again, it felt good." He lowered his chin a bit so our eyes were
nearly level. "Are you sure you're okay about him coming for visits?"

"He's your dad."

"He's also an ex-con."

"I'll admit, when you first mentioned that your dad was in jail,
I was a bit nervous. I don't know you. You don't know me and we're
in pretty close quarters here. Not to mention I've never met anyone
who's been a guest of the state, but I get a good vibe from you and
you clearly love your dad, so I'm following your lead on this."

It was because I was staring at him that I saw his reaction, even
as slight as it was, to my observation regarding his affection for his
dad. "I don't think it's fair to leave you with that impression. I barely
know my dad."

"I won't argue that, you may even feel resentful and bitter since
twenty-five years is a lot of time to lose, but there's love there too or
you wouldn't have picked him up today. And I know this because my
sister hates my father, she'd step over his body before offering him
aid."

"Why?"

"My father is very selfish. You probably know your dad better
than I know mine and my dad doesn't have the excuse of being incarcerated for the past twenty-five years."

He seemed to have a thought on that, one I was curious to hear
since he looked annoyed, but I didn't want to think about my dad, let
alone talk about him. "What does a man do as his first act as a free

man?"

"I took him to a little Italian place that has the most amazing food."

"Yeah, food. I think that'd be my first move too."

Rafe shifted a bit, his green eyes flashing in the most mischievous way. "Really, food first?"

A tingle started at my head and went clear down to my toes. If Rafe were an option, food would definitely be a distant second but to him I said, "That would be a close second."

He laughed, the sound so fabulous, the tingle was replaced with a heat that damn near burned me. "If he ever gets a craving for something sweet, let me know."

"Yeah?" But it was the way he said it, a familiarity that I really wished we had.

He was involved with someone and sitting out here like this, sharing like we were, it'd be easy to forget that. Standing, I rubbed Loki's head. "Absolutely, anytime. I think I'll try for sleep. Night, Rafe."

"Night, Avery."

CHAPTER ELEVEN

RAFE

Sitting at the bar in Allegro, I waited for Lucien to finish his conversation with his bartender Tara, so we could discuss what Josh had learned about the two who had done the robbery with Dad. Learning there was still interest in the case, I grew more curious about how they died. Dad didn't think there was anything to worry about, I was of a similar mindset since twenty-five years was a long time—the dust had settled—but it couldn't hurt to have the full story. My thoughts drifted to Avery. Coming home last night after such an intense day and having her to talk to, felt good. I hadn't been completely sold on the idea of someone invading my personal space, and Avery, despite her words that I wouldn't even know she was there, was a bright presence you couldn't ignore and yet I liked that she was what she appeared—sweet, thoughtful, a bit of a nut, but she listened and she cared. And her penchant for getting herself into trouble, it didn't annoy me; I actually looked forward to discovering what crazy scheme she came up with next. Uninhibited and free, she lived life with abandon and I'd admired her for that. The fact that I was also in a constant state of arousal around her didn't hurt. Just visualizing peeling her clothes from her body to the prize underneath was keeping me up at night, but Avery was also my tenant and she worked for a friend, which could be tricky if things didn't go well. I couldn't lie though; the sexual tension combined with genuinely liking her was a heady fucking combination.

I was pulled from those thoughts when someone settled next to me. Darcy. She'd been married to Lucien for three years. Even with the passing of time, and the birth of their daughter, sparks still flew when they were in a room together. I was happy for Lucien and Darcy, happy that they had found their way back to each other.

"Hey, Rafe. What brings you here?"

"I was hoping to have a few words with Lucien."

She studied me, her blue eyes assessing. "I like Avery."

"I like her too."

"How often does she bake for you?"

I couldn't help but grin; Darcy was practically drooling at the idea. "She isn't baking for me, she's practicing and I get to eat it. And she practices a lot."

Darcy's head cocked, but what she was thinking she kept to herself. Then she said, "I was surprised to see Melody joining us the other night."

Here we go.

"Seems coincidental, Melody's sudden interest in hanging with us and Avery's arrival."

"What's on your mind, Darcy?"

"Me?"

Turning to her, I held her feigned bewildered stare. "Spill."

"I'm going to be brutally honest."

"When aren't you?"

The woman had the nerve to smile. "You, Trace and Lucien are friends because you're a lot alike. Lucien is private, but he has his circle of friends who mean something to him. As his wife, those friends mean something to me because they're important to him. I know you've only been with Melody a short while, but she's not made any attempt to get to know us. You'd think she'd show some interest in what's important to you. Hell, I know more about Avery than I do Melody and I've seen Avery exactly twice."

"Avery's more outgoing."

"It's more than that and I know you're smart enough to know that."

"I'll give you that, but I'm not looking to put a ring on Melody's finger."

"I get that, but even if all you ever want is someone on your arm and in your bed, when you really like the person you're dating, it makes it all the more sweet."

I knew she was right, suspected she was referring to Avery being that someone else every bit as much as me. "I appreciate your concern and because I do, I'm going to share something with you."

"Yeah?"

"I've already been thinking about all of that."

"Really?"

"Yes, but I need to talk with Melody. Do you get what I'm saying?"

"Oh, I get it." And then she reached for my hand. "You deserve more."

Women seriously needed to come with an instruction manual and a bottle of whiskey. Thank God Lucien walked down the bar, stopping in front of his wife. Without missing a beat, he wrapped his hand around her neck and pulled her to him. Looking down at my beer, I grinned. Sorry son of a bitch was completely besotted with his wife. Not that I could blame him. Darcy was great. And for whatever reason, she loved Lucien to distraction.

"Wife."

"Husband."

Sensing Lucien's attention, I shifted mine to him. "What brings you here?"

"Do you have a minute to talk?"

"Yeah." Turning back to Darcy, his voice changed, turned softer. Yep, totally whipped. "Wait for me. I won't be long."

The smile Darcy offered in reply even I felt the effect.

Lucien moved to the end of the bar, I stood to follow him, but said to Darcy, "You and Ember should visit Avery again. Outside of her sister, she doesn't get visitors."

"Taking an interest in your tenant?"

"Maybe."

The look I got in response was priceless. Her chin practically touched the bar top. If she only knew how much of an interest I had in my tenant, she'd be plotting.

Following Lucien to his office, I settled in the chair across from him.

"You want to know what Josh learned." He wasn't asking.

"Yeah."

"Lucas Steele, the mastermind behind the robbery, was no choir boy. He'd worked countless robberies in the area, usually selecting a person down on their luck to work with him, this person often was the one arrested."

"So it's likely had Dad not turned himself in, Lucas would have fingered him."

"Probably."

"What happened to Lucas and Jackson?"

"Don't know. They never caught the killer. It's a cold case, so there's not much effort being made until new evidence comes to light. What Josh did learn, while retracing Lucas's last steps, according to the testimony of the bank manager, Lucas demanded access to the vault. However, he didn't go for the money he went to the security boxes. Even stranger he only wanted access to one of those boxes."

"Dad mentioned the other day that he'd heard some rumblings that there may be people interested in talking to him about the job."

"That's interesting. Makes you wonder what was in the box."

"So whose box did Lucas want access to?"

"Jeremy Paddington."

"Who the fuck is Jeremy Paddington?"

"No clue. Josh is still working on it. Is your dad concerned?"

"No, but two people died, I don't think he should dismiss the rumors completely."

"True. How's he doing, your dad?"

"Happy to be out. I took him to lunch, something we take for granted, but to him it was like tasting food for the first time. Anyway, Josh learns anything more, let me know."

"You'll be the first."

Rising, I headed for the door. "How's Avery feeling? She was definitely impaired at Allegro."

"Little worse for the wear, but she's good."

"I like her."

"Yeah, so does Darcy. I get the feeling you're trying to tell me something too."

"Only that sometimes we can't see what's staring us right in the face. Just making sure you're looking. When I hear from Josh, I'll call."

I was looking; I was most definitely looking.

Returning from my chat with Lucien, I pulled into the drive and was greeted to the sight of Avery and Loki playing fetch. Well, it wasn't really fetch since Loki didn't bring the stick back to Avery. I saw the stockpile he horded near a tree. Turning over Darcy and Lucien's sage advice, I tried to figure Avery out. She was sweet, kind, could bake desserts that made a man want to weep and she was a looker, so where were the men? Outside of her sister, no one had visited her. I understood wanting to keep your circle of friends small, but the men should be pounding down her door. The thought that she had a man had my hands fisting. Where the hell was he? Why hadn't he helped her settle in? Why hadn't he visited? Or branded her as his so everyone around knew it? I was inclined to think she didn't have a man, but she had that god-awful car and someone didn't keep a piece of shit like that unless it held meaning. Suddenly, I really wanted to know more about my tenant—personal things that I had no business asking and yet I planned to ask all the same. Climbing from my truck, I heard her instruction to Loki.

"You're supposed to bring it back to me so I can throw it again." Loki's head tilted, studying her, but he still didn't bring the stick back. I headed over to them.

"I see Loki is as cooperative with you when it comes to fetch as he is with me."

"Yeah, he's being very difficult."

She sounded really put out, deceiving since she was barely able to contain the grin.

She searched around for more sticks and when I realized my gaze was fixed on her ass, I shifted it but not before my dick stirred. "How did you get into baking?"

Her head snapped up at that, surprised by the question and, if I wasn't reading her wrong, touched that I asked. "I've always loved baking. I baked my first batch of cookies at six. The need to create, you must understand that, the feeling of visualizing something and creating it with your own hands. I just happen to also like eating what I make since I adore sweets."

"From what I've tasted, I don't blame you for wanting to eat what you bake."

Pink tinged her cheeks, her hand unconsciously going to the rogue lock of hair that had slipped from the knot she had her hair twisted up in, tucking it behind her ear. She was lovely: sweet, refreshing with a vein of innocence that was very appealing, so where the hell was her man?

I was about to demand an answer to that when she asked, "What about you? How did you get into woodworking?"

It was a reasonable question, even logical given my question to her and yet those words from this woman profoundly impacted me. Sometimes the greatest life lessons came in the most unusual ways. And I was having one now, standing in my yard, watching as Avery played catch with my uncooperative dog. She showed more thirst for life watching my dog horde his sticks, than I showed for the most meaningful moments in mine. Melody was the perfect example, my own girlfriend had never once asked me about my work and more fucked up, I had no interest in sharing that part of my life with her.

I had been going through the motions of living, but I hadn't actually been living. And I think if I were being honest, I'd been in that mode since I was a kid.

She studied me expectantly. I answered her honestly. "Wood shop class. Loved the smell of the wood when cut, the feel of the wood after a sanding. My first piece was a set of bookends, simple design that I stained a dark oak. I've had the bug ever since."

"Your work is exquisite."

Hearing that from her had my chest feeling a bit tight and coming as a one-two punch with my earlier observation, knocked me off-balance so I retreated. "I've got work."

And yet I didn't get anything done because my thoughts were still outside with Avery. I needed to stop dragging my feet and take a play from Avery's book and the first step in doing that was to break it off with Melody.

Arriving at Melody's condo, I stood at the call box; tension tightened my muscles and had the start of a headache threatening. I'd no idea how she was going to take me breaking it off with her, and by that how crazy she was going to get, but it was time.

She didn't know I was coming otherwise she'd have worked up excuses and arguments, which would turn what was bound to be unpleasant, nasty. Ringing her apartment, I knew she was home; she was usually home. She didn't work; her telling everyone she was interviewing was bullshit. She hadn't been on an interview yet. I hadn't called her on it, didn't want her to lose face, but it was just another symptom of the problem.

It took surprisingly long for her to answer; she was probably still sleeping. "Hello?"

"It's Rafe. Can I come up?"

"Rafe." She had a tone, knew she intended to make me pay for the other night before she let it go. Too bad for her I didn't give a shit if she did or didn't. "Hold on."

The door buzzed open.

When I reached her apartment, she stood in the threshold dressed in only a sexy little lace number. "Come in."

Her ass swayed, the silk clinging in a very nice way as she moved deeper into her apartment. And yes I looked because I wasn't dead.

She turned when she reached the kitchen, her hips cocking, a smile touching her lips. "What are you doing here? After the other night, I'm not sure I should have let you up."

"What was that shit at Allegro?"

"Excuse me?"

"You never come out with my friends and when you do, you get drunk the first hour and demand we leave."

Looking and really seeing her, I saw the feigned innocence and it grated that I hadn't seen it before. "The drinks went to my head."

"Bullshit."

She switched tactics. "Okay, honesty. I don't like that you have that woman living right outside your back door."

Hearing her call Avery *that woman* stirred my temper. "Are you serious?"

"Yes, I'm serious. You have a beautiful, young woman living on your property within walking distance of your bedroom. Any woman dating you would be pissed about that."

"If I'm with someone, I don't fuck around. If you knew me, you'd know that. We've been together long enough, Melody, you should fucking know me."

"Don't give me that. How would you feel if I had a hot man living with me?"

"She's not living with me, she's renting my carriage house."

"Same difference."

"No, it's not the same."

"I don't like it, Rafe."

"Why? You think the temptation is too great and I'm just some rutting dog?"

"Too great?"

Figured, she was accusing me of being a cheater, but she narrowed in on the fact that I called the temptation that Avery posed as great.

"You and I were fine until she showed up."

That wasn't true, but I hadn't had the motivation to end things until Avery. "This isn't about Avery."

"I think it is."

"It's about your games, your lies and how I'm done."

"What games?"

"Like the one you're playing right now. You know damn well what I'm talking about. Your lies about interviewing, that shit with Avery, the constant dodging of my friends...do I need to go on?"

Her fingers turned white with how hard she held the edge of the counter. "Are you breaking up with me?"

"Yeah, I am."

Again the tactic change, words weren't working so she tried something else. She walked around the counter to stand just in front of me. Her fingers moved to my chest, a light stroke as she looked up at me through her lashes, "Let's not let this little lacy number go unused, let me remind you of how good we are in the bedroom."

She wasn't wrong; the sex had been great. Like I'd said, killer blowjobs. Never knew a woman to like sucking dick like Melody. She got off on it, had on many occasions come from nothing more than having my cock in her mouth. But not even the sex was tempting enough to make me stay.

"It's over, Melody. Take care of yourself."

I had momentarily stunned her, since she made not one move to stop me when I walked to the door. She found her voice though, as the door was closing, by the string of curses she hurled at me.

chapter twelve

Avery

rriving an hour early for my first day of work, I felt like a
little kid on Christmas morning. I had set my alarm for
six, but I was up at four—excitement and nerves keeping me from
sleep. I showered and dressed and still I had time to kill so I baked
some cupcakes and left them for Rafe when I collected Loki for our
walk. I balanced my checkbook and even re-arranged the furniture
in the living room before I finally headed off to work. Setting up
my tools, I reminded myself of an operating room nurse, organizing
the instruments in the exact manner the doctor preferred. After my
workstation was set up, I checked the refrigerator and pantry three
times to ensure all the ingredients for the night's offerings had been
purchased. Chef arrived shortly after me, a knowing grin on his face
when he stepped into the kitchen.

"Couldn't sleep?"

"No."

"First days are both exciting and terrifying. You've got this, Avery.
Tina and Lee are our new interns who I've assigned to you. Both
have impressive resumes and strong recommendations. I'll let them

introduce themselves. The ovens run a little cool, which I believe you picked up on during your interview, so plan accordingly. Good luck. I look forward to tasting your creations."

"Thank you." But Francois had already started back to the other side of the kitchen. Tina and Lee arrived shortly after Chef, both looked to be fresh out of college, eager and ready. Tina had a shock of red hair, freckles and big hazel eyes. Lee had dark mocha skin but the palest blue eyes. I didn't know what he had in his gene pool, but he had definitely gotten all the best ones.

"Why don't we start off with you sharing a little about yourselves?"

Tina answered first, not surprising since she definitely was the hare to Lee's tortoise. "I'm Tina. I just graduated from NYU with a degree in Culinary Arts, my focus pastries. I'm so excited to be working with you."

Tina was practically bouncing off the walls; her enthusiasm was awesome if not a bit exhausting. Her hair was pulled back in a bun, smart, but with how her head bobbled on her neck, I was surprised it stayed in place. Her hands were in front of her, her fingers twisting around each other, an indication that her bubbly personality stemmed, in some part, from nerves.

"Have you ever worked in a professional kitchen, Tina?"

"No."

"Me either."

Her mouth opened to respond but nothing came out. It took her a minute before she said, "Really? This is your first time too?"

"Yep. We'll learn together."

"Cool."

"In your studies is there anything in particular you really enjoyed, or would like to learn more about?"

"Tempering chocolate, I haven't quite gotten the hang of it."

"We can work on that. And you, Lee?"

"I studied at C.I.A., like you. I like bold flavors, the contrast of spicy and sweet. I haven't gotten the handle on preparing phyllo dough."

"That's tricky, phyllo, most don't bother with making it and have reliable vendors. Here we'll be making it. I've a few tips. So for tonight, to complement Chef's offerings, we're making a pear/almond cheesecake, tart cherry torte with hazelnut brittle and a vanilla bean cake with a mango/kumquat filling and a whipped cream icing. I have the recipes here. Each of us will take one. I'm going to watch your technique to make sure we get the desired end product. Select the dessert you want, here's the ingredients list for each. Once we've perfected the process, we'll get started on producing them in bulk. Sound good?"

"Yeah."

"Let's get started and guys, first day jitters aside, let's have fun."

"You got it." Lee said, Tina agreed by bobbing her head and then they were gone, darting off to the pantry.

Unlike in a home kitchen, everything was on the large side, the mixer, the bags of flour and sugar. The butter came in sixty-eight-pound blocks. For baking, it was imperative to get the measurements correct. Tina, Lee and I measured and brought to room temperature our ingredients and then the fun part started. Both were very hard working, the ease in which they worked the recipes had most of my nervous energy fading. The test desserts turned out perfectly and that's when the real work started. Instead of making one cake, we made trays of cakes that baked in the walk-in ovens, layered countless cakes with vats of mango/kumquat filling, baked up mounds of hazelnut brittle, and plated countless desserts being careful that regardless of who plated the dish, all looked uniform. What I found the hardest, something you aren't prepared for until you're in the middle of it, the turnaround, even for desserts, was like getting whiplash. And standing for nine hours was hard as hell on the back. And still I loved every second.

Kyle appeared in the middle of shift, carrying a tray with four glasses of champagne. After handing one to each of us, he lifted his. "To your first day."

Tina giggled and it didn't take a genius to know that Kyle was the reason for it. Lee drank the champagne in one long swallow, before getting back to work.

"Thanks, Kyle." Taking a sip, I nearly moaned in pleasure. "The good stuff."

"Cristal."

I almost dropped the glass. "Cristal? Would it be unseemly for me to lick the glass?"

"There's more out front. I'll bring it back."

"Are you going to get in trouble? That's an expensive bottle."

"Trace was the one who suggested I bring you some libation and in what form."

Happiness settled over me with that insight. "I really like Trace."

Kyle laughed and turned to leave. "I'll bring the bottle back."

"And I'll be sure to drink it."

"Good girl." He stopped at the door. "Seriously, from what I've been hearing, you killed it tonight. Congrats."

Trying to adequately express what Kyle's words meant to me just wasn't happening and so instead I settled for a heartfelt, "Thank you."

The night was settling down, Tina and Lee looked like I felt, exhausted but proud of the work we'd done. "How are you both feeling?"

"Happily tired." That came from Tina.

"Hungry," Lee responded.

"In a few weeks, we'll start staff meetings. Ideas are encouraged though I will be testing all suggestions, tweaking etc. Great job tonight. I think considering it's the first time we've worked together, we did an outstanding job."

"Agreed. If there are leftovers, I want to try that cheesecake." Lee really wasn't kidding about being hungry.

"You'll get some, I worked in a ten percent surplus when I planned out the quantities for the raw ingredients."

"Sweet."

Toward the end of the evening, Trace appeared. I knew he was in the dining area, thanks to his generous gift, but I didn't know if he was dining or mingling with the guests. Even dressed in an elegant suit, there was no denying the hard edge of the man.

"How was your first day?"

"I'm going to need better shoes, but it was...I really don't have words. And thank you." I gestured to the bottle of Cristal that I kicked. "That was delicious."

"You earned it. I had the cherry torte. Ember had the vanilla cake. Now *they* were delicious."

He was here to eat; he didn't seem the type to mingle with guests.

Gesturing across the counter I said, "I couldn't have done it without Tina and Lee."

"Nice work." Trace said to my interns; Tina thanked Trace profusely while Lee nodded his head and replied with a quiet thank you.

And then Trace's attention was back on me. "There's a staff meeting on Friday at ten am."

"I'll be there."

"How are you getting home?"

"My car is out back."

"Good. See you tomorrow."

Trace stopped to say a few words to Chef before disappearing through the swing door. Chef turned, his eyes found mine. "Nice work tonight."

Chef Moree just complimented my work, incredible. "Thank you."

After shift, I stepped out back and took a moment to enjoy the cool night air on my overheated skin, so I didn't immediately see Rafe. And when he did come into focus, I couldn't take my eyes off him. He was dressed in a beautiful black suit, the pale green shirt opened at the collar, his hair back in a ponytail. He was exquisite and he was leaning against my dirty car.

"You're going to get dirty."

In reply, his brow arched.

And then my brain caught up and my heart squeezed because Rafe had dined at Clover for my first night.

"The cheesecake was incredible."

"You came for my first night?"

His smile was his only answer and in that moment he claimed a little piece of my heart.

"So tell me all about your first day?" Mom asked as I lay in bed the following morning. It had been a fabulous first day, made even more so seeing Rafe waiting for me. He had never mentioned that he was coming which made the gesture so much sweeter. Especially since no one in my family could make it, I hadn't anyone to share the momentous occasion with until I stepped out that door and saw Rafe. Sure I'd been engaging in harmless lusting after my landlord, but after last night I could admit my feelings went a bit deeper. I wanted to share Rafe's gesture with Mom, but her good-natured meddling would start and I wasn't prepared to deal with that just yet.

"It was incredible. I have a team dedicated to me; they're quick studies. It didn't take long at all before we found a rhythm. The oven, you walk into it. Oh, and Trace and Francois both loved the desserts."

"A success, I'm not surprised."

"I've already met Chef Moree's sous chef, Terry, and we discussed the upcoming week's menu in detail so I can prepare desserts that will complement Chef's offerings. Each night I supply the list to the runners who are responsible for supplying the raw ingredients. I think I'll join them occasionally because I really want to check out the markets, but it's getting up at four to get there by five so we can get to the market when it opens at 5:30am that will keep my visits to just occasional."

"That is early, but I imagine it's wonderful. All the scents and sights."

"So where are you now, Virginia Beach?"

"Just left, we're on our way to the Outer Banks."

"What's it like just the two of you in that large tin can?"

"You know I wasn't really thrilled with the idea of the RV, but I have got to tell you Avery, I adore being cooped up with Harold. It's a testament to our relationship that we don't grate on the other's nerves. I really did score the second time around."

"You sure did. Speaking of second time around, I saw Dolly in town last week."

"Trollop."

"Mom!"

"She is and you know she is. She cut your father's hair for Christ's sake and now he's married to her, living above his means and talking about starting another—"

"Another what? He wants kids with the wicked stepmom?"

"I'm sorry. I didn't mean to blurt it out like that."

I couldn't lie, that news hurt. "How do you know?"

"Your father called me. I talk more to the man now that I'm no longer married to him. He wanted to know what I thought. Can you believe it? He's asking me advice on family planning. Honestly, I don't see Dolly lasting. She'll grow tired of your father and move on to a younger, richer man. I didn't have the heart to tell him that though. I did mention that he should discuss it with you and Nat. That suggestion completely took him by surprise."

"Of course it did. I think he forgets he has kids."

"He loves you both, he's just very self-absorbed, which is not a good trait for a parent. Did you speak with Dolly?"

The idea that my dad was looking to have another kid when he sucked the first time around had hurt morphing into bitterness. As if he'd be a better father now. Moving on from that subject, since I could definitely wallow, I said, "It was a typical Dolly conversation, twenty questions and disbelief in the answers."

"I don't understand why she acts so high and mighty when she knows we know where she comes from."

"Social climbers forget their roots, or so I've been told."

"Are you okay about your father's family planning?"

"It's a shock and not a good one, but Dolly's young so the idea that she might want a family has occurred to me. Hearing he's actually thinking about it though, that hurts."

"I'm so sorry, Avery."

"Does Nat know?"

"Yeah, but unlike you, she gave up on your dad a long time ago."

"I'm beginning to understand her attitude. He makes it very hard."

"I'm here if you want to vent. Now changing the subject to a more interesting one, the pictures of the carriage house are unbelievable, but I have to say Avery, that Rafe is sexy."

"Mom!"

"I might be sixty, but I'm still a hot-blooded American woman and I can appreciate beauty just the same as you and Nat. What's he like? Nice? Arrogant?"

As much as I wanted to gossip with my mom about Rafe, I had to get to work. "He's very nice, but I can't get into that now. I've got to get ready for work. I'll call you later in the week."

"Knock them dead. We'll send you some snapshots of the Outer Banks."

"I'd like that. Tell Harold I said hi."

"Will do."

After showering and dressing, I headed to my car eager to get to Clover so I could start prepping for the night's offerings. Rafe appeared, walking the distance to me.

"Hey, Avery."

"Morning."

"You off to work?"

"I am."

"I'm glad I caught you. I've changed the alarm codes for the front gates and the main house. I wanted to make sure you had them. Do you want me to write them down?"

"No, you can just tell me."

"Are you sure?"

"Yeah, Working with measurements, I've become quite good at remembering numbers."

He gave me the codes. "I should be home, so call me if you forget."

"Will do." I wanted to know why he was changing the codes, but he didn't seem inclined to tell me. Asking seemed rude. "I'll see you later." I started away from him but I didn't get far before I stopped and looked back at him. He still stood there, hands in his pockets, watching me. "Thanks for coming last night. It meant so much more than you can know."

"I wouldn't have missed it." But it was the tender look in his eyes that had my heart beating faster. He started for his workshop but called from over his shoulder. "If there are leftovers, bring some home."

Home. I liked hearing him say that, liked it far more than I should.

My muscles ached; the heat from the shower helped to ease some of the pain. We had a few glitches tonight. The one mixer burned out; Tina had slightly over-cooked the caramel sauce. Most people wouldn't have noticed, but when the meal was upward of several hundred dollars, you didn't serve slightly scorched caramel sauce with your dark chocolate molten cake. All in all though, it had been another successful and satisfying day. But my back was killing me. On my next day off, I needed to buy more comfortable shoes.

I had just lathered my hair with shampoo when the water temperature went ice-cold. I screamed, the action instinctual because it felt like a thousand little needles stabbing me under the skin. I hadn't realized how loudly I had screamed until I heard the pounding on my front door, followed quickly with Rafe's worried voice. Jess's suggestion came flooding back to me on how I could ensnare my landlord by claiming the water had stopped working while I was in the middle of a shower. And it was because my thoughts had taken a radical detour that I didn't react fast enough to grab for the towel before Rafe came slamming into the bathroom. Thank God, the shower stall had frosted glass, so I wasn't completely on show for him.

"Avery," he said in a strangled whisper as understanding slowly dawned.

"The water went ice-cold."

"You're not hurt?"

Embarrassment aside, it was nice having him rush to my aid because he thought I'd been hurt. I'd never had that before, a man looking out for me. "Not hurt, just freezing."

He moved, reaching for my towel before opening the door enough to hand it to me. "Do you have a robe?"

"In the bedroom closet."

He disappeared only to return a few minutes later. "You can finish your shower in my bathroom while I check on the hot water heater."

I wrapped the towel around my head so the shampoo didn't drip into my eyes and pulled on the robe. Stepping from the stall, Rafe made no move to leave. His focus moved down my body, his lips turning up on the one side. "That's a good look on you."

"Right." I thought he was being sarcastic, but when those green eyes found mine, I discovered I was wrong on that account. And that knowledge had my body growing warm to a nearly combustible level.

"Go, shower. I'll see what I can do about the heater. If I need to order a new one, you can shower at my place until the unit is replaced."

It was me who made no move to leave because now I was imagining showering in Rafe's bathroom, preferably while he was showering too.

He made a sound in the back of his throat, a hungry sound that incited a hunger in me; a craving for something I suspected just sampling would be my downfall. And since the man was involved with someone, even a sample was out of the question. I nearly tripped over my own feet in my haste to leave.

"Thanks for letting me use your shower."

I didn't wait around for his reply. And as I fled to safety, I noted the weakness in my knees and the pounding of my heart and knew I was sliding down a slope I had no business being on. And even knowing it was wrong there was a part of me that wanted to slide the rest of the way.

chapter thirteen

Avery

Almost a full week had passed since the shower incident. I hadn't been able to get that moment out of my head, not that I put a great deal of effort in trying to get it out of my head. In fact, I went out of my way to ponder it in detail, the dawning reality that the attraction wasn't one-sided. Just thinking about him caused chills to shoot down my arms even as a heat scorched my blood that damn near liquefied my insides. Of course, he was involved with someone and that put a damper on my very pleasant daydreams. Though I wasn't entirely sure he was still with her since she hadn't been around since that night at Allegro. Either way, he was my landlord and getting involved seemed like a bad idea. Trouble was, I was beginning to really like that particular bad idea.

I was running errands on my day off because I was in desperate need of groceries. I had worked six full days—long, exhausting, tough on the back, exhilarating, thrilling and fantastic days. My team was great, hardworking and eager, but more they weren't waiting for me to mess up so they could takeover. Chef Moree stayed back and let me lead and his show of confidence added to mine. All in all, my first week of work had rocked.

Returning to the house, I was surprised to see someone standing at the gates. The man turned and there was no denying he was related to Rafe. With the exception of his hair being buzzed, he could be Rafe's older twin. His father. I waited for the nerves to kick in knowing that he was an ex-con, but seeing so much of Rafe in him, I instinctively took a liking to him. I pulled up to the gates, threw my car in park and rolled down the window: an activity that took about twenty-five minutes since my car was thirty-two years old. The man grinned, the same grin I had seen on Rafe's face.

"You're Rafe's dad."

"Guilty. Liam McKenzie." He even sounded like him.

"Is he expecting you?"

"No. Are you his girlfriend?"

I wish. "No, tenant. I'm renting the carriage house. Would you like to come inside and wait? I imagine he'll be back soon, he's probably making a delivery."

He hesitated, looking a bit conflicted, before he said, "Maybe I should come back."

"Why?"

He rubbed a hand over his shaved head as he regarded me from the corner of his eye. "Did Rafe mention anything about me?"

"Yeah."

"That I was in prison?"

"Yep."

"And you're still inviting me in?"

"I'm guessing that's not the reaction you're used to."

"No."

"I don't know you, but I know Rafe. This is his home and he has made it clear you're welcome here. I have the day off and a freshly baked apple pie sitting on my counter. If you want to help me eat that pie while you wait, it would be doing me a solid since otherwise I'm likely to eat it all myself."

"Are you sure?"

And even trying to stay upbeat, I was pissed. Sure I didn't know this man, but what the hell kind of reception had he been getting that he was so hesitant now? "Yes, very sure."

He flashed me a smile before coming around to the passenger's side and folded his large, and immensely muscular, frame into my car. His gaze sliced to me. "1984?"

"Yeah, how'd you know?"

"I used to work on cars back in the day.".

Pulling up to the garage, we parked and Liam looked how I probably had the first time I'd seen the place—awestruck. "Hard to believe we're in the Bronx."

"My exact words. I'm just going to run to the house to get Loki."

"Loki?"

"Rafe's dog."

Loki was eager to see me, even jumped a bit in greeting. "We have a guest." I led him across the yard to where Liam waited. "This is Loki."

Loki eyed the newcomer, taking his measure, and then he did something I had never seen him do, an action that required energy—something he staunchly conserved—he jumped up, put his paws on Liam's chest and started licking him.

"He likes you." Having shared as many walks as I had with Loki, witnessing his reaction to people, I believed him to be an excellent judge of character.

"The feeling is mutual."

I wanted to give Liam the tour, but it wasn't my place so instead I invited him inside and started the coffee. After I put the pie in the oven to warm, I headed to the freezer since I liked a little vanilla ice cream with my warm apple pie. "I have vanilla ice cream too. It's homemade, so it's a bit different than what you're used to. Would you like some?"

"Please." Liam's attention was on the recipes I had lying on the counter. "Are you a baker?"

"Yes. I just finished my first full week as the pastry chef for a restaurant in town."

"You create those desserts that look like art?"

"I try, the combination of beauty and taste."

"So you're an artist of sugar."

I couldn't help the smile since I loved that analogy. "Exactly."

"And how did you know you wanted to do that?"

"I love sweet things, love creating sweet things that morphed into imaging new sweet things."

"How was your first week?"

A lump formed in my throat at this exchange because this man, who I just met, was showing more of an interest in my life than my own father. I forced the words past the ache, tried maybe a little too hard for happy. "It was a great week. I have a wonderful team who works well together. And outside of coordinating with the executive chef's menu, I'm only limited by my imagination. It's a dream job."

The fact that he picked up on the change in me, evident in the way his eyes grew assessing, hurt too. He didn't pry and instead said, "I'm in for a treat then."

Rafe's father, having met the son, shouldn't have surprised me but instead of the hardened closed-off man I expected, after the life he'd led, he was surprisingly easy-going. And I found myself as interested in him as he appeared to be in me. Though, in fairness, the man likely was only interested in me since he'd been locked away for so long so any interaction was probably welcomed.

That knowledge didn't stop me from asking. "If I'm out of line, I apologize, but your hesitation earlier…how has it been acclimating after being incarcerated for so long?"

"In some sense it's been fucking incredible, as you can imagine. I have very few restrictions and outside of my parole office, I'm in charge of my life again. But in some ways it's been difficult. You get used to life a certain way: told what to do, when and for how long, and as confining as that is, you get used to it. On the outside, you have to find your own way; no one is there to tell you what, when and how long. Not to mention you're battling not just your own demons—like the insecurities that stem from your own doubts as to your ability to cope with life on the outside—but the prejudices of people who would prefer if you'd stayed behind bars. So even breathing air as a free man—a fucking fantastic thing—readjusting to the world when you have the stigma of being an ex-con is not an easy adjustment."

My heart went out to him because I could imagine the difficulties, seeing how hard it had been for him to accept my invitation, but before I could comment he asked, "You mentioned Rafe was making a delivery, his furniture?"

"Yeah, have you seen his work?"

"No." There was regret threaded through that reply.

"He made the tables in the living room and he restored this carriage house and the main house. There are pictures in the front room that show the before for this place."

Liam walked to the pictures and studied them before taking in the space now. "He did this work by himself?"

"Yeah. He gave me the tour when I first moved in, explained how he'd been at it for years, but the results are so worth the effort. Wait until you see the main house."

"I look forward to Rafe showing me. How long have you lived here?"

"A little over a month."

He actually exhaled, like in relief. "I'm happy to hear that."

"Why?"

"Because if you'd been here longer and my son hasn't made his move, he clearly has something wrong with him."

"He has a girlfriend."

Liam had a thought on that and whether he intended to share or not, I'd never know because the timer on the oven went off. "Pie's done."

An hour later, Rafe still hadn't returned and I had the sense that Liam didn't want to over-stay his welcome. I walked with him to the front gates. "Thank you. I haven't eaten something that incredible in far too long."

"I enjoyed the company. I'll let Rafe know you stopped by."

He started down the drive, but stopped and looked back at me. "Is he happy?"

The genuine interest it seemed Liam had for the answer hit me hard because my dad had never once asked that question of Nat or me. "I don't know him all that well, but I think so. Sometimes he seems a bit lonely."

He nodded his head in acknowledgment of my words yet his thoughts were his own and then he said, "Thanks for keeping me company."

It was Liam who looked lonely now, his words coming back to me about the challenges of fitting back into society. All that time waiting to be free and then dropped in a world where many wanted you back behind bars. I didn't know him, but seeing the pride he obviously felt for his son and his concern over Rafe's happiness had the next words tumbling out. "Anytime. I mean that. You're welcome to visit me whenever you want."

"I'd like that."

"Do you have a cell?"

He handed me his cell that he'd taken from his pocket. "I still haven't gotten used to this. When I went away, cell phones were huge with antennas. These look like something out of *Star Trek*."

"And every year they get smaller but are capable of doing more."

"I can't help but think of *Terminator* and the danger of too much automation—all your info just floating around in cyberspace. You can do electronic bill pay, right from your checking account. It's a little too much for me."

"I feel the same. I still use actual checks." I punched my number into his phone. "Whenever you get a hankering for something sweet, call me."

Reaching for his phone, his expression changed and his next words sounded almost dire. "Next time you see a stranger at the gate, don't engage them. Keep driving and call Rafe. Promise me, Avery."

A chill worked down my spine because the warning came out of left field. "Okay, I promise."

And then he strolled away while I stood with Loki and watched until I couldn't see him anymore.

"I agree with you, Loki, orange and chocolate are wonderful together, but I want something that's not cake."

Loki and I were lying, head-to-head, on the sofa while I worked out some ideas for new recipes. Since he seemed to respond when I included him in my thinking, I did it often. He liked me, always waiting at the front door for me to let him in, greeting me warmly when I came for him on the days I got home before Rafe. Loki and I had been for a walk earlier, after Liam had departed, and having exhausted Loki's daily limit of exercise we lounged about.

"I'm toying with the idea of a chocolate tray, custom-made chocolates. Unique pairings, maybe even offering wine to complement the flavors."

The knock at the door had my head peeking up over the sofa back to see Rafe filling the doorway. There was the strangest expression on his face. "Sorry to interrupt, but have you seen Loki?" Even his tone seemed off. I wondered if he had had a fight with Melody.

"Yeah, he's right here. Come in."

The screen door swung close as Rafe entered the living room, a space that seemed so much smaller with him in it. "You were just talking to Loki?"

I couldn't tell if he was incredulous or humored by the thought of Loki and me engaging in conversation. "Yeah. He never answers though. We were tossing around dessert ideas."

As I watched, the tension that had tightened his shoulders seemed to roll right off him, his demeanor changing from guarded to relaxed. I couldn't help feeling slightly giddy because I had the distinct impression he thought I had a man over and even more unbelievable, he didn't appear to like that idea in the least. And *I* liked that he didn't like it.

"We?" There was definitely humor in that one word.

"You've never chatted with him?"

"No, I talk to him all the time, I'm just surprised you are."

"Why?"

He looked as if he was going to answer, but held back.

"You missed your dad."

Surprise flashed over his face. "What?"

"He was here earlier to see you. He waited for a bit, I gave him pie, but he had to go so…"

"He was here?"

"Yeah. Is that okay?"

"Yeah, no I'm just sorry I missed him."

"He was lovely and very interested in you, if you were happy. He loves what you've done with the carriage house and is eager for the tour of the main house."

I was surprised by the look that swept his face at my words; he looked conflicted. "Are you okay, Rafe?"

"It's just weird. It's been so long. I kind of thought I outgrew wanting approval from my dad, but I guess not."

"He said something else before he left. He told me the next time I see a stranger at the gate I shouldn't engage him and call you. Any idea why he'd say that?"

Rafe's demeanor changed instantly—fun-loving chased away by wary. "That was another reason why I stopped by. I wanted to mention that I've recently learned there are people interested in Dad and his part in the robbery."

I wasn't sure what I felt more, concerned or confused. Was that why he had changed the codes on the gates and main house? "It seems odd that there would still be interest so many years later."

"Our thoughts exactly."

"You mentioned before that the people who did the job with your dad were killed."

"Yeah, a few days after the robbery. The case was never closed." He stepped closer to me, but it was the concern coming off him, for me, that I liked…a lot. "Are you worried?"

"I'm not sure because whatever this is, someone was willing to kill for it. Maybe there's reason to worry."

Dangerous was how he looked in response. Fierce. "You're safe here, but if you want me to help you find another place to—"

I didn't let him finish that sentence; the thought of leaving was like taking a kick to the gut. "I'm not going anywhere."

He seemed to like the idea of me leaving about as well as me since the scowl lifted from his expression at my insistence on staying. Had I been alone, I'd be doing that booty wiggle he liked so much.

"Besides, this place is like Fort Knox and we've got this incredible guard dog."

And Loki, right on cue, snored loud and long.

Rafe chuckled. "Yep, he's fierce."

RAFE

I was still grinning when I reached my workshop, Avery the cause. I'd never met anyone like her. That day in her bathroom was burned onto my brain. A robe, a thin layer of cotton had separated all of her from me. It took will to keep my hands at my sides and not reach for her, pushing the fabric off her shoulders and tasting her. God, I wanted her taste on my tongue. But what changed simple lust and craving into something a whole hell of a lot more was her compassion. Even knowing where Dad had spent the past twenty-five years, she hadn't turned him away; she had made him feel at home. I was coming to learn there were many facets that made up Avery Collins and I liked every single one. And even knowing the attraction was mutual—the air damn near sizzled when we were together—getting involved with my tenant seemed like a really bad idea, but it was getting harder and harder for me to convince myself of that.

Moving deeper into the barn, to where I had a small weight room setup, I pulled off my tee and started working the punching bag that hung from one of the rafters. Dad's warning to Avery concerned me, had someone approached him? The case file on the robbery was pretty vague because to the police it was exactly what it appeared to be, a robbery gone wrong. If Dad was right though and the robbery had been used to cover up the real crime, what or who had been the target? We needed to find out how Jeremy Paddington and his security box tied into all of this.

The knock on the barn door pulled me from my thoughts. Twisting my neck, Avery stood about twenty feet from me. She looked as if she was rooted to the floor. Her eyes were moving down my body, her thorough inspection had my dick growing hard.

"I'm sorry. I just…" she gestured to the plate she held. "…I was making lunch and thought you might like some. I'll leave it over there."

Her footing was a bit unsure and I couldn't help the grin because it was nice seeing the confirmation that I wasn't the only one harboring thoughts that would likely lead to trouble.

"Thanks, Avery."

She looked back at me, but her gaze was on my chest, which turned my grin into a shit-eating smile. Her focus eventually reached my face, her cheeks turning red when she saw I'd read her thoughts.

"You're welcome." She managed before she hurried away as if the place was on fire. Turning back to the bag, I started hammering at it again but this time what I was working through was far more pleasant to ponder.

"Sorry I missed you earlier." Dad and I sat at the bar at a local dive. The cold beer hit the spot after the long day I'd put in.

"Avery, she's adorable and damn that woman knows how to bake a pie."

"Yeah, she does."

"She just invited me in. Didn't know me, only that I was your father, but she opened up her home to me. Sweet, but that kind of innocence can get her in trouble."

Something shifted in me, a stirring…a warning. "I know."

"She gave me her cell number too, told me to stop by whenever I was in the mood for something sweet."

"That sounds like Avery."

"It's refreshing and worrisome. The man who's lucky enough to snag her will have more than his share of gray hair keeping that tender heart from getting squashed."

I wanted that man to be me; the intensity of how badly surprised me. But now wasn't the time to ponder the delectable Avery.

I changed the subject, "How are you doing?"

He didn't immediately answer, studied me in that way he had, knew he saw far more than I wanted, but instead of prying he answered my question. "Some people have a really hard time adjusting to life after being away for so long, and there is some of that I'm not going to lie, but I love having the fucking window open, and getting to eat and piss whenever the hell I want. My apartment is shit, but it's my shit, my place. I had McDonalds last night, a big Mac with cheese and goddamn was that good."

I didn't need a lifetime locked away to think McDonalds was good. "Any luck with finding a job."

"Not yet, but my parole officer has a few contacts he's reaching out to."

"Earlier you gave Avery a warning."

"Yeah, shouldn't I have?"

"No, it's fine but has anyone approached you since you've been out?"

"No, just wanted her to be cautious. Being the way she is, she could welcome trouble and not even know it."

A shiver worked down my spine at the idea of Avery in trouble. Not on my fucking watch. Speaking of which, "I asked a PI to look into your case. You were right, Lucas was after something, wanted access to a security box belonging to a Jeremy Paddington."

"Who the fuck is that?"

"My question exactly. Josh is looking deeper into it."

"So there had been more to that job. Son of a bitch." And even pissed he seemed to move from that with ease to ask, "So what is the deal with Avery?"

He was like a dog with a bone. "Meaning?"

"You seriously aren't going to explore that?"

"She's my tenant."

"So what. She's beautiful, sweet and bakes like an angel. I'm surprised you haven't already."

Not for a lack of wanting to. "You're playing matchmaker? You've been out for like a week."

"Hey, I've learned the hard way to appreciate what you've got, to grab for what you want."

"Avery's great, but I just recently ended a relationship. Plus, she's my tenant. I think it'd be wise to keep it just business."

I felt his stare as I took a pull from my beer. Turning my head to him he seemed to be grinning at a joke aimed at me. A suspicion confirmed when he said, "A sexy and incredibly sweet woman, who bakes like a goddess, lives right outside your back door and you're going to keep the relationship all business." He took a pull from his beer before adding, "Well, good luck with that."

And even as I formed my protest, deep down I knew Dad was right, Avery was just too tempting.

Avery

"Honestly, Loki, you could have totally caught that. You didn't even try." Glaring down at the big goof, sitting under the tree, I swear he was grinning at me. And why not, he failed to catch a perfectly good pass and now I was up in a tree retrieving his Frisbee. I seriously wanted to come back as a dog like Loki. Lucky bastard.

"I'm going to fall out of this tree and crack my skull and then you're going to feel guilty. I promise you Loki, you'll miss me when I'm gone."

Reaching the Frisbee, I looked down to toss it and realized for the first time just how far up I'd climbed. I couldn't deny, I was thrilled with my very nimble, monkey-like ways, but being stuck high up in a tree was not the best time to learn you were afraid of heights.

Curling my fingers around the tree branch, I closed my eyes on a wave of dizziness. I was in a pickle because I couldn't get myself to move. It was like my entire body just froze in place, too terrified to shift even slightly for fear I'd lose my footing and crash down in a bone-breaking fall.

I shouldn't have climbed the tree when Rafe wasn't home. I had thought that, right before I climbed the tree, how I shouldn't climb the tree in case something should happen. But I didn't listen to myself and climbed the damn tree anyway. Taking a few deep breaths I forced myself to stop panicking. I climbed up this high; surely, I could climb back down and yet my body refused to listen to the instructions from my brain.

I'm not sure how long I stood in the tree, frozen in place, losing blood in my fingers with how tightly I held onto the branch; I'd probably lose them or the whole hand. It would serve me right, climbing a damn tree when no one was home. And then Loki barked at the same time I heard the front gates opening. Joy and relief hit first, but following just after was chagrin—Nat would be proud of my ever-growing vocabulary. This was the fourth time Rafe had to rescue me. Maybe I should just stay up in this tree. I had read once an adult human body took eight to twelve years to completely decompose. They'd find me when my bones started falling out of the tree. Would Rafe even remember who I was: the crazy chick that had lived in his carriage house for all of a month and a half before disappearing without a trace?

His truck pulled up next to my car and Rafe climbed out. He saw Loki immediately.

"Hey, buddy. What are you doing?"

Loki barked, which I thought was adorable that he was trying to tell his daddy that the crazy lady he rented his carriage house to was pretending to be a squirrel. Even frozen in terror, I did enjoy the way Rafe's body moved as he came to stand next to Loki. And then that head tilted back and those green eyes landed on me. The sexiest smile spread over his face as he pushed his hands into the front pockets of his jeans and rolled back on his heels.

"Hey, Avery. Let me guess. Your interpretation of a bird?"

He was referring to my flippant answer of imitating a spider the day of the fence incident. Of course he'd remember that. "Cute. If you must know, Loki and I were playing Frisbee and he didn't apply himself to lunge for the Frisbee and so I had to retrieve it."

"Playing Frisbee at dusk is probably not the best time to be playing."

"It wasn't dusk when we started."

The smile stripped from his face, all humor fled. "How long have you been up there?"

"Well, if I used the sun as a guide, a long freaking time."

"Jesus Christ. I'll get the ladder."

A ladder wasn't going to help since my muscles had atrophied. I thought it took longer for muscles to disintegrate due to lack of use. Who knew?

Rafe climbed up to meet me halfway, but I couldn't move.

"Avery, you need to come to me."

"I can't."

"Baby, I can't reach you and climbing up there and getting us both caught in the tree isn't an option."

"It would take twelve years for us to decompose, we'd have to die first and I heard that can take up to fifty days."

"I'm not planning on decomposing anytime soon and I don't want your body decomposing in my tree either."

"Why not?" I was actually pissed that he didn't want me to decompose in his tree. What was wrong with my body that it wasn't good enough to decompose in his tree? I was working myself up into a good rant; he defused my craziness when he added, "And not see your booty dance again, no way."

Oh. Oh…"Are you objectifying me?"

"Are you seriously starting a fight because I'm trying to rescue you from a tree? I can call 911 and let the firemen do this, which will likely end up on the news so everyone will know the new pastry chef at Clover thinks she's a cat."

"You wouldn't."

"If you don't move your ass down here, you aren't leaving me much of a choice."

"You can be quite bossy, do you know that?"

"And you have a tendency of putting yourself in ridiculous situations."

It was instinct to counter his comment, the haggler in me, but he was right. I did get into more than my share of ridiculous situations. And I knew exactly when I started engaging in foolish stunts; it was right around the time my dad forgot he had kids. Being silly surely would gain his attention and by extension his affection. It didn't, but now recklessness was kind of programmed into my DNA. Damn Dad.

"You're right. I've been up here a while, my limbs are numb, so if I start to fall, get out of the way. No reason for both of us to die on this fine evening."

"You're not going to die."

"I'm dying, either from the fall or humiliation, there's just no stopping that."

"I won't let you fall."

And somehow I knew he really wouldn't. Focusing on moving one leg at a time, it took a few starts to actually get my legs to listen to the command from my brain, but if I kept Rafe in sight, I didn't freeze up in fear. As soon as I was close enough, he wrapped his arm around my waist, pressing me up against him.

"You okay?"

"Yeah, this humiliation will only last a couple years."

"I think it's very you, retrieving Loki's toy."

"What does that mean?"

"Fucking sweet."

I wanted so badly to ask what was up with Melody. But I didn't want to ruin the moment, particularly since I'd gone boneless hearing him call me baby. In an attempt to hide my real thoughts, I tried for stern when I said, "He should have caught it."

"You should have waited."

"I know."

"Let's climb down and I'll pour you a drink."

"I like this idea."

I waited until he reached the ground before I followed after. As soon as my feet hit solid ground, I was tempted to drop to my knees. Loki appeared, rubbing his head against my leg.

"It wasn't your fault, Loki."

Rafe put the ladder away before returning to me and reaching for my hand. "Are you sure you're okay?"

"Yeah, thanks for saving me again."

He chuckled as he started pulling me toward his house. "Even if I did keep you waiting?"

"You got me out of the tree, so I'll forgive you."

He held the door open for me, our bodies brushed as I passed him. His harsh exhale could have come from me, the sensation where our bodies touched tingled in a very, very pleasant way.

His voice pitched deeper, had an edge when he said, "I'll work on my timing."

"And I'll keep my feet on the ground."

Halfway to work, I realized I had forgotten the bowls I had ordered specifically for the spun sugar domes for tonight's pistachio meringues. I debated about turning around, since I could probably find something similar at the restaurant, but I wasn't that far from home and they really were the perfect size.

More than once I replayed the encounter with Rafe from last night. I should have been mortified—he was right I did have a penchant for putting myself in ridiculous situations—but I wasn't. It was a really good memory, particularly recalling the electricity that zapped the air when our bodies brushed. That wasn't even the part I liked the most when I was around him—the chemistry that singed the air. I just liked him. Being around him was easy; talking was comfortable. I wanted to ask him about Melody, but how exactly did I bring up that subject?

Turning onto Rafe's street, I had made good time. I was lucky my start time was two because had I been caught up in the morning traffic, it wouldn't have been worth coming back. And that would have been a shame because the bowl proportion to the meringue was perfect. Reaching Rafe's house, I just drove right past it because Melody stood at the gates. Speaking of the devil. My heart dropped seeing her. I had convinced myself they weren't together any more, particularly since Rafe's behavior toward me had changed, grown more intense, but for her to be here, maybe I was wrong on that account. Either way, I had absolutely no interest in talking with her. Turning around, I parked across the street and waited for her to leave. Rafe wasn't home; he had left before me in search of the perfect exotic wood for a new project. His words.

Five minutes past and she still stood there. The drive was easy enough to see, Rafe's truck wasn't there. Why the hell was she lingering? If I thought that was odd, her next move was bizarre. She grabbed the gates and started pulling on them. Clearly frustrated that she couldn't get them open. Rafe had changed the codes. Had he not told her? As his girlfriend you'd think she'd be the first person he'd give the codes to. Maybe he was single. I couldn't help the excitement that fluttered in my stomach at that thought or the knot that quickly followed. If he were single, why wouldn't he have shared that with me unless I was reading more into the dynamic between us?

Pushing aside that unpleasant thought, I grew impatient. If Melody loitered much longer, I'd have to forget about the bowls because there was no way I was engaging that woman in conversation. A minute or so passed before she turned and headed down the street. It was only then that I noticed her convertible parked two houses down. If she'd been visiting Rafe, why wouldn't she have pulled her car up to the gates and waited for him to open them?

She drove right by my car. I was tempted to duck, but it was highly unlikely she'd recognize my car or me. As she passed, I saw that she was on the phone. She looked pissed. And even having no idea what I'd just witnessed, I derived a sick kind of pleasure seeing her not getting whatever it was she wanted.

A glance at my watch and I forgot all about Melody. I had to get those bowls and get to work.

CHAPTER FOURTEEN

RAFE

Pulling into my driveway, it was late, so I was surprised to see Avery outside. She had a blanket on the ground, one wrapped around her shoulders and she was looking up at the stars. Loki was next to her, a blanket over him, and based on how still he was I knew he was sleeping, likely snoring. Every time I thought about Avery up in that tree, I wanted to laugh out loud almost as much as I wanted to holler some sense into her. Dad was right about the gray hair, she wasn't mine and I felt the stress of keeping her safe...from herself. More startling, the fact that she wasn't mine made me feel almost homicidal. And she had said I wouldn't even know she was here.

Climbing from my truck, I walked over to join her. Seeing me, she called a greeting.

"What are you still doing outside? It's freezing."

"The sky is so clear, look at those stars. Mom called, told me to check out the sky. She does that sometimes, reminds me to look up. I tend to forget."

Where was her mom? Why hadn't she helped Avery move in or come for a visit? Telling her to look up was all well and good, but her daughter just made a major move and none of her family had been there except her sister. And the woman was a freaking brain surgeon and still she carved out time to show her support. Avery clearly had no trouble reading my thoughts.

"You're wondering where she is."

"Yeah, but let's move this inside. You're making me cold. I'll make you hot chocolate."

A slight smile before she asked, "With marshmallows?"

She asked that much in the way I'd heard Faith and Emily ask it. "Yeah, with marshmallows."

She tilted her head, "You have marshmallows?"

"My friends' kids love them."

"So it's not because you're harboring a secret marshmallow fetish?"

Fucking adorable. "No."

She stood, which had Loki stirring from his slumber. We both reached for the blanket draped on him, our fingers brushing, and damn it all but just that light brush had my balls tightening. Her scent, she smelled like cocoa. Her big green eyes held no secrets; what she was thinking was right there for me to see. She felt it too. I wanted her pressed against me, wanted to bury my face in her neck and just breathe her in. Instead, I put a collar on my raging lust and helped her collect her things before leading her inside.

Once we settled in the kitchen Avery filled me in on her absent family. "Mom is driving cross country in an RV with Harold, my stepdad. She was really upset when she learned about the interview and subsequent move, but they've been planning their trip for almost a year."

Filling the kettle with water, I set it on the stove. Couldn't help but feel relief that her mom had a reason for her absence especially after the small glimpse Avery had given me about her dad. And the fact that I cared was just another reason why I knew the battle I was fighting to keep my distance wasn't one I'd be winning—not when everything in me wanted to close the distance between us and kiss her. When I realized my focus was on her lips, I jerked my gaze back to her face. She studied me in much the way I did her. And since my blood was now rapidly moving south, I grabbed at any subject for a distraction. "Is your mom an outdoorsmen?"

Avery laughed, the sound so carefree and natural I couldn't help but grin in response even as my cock grew hard. "Mom, no. She's a room service kind of woman. Not necessarily pricey but when she's on vacation she doesn't want to have to cook or clean. It's been a dream of Harold's for a long time though and since Mom loves him, she didn't even hesitate. I love that she found Harold, they're so perfect for each other."

"Sounds like it. And your dad, where's he?"

Her easy smiled dimmed, her eyes losing some of their sparkle. And even knowing she didn't have a great relationship with her dad— the man was clearly a moron—seeing just how hard Avery took her father's neglect caused a surge of protectiveness in me. I wanted to hunt her dad down and beat some sense into him.

"Like I've mentioned, my dad is a selfish man. We've never been close despite my efforts to change that. You have a closer relationship with your father and he's been away for so long. He and Mom were like oil and water. I don't understand why he remarried; he really doesn't seem to need anyone. But he did, to a woman who is only six years older than me. She's vile, but she doesn't demand conversation or companionship, as long as she gets her hair and nails done and has a credit card she's happy."

So not just a disinterested father, but a bitch of stepmom too. Before I could offer a response, she asked, "What was it like for you with your dad being away? I mean if that's okay to ask."

"At first, it was hard. I was nine and had lost my dad and my home. When I entered my teenage years I was the typical, angry at the world, kid. But my dad and I, even having so many years that separated us, somehow we're managing to find our way back."

"He loves you. You can see that very clearly."

I hadn't expected her to say that, was even more surprised at how much I wanted that observation to be true. When the kettle whistled, I poured the hot water in the mug and stirred the hot chocolate.

"How many marshmallows?"

"I'll tell you when."

And she did when there were at least twenty little marshmallows in her mug. "You weren't kidding about liking marshmallows."

She flashed me a smile. "What can I say? I like sweet things."

She wasn't the only one.

Avery

Fall was in the air, it was my day off and I had pumpkin treats baking. While I waited, I decided to plant up a few pots I had picked up at the local garden center. The mums, asters and millets looked so festive. I even had cornstalks, hay and pumpkins arranged at the front door of the carriage house. Loki sat at my feet, as I arranged and rearranged the pumpkins and plants to get the exact look I was going for.

Rafe had been gone most of the day, returning about an hour ago. He called a greeting to Loki and me before he changed into sweats and a tee and headed into the barn. Seeing him that day in the barn, working the bag without a shirt. If only you could print mental images I'd have that one papering the bedroom walls. I should have told him last night about Melody's visit. It had been on the tip of my tongue, but I hadn't wanted to bring her into the moment because talk about a buzz-kill. I'd have to tell him, he needed to know she'd been here and I needed to know if they were still together, if all the flirty banter between Rafe and me was just that and not a prelude to something so much better.

"He's very sexy, your daddy. You might not see it being male and all but truly, he's enough to turn a straight man gay. I could look at him all day."

Loki's head lifted, his black eyes regarded me.

"I realize I'm objectifying your daddy, but when a man looks like him, he has to expect it."

Loki shifted; I reached over and rubbed his head. "You have no idea what I'm saying."

"Probably not."

And that didn't come from Loki. The head drop was instinctual; Rafe was behind me. It was like the man had a super power of always being present when I was at my silliest. Studying the flowerpot, I wondered if I could get my head in there too.

It took effort, great effort, to turn my head; my eyes landed first on Rafe's feet, up his legs in those sweats that had places on my body aching in ways they never had, up his stomach to the tee that clung to his heated skin leaving nothing to the imagination. And unlike my moment, when I first arrived, of cotton sticking to my body, he looked edible. Reaching his face, I swear I almost lost consciousness because the man was smiling at me in the naughtiest way. If there was any question as to whether he heard what it was Loki and I were discussing, there wasn't any more. Those made of weaker stock would crumble right now, but not me. I rallied and tried for my best clueless expression—one that looked a lot like Nat's usual expression.

"Hey, Rafe."

"Avery. Smells good."

So do you. I could see the sweat beading on his neck and how I wanted my tongue there. I was getting turned on, so I tried to pull myself together. I'd wait until later to have my dirty thoughts about my landlord when I could actually do something about the aches he stirred. And then I realized what I was thinking while he stood over me as I contemplated it. Could he read minds? From the way his eyes turned darker, I had a terrible suspicion he could.

Realizing I hadn't answered him and not wanting him to pry into my brain to read any more of my wicked thoughts, I practically shouted at him. "Pumpkin scones. That's what you're smelling."

"Do you need me to taste them?"

My eyes widened and I think my jaw dropped because as innocent as his comment seemed, there was definitely a sexual innuendo in the way that he said it. And though I was out of my depths, it didn't stop me from saying, "If you think you can handle something as sinful as my pumpkin scones."

Humor marched across his face. "Don't know, but I sure as hell would like to give them a try."

And in my head my scones actually meant my breasts, and just thinking about that mouth on me, I wanted to weep.

"I'm going to shower, call me when they're done."

He was going to shower, of course he was. I wanted to say there was a perfectly usable hose right here why go inside and shower? I'd even hold the hose for him. Instead, I waved at him in a noncommittal way because I was about to expire from raging lust. No need for him to see that. "I'll give a holler."

Give a holler? Where was Nat's deadly knife when I could actually use it?

"Looking forward to tasting...your scones."

Oh I didn't imagine that hesitation, the emphasis he put on *your*. Being me and not knowing when to say when I replied, "Looking forward to you tasting them." And then I thought of Melody and Rafe's penchant for flirting, having witnessed his banter with Mrs. Milner. It was all in good fun for Rafe, for me it skirted too close to the danger zone. My raging lust evaporated like I'd been doused with a bucket of ice water.

My tone turned neutral, a fact not lost on Rafe. "I'll leave a few on the counter in your kitchen."

He stopped walking, his upper body twisting as his gaze searched mine. "What just happened?"

How did I answer that? It was the perfect opportunity to tell him about Melody, but I didn't. A part of me wanted him to broach the subject of her first, especially since what we were doing was so much more than flirting and he knew I knew about her. So instead of answering him, I went with the time-honored classic. "I'm getting a headache." Yep, I used the old headache ploy. A strategic genius, I was not.

He didn't buy it; I could practically see the bubble over his head. Instead, he said, "Do you need anything for it?"

You. I almost said, but bit my lip and shook my head no.

"Night, Avery."

"Night, Rafe."

He'd just reached his door when he called to me. "Oh, and Avery?"

"Yeah."

"I'm not with Melody anymore."

Oh my God, he *could* read minds. And as I mentally recalled every thought I'd ever had when in his company, he added, "I really want to taste your scones."

And then he winked at me before disappearing into his house. I stood motionless as the full impact of his statement hit me. He wasn't with Melody anymore and he wanted to taste my scones. Oh, hell yeah. And even riding that high, I couldn't help but wonder if he wasn't with Melody anymore then why the hell had she been at his gate?

chapter fifteen

Avery

I was on a break when I noticed I missed a call, but it was whom the call was from that had me staring at the screen in disbelief—my father. He hadn't voluntarily called me...ever. I couldn't lie; I was tempted to ignore his call, since he was so very good at ignoring mine, but rudeness didn't come as easily to me.

He answered on the second ring. "Avery."

So like him, no greeting. "Hi Dad."

"I'm sorry to call you out of the blue, but I wondered if you had time to talk today."

Talk was code for wanting something; unease moved through me because the request was likely coming from Dolly and still I heard myself saying, "I have a dinner break coming up at four."

"Okay, I'll swing by and we'll grab a bite."

As surprised and apprehensive as I was, excitement sparked too because we were going to dinner.

"I'm working at Clover."

"I know. I'll see you at four."

He clicked off before I could reply.

At four I stepped outside and my dad was there, working on his phone. His head lifted and he smiled. "Avery."

"Dad."

Nat shared his coloring, blond hair and blue eyes. Tall, fit, my dad was a good-looking man. "Do you have any preference on where we eat?"

"No."

"There's a great deli just down the street. How about we go there?"

"Sure." It didn't escape my notice how awkward our conversation was and how terribly uncomfortable I felt around my own dad.

"How's the job?" he asked.

"Wonderful. I love the freedom and the creativity that's encouraged."

"I'm happy to hear that. I've a business associate who mentioned he dined at Clover the other night and the raspberry rum tart was, his words, out of this world."

Pride gushed through me not only at the compliment but that my dad was the one to tell me. Rafe had been right, even as adults, children still sought the approval and praise of their parents.

Reaching the deli, we ordered our food and settled at a table. "So your mom and Harold are on their trip?"

"Yeah, she's having the time of her life."

"That surprises me, I'd never have thought your mom would enjoy something like that."

"She didn't either, but it isn't so much the activity but the person she's sharing it with that she adores." Yes, it was a little dig, but he had it coming.

He brushed right past that when he said, "I'm happy to hear that. And you're staying in Riverdale?"

My stomach twisted because I hated that I was right. Whatever this was, Dolly had put him up to it.

"I'm renting the carriage house of a friend of my boss's."

"Nice."

"So what's new with you, Dad?"

He looked up from his sandwich and it was the first time during our reunion that he looked nervous. "Well, actually I do have news."

My stomach squeezed.

"Dolly's pregnant."

My pastrami on rye soured in my stomach. Working to control my reaction to that news was hard, but I sucked it up and pasted a smile on my lips. "Congratulations."

"Thanks. It's a bit daunting becoming a father again at sixty, but Dolly really wants a family."

Again? Well yeah it kind of was again since he stopped acting like a father years ago. Bitterness burned through me. Instead, I just smiled and nodded.

"Anyway, to the reason why I wanted to see you. Dolly's hope is that you'll have an active role in our child's life."

Irritation and annoyance lit through me, as if I was the one who'd been keeping my distance. "As your daughter, it's kind of a given I'll be a part of your child's life."

"No, I realize that. What I mean to say is she wants to have a baby shower and she's hoping that as the sister, you'll throw it."

It took me a minute for understanding to dawn and I couldn't lie, hurt hit first knowing that had he not this request to make of me, my dad never would have called. Anger quickly replaced hurt that my dad could be such a blind fool when it came to his scheming bitch of a wife. "And does she have a preference for where this shower should be thrown?"

"As a matter of fact, yes. She'd like to have it at Clover and knowing how hard it is to get in there, she was hoping you could set it up."

My voice turned deadly quiet; Mom would have known I was just barely holding onto my temper, so would've Nat, hell, even Harold would have picked up on it, but my dad hadn't a clue. "So she'd like for me to ask for special treatment from my boss, whom I've only just started working for, so she can show off to all her friends at Clover. Am I getting this right?"

Dad's brow furrowed, he was seriously living in a hole when it came to his wife. "I don't think she's being that calculating, Avery. It's just an opportunity."

"And if I worked at say, Applebee's, would she still like for me to have an active role in my sibling's life and host the baby shower? What about Nat, not interested in having the shower in an OR?"

Temper, I saw it rolling over his features. This little chat wasn't going the way he wanted. "I think you're being unfair to your stepmother."

That was it; I lost it. "She is not my stepmother. She's your new wife. I have a mother whom I love dearly. As far as your wife, the only one who doesn't clearly see your wife's actions is you. I will not be hosting her shower, in fact as soon as I get back to Clover I will do everything in my power to make certain it will be a cold day in Hell before Dolly gets to strut her low-class ass in my place of employment."

"Avery!"

"You haven't called me in years, you haven't been a father for even longer, but you call me out of the blue, playing on my emotional need to have you in my life, to get your new wife what she wants even if that means using me to do it." I stood, my body just shaking with rage. "Good luck with baby number three; you sucked being a father with Nat and me, maybe you'll have better luck with this one."

Tossing a twenty on the table, I walked out with my head held high until I reached the corner and then it all just crashed down on me. How badly I wanted my dad in my life and how he'd only ever been one huge disappointment. I cried, big fat tears because I'd finally had reached my limit, had finally come to the place where Nat was. I was done trying. When I returned to Clover I looked like a puffer fish, a fact not lost on Trace.

"Avery, what's wrong?"

Wiping at my eyes, I took a few deep breaths to seek the calm I needed before I said, "I just saw my father. This is out of line, but I'm going to say it anyway. If you should get a request to host a baby shower for a Dolly Collins, it would be a huge favor to me if you turned that shit down."

"A relation of yours?"

"My father's new wife."

Understanding moved over his face. "Consider it done."

"Just like that?"

"For you to come back looking like that, knowing what I do about you, yeah, just like that."

Even wallowing in misery, Trace's opinion of me had a smile breaking over my face. "Thank you."

"No problem. I'm even prepared to throw them physically from the building." He offered that tidbit with a grin.

I laughed at the thought of Trace chucking Dolly out the front door of Clover, pregnant and all. "I don't think it will come to that." Even though there was a part of me that really wished it did.

I didn't go right home after work, went to Allegro and bellied up to the bar. Signaling for a drink, I downed the first glass of wine and ordered a second. Feeling the alcohol in my blood was nice, took a bit of the sting out of the emotions stirred by the conversation with my dad.

I had tried, really had tried to see the good in him, but I was done. He hadn't even seen it; the manipulation his wife was pulling on him and his daughter and here the man was talking about becoming a father again and with that woman as the mother. Unbelievable.

Tara approached; she must have been working the other side of the bar. "Avery, right?"

"Yeah. How are you, Tara?"

"Good. Staying busy."

"Are Darcy and Lucien here?"

"Nah, they skipped out early, had some preschool thing for Emily. Oh, someone's signaling me. I'll be back."

As she made her leave, a man settled next to me. Glancing over, my eyes collided with his. He was hot, kind of like Elijah from *The Originals*. "Hey."

He had a nice voice. "Hi."

"Can I get you a drink?"

The point of being here was to forget the situation with my dad. If a sexy man wanted to help me with that, who was I to argue? "Sure."

"What are you drinking?"

I had been drinking wine, but I wanted something more potent. "A mind eraser." They were good, tasted like liquid sweet-tarts.

He signaled the other bartender working with Tara and placed my order before he turned his dark eyes on me. "I'm Marco."

"Avery."

"Did you just get off work?"

"Yeah. I needed to unwind."

"Where do you work?"

"A restaurant not far from here."

"With a face like that, you must be the hostess?"

He was a good-looking man and he was trying, but in my head all I saw was Rafe. His laugh, his smile, the way his eyes twinkled when he was being mischievous. This poor guy didn't stand a chance, but conversing with him would keep thoughts of my dad at bay. "Pastry chef."

"Really? Is that job as interesting as it sounds?"

"And then some. It's like art with sugar." Liam's description of my job was very fitting.

He chuckled and it was a nice sound.

"What about you? What do you do?"

"Security specialist." He must have seen the question in my expression when he added, "I work for a firm installing security systems."

"I bet you have a huge client-base in this area."

"Our biggest. So you said you were here to unwind, is that code for a bad day?"

"Not a bad day, just a bad situation."

"How bad? On a scale from one to ten, ten being totally shitty."

"An eleven."

"Oh man, I'm sorry."

"Sadly, it comes as no surprise. I have become entirely too used to bad situations of this kind." I flashed him a smile as I finished off my mind eraser, "A little help forgetting, always a plus."

"How are you getting home?"

"Cab."

"Then I'll get us another round."

I woke face down on my bed, still dressed in yesterday's clothes. My mouth was dry, I had to pee and my head was pounding. Damn those mind erasers, had the name for a reason. Climbing from bed, I realized the pounding wasn't my head but someone at the door.

"Stop pounding." A sharp pain stabbed my aching brain, which only served to spark my temper.

Pulling the door open, Rafe stood there and he looked dangerous.

"It's too early for this. Come back next week." I tried to close the door, but his foot stopped that action.

Focusing on his foot was hard since I was still slightly drunk. "Could you move that?"

"Who was the guy?"

"What guy?"

Now he looked both dangerous and really freaking mad. "The one who saw you home at three in the morning."

Someone saw me home? Wait, my car wasn't here? Moving past Rafe, I peered over to the drive and, yep, my car wasn't there. Well, that was good; I didn't drive while drunk.

"Avery?"

Focusing on the question, the night started coming back to me. Marco. Right, we shared a cab. I had been so far gone he'd hadn't been comfortable with me in a cab alone.

"Marco."

"Who the fuck is Marco?"

Surprised at the anger coming from him, I didn't answer immediately. He didn't like my hesitation because he got up in my face, so close his breath fanned out over my cheeks and as hard as I tried to bite down on the moan, it couldn't be stopped because he smelled so good. Edible.

"Who's Marco?"

My thoughts were a bit scattered because instead of answering him I asked a question. "How do you know someone brought me home?"

"I saw it on the cameras, the alarm buzzed when the gate opened."

Ah, good to know.

"Who's Marco, Avery?"

"A nice man I met at a bar."

I was still in a bit of a haze, so I wasn't picking up on the subtle nuances coming from Rafe. "Were you on a date?"

Bile burned the back of my throat, damn mind erasers…wait, what? A date? And even feeling like death, I couldn't help the grin because Rafe looked jealous. It was tempting to tease him a bit, but then had the roles been reversed I wouldn't have found the situation funny in the least. "No. I went to Allegro to drink my troubles away. He was nice, didn't want me in a cab alone in my condition. Come in, I'll put on some coffee, since I didn't set the machine last night, but first I have to pee."

I didn't wait for him to accept my invite and disappeared down the hall to take care of business and to change from my work clothes to my comfy sweats. When I returned, Rafe was already brewing the coffee. I settled at the counter, Rafe leaned over it, right in my face.

"Call me the next time you find yourself needing a ride."

"But it was late. You—"

"Avery, don't fucking argue. You call me the next time. Understand?"

High-handed, absolutely, and still every part of me loved that he was being high-handed. "I'll call you."

"How about an omelet?" Gracious too, Nat would have ridden my ass for an hour on my poor judgment. And I could admit that I'd been reckless last night. Luckily for me it all ended well.

My stomach growled in answer. "Please, I'm starving."

As he walked to the fridge, he asked, "What troubles were you drinking away?"

"Just stuff with my dad."

"What stuff?"

"He called me out of the blue yesterday and invited me out for a bite to eat. Foolish little me thought he was finally reaching out, but he was there at the request of his wife. They're pregnant and they were hoping I could arrange to have her baby shower at Clover since I work there. The sad part is he doesn't see it, her manipulation and worse how her manipulation hurts Nat and me."

"Assholes. What did you tell him?"

I didn't answer right away, just took a moment to appreciate Rafe's outrage on my behalf. "I told him it would be a cold day in Hell before Dolly had her baby shower at Clover. I even asked Trace to decline the request if one should be made."

"Good for you." He stopped beating the eggs, his focus completely on me. "Your car, it's from him isn't it?"

"Yeah."

Understanding looked back at me, but he tried for levity when he said, "There had to be a reason you kept that ugly piece of shit."

And despite feeling melancholy, I felt my lips turning up into a smile. "My car is not ugly."

"Baby, your car is hideous."

"It's vintage."

"Vintage shit."

"I don't have words." And even as I smiled, my heart hurt because it was an ugly car and I had kept it for far longer than I should have, I had kept it for him. But after his latest parental failure, even that memory didn't improve my opinion of him.

Rafe touched my chin, lifting my face to his. "I'd like to say one day he'll realize what an ass he's being, one day he'll man up and be the father you deserve, but it's likely he'll never get there. The happy memory you have when you look at your car, that's what makes your car beautiful."

I wanted to lean into him, wanted to press my mouth to his, wanted to feel his strong arms pulling me close. He brushed my cheek with his thumb before he focused back on the eggs.

My voice was thick, husky, when I asked, "What kind of omelet are you making me?"

"Western."

"Ham, onions, peppers, mushrooms and cheese?"

"Yep."

"Yummy."

The sizzle of the butter in the pan, the fragrant scent that assailed me had my stomach growling again, loud and long. A fact not lost on Rafe. "You are hungry."

"Oh my God. How sexy am I, dressed like this and having a stomach attempting communication outside the body. Maybe you should put the oven on so I can stick my head in it."

Rafe glanced at me, the bowl of eggs in his hand, but I hadn't a clue what he was thinking.

"What?"

He shook his head, like in confusion or maybe disbelief, before he poured the eggs into the pan. And on cue, my stomach responded with a loud approving rumble. He was rather skilled at making an omelet, even flipping it to cook the top. Another pan was sautéing the onions, peppers, mushrooms and ham. Scooping the filling onto the egg, he sprinkled cheese, cracked pepper and a hint of salt before folding it. He slid the omelet onto a plate and placed the heavenly concoction right in front of me. Digging a fork from the drawer, he set it next to the plate.

"Avery?"

Drool pooled in my mouth, smelling the incredible scents wafting up in the steam, so it took effort to move my focus from the omelet to Rafe.

"You're the sexiest woman I've ever seen, even more so dressed like that."

If I weren't sitting, I'd be on the floor right now. Did he just say that? I never felt sexy before, but I felt it now with those green eyes looking with such unabashed heat. To cover just how much those words meant to me, I teasingly replied, "I think the heat from the stove has fried your brain."

"And I think you should just shut up, understand that I'm right and eat your omelet."

"All right, Mr. Bossy." But I was grinning like a fool.

chapter sixteen

Avery

It's incredible. I'm only limited by my imagination, literally. If I can think it up, cost is no issue. I have a team, two sous chefs." Sitting at the local café, taking my meal break, I chatted on the phone with Jessica.

"You have a team?"

"Crazy right?" An odd sensation caused the hair on my arms to stand on end, the sensation so powerful I actually peered over my shoulder to see who was staring at me. Distracted, I missed Jessica's question.

Picking up on my inattention, she jarred me from my scan of the place when she practically bellowed, "Avery!"

"I'm sorry."

"What's going on?"

"I don't know, probably nothing, but it feels like someone's watching me."

"Where are you?"

"Down the street from Clover."

"Maybe someone's just checking you out."

"Maybe."

Her voice went from teasing to serious. "Are you getting a bad feeling?"

"A little."

"The city scares me."

"I've never had an issue, doesn't mean I won't, but this is definitely a new experience. A little creepy."

"But you don't see anyone outwardly looking at you?"

"No, but the place is pretty crowded and there are a lot of tables concealed from me."

"Are you worried?"

"Worried, no, but definitely wary. As long as I don't go walking to the rest room alone and I don't inexplicably say *I'll be back* because, as you know, in movies—outside of Arnold—those people never come back, I should be okay."

"You're so weird. Maybe it's a customer from Clover, a woman who you've increased her dress size and now she wants payback."

"I'm weird? Have you and Nat been spending time together? You're beginning to sound just like her."

Her only response was a laugh. Focusing on Jessica, I tried to ignore the prickling my skin was doing. "Did you get a hotel?"

"Yep. Kit plans to take Aidan to a football game on one of the days. So tell me about Rafe?"

"He's not with Melody anymore."

"He told you that?"

"We were flirting and in the middle of it I remembered Melody, it kind of put a damper on it for me. I feigned a headache, he saw right through me. Told me he wasn't with her anymore and really wanted to taste my scones."

"You're scones?"

"Code for wanting to taste me."

"Oh my God."

"Yeah. I've been kind of floating around since, my head isn't functioning as well as it should. But when you've got a man like that wanting to taste your scones, I think I'm entitled to be a bit loopy."

"You can say that again."

"What was weird though, I saw Melody a few days before that attempting to get onto his property. If they aren't together, why was she there?"

"Good question. What did he say?"

"I didn't tell him. I intended to but then my dad called."

"What?"

"Yeah, he wanted to have dinner but really he wanted me to set up a baby shower for Dolly at Clover."

"He did not."

"He did. He even got annoyed with me when I told him where he could stick his baby shower."

"Unbelievable."

"It was the kick I needed. I've officially joined the ranks with Nat. I'm done."

"I'm sorry, but sometimes relationships are toxic and it's healthier to let them go."

"You're right. It just hurts that my dad is my toxic relationship." I had an incoming call. "I've got another call. We'll talk soon."

"Be safe, Avery. And no worries about your dad, you've got a kick-ass mom and an awesome stepdad."

"So true. Kiss the boys."

"Always."

Disconnecting with Jess, I saw it was Ember. "Ember? Is everything okay?"

"Yeah, I just wanted to invite you to dinner on Saturday. Trace insisted, said your sous chefs could handle things for the night."

I wasn't going to argue, it'd been an age since I'd been to a dinner party and for it to be at Ember's meant that Rafe would be there too. I didn't hide my excitement. "I'd love that."

"Can you bring dessert?"

"Like you need to ask. How many people are you expecting?"

"About twenty."

Not just a dinner party, but a big dinner party. I couldn't wait. I'd never gone so long between social gatherings, I was beginning to feel like a hermit. "I'll be sure to bring enough so there are leftovers for you and the family."

"I was hoping you'd suggest that."

"Thanks for including me. I used to have dinner with my girl-friend all the time, I miss it."

"Darcy and I want to pick your brain about Rafe."

"Ugh."

She laughed. "Kidding, well not entirely kidding." Her next words were spoken with unfeigned sincerity. "We're looking forward to see-ing you."

"Me too. See you on Saturday."

A half an hour later when I headed back to work, the pricking sensation had stopped.

Sitting outside, I listened to the sound of power tools coming from Rafe's barn. He'd been at it for a few hours. It wasn't quite lunchtime, but I wanted to offer him lunch as a thank you for the breakfast he'd made me the other day.

Entering the barn to the scent of freshly cut wood, I spotted Rafe working with a power tool I didn't know the name of. His focus was incredible, the ease in which he worked equally so. I hadn't made a sound and still Rafe's head turned, his eyes catching mine.

"Sorry to interrupt, I was about to make lunch and wanted to know if you'd like some."

He straightened from his position and turned more fully to me. He was in those faded jeans again; I wanted to see him in those and nothing else, preferably while moving toward me with the intent of spending hours wearing no clothes at all. And then remembering he may have the ability to read minds, I emptied mine.

"I'd like that, but I want to finish these cuts first. Why don't you stay? Together we'll get it done faster and then I'll help you with lunch."

Um, so he hadn't read my lustful thoughts; it said a lot about me that I was disappointed about that, but not for long with him seeming to want my company as much as I wanted his. "Okay, but fair warning, I don't know the first thing about woodworking."

His lips curved up. "I'll teach you what you need to know."

He handed me a pair of goggles, our fingers brushed which had the hair on my arms standing on end from the electric current that burned through me at the contact. I wasn't alone in feeling that heat, his eyes turned dark as his focus shifted to my lips. To say he looked hungry was definitely an understatement.

"Safety is the first and most important lesson when working with any power tools." He rested his hand on the saw he'd been using. "This is a miter saw, it makes the angle cuts to frame out the bookcases. This is a miter box to help guide the cuts; the angles I'm cutting are not standard since the ceilings in the house are not square. I've already made the first cut. We need to cut these." He gestured to a pile of long rectangular boards stacked on a pair of sawhorses. "Then we'll use wood glue to attach the pieces and clamp the corners so the glue can set."

"Are these for the library?"

"Yeah." He moved the piece he had cut and reached for another, setting it along the miter box. "I'm going to turn on the saw. When you're ready, bring the blade down slowly. Let the blade do the work."

"Okay."

The saw kicked on, and my heart jumped because it was a bit scary seeing that blade spinning and knowing the damage it could cause. Rafe helped to hold the piece steady as I lowered the blade. The saw cut the wood like a hot knife through butter. Rafe certainly kept his tools in excellent shape. Once I'd cut all the way through, I lifted the blade. Rafe cut the power.

"Nice job."

"Even for as loud as it is, it's oddly calming, almost hypnotic."

"I've always thought that too. Are you ready to do another?"

"Absolutely."

For the next hour, we worked through the pile of wood, making the cuts and then gluing and clamping the pieces together. After, we cleaned up his workshop before we headed to my place for lunch.

"I was going to whip up a chicken salad with cranberries, walnuts and honey. I made whole grain bread earlier."

"Sounds great. Can I use your bath to wash up?"

I liked the thought of Rafe in my bath washing up. Would like it even more if I were in there with him. "Yeah, there are extra towels in the closet."

Pulling the chicken I had roasted yesterday morning from the refrigerator, I started removing the meat from the bones. I heard as the water turned on and I gave myself a moment to imagine Rafe stripping down, knowing he wasn't really doing that, but I so enjoyed the visual. I was fairly turned on when Rafe came back into the kitchen. I couldn't look at him for fear he'd see that I'd been envisioning him naked, so I focused on mixing the chicken with the mayo and honey like I was working with nitroglycerin. I offered, "There are drinks in the fridge. Help yourself."

"Thanks. You want something?"

"A beer would be nice."

He popped the top off one and placed it next to me. I asked, "What kind of wood was that?"

"Mahogany."

"It's beautiful. I don't imagine you're going to stain it."

"No, just some polyurethane to bring out the natural striations in the wood."

"Thanks for letting me help. That was fun."

"Thanks for lunch." He leaned up against the counter next to me, holding his beer with his thumb and pointer finger. "So how's work? What kind of boss is Trace?"

He was digging, looking for dirt that he could use to rib his friend, but I had to disappoint him because Trace was an excellent boss. "He's great. He demands excellence, but as long as you're giving him that, he's hands-off. I wasn't sure how it would be working for him because he seems more like a fighter than restaurateur, especially after I did a little research on him prior to my interview."

"You did?"

Embarrassed that I admitted it, I didn't back down because the pin had been pulled. "I wanted to be prepared, wanted to know my audience. I even took a class at his cooking school just to see what he was like. Brought Nat, that was a mistake."

"Why was bringing Nat a mistake?"

"She's a clown and drew attention, Trace's actually, when the whole point was to be on the down low. It's amazing to me how someone so scattered and wacky can operate on brains."

"Yeah, about that. What made her want to be a brain surgeon?"

"I think she's a zombie and she uses her occupation as a way to eat. I could be wrong, since I've never been in the operating room with her, but it's the only thing that makes sense to me."

A grin appeared on his lips before he took a pull from his beer. "Does she tease you as much as you tease her?"

"She teases me more, but in all seriousness I think she chose her occupation because our Nana had a brain aneurysm and it killed her. We were all really close, but Nat and Nana were like two peas in a pod. She couldn't save Nana but she can save other people's Nanas."

Looking up from what I was doing, I discovered I had Rafe's complete attention. "To look at you and your sister, you look opposite, but you're a lot alike."

"Yeah, we are. She's older, but it never felt like she was older. She wasn't one for pulling the age card as kids. You don't have siblings, do you?"

"No, but I have Trace and Lucien and we've known each other since we were kids so they kind of feel like my brothers."

"The three of you together, there was likely a stream of heart-broken girls in your wake." And then I realized I said that out loud and since I had already stuck my foot in my mouth I added, "I'm just saying your fairy godmother should be given a citation or something for being so free with her wand."

"Wand?"

In answer to that, I lifted the spoon I was using and waved it in true fairy godmother fashion. "Her beauty wand."

Heat, raw and primal, flashed in his eyes, and my mouth went dry as my skin started to tingle. And then he said, "You're goofy."

"Maybe, but the probability of all that hotness focused in one area, it's just not statistically possible. So either you're undead, because we all know the undead are notorious for being hot, or you have a rogue fairy godmother who is not shy about sharing the wealth."

"Totally goofy." Rafe said on a laugh, but the smile he gave me after was proof that he liked my goofy.

"Watching you work, the effortless way you move through a project is really impressive. How long have you been a woodcrafter?"

"About ten years, the business really took off about seven years ago. I imagine my focus is a lot like yours in the kitchen, second nature."

"Yeah, but you're creating pieces that in a hundred years will still be around. You're creating a legacy, that's enviable."

"And you're not? Sure what you create doesn't last, but for that moment you're creating memories. People view my creations, but people taste yours and having tasted some of your desserts, they are definitely memorable."

I'd stopped scooping the chicken salad onto the bread and just stared at him because that was, hands down, the nicest compliment I had ever been given. "Thank you."

My breath stilled in my lungs as he touched a lock of my hair that had fallen from the knot. "You're welcome."

Talk about memorable moments. I couldn't even form a reply. I wanted to kiss him, wanted to bridge the distance between us and press my mouth to his. And maybe I was being fanciful, but he looked to be battling the same urge.

He recovered faster than me when he said, "Looks good. I'll get the plates."

CHAPTER SEVENTEEN

RAFE

I'd just finished putting the last coat of poly on the bookcase Avery and I made when I heard Loki bark a second before Avery's slightly hysterical laughter. It was early, before eight, but Avery was already up. Stepping from the barn, the sight that greeted me had a smile pulling at my mouth, even as envy burned through me. The fact that I was envious of my dog was seriously messed up. Avery lay on her back while Loki tried to lick her face, an action she was attempting to avoid at all costs. The image slammed into me, so vividly, her on her back and my body over hers. *I* wanted to lick her: every single inch. I knew she wanted me too. And even with all that sexual tension between us, the woman was hilarious. That entire conversation on fairy godmothers and her sister being a zombie was a riot. I was attracted to her, absolutely, you'd have to be a eunuch not to be, but her personality was almost sexier.

"You've licked your butt with that tongue. Stop it you fiend." Her order was barely audible through her laughter. Her head turned, her bright eyes found mine. "Don't just stand there, help me." And though she issued a command, it didn't really come off as one with her giggling like she was.

I didn't really want to get involved. She looked adorable, lying there with my huge dog trying to eat her whole. I wondered what Avery would do if I took his place? The thought was so tempting I almost threw caution to the wind.

Instead I ordered, "Loki, stop."

And my dog, he clearly was of a similar mindset of not wanting me to get involved, because he merely glanced over at me before he continued to lick Avery.

"Loki, come."

He reacted then, following the command, but he did so very reluctantly. Avery didn't move, just lay there, still laughing, her hair had fallen out of the knot thing she always had it pulled up in. Her gaze moved from Loki and me to the sky, her expression turning almost serene. The temptation to look up and see what put that look on her face nearly had me doing so.

"How's work?" It was kind of a lame-ass question, we'd talked about her work yesterday, but that happened when the blood in your brain headed south—a condition occurring more and more when I was in her presence.

Her green eyes turned to me. "Awesome. I have a team, two sous chefs. I can't get my head around that. Me, who just started my first professional job as a chef and I have a team." She rolled and stood, the movement fluid, really fucking sexy and completely unconsciously done. She pulled her hair back while answering. "They look at me like I can split the atom and perform brain surgery at the same time."

"Can you?"

She looked mischievous when she replied, "Not yet."

Her lower lip begged to be bitten, fuller than the top one and perfectly shaped. Dragging my eyes from her lips, since I felt my jeans getting tighter, I managed to lift my gaze to hers when she asked, "Have you finished the bookcase?"

"Yeah."

"How many more do you have to make?"

"Four."

"I'll help with those too, if you want."

After yesterday, the thought of working with her again was very appealing. "I'd like that."

"Cool. I have the sketches for the gardens. Fall is for planting, so it's a good time to get to work on them."

"Do you have time to look them over now?"

"Sure, but I'll need to multitask. Ember called earlier in the week and invited me to dinner tomorrow. I'm bringing dessert."

The thought of her among my friends appealed too, a whole hell of a lot. "We can drive over together."

For just a split second, I caught her unguarded reaction to my suggestion and I liked every single expression that swept her face. "I'd like that."

Her and me in my truck, yeah I fucking liked that idea too, more specifically the trouble we could get into. Changing the subject before my IQ dropped any lower I asked, "What are you making for dessert?"

"A chocolate caramel cake, layers of dense chocolate cake and creamy caramel with a rich chocolate buttercream icing. I need to make three. Normally I'd bake them the day of, but I have found with this recipe it tastes better the next day since the caramel is absorbed into the chocolate cake."

"I'll help, but with your guidance because I don't know the first thing about baking."

"No worries, I'll teach you everything you need to know." She said that with a wink because she'd used my own words back at me.

We headed inside where Loki settled on the sofa. Avery started pulling pans from the cabinets. "Can you get six pounds of butter and the cream from the refrigerator?"

"Six pounds of butter? You have six pounds of butter?"

"I always have at least six pounds, but I'm making the caramel so I've double that. I bake, butter is in everything."

That was true enough, but going through that much butter she should probably get herself a cow or two. I got distracted when Avery bent in half to get something from one of the lower cabinets. Her ass in those sweats, Jesus I wanted a piece of that. Not surprising, since I seemed to revert back to a teenager whenever she was around, my dick grew hard and my hands actually itched to grab her hips so I could pull her to me and make us both happy. In an attempt to not succumb to the horny adolescent I had been reduced to, I turned and moved deeper into the refrigerator and pictured Sister Margaret naked; the cantankerous old nun from my days at St. Agnes orphanage, who at ninety-eight was still a ball-buster. Yep, that worked every time.

"Are you going to climb into the refrigerator?"

"Smart ass."

Her only response to that was a saucy smile. "Before we get started, here are the sketches." She slid a few sheets in front of me, and damn but she'd been serious about knowing what she was doing. She'd drawn the house, really well too, and the gardens she proposed. The other pages showed in more detail each garden bed and what plants went where. Pictures were included of all the plant material she recommended.

"These are amazing."

Her head lifted and the warmest smile touched her lips. She stirred my blood like no one ever had, but she also brought a peace that was nearly as good. Dad was right; I never stood a chance with my attempt to stay away from her.

And accepting my fate, I gave in to the hunger to have her near. "Are you free on Sunday?"

"Yeah."

"Let's hit the nursery and order the plants."

If possible, her smile grew even warmer. "Sounds good. I can work on the gardens in the evenings."

"We'll work on the gardens."

The look she gave me shifted something in me, something I didn't appreciate at the time but was irrevocable all the same.

"We need to measure out the dry and wet ingredients. Which do you want, wet or dry?"

We were talking about cake but the image of Avery, naked in my bed, wet for me, turned me hard again.

Tamping down on that before I dragged her across the quartz countertop and took her right there, I replied, "I'll take dry."

She jotted down the dry ingredients and their proportions and slid the paper to me. "All of that can be found in the pantry." And as I worked on that, she measured out the buttermilk, the butter and the vanilla. Melted the chocolate, added the sugar to sweeten it.

"The baking powder, salt and flour can be blended. The sugar we'll cream with the butter before adding the eggs and then we'll alternate between the flour and the buttermilk until everything is incorporated. Can you start creaming the butter while I prepare the pans?"

"Sure."

"When it turns a pale yellow and has increased in volume you can add the eggs."

"We're not going to get to eat this, that seems cruel."

"I have an apple/cranberry pie in the freezer."

"That'll do."

I was watching her move around the kitchen, not really paying attention to what I was doing. And wanting her closer, I asked, "Is this good?"

She peered into the bowl, the scent of cocoa wafting up to me. I swear the woman smelled like cocoa and not because she just melted chocolate. It was like her natural scent. It drove me crazy. "Looks good."

She looked good. I didn't know how much longer I could keep from kissing her. I wanted her curves pressed up against me, wanted her taste on my tongue, wanted to feel as she let go and gave in to the passion I knew simmered under the surface.

"You can add the eggs and then the extra yokes. And that's what's going to make this cake airy and light. And the chocolate is cool enough now, so you can add that and then alternate between the flour and the buttermilk."

When done, she poured the batter evenly into the pans and set them in the oven. "I'll defrost the pie and you can start measuring the dry ingredients again. After the cakes are done I'll show you how to make homemade caramel. As a thank you, I'll whip you up something for dinner before I have to go to work."

Yeah, I wasn't going to be able to keep from kissing her for much longer. So fucking sweet.

Avery

As soon as the door opened at Ember and Trace's, we were greeted to a wall of noise. Everyone else seemed to already be there. Rafe was just beside me, two cake holders in one hand, and Loki's leash in the other.

"You made it!" Ember reached for the cakes from Rafe. "And you brought lots of dessert. Leftovers!"

I felt Rafe's hand on the small of my back, his touch light and yet it burned clear down to my bones. Stepping into the apartment, I took a moment to just observe. Lucien was across the room, Darcy pressed up against his side, her hand being held in his and on his shoulders was Emily, who was pulling on her daddy's hair and squealing in delight. Two older men were talking with Lucien; both obviously were related to Ember. Another woman, also older, stood with a tall, dark-haired man. She had to be Trace's mom because they had the same eyes. And with them was another woman about Ember and Darcy's age, but with how she gestured and moved she seemed younger than she looked. There were two guys, teenagers, one looked just like Lucien and the other looked remarkably like Trace. Kyle was there, talking to Tara, the bartender from Allegro. And on the sofa was a nun; I knew this because she was dressed in a habit. But what had me unable to pull my focus from her was that she looked to be about 120 years old. She must have sensed my stare because her head twisted, and very sharp and alert eyes settled on me. I'd been staring, it was rude, so I waved. She didn't return it.

"Okay, going around the room. You know Lucien, Darcy and Emily. They're talking to my dad, Shawn, the man on the right, and my uncle Josh. Kyle and Tara, whom you've met, the tall man there is Vincent Gowan and he's married to Trace's mom, Victoria. And the woman with them is Chelsea, Trace's sister. She's a few years older than me, but she was in an accident when she was younger and suffered some brain trauma. Those two clowns are Brandon and Seth. Brandon is Lucien and Darcy's son and Seth is Trace's cousin in a convoluted way. And the woman on the sofa is Sister Margaret. She played a pretty big role in getting Lucien and Darcy reunited with their son."

"Sounds like a story there."

"Yeah, there is. Let's put these in the kitchen." She looked passed me to Rafe. "We'll be right back. You want a beer?"

"Yeah, thanks Ember."

Their kitchen was fantastic. All Clad pots and pans hanging from the pot rack, a subzero refrigerator, soapstone countertops and plenty of room for multiple people to work and not bang elbows. "Oh my God, I'd sleep in this kitchen."

Ember glanced around the room, someone obviously not a cook enthusiast. A suspicion confirmed when she said, "This is Trace's domain."

"I like it."

"So you arrived with Rafe." She bumped her shoulder into mine just as Darcy appeared.

"You came with Rafe. Progress." Darcy and Ember clearly shared a brain.

"You both need to get a hobby."

"You have that sexy man sharing space with you. You need to come up with a plan." Darcy was in the mood to play matchmaker apparently.

"If you don't come up with a plan, you must be an idiot." Sister Margaret said as she walked into the kitchen.

"She comes across mean because she is mean." Darcy's comment had my jaw dropping.

"What is it with you younger folks, dropping your jaws like nitwits. Close that up girl, I don't need to see your tonsils."

Did she just say that to me? She was a nun, I should show respect, but the words came out before I could censor myself. "You're charming. So when do they put you back in your sarcophagus?"

Rafe and Trace strolled into the kitchen as I asked that. Both stopped and looked from me to Sister Margaret, whose expression I could not read at all. Thinking I might be about to have my hands slapped with a ruler, I contemplated taking a step back but showing weakness was not something I did. And then the woman made a sound; it was an awkward sound so it took a minute to realize she was laughing. And me being me said, "You either smoke entirely too much or you seriously need to laugh more."

Trace chuckled, Rafe grinned and Darcy and Ember both dropped their jaws and honestly, I kind of understood Sister Margaret's comment. Her beady eyes were glued to me and then she laughed again. "I like you. Wherever did you find her, Ember?"

"Trace did. She's his new pastry chef."

"Sassy and can cook. You better snatch this one up, Rafe, before she gets away."

The room fell silent again for a completely different reason and feeling awkward, I was about to exit stage left when Rafe softly replied. "I think you might be right."

He winked at me before taking the beer from Trace and walking from the room.

"Did he just say that?" Darcy asked.

"He did." Ember confirmed.

Sister Margaret's contribution, "Please, they're hot for each other. A blind man can see that."

Dinner was served in the living room on a table clearly purchased for these large dinner parties. And even with the addition of a table nearly the size of the one depicted in Leonardo da Vinci's *The Last Supper*, the apartment wasn't crowded; people were still able to freely move around the space. And they lived on the Upper East Side. Amazing.

I had been seated next to Sister Margaret and Trace; Rafe was across from me. And even as I listened to the conversation that moved around the table, my head was still in the kitchen hearing Rafe's reply to Sister Margaret. Hearing him suggest that he should make his move, teasing or not, I wanted him to make a move. And it was thinking about all the ways he could that had an ache forming between my legs. A throbbing would be a better description. Shifting in my seat, hoping to ease it, Sister Margaret elbowed me in the arm.

"What's wrong with you, moving around like that in your chair? You got ants in your pants?"

Not ants, something so much better. My gaze collided with Rafe's, and honestly it looked as if he knew exactly what afflicted me. And even as my cheeks burned, moisture accompanied the ache. I physically lusted after a man while being seated next to a nun. I was going to Hell, or at the very least purgatory. Turning my attention to Sister Margaret it was to find her grinning. Narrowing my eyes at her, I realized she also knew why I shifted as I did in my chair. Her expression changed slightly, acknowledging that she knew I knew.

"You're a wicked woman."

"That's not a nice thing to say." And yet her expression contradicted her words because she was smiling like a deranged clown.

After dinner, I tried to help clean up but Ember and Darcy pushed me from the kitchen, told me I should go find Rafe. I didn't really need an excuse to settle in next to him. So I did, spotted him across the room talking with Ember's dad, uncle and Lucien. As soon as I approached, all four heads turned in my direction. It seemed serious, whatever they were discussing, and I gathered they didn't want me to overhear by the way they all shifted their attention to me.

"I didn't mean to interrupt."

Before I could retreat, Rafe reached for my hand. "Avery is renting the carriage house. She's met my dad and knows about his past, she should probably hear this. Josh has been looking into the robbery, specifically the two others involved."

When he'd mentioned this the last time, I'd felt uneasy. Now I felt a bit more than that because clearly this wasn't just a passing interest. "I'm guessing by the fact that you're looking into it, you're more concerned than you let on."

"The pieces don't fit and that bothers me."

"I can understand that as it involves your dad."

Josh filled me in. "I didn't find out much, Jeremy Paddington worked a low level tech job at a shipping company, Morton Shipping. For all intent and purposes he was a regular guy, in debt and behind on his mortgage. The only information remotely interesting is that he died not long before his box at the bank was broken into. A mugging."

"He dies and his box gets broken into, seems suspect."

I had to agree with Lucien.

"Agreed. I'm looking deeper into the mugging." Josh replied.

Shawn's attention was redirected when Faith ran over and wrapped her arms around his leg. "Up, Poppy."

Josh's voice grew soft and a touch sad. "She looks just like Ember did as a kid, the spitting image of my sister."

Ember's mom Mandy, I had learned, had died in a hit and run when Ember was three. For a group of people who had known more than their share of grief, it was beautiful to see the family they'd all become.

Josh and Shawn were pulled away to play with the girls and Lucien went in search of Darcy. Rafe squeezed my hand. "You okay?"

"I like your friends."

"Yeah, they're pretty great."

I understood better Rafe's interest in the robbery because I found myself curious. "What do you think was in Jeremy's box?"

His expression turned hard and I regretted asking. "I don't know. And was the person who hired Lucas the same person who killed him or was there another interested party who got to it first?"

"I don't get the sense your dad knew what he was getting himself into."

"No, he didn't. Of that I'm certain."

"It was good he turned himself in, considering what happened to his accomplices."

"Yeah."

Our conversation was cut short when Ember called, "Dessert."

Rafe was still holding my hand, he seemed to be as surprised by that as me. I thought he'd release it, but he didn't. He held it tighter as he escorted me to the table.

I sat on the sofa and had one brown-haired head resting on one leg and one black-haired head resting on the other. I had become Faith and Emily's new best friend because I created, 'yummy sweet things'. I was as tired as they were, but I couldn't pull my gaze from the people sitting around the table. Most of the guests had left and Chelsea had gone to bed a while ago. It was only Lucien, Darcy, Rafe and Kyle who shared the table with Trace and Ember. The affection between the six of them was undeniable. It was beautiful and in that moment, I missed my mom, Nat and Jessica terribly. The last time I spoke to Mom, they were heading to New Orleans. I couldn't imagine either of them in that city, but I looked forward to hearing the stories.

I must have dozed off because the next thing I remembered was Rafe hunching down in front of me, gently stroking my cheek with his finger.

"Ready to go?"

"I fell asleep, didn't I?"

"It's okay, you had a long week."

"Loki?"

"Already leashed." He reached for my hands and helped me to my feet. Both the girls were sound asleep in their dads' arms.

Moving to the door, Ember and Darcy weren't able to hide their enthusiasm at the sight of Rafe and me. I was too tired to tease them but I did say. "Thanks for including me. I really enjoyed myself."

"You're officially invited to all our dinner parties and you're on dessert patrol because that cake was freaking awesome." Ember said.

Darcy followed with, "Yeah, it was. The next one is at our house."

"See you Monday, Avery."

"Night, Trace. You've got a beautiful family." My eyes moved to Lucien, "You both do."

Trace's arm slipped around his wife's shoulders, his attention on Ember. Ember's reaction was sweet. She blushed but at the same time it looked as if she wanted to climb her husband like a tree.

"Night, Avery." Lucien whispered so he didn't wake his daughter.

I didn't really remember the walk to the truck or the ride home. I remembered Rafe walking me to the door though. He unlocked it for me and held it open and then he touched my face, his finger brushing lightly down my jaw before his thumb stroked my lower lip.

"Night, Avery."

"Night, Rafe."

Somehow I made it to my bed, fell face first without even changing. And when I dreamed, I dreamt of Rafe and me hosting a dinner party: one with his friends and mine, our child sleeping in her daddy's arms.

CHAPTER EIGHTEEN

RAFE

Avery and I had plans to hit the nursery today but based on how late we got home last night and how tired she'd been, I wasn't expecting to see her until later in the morning. I could get a few hours of work in.

Loki stood by the back door waiting for me to let him out, but it wasn't nature calling that had him so eager. He and I shared the same affliction. Avery. He seemed to crave her company as much as I did. Unfortunately for me, I couldn't drop my ass down on her front step until she came to let me in. Though, the idea held more appeal than it should. And here I snickered at the idea of Lucien being whipped. Who the hell was I kidding? He, at least, was getting sex from the object of his obsession, me I only got dessert—delicious as all hell dessert, but my cravings went deeper. Last night when she fell asleep with Emily and Faith, I had the strangest reaction to that. For a moment, it wasn't Trace and Lucien's kids but my own, ours, she cuddled with. That had never happened to me before, wasn't even sure I wanted kids, but I felt the pull last night seeing her with Faith and Emily.

She lived here though and if it didn't work out between us it'd be awkward. Of course, if it did work...

I stopped myself because I was beginning to sound like a woman. Grabbing a cup of coffee, I headed outside only to stop at the sight of Avery sitting on the front step of the carriage house. She was dressed for the day, jeans and sweater, her hair up, Chucks on her feet. As soon as she spotted me, she smiled and the thought of waking up to that smile every day hit me in the gut, in a really fucking nice way.

"Morning." She stood and met me halfway.

"I wasn't expecting you up so early with how tired you were last night."

"I'm used to getting up early, my internal clock is still set to the days when I worked at the bakery at home."

"Have you had coffee?"

"Yeah. Are you heading to your workshop?"

"I was, but only because I thought you'd still be asleep."

She shifted, her cheeks turning rosy. I didn't know why she was flustered or why the sight of her flustered had my balls tightening. But I did know I was fooling myself believing I had a choice when it came to Avery.

"I had a thought and if you can't, I understand but the nursery opens at nine and after I wondered if you'd be interested in going to Coney Island with me. I've never been and I'd really like to see it."

She seemed nervous, as if she was accustomed to asking for something and being told no. How could anyone say no to her? And how the hell was it that this vivacious beauty was alone?

"Yeah, I'll take you to Coney Island."

Her face just lit up but instead of bringing a smile, I felt really fucking pissed; enough that I asked her. "Where are your girlfriends?"

If she was taken off guard with that question, I couldn't tell. "I have Jessica, we've been best friends since grade school, but she's married with a toddler, so it's hard for her to visit. We talk on the phone all the time and she and her family are visiting in December. But outside of her, I don't have any other friends I'd climb out of bed for at two in the morning to help bury the body."

"And the men?"

"What men?"

"Looking like that, there are always men."

Her expression was comical; she thought I was teasing her. "I'm serious, Avery. Where are the men?"

"Are you saying you want there to be men?" Annoyance rang through her words and I liked that I'd stoked her anger because, quite frankly, the thought of her with someone else stirred my own.

"No, I'm saying how the hell can there not be any."

She understood that if the blush that covered her face was any indication. "Never found anyone worth the effort."

I liked hearing that, enough that I did actually tease her when I said, "No surprise visits then from exes still holding a torch?"

"A torch for me, please."

She'd done that before, the subtle disparaging of herself. I didn't like it then, liked it less now. "You're a smart, talented and extremely sexy woman. Whomever it was in your world who made you doubt that is a fucking asshole."

Her eyes widened in surprise then turned warm, hinting at just how deep that comment hit. "Thank you."

And seeing that look only pissed me off more. "Nothing to thank me for. Only saying what anyone, without their head in their ass, would see—a funny, smart and beautiful woman who makes some seriously incredible, kill all your friends to horde for yourself, desserts."

Her pupils dilated, her cheeks turned pink again and her pulse pounded in her neck, I could see that from where I stood. She swallowed and I watched the movement of her throat, wanting to taste her right where her neck met her shoulder. It was so tempting I found I was actually leaning in. When my gaze shifted to hers, her tongue darted out to touch the corner of her mouth. Her voice was pure sex. "You think I'm funny?"

It took me a minute to catch on to her teasing—caught in the haze of lust that seemed to have overcome both of us—I laughed out loud because to all her qualities, I had one more to add. She really was a goof.

"You're a goof."

"You've called me that before. I've been called worse."

"Bring a jacket, it gets cold on the pier. I'll get Loki settled and then we'll go."

"Okay." She turned toward the carriage house, but stopped and called back at me. "I'd help you bury the body."

Before I could reply, she disappeared inside. Pulling a hand through my hair, I looked down at Loki who stared after Avery in longing. "Yeah, I like her too boy, a whole hell of a lot."

I learned something else about Avery while we shopped at the nursery. She could be a pit bull when she wanted to be. We decided to do the landscaping in phases, the first being the front yard. For the plants, the fertilizer, the mulch and the delivery the cost was upwards of two grand, she was determined to get it for just over a grand. Avery, who could have smiled and batted her lashes at the nursery owner and gotten whatever she wanted, chose to go another route. Tigress was a good description, unrelenting, unyielding and the cub she sought to protect was my wallet. And there I stood with this five foot two slip of a woman, going toe-to-toe with a man who seemed to derive as much joy from haggling as Avery. I should have felt emasculated, but instead I couldn't keep from grinning.

"You sell them to us, you won't have to store them, which leaves room in your greenhouses for new plantings."

"Come Spring, people are more eager to plant after a long winter, I could double my prices and still sell."

"Yeah, but we've got the long, cold winter coming and outside of Christmas with poinsettias and tree sales, you're looking at a lean season. Plus, this is only phase one, we have several phases and developing good customer relations will ensure we come here for not only the completion of our project but yearly maintenance and expansion."

Her eyes darted to me, a grin tugging at her mouth. She was having the time of her life. Turning to the man, who honest to God looked a bit like Loki had this morning, I knew Avery totally had him.

"You drive a hard bargain young lady, but you've got yourself a deal. $1200 including delivery."

"Awesome."

"Let's go write it up." He led us into the greenhouse where he had the cash register, but peered at Avery from over his shoulder. "I'd have let you have it for $1000."

Her smile was cocky. "I'd have taken it for $1500."

To this, the man tilted back his head and roared with laughter.

In the car on the way to Coney Island, Avery was like a firecracker with a lit fuse, bouncing around in her seat. "I can't believe he caved and so easily. I can't wait to tell Mom."

"Is she the one who taught you how to haggle?"

"Yeah, she haggles for everything including groceries at the Acme."

"Seriously?"

"Oh, yeah. She's a nut and it's not that she needs to watch the budget, she just likes it."

"Well, I think she'd have been impressed. I was, you enjoyed every second of that."

"I really did. Now I'm hungry."

Glancing at her, she was in profile as she looked out the side window. Wanting to see how her hair looked down, I reached for the elastic and tugged it out. The action caught her by surprise; her head turning to me in confusion, but shyness quickly took its place. Her hair was red, a dark mahogany red, thick, straight and long enough to fall past her shoulders. Beautiful.

"Why don't you ever wear it down?"

"I'm usually in the kitchen."

"Hair like that needs to be down."

She didn't reply, but she didn't pull her hair back up either. I grinned.

"Will you go on the rides with me?" She asked some time later.

"Yeah."

"First we need hot dogs from Nathans."

"Nowhere better to eat."

"With everything."

"Agreed." Her focus was out the side window again, her hair now curtaining her face—a definite negative to her hair down. "Avery?"

Our eyes met.

"I'd help you bury the body too."

The sweetest smile touched her lips, the meaning behind my words not lost on her. And then she said, "That's good because there's probably going to be one sooner than later."

I almost ran the truck off the road. "What?"

"My stepmother, I'm thinking about offing her."

What was even more comical than sweet Avery plotting her stepmother's demise was the expression on her face. She was completely serious. "She's really that bad?"

"Yeah. She hates me and she's a bitch. I want to stab her in the eye with her designer heels. I don't think that makes me a bad person. I really don't. I mean I've never wanted to kill someone with her own shoes before. It's her, she brings it out in me."

Yep, she was goofy.

Avery

He'd help me bury the body. I felt a bit giddy thinking about his declaration, but I didn't have long to ponder his words because we were strapped in a roller coaster that was climbing high. I loved roller coasters because they scared the crap out of me. Rafe sat next to me, his body relaxed, his fingers not gripping the pole to the point that his knuckles stood out in drastic contrast like mine were doing. To look at him, you'd think he was sitting in his living room watching a ball game.

"Aren't you even a little bit scared?"

Those eyes found mine. "No. Are you?"

"Terrified."

Concern moved over his expression. "I thought you wanted to do this."

"I do."

"Even though you're terrified?"

"Especially because I'm terrified. Makes the experience that much better, conquering the fear to experience the pleasure."

His focus moved to my mouth and I suspected he was thinking about doing his own conquering. I didn't know what was going on between us, but I didn't want it to stop. Hell, I wanted so much more, wanted him to kiss me, wanted him to unleash what he seemed to be holding under very tight control.

And then we crested the top of the drop. Peering down, my stomach moved up into my throat, my heart pounded so hard it hurt and then we were falling. And even screaming my head off, I felt Rafe's hand covering mine, his fingers threading through my own. And in that moment, I knew I was falling in love with him.

I felt off-balanced when we exited the ride and it had nothing to do with the roller coaster. Crushing on Rafe was cool, flirting with Rafe was fun, liking Rafe was wonderful, but feeling the way I did about him scared me a bit because I'd never been in love. I suddenly found myself in uncharted water and I wasn't entirely sure how to navigate it.

"You okay?"

I was okay, terrified, but definitely okay and also not ready for him to know just how far I'd fallen so I tried for cool. "That was fun."

"I think I'm deaf in my right ear."

"Sorry."

"Worth it though. You weren't kidding that you liked roller coasters. You game to ride another?"

"Are you kidding? You'll have to drag me out of this place."

"All right. Then let's do it." His hand reached for mine again, linking our fingers, before pulling me to the next ride. Maybe I wasn't falling in love, I may have already fallen.

"Hungry?" Rafe asked as the gates to the park locked behind us. We really had stayed until they kicked us out. My love of roller coasters reached a whole new level, sitting next to Rafe, his big powerful body pressed against mine while he held my hand. And now he wanted to feed me. Best day ever!

"Yeah, starving."

"Pizza?"

"I could get a slice."

"Not a slice. They don't do slices where we're going."

"So you're saying I have an excuse to eat more than one slice of pizza. Yeah, let me work up an objection."

Rafe laughed, I loved his laugh. We started for his truck; he reached for my hand. My eyes flew to his. "I've held it all day, don't see any reason to stop now."

The distinct 'splat' noise was my heart. "Again, let me work up an objection."

When we reached the pizza place I was seriously disappointed to see the line was down the street because my stomach was growling.

"That sucks."

"What? The line?"

"Yeah."

"Not a problem."

"Based on that line, we won't be eating until midnight."

"True, if we were waiting in the line."

"We're not waiting in the line? Are we going to sneak in?"

"You want to cap off the day of haggling and near-death experiences with a felony?"

"If it means I get pizza that's worth waiting in a line like that, oh, hell yeah."

Humor looked back at me. "I know the owner."

"Even better."

He parked in the employee parking, before coming around and helping me down. Again he took my hand and led us to the back door. It opened; the man that greeted us was huge, with tats down his arms, and the most incredible dark brown eyes. Seeing Rafe, he smiled before pulling him in for a hug.

"Hey man. How are you?"

"Alcide, I'm good. This is Avery, Avery the man behind the pizza."

That fairy godmother—unbelievable. "Hi." Kind of lame but the man looked like Adonis and the scents coming from his kitchen made me want to weep.

To say I was surprised when he yanked me close and hugged me hard would be fair. "Nice to meet you, Avery."

"Likewise." I didn't say more since at that moment a pizza must have just been pulled from the ovens because the mouthwatering smell that wafted out to us had me blurting out. "Oh my God, that smells incredible."

"Let's get you settled, so you can dig into a pie."

"I really like this plan."

Walking through the kitchen to the dining area, I took it all in— the wood-burning stoves, the simmering sauce, the mouthwatering toppings. "I could live back here. I mean seriously, drag in a mattress and I'm good."

Rafe's eyes caught mine. "Goof."

Alcide led us to a table in a corner and though the place was packed, the location felt intimate.

"Beer?" Alcide asked.

Rafe looked at me for agreement before he said, "Yeah." He didn't even open the menu. "Do you trust me?"

"Yep."

"Large pie, garlic, onion, ham and olives."

"You got it."

Watching as Alcide walked away, I asked, "How do you know him?"

"He lived at St. Agnes for a time."

"St. Agnes?"

"The orphanage where I lived when I was a teen. Alcide's parents died in a car crash, he lived with his grandmother but when she died, he didn't have any other family. It was a good place and Sister Anne was wonderful, until she died. Cancer. Lucien was very close to her. He still has an annual event every year to raise funds for St. Agnes. Anyway, Alcide's grandmother left him a nice nest egg, he opened this place."

"And based on the crowds and the scents, he has a success on his hands."

"Yeah, he keeps it simple, doesn't do all the fancy toppings and crusts, just your basic pie with the best ingredients available. It works."

"I can't wait to try it." Catching his eyes, I added, "Thank you for today. I haven't had this much fun in a long time."

"Me too."

On the way home, I had trouble keeping my eyes open. The pizza had been incredible; we ate the whole pie. I had never eaten an entire pie in my life, but we devoured it.

"Alcide has another loyal customer. That was amazing."

"You're tired."

"I am. I think I might sleep for a year."

"Do you want to watch a movie when we get back?"

Butterflies danced in my stomach, he didn't seem to want the day to end any more than I did. "I'd like that. Something scary."

"Scary?"

"I never get to watch scary movies because blankets aren't enough. And Nat, she just taunts me. Nothing scares her. It's unnatural."

"Okay, we'll watch something scary. And if you get too scared, you're welcome to climb into my lap."

My body throbbed, my reply instinctual. "I may crawl into your lap regardless."

He liked that idea, looked as if he wanted to pull me into his lap now. Yep, best freaking day ever.

RAFE

I didn't understand why the woman liked watching horror movies because she wasn't watching this one, not with the blanket over her head. Every once in a while she peeked out the side, screamed and hid again. She was adorable and really fucking sexy. She had crawled into my lap, her ass on my thigh, her soft breast brushing against my chest. The sweetest torture and a test of will because every instinct in me was demanding I press her back into the sofa, settle between her legs and take what I'd been craving.

"She was told not to go down there. Why is it when people are told not to do something they do the very thing they're told not to?"

"Temptation." And damn did I know about temptation having her luscious body pressing up against me.

She peeked out of her blanket; her eyes found mine as humor faded into desire—her pupils dilated, her breath hitched. Her focus moved to my mouth, her tongue appeared, just the tip touching the center of her top lip. Like I was her favorite flavor and she was about to indulge in a taste. Holy shit I was so fucking hard, wanted to drag her leg over my hips, settle her on my cock and make us both happy. Then she leaned into me and lifted her lips to mine; sexy as all hell, but it was the vein of innocence in the hesitant move that had a far more powerful emotion slamming into me. I didn't want to just take her; I wanted to cherish her. Curling my fingers around her neck, my thumb stroking the pulse point that beat erratically, I leaned in. Even her breath smelled like cocoa, fanning over me, as her breathing grew heavier with anticipation. And just when I was finally going to taste her, my phone rang snapping us both out of the moment. Growling, I wanted to toss the fucking thing across the room, wanted to commit murder when I saw who was calling.

"What the fuck!"

"Rafe?"

"It's Melody."

Now she looked about as pissed as me. "Her timing is impeccable. Are you going to answer it?"

"No."

"As much as I can't believe I'm saying this, it's late, she may be in trouble."

"And that's my problem, why?"

"She doesn't strike me as a person who has a lot of people she could call for help."

God, she was sweet. "We're finishing what we started."

Her expression turned soft and so fucking sexy. "I was hoping we would. Do you want me to pause the movie?"

"No, I'll be right back."

Moving down the hall, I snarled into my phone, "You better be dying."

"I'm lying in my bed, naked, touching myself and thinking of you. Won't you come over and ease the ache?"

"Fuck me."

"That's the point."

"Have some pride woman."

"I miss your cock. I want it in my mouth. I miss sucking you off."

"You're home?"

"Yeah, babe. Home, naked and wet."

"And aching? Are you aching for me, Melody?"

"Yeah, baby. Oh God, yeah."

"Take a cold shower and lose my number." Hanging up I walked back into the living room.

"Crazy bit..." I stopped just inside the room seeing Avery asleep, curled on my sofa with her cheek resting on her hands. My disappointment was visceral. Turning my phone off, I slid behind her on the sofa, pulling her back to my chest. It wasn't how I'd hoped the evening would end, but I'd take Avery anyway I could get her.

Avery

I had fallen asleep. Rafe and I had come so close to giving in, the look in his eyes, just the memory of it made me weak in the knees. It had been the single most beautiful and erotic moment of my life. And then that bitch Melody called. I had only intended to rest my head, but I'd fallen asleep. I woke in my bed. He'd carried me home and put me to bed. And I had missed it; my romance-book moment and I had slept through it. He had even set my coffeemaker, so I woke to the heavenly scent of my favorite brew. I had intended to apologize for my narcolepsy, but when I stepped outside this morning his truck was gone. And so here I was at work, hours later, but my head was still on last night and that magical moment that had been all too fleeting.

"Hey, Avery."

Kyle stepped into the kitchen. Glancing up from the chocolate I was shaving, my greeting died on my lips because he looked irritated. "What's wrong?"

"Melody is out front for you."

That didn't garner a reaction at first because those six words together made absolutely no sense. Based on Kyle's expression, he thought the same. "Melody?"

"I told her you were working, but she said it wouldn't take long."

The nerve of her to bother me at work shouldn't have surprised me, but it did. Granted, the restaurant wasn't yet open for dinner, but still. Not cool and I intended to tell her as much. "I'll be out in a minute."

By the time I was heading into the dining area, my temper was simmering. And not just because of her coming to my work, but because had she not called, Rafe and I would have spent the rest of our evening locked at the lips and potentially other places. The chick was a pain in the ass.

As soon as I reached her, knowing just what her phone call last night had cost me, it took all I had to not snarl at her. "Melody."

"I know you're working, but could we talk for a minute?"

"One minute, Melody, because I *am* working."

She moved toward the bar, Kyle was kind enough to give us privacy. Not that he needed to do that for my benefit.

"Have you ever been in love?"

Oh my God, was she serious? She wanted to have a heart-to-heart with me? "I don't have time for this, Melody."

Temper flashed in those unusual eyes, but she recovered quickly. "I'm sorry, it's just that I messed up with Rafe and being away from him I've come to realize I love him. I want to try to make it right."

Everything in me recoiled at her words, but to her I said, "This involves me how?"

"Rafe is hardheaded, one of the things I love most about him."

She thought Rafe was hardheaded, I didn't find that to be the case at all.

"I need to talk to him, need him to listen, so I wanted to surprise him with dinner tonight. If I'm there, he'll be more inclined to hear me out. Can you help me, Avery, and give me the alarm codes for his house?"

Her request for his codes jarred me right out of the pretty little picture she'd just painted. What was she after? "Excuse me?"

"I know this seems out of the blue, but we talked last night. Actually..." her smile had a chill working down my spine, "we did more than talk. I think after last night he'll be more receptive to what I have to say."

Even trusting that nothing happened, her implication twisted in my gut. Whatever her game, I wasn't playing. "I'm not comfortable giving out his alarm codes."

She didn't recover from her temper spike as easily this time, her 'let's be girlfriends' façade was cracking. "Come on, we're both women. Help me out here."

"I'm sorry you wasted your time, but like I said Melody, I'm not comfortable giving out that information." The mature course of action would have been to leave it at that, but I was only human and couldn't resist a subtle dig. "If Rafe wanted you to have them, he'd have given them to you."

Her feigned sweetness dissolved; I'd pissed her off with that comment just as I had intended. She wasn't subtle in her reply. "The mouth on that man. I thought nothing could top the way he tongues me to orgasm, but he's got such a dirty mouth. I never came as hard as I did last night."

I felt as the blood drained from my face, she noticed it too when her red lips curled up into a nasty smile. I trusted Rafe, especially after the day we shared, and still the visual she put in my head made my stomach turn. What was Melody's end game? Coming here and trying to incite me? She had to know I'd be sharing this encounter with Rafe. What the hell was she after?

"He fucks like a god, doesn't he? I can't get enough of that cock. Love swallowing him down my throat, I'm wet now just thinking about it." Surprise was quickly replaced with smugness, when she tilted her head and laughed. "Oh my God, he hasn't fucked you."

Her intention was to rile me up, but her words did just the opposite. Sex was all she got from him, she didn't know him the way I did, and that made me feel smug—enough that I smiled at her wickedly, which baffled her when her own sneer faded into confusion.

Kyle appeared, his timing too perfect. He'd been out of sight, but he'd stayed close enough in case there was a problem. Clearly he knew enough about Melody to expect a problem. "I'll show you to the door."

What could she do, but follow after him. It didn't prevent her from staring daggers at me though. After locking the door behind her, Kyle strolled over. "You okay?"

Putting aside her childish attempt to make me jealous, what the hell had that been about? "Yeah. Confused, but I'm fine."

"That woman is whacked."

He wasn't wrong.

There was just enough time to meet Nat for a bite to eat before Clover opened for dinner. We were in a little café not far from my work; Tyler was joining us, but was running a bit late and told us not to wait for him. We placed our orders and then I filled Nat in on the odd visit from Melody.

"What a bitch!"

"Understatement. And get this, a couple weeks ago I forgot something on my way to work and when I backtracked to Rafe's, Melody was there. Rafe wasn't—his truck wasn't in the drive—and yet she was trying to get in, showing obvious signs of frustration when she couldn't. Puts an interesting spin on her visit today. Why is she so desperate to get into her ex's house?"

"What did Rafe say?"

"I haven't told him yet."

"She has to know you'll be sharing this with Rafe and that he's going to be pissed. What's she hoping to accomplish?"

"I really think she wants inside his house. Why? I don't know. But her graphic imagery was done out of spite. I pissed her off; so she hit me where she knew it would hurt. It would seem her vindictiveness is greater than her fear of the consequences."

"It's fucked up and nasty."

"True, but there's so much more to Rafe and I'd bet money she's never seen it. So yeah, thinking about them having sex isn't pleasant, but knowing she never really knew the man behind the hot guy makes *me* feel smug."

"There's that optimist I love so much, but you need to tell Rafe about her visit today and that day at his house."

"I agree."

"Onto a more pleasant topic, I'm glad you and Rafe are finally coming to your senses because the air practically hums when you two are together. It would be a crime for you not to explore that chemistry. So tell me about yesterday."

I was happy for the change of subject, it was infinitely more pleasant than talk of Melody. "We went to the nursery, he loves my plans for the gardens."

"You're doing the gardens?"

"Yeah, and I even haggled a really great price with the garden center."

"Mom would be proud."

"We spent the day at Coney Island and then he took me for pizza at his friend's place."

"And you finished the day with a movie. Based on that smile, I'm guessing it was a perfect day."

"It really was."

She reached for my hand, covering it with hers. "I'm happy for you, so tell me about this almost kiss."

"It was more than that, Nat. It was as close to a perfect moment that I've ever had."

Nat understood. "So why didn't you kiss?"

"Melody called. I swear it's like the chick has a camera on us."

"She really sounds like an asshole."

"She is."

"Get her in my OR, I'll take care of it."

I couldn't help the laugh because I could see it now, Nat looking much like Dr. Frankenstein, that deranged smile on her face as she played around with Melody's brain. "I'd pay to see that."

"When I met him, I liked the way he stared at you—like you were the most fascinating person on the planet. And, outside of me, you are."

"You're a clown."

"But seriously, even then there was something that smoldered between the two of you. I'm glad you're finally acting on it."

"We haven't, but we're getting there."

"When you do, I want details, spare nothing." Her eyes moved from me to the door as a smile spread over her face. "There's Tyler." She waved and in the next minute a man appeared. Even in a suit, the man was sexy and he stared at my sister like she was a hot fudge sundae.

"Avery, this is Tyler, Tyler, my sister, Avery."

He didn't immediately take a seat; he waited until he was invited. What a gentleman. "Please join us." I said.

He unbuttoned his suit jacket and as graceful as a large-muscled man could be, settled in the chair opposite Nat. The smile he gave her had my heart fluttering.

"Sorry I'm late. I got caught up at work." He signaled the waitress and ordered a salad, grilled chicken and water. With the body he had, I understood the healthy pick though I had to say, I liked that Rafe ate whatever he wanted and kept his body up through manual labor.

"It's nice to finally meet you Tyler."

"And you."

"As Nat's sister, it's my job to ask questions of the man who's caught her eye."

Nat glared at me. "You are having entirely too much fun with this."

"And you wouldn't do it to me if you had the chance?"

She didn't answer; she didn't have to because we both knew the answer.

"It's okay, Nat. I'd be disappointed if Avery didn't have questions."

The immature part of me wanting to rub that in, but I didn't and instead asked Tyler, "What do you do?"

"Personal trainer."

"That explains your very healthy lunch. Why are you in a suit?"

"I own a gym and am meeting with potential investors."

"So not just a trainer, but a businessman. I like that. What's the one thing you like most about Nat?"

"Avery!"

"What? It's a fair question."

Tyler reached for Nat's hand. "She's right. It's a fair question." Meeting my gaze, he said, "I like everything about your sister—her humor, her brain, her body, her face, but I think what I like the most is when I'm with her there's nowhere else I want to be."

Nat turned to goo, I actually watched as she morphed into a sappy mess and I completely understood.

"I like you, Tyler. You have my approval."

"And I'm happy to have it." And then he only had eyes for Nat, studying her face like he was committing it to memory. I really liked the way he looked at her. "How was Mr. McNalley's surgery?" he asked.

Nat's expression was one I knew well, since I often found myself giving the same to Rafe. Not just happiness and contentment but connected. Nat was head over heels for this guy. "He pulled through with flying colors."

The hand he held he brought to his lips and pressed a kiss in her palm. "I'm so happy to hear that."

I settled back in my chair and grinned one of Nat's grins because my sister was in love.

After work, I stepped outside and was greeted to the sight of Rafe leaning against his truck, his hands in the front pockets of his jeans. His head turned, those eyes caught mine as a smile curved his lips. Last night came back, every exquisite detail. I grew warm under my clothes as my blood heated. And as beautiful as the sight before me was and the memory it stirred, the ugly conversation with Melody came rushing back too. He needed to know about her visit and when he did, he wouldn't be smiling.

Before I could open my mouth, he said, "I've been thinking about you all day, needed to see you. Ride with me. I'll bring you back to-morrow. Your car is in no danger of being stolen."

I felt like Nat did earlier, turning all sappy, because I was turning so now. To hide how much those words affected me I said, "Grief about my car, still?"

"You need to upgrade, if for no other reason than safety."

It was a valid point and after my last confrontation with Dad, I was seriously considering it. "I'm thinking about it."

"Really?"

"It's time."

He knew what I was admitting to, that I was finally accepting defeat. His features turned hard, but his voice was soft when he said, "I'll take you whenever you're ready."

"Thanks." I could totally relate to Tyler's sentiment regarding Nat because when I was with Rafe there was nowhere else I wanted to be. "I fell asleep last night."

"You did."

"I'm sorry."

An edge came into his voice, a hardness that surprised me. "Don't be."

"She stopped by today."

I had never in my life seen someone lose it as quickly as Rafe did in response to that statement. "Are you fucking kidding me?"

"She tried, at first, to be nice. Played on the fact that I was a 'girl-friend' to get me to help her out."

"With what?"

"She wanted to surprise you with dinner, hoped you could talk out your differences. She asked me to give her the codes for the alarm, so she could put her plan into motion."

The image of someone with steam coming from his ears popped into my head. If we were animated, that would be Rafe right now. I continued on. "I wouldn't give them to her and then she turned ugly, said some really vile things before Kyle showed her to the door."

"What things?"

"It isn't nec—"

"What things, Avery?"

"She claimed you had phone sex last night, detailed for me how much she liked your tongue and your..."

My words dried up because Rafe was beyond angry, even furious. For as laid-back as he was, when in temper he was formidable and seriously scary.

Pushing off his truck, he started to pace. He was clearly working hard to pull his temper in and then he stopped suddenly, his gaze slicing to me. "You didn't believe her." He wasn't asking.

"Of course not."

His expression changed slightly, the hard lines around his eyes softened. And as much as I wanted that look to linger, he needed to hear the rest.

"Not to send you on a murdering rampage, but I saw her a few weeks back as well after you had changed the codes. She was trying to get into your house even though you weren't home."

It wasn't so much anger as it was suspicion shifting his features. He was as curious as me about her motives.

I hadn't meant to ask, even though I really wanted to know, but I found the words tumbling out anyway. "Knowing what I do about you, which I realize isn't a lot, but I'm guessing she wasn't always like...well, what she's like now."

"Maybe she was and was just better at hiding it, but I didn't see it. If you asked Lucien and Darcy though, they'd likely tell you something different. They never liked her."

"I never did either, but again my opinion is based on more than her personality."

That earned me a grin, his temper not gone but he was moving past it. "I'll take care of Melody, but thank you for not giving her the codes."

"I figured if you wanted her to have them, she'd have them."

"You figured right. Did you have a good night?"

And since I wanted him to move past his anger too, wanted to get back to the dynamic of when I first stepped outside, I happily shared about my evening. "It was an awesome night. My take on gooseberry cobbler was a hit. I really like my sister's boyfriend and I ended work having you standing here offering me a ride home."

Based on how he undressed me with his eyes, he wanted a different kind of ride. I was totally game for that, but I was exhausted and when we did have sex for the first time, I wanted to be well rested because once I had a taste of him I suspected it'd be a long time before I was sated. He read my mind, scary how he did that. "You look tired."

"I am."

"I'm not going to lie. I've thought of nothing but finishing what we started last night, but when I get you in my bed it's going to take hours."

Oh my God, my entire body tingled and burned. "I'm not feeling all that tired anymore."

A look that hot should have incinerated me where I stood. "There's no rush, Avery. The longer the wait, the hungrier I'll be."

"Keep talking like that and I'm going to get reckless."

"I think I'd like you reckless."

I wanted to weep.

Touching my elbow, he led me to his truck. "Are you hungry?" Wicked man was enjoying turning me on.

"You know that I am."

Smiling devilishly he said, "I'll make you an omelet."

Holding his naughty gaze, I replied, "Yeah, we can start with that."

Reaching the house, Rafe parked and climbed from the truck before coming around to help me. Not that I needed help, he was just being a gentleman. Standing so close to him, feeling the heat from his body, my mouth went dry. "I'm going to change. I'll be over in a minute."

"I'll let Loki out."

Neither of us moved though; rooted was a good word for my feet and their sudden unwillingness to listen to my brain, not that my brain was putting a great deal of effort in.

Rafe moved first, stepping even closer to me. My pulse pounded, my heart slammed against my ribs. Large, warm hands cradled my face, his palms on my cheeks, his fingers threading through my hair holding me in possession and tenderness. His head dipped, his soft breath teased me, the little hitch in his breathing when his lips descended, the growl, deep in his throat when his lips brushed softly over mine. I felt like a flower, blooming in that moment, the unfurling of myself that I never realized I held in until this man unlocked it with nothing more than a delicate kiss. For just a second I was trapped in that one, perfect moment. His fingers tightened, his body pressed tight against mine, his mouth opening to more fully taste me. Gripping the waistband of his jeans to keep myself upright, his tongue swept my mouth, tangled with my own. I knew with a clarity that terrified me, having only sampled his taste, it would be the one I would always crave.

His eyes were dark, like a forest at night, when he looked at me.

"I'll start dinner."

"Kay."

His lips turned up on the one side, his eyes dancing with humor as he turned me toward my door. "Get changed."

"Kay."

I moved, but I felt off balance. Reaching my door, Rafe added, "That kiss, totally worth the wait."

"You can say that again."

After dinner, Rafe and I walked Loki, before saying good night. Standing on the stoop of the carriage house, Loki sniffing the grass around us, I asked, "Do you want to come in? Maybe watch a movie?"

"I do, but I won't."

"Why?"

"It's taking all the will power I have to keep from pushing you through that door and discovering for myself just how sweet you are. But you're exhausted."

The idea of seeing Rafe naked brought on a surge of energy, along with a few other things. "I'm not that tired."

Rubbing his thumb over my lower lip, his eyes followed the motion, he said, "You're exhausted."

Further discussion was halted when his mouth sealed over mine. Rational thought flew right out of my head since my brain had now melted into a mushy, useless puddle in my skull.

Even after his lips left mine, I didn't have the will to open my eyes because I was too busy savoring his taste on my tongue.

"Night, Avery."

"Goodnight, Rafe." I may have been a bit breathless when I replied, became even more so when I opened my eyes to see Rafe walking back to his house in all that magnificent, sexy wonder. Loki trotted along beside him. I needed another shower.

chapter nineteen

Avery

In the morning I woke, and just lay in bed thinking about last night. Remembering Rafe's kisses caused excitement to flutter just behind my ribcage as I traced my lips, the memory of his taste teasing me. I loved the beginning of a relationship—the newness, the thrill, the all-consuming need to be near the one who occupied your thoughts. And Rafe lived right outside my door. I loved my new home.

Climbing from bed, I headed to the bathroom to take care of my morning rituals before I poured myself a cup of coffee and went in search of him. As usual, Loki sat on my front stoop.

"Morning, Loki."

He lifted his head, his tail wagging. The muffled sound of power tools came from the barn. Rafe was dedicated to his craft; every morning when I woke he was already hard at work. And that dedication showed. The man was an artist.

Stepping into the barn, I was treated to the sight of Rafe bent over a long strip of wood; the muscles of his back stretched the cotton of his tee in the most mouthwatering way. He knew I was there—as aware of me as I was of him—because he shut down the saw to greet me. "Morning."

"Good morning."

He didn't approach, but the way he regarded me was reminiscent of how Tyler had looked at Nat yesterday. There was more than lust in his gaze. "Have dinner with me tonight."

Like he had to ask and feeling playful, I teased, "A date?"

"Yeah, a date."

"And you're going to feed me?"

He looked downright wicked when he replied. "I'm hoping in more ways than one."

And with that veiled promise, I was incapable of keeping up the flirty repartee. "I like this plan."

Even knowing what his words had done to me, he was gracious to not call me on it. "Anything you don't eat?"

"I'm not a fan of sushi."

"That makes two of us."

Knowing we'd be ending the day having sex and all the feels that knowledge stirred, it was the easiness of being around him that I craved even more. "Have you had your coffee?"

"Not yet."

"Do you want me to get you some?"

He moved then, right into me and the look in his eyes had the butterflies in my stomach doing the pole vault. He looked hungry. He didn't stop until he was pressed up against me. His fingers laced through my hair, tilting my head back for his kiss and when his tongue swept my mouth, my knees buckled. I nearly dropped my mug, the need to hold him, to pull him closer, was powerful. Insatiable was how he kissed me, as if he was savoring my taste, owning it, possessing it. I never knew a kiss could be consuming…addictive.

"You're as sweet as your desserts."

"I don't think my legs work anymore."

He flashed me a grin. "Don't tempt me, Avery. I want to carry you back to your room and spend the next forty-eight hours devouring you, but you have work."

"Devouring me, that sounds nice."

"It'll be way more than nice." That was said with more than a little cockiness, the look that accompanied it was adorably smug.

"I bet. If you kiss like that, I can't wait to see how you do other…"

His hold on me tightened a second before he released me and took a step away. "You're too tempting."

Unconsciously I glanced down at my sweats, not really understanding what it was he saw. I mean I knew I was attractive, but tempting. I didn't see that. He seemed to read my mind when his head shook in disbelief.

"You don't see it?"

"See what?"

"How sexy you are."

"Sexy? This is sexy?"

"Absolutely."

"You're serious. I think maybe you've got some kind of glasses on when you're looking at me, but keep them on. I like it."

"You really are a goof."

"But a sexy goof."

He looked up at the barn ceiling when he said, "She's killing me. Go before I lock you away for the next two days."

"With you?"

"Yeah."

"Naked and in bed?"

He growled now. I liked it. "Yeah."

"I'm not really seeing the incentive to leave. I like the idea of two days locked away with you in bed, naked."

"And your job?"

"Oh, so you're going to use logic."

He laughed, the sound wrapping around me like a blanket. "When you're ready, I'll drive you to work."

It took me a second to remember we had left my car at Clover. "Okay."

"And I'll come for you at nine tonight."

"Okay."

"And after dinner I'm going to peel your clothes from you and taste every inch."

Easy, natural…yes, I felt that with him, but I also felt hot, edgy and wet. Just thinking about him devouring me, I had no words.

"Every inch, Avery. Think about that while you're making your desserts."

"You're a wicked man, Rafe McKenzie."

"Good of you to notice, Avery Collins."

"I'm going to take a very cold shower now."

"Enjoy." Somehow he purred that.

"Wicked."

His laugh followed me out.

After I showered and dressed, I collected my things only to find Rafe waiting near his truck when I stepped outside. He knew my schedule and knowing he stopped his own work to make sure I got to my work on time was almost nicer than his kiss. Almost.

He helped me into his truck before he said, "You'll probably want to come home before we go to dinner."

"Yeah, I'll need a shower. I can drive myself home."

"I'll come for you, I'll arrange to have your car brought back here."

"Are you sure? It really isn't a big deal."

"I want you in my truck, I'll get your car home."

And I wanted to be in his truck so there was no point in arguing the point. "Okay."

He closed my door on a grin.

Halfway through the evening, the maître d' entered the kitchen. "A couple at table ten would like to offer their compliments."

It was the first time I had been summoned into the dining area to receive compliments on my work. I had received compliments; the wait staff shared them from time to time, but to actually be requested tableside was a first. My hands shook as I made my way into the dining area and the very attractive couple seated at table ten.

"Good evening. I'm Avery Collins, the executive pastry chef."

The woman studied me for a few seconds, her gaze not critical but definitely interested. She was attractive, dark brown hair, pale green eyes and dressed from head to toe in some fabulous designer. The gentleman with her was older than her fifty or so years, distinguished in a suit clearly tailored just for him. He had what was left of the walnut cake on his plate. Her plate was nearly cleaned of the pumpkin torte.

"Our dinners were perfectly prepared and the desserts were just divine."

"Thank you."

"The walnut cake was outstanding as you can see. This is our first time dining here, but it won't be our last." The gentleman added.

"Thank you, I'll pass on your compliments to the kitchen."

"Have you worked here long?" The woman asked.

"No, just a few weeks."

"Well, I can't wait to see what you come up with after you've been here longer, since I can't imagine you topping this."

Pride burned through me, affirmation that I had found my calling. "I'm enjoying pushing the boundaries of flavors, finding the unique combinations that work."

"You've definitely got a gift, Ms. Collins."

"Thank you—"

The man's cell cut me off; the expression on his face when he saw who was calling was chilling. The dynamic at the table changed, the happy energy replaced with tension.

"We need to go, Allie." He said at the same time he flagged down their waiter.

She nodded her head before her gaze returned to me. "Congratulations on a wonderful success."

In less than a minute, they were walking out the door.

Rafe arrived exactly at nine. As soon as our eyes locked, his promise from earlier about tasting every inch of me had a naughty grin curving my lips.

He moved toward me, but said nothing. If my grin was naughty, his was downright sinful. And then the wicked man said, "I'm really hungry."

I'd often read in romance novels about the woman's body clenching in desire. I had no idea what that meant, but I got it now. I ached everywhere. "You keep talking and looking at me like that and we aren't going to make dinner."

His fingertip ran from my neck, down to my shoulder sparking a trail of heat in its wake. "Promise?"

I had to change the subject before I did something uncharacteristic like jump him in the parking lot. "I was called out to the dining area to receive compliments on my desserts. That's a first for me."

He had the nerve to ask. "Changing the subject?"

"That or get arrested for lewd behavior."

He moved into me, his chest rising and falling as his breathing grew a bit erratic. I couldn't pull my eyes from him, my mouth watered and I wanted nothing more than to get incredibly inappropriate in the parking lot.

"Congratulations."

"Um...wait, what?"

He chuckled as he pulled the elastic from my hair. "On the table-side compliment."

Right. It was amazing how your brain stopped working when it wasn't being supplied with blood. "Thank you."

He held open the door to his truck. "Ready?"

"Very." As soon as I took my seat, he leaned over and traced my lips with his tongue. I moaned, it could not be stopped, and pressed my legs together because I actually experienced a mini orgasm. Yep, right there in his truck. He knew too, the sexy sound that rumbled in the back of his throat prolonged the spasm. "Fuck. You just came."

I should have felt embarrassed; I didn't though, just really, really turned on.

"Do you know how badly I want to taste you right now? I want to spread you wide and bury my tongue between your legs."

"You're going to make me come again."

He was thinking about it, dragging me into the back of his truck and what was worse, I was seriously thinking about letting him.

His mouth closed over mine, his tongue driving past my lips as he all but swallowed me whole. His cock was pressing against my thigh and I wanted that, God did I want that. Yanking his mouth away, he gulped air as if in an attempt to cool off. He held my heavy-lidded stare. "Dinner first and then you're going to come again in my mouth."

I likely would not be living through this evening and I so could not wait.

We returned home and while Rafe took Loki for a walk, I showered, a really cold shower, and changed. I was done before he returned, but in fairness I had taken the fastest shower of my life. My thinking, the sooner we ate, the sooner we came home and got naked. I sat in one of my chairs refusing to give in to my lustful thoughts because I'd never make it through dinner. Instead I pondered the addition of a vegetable garden by the back door. Yes, that was a safe subject to contemplate. Loki came trotting up the drive, right to me. He seemed to have more energy than he did when I first arrived and even so, he dropped down on his butt as soon as he reached me.

"Did you have a nice walk?" I asked that of Loki, his attempt to lick me I took as a yes. Rafe appeared not long after, my attention shifted from the affectionate fur ball next to me to his sexy as hell human. I loved the way he moved, deliberate but with a graceful flow that had visions of that body over me, in me, moving in just the right rhythm. He was dressed in jeans but they were darker, his button down shirt was a grayish/green and the black boots were nicer than the ones he normally wore. After dinner I was going to lick every inch of the body under those clothes, so much for not giving in to my lustful thoughts.

As soon as he saw me, he didn't hide the inspection he gave me, one that started at the tip of my head and moved slowly down my body to my toes. I was dressed in black: pants, cropped sweater and boots. My hair was down since I knew how much he liked that.

"You're beautiful."

His compliment settled very comfortably in the center of my chest.

"Let me get Loki settled and we'll go."

Joining him, he reached for my hand as we walked to his house. "What would you think about a vegetable garden here?"

If he was surprised by the question, considering that really wasn't where my thoughts were, I couldn't tell. "Does it get enough sun?"

"Plenty."

"Sounds good. I guess that's phase five?" he asked in humor.

"It is. Giovanni will be so happy."

Rafe stopped walking, his expression indiscernible. "Who's Giovanni?"

"The owner of the garden center."

"When did you get his name?"

"As soon as we arrived. That's the first and most important step in haggling, familiarity with the one you're haggling with."

He chuckled as we resumed our walk to the back door. "Good to know."

Once we entered, Rafe walked to the pantry to get Loki's dinner. I moved into the living room, loved the feel of the room. As I stood studying one of the pictures he had on the wall, I felt Rafe behind me seconds before his hands settled on my hips. Chills danced down my arms, his warm breath bringing goosebumps, right before he touched his lips to the spot at the curve of my neck. Tingles swept through me and as his lips moved over my shoulder, the tingles followed. My body burned and yet felt chilled all at once.

His hold on me tightened as he pulled me back against him. I felt him, hard and thick, against the small of my back, which elicited a whimper from deep in my throat.

"I can't tell you how long I've wanted to taste you right here." He whispered as he kissed me in the same spot, his tongue darting out for a taste.

Tilting my head to offer him more, I leaned back into him. His fingers caressed the bare skin at my hip. "Please don't stop." I was going to come again just from his mouth on my neck.

His hands roamed under my sweater, up my sides, to my breasts where he brushed his thumb over the hard nipple.

"Fuck." That one word from his mouth was the sexiest sound I'd ever heard. "I can't wait. Dessert first," he said, right as he grabbed my sweater and lifted it up over my head. Even though there was a chill in the air, I was burning up. His hands over my skin felt so incredible. He flicked the clasp on my bra at the same time he turned me to him, his eyes on my breasts that spilled out into his hands.

"So fucking beautiful." And to emphasize that point, he touched his tongue to me. I was aching, a throbbing ache that begged to be soothed. Pressing me back against the wall, he sucked me deep into his mouth as he worked the snap on my pants. Moving to the neglected breast, his fingers traced the skin where my panties met my hips. Dropping to his knees, my heart galloped in my chest because I wanted his mouth on me, could think of nothing else. He pulled my pants down and I moaned, and just as I stepped out of them, he buried his face between my legs.

"Oh God, yes." Opening my legs wider for him, his hands splayed on my ass as he pulled me closer. His hot mouth settled over my clit through the silk of my panties. Lacing my fingers though his hair, my head fell back against the wall and my legs shook as my stomach knotted with lust.

"So fucking sweet." His warm breath across the part of me that throbbed caused a surge of moisture.

He inhaled and moaned before he growled, "Sorry." In the next second, he ripped my panties from me and drove his tongue in deep.

My eyes rolled into the back of my head and my legs were now useless. I was being held up by Rafe's hands on my ass and his mouth. My hips worked though, as I moved into his mouth, grinding myself against him as my body crested on the cusp of an orgasm that I knew would blow every other orgasm I'd ever had right out of the water. Just seconds before glorious release, Rafe's mouth was gone.

He stood, hooked his arm around my waist and lifted me into his arms. "Not yet."

It was while he walked us to his room that I realized I was completely naked and he was fully clothed.

"You're wearing too many clothes."

"Agreed."

He dropped me to my feet at the foot of his bed. "Can you help me with that?"

Ahh…yeah.

My fingers were shaking when I started unbuttoning his shirt. When I spread it open and pulled it down his arms, flawless tan skin pulled tight over hard muscle met my gaze. I ran my fingertips down his chest and his muscles flexed in response. His abs, my fingers traced those muscles and then I traced them again with my tongue.

Looking at him, his eyes were hot and I could feel his cock, hard in his jeans, pressing against my tummy. Slowly I worked the snap, lowered the zipper, and pulled his jeans down enough to free him. Seeing him, little trembles went off in my body, so perfectly formed, hard and ready. Touching the tip with my tongue, we both moaned. Kneeling in front of him, I gripped the base and slid my hand up his shaft as I worked the tip with my tongue. The sound coming from him was like an aphrodisiac, encouraging me to be bolder. Fondling the heavy sac between his legs, I closed my lips around the tip, before I slowly pulled him deeper until I could practically feel him at the back of my throat. God he tasted good.

His hips moved, his fingers in my hair tightened and mine on his ass dug into his flesh leaving crescent shapes I was sure. I wanted him to come in my mouth, wanted to taste him, but he moved, grabbing me under the arms and tossing me on the bed before he pounced. His mouth slammed down on mine as his fingers curled around my thighs, spreading me wide. He rubbed himself over me, but I wanted him inside me.

"Rafe, please."

Reaching for his bedside table, he grabbed a condom, unwrapped it and rolled it on and then he was right there, exactly where I wanted him.

Locking eyes, he said nothing as he slowly pushed forward, stretching me wide as he sank himself deep in an excruciatingly slow pace. His gaze shifted, but I didn't know where to look—his eyes that were hot and fixed on where we were connected, his chest and arms as he held himself over me, the muscles flexing as he moved or lower to where his cock filled me, claimed me with every shift of his hips. Arching my spine, I took him deeper, as my hips lifted to take even more. We moved, reaching together for climax, and when it crashed over me I cried out as my body splintered apart into tiny little pieces. His focus shifted to my face, seeming to derive pleasure from witnessing me come. He was holding back, knew he was when his movements became harder, deeper and then he lowered his head and kissed me: a deep, open mouth kiss just as he seated himself seconds before his body shuddered in release. Sucking my lower lip into his mouth, he caught it between his teeth, applying enough pressure to make it hurt so good.

Wrapping my legs around his waist, so he couldn't move, I held his stare. "I've always believed in dessert first."

He laughed, causing pleasant shivers since he was still inside me and, surprisingly, hard.

"I should feed you." He brushed his lips down my neck before he added, "And then I'm eating you again."

I so loved this plan.

It was late, hours after round two and three. We'd fallen asleep but Rafe wasn't sleeping now. His body was tense, primed.

"Rafe?"

It was only then that I heard Loki growling from his spot at the foot of the bed. "The silent perimeter alarm has been tripped."

Lifting my head, I saw the lights on the panel. He climbed from bed, grabbed his jeans and pulled them on. "Stay here. The cops will be here any minute, a call goes to dispatch when the alarm is tripped."

"Shouldn't you stay here too?" Fear was pushing back exhaustion.

If people were in the house, Rafe shouldn't be confronting the intruders, should he? What if they had guns?

He reached for a baseball bat he had next to his bed, his expression scary when he looked back at me. "Stay here."

"Okay."

He disappeared, my heart moved into my throat as I strained my ears to hear what was happening beyond the door. It felt like eternity before I heard the sound of sirens coming from down the street. A few minutes later, Rafe returned.

"Whoever it was, they're gone now."

Unease and irritation moved through me. "Do you think it was Melody?"

He did, by the dark look that swept his face. "Probably. Hopefully the camera caught something."

"You have cameras outside?"

"Yeah on the gates, the entrances to the main house, the barn and the carriage house."

He placed the bat against the wall before settling on the bed next to me. "The cops are going to be here any second, you might want to dress."

I'd forgotten I was naked, too worried about him to care.

Running his finger along my jaw, his eyes tracking the motion before they lifted to mine. "One of these days I will actually get you to dinner."

"What we did was so much better than dinner."

The slight smile that curved his mouth nearly melted my heart. "Agreed."

The doorbell had Rafe's expression switching from tender to dangerous. "If you'd rather go back to sleep, I won't be long."

"I'd like to stay here."

"Okay." He kissed me again before he started from the room. "Rafe."

He stopped at the door and looked back at me. "Yeah."

"Wake me when you come back."

Hungry was how he looked now. "Absolutely."

CHAPTER TWENTY

RAFE

"Did the camera get anything?" Lucien asked the following day and though I heard him, my thoughts were on Avery and last night. God she was sweet, every inch of her. I couldn't get enough. Craved her, a hunger I couldn't seem to appease. She'd left earlier for work and the sight of her pulling down my drive had me feeling almost primitive. And as fantastic as the sex had been, it wasn't the sex that had wrangled my heart like a cowboy roping in a steer. It was Avery—that guileless, witty and sweet woman who had absolutely no idea of her appeal.

"Earth to Rafe."

Pulling a hand through my hair, I turned to Lucien who had that look; the bastard missed nothing.

"Sorry I missed Avery this morning."

Fishing for info, I wasn't about to make it easy for him. "The cameras didn't get anything. Whoever it was knew where the cameras were positioned, even the angles, so clearly they'd been here before to case the place."

"I don't like the sound of that." Lucien wasn't teasing now.

"I think it was Melody."

I hadn't seen that dark expression on Lucien in a while. "Why do you say that?"

"She visited Avery at work the other day and asked her for the codes. And Avery mentioned she'd seen Melody at my gates a few weeks back, trying to get onto my property when I wasn't home."

"What the fuck for?"

I didn't answer, knew Lucien wasn't really asking since it was pretty obvious what Melody was after.

"You ended that."

"Yeah, but Melody is apparently not on board."

"You need to handle that shit."

"I know; I'm working on it."

"Does Avery know about the attempted break in?"

"Yeah."

"It was close to three in the morning, right?"

Nosey bastard. "Yeah."

"I guess it was the sirens that woke her."

"You're sounding more like your wife, you know that, right?"

"Just curious how your tenant heard about the break in."

"Well, you can remain curious."

"All the answer I need. We're all going to Allegro on Saturday to hear Kyle's band."

"We'll be there."

"*We.* I like hearing that, brother." Not as much as I liked saying it. Lucien headed for the door after placing his mug in the sink. "I need to get to work. Call me if you need me."

"Will do."

I had work too, and as much as I wanted to spend the day in my workshop thinking about all the things I planned on doing to Avery when I got her back in my bed, first I had to handle Melody. "Fucking hell."

This had been a mistake. Reasoning with someone who wasn't reasonable made about as much sense as banging your fucking head into a wall. My brilliant plan, confront Melody in person and tell her to back off. Somehow I thought face-to-face would have more impact. Clearly banging my head against the wall might be in order to jar my brain into working. As soon as she opened the door, she threw herself at me. I swear to God, she turned into an octopus because there were way more than four limbs wrapped around me. Prying myself loose took time and all the while Melody was attempting to eat me whole. Christ.

"I knew you'd come around."

Finally breaking free, I moved as far from her as possible. When she made a move toward me, I put my hand out and snarled. "Stay over there."

"Why? We'll have so much more fun close and naked."

"We're not getting naked."

She pouted; had I ever thought that was sexy? I might need to have my head examined. Luckily for me I knew a brain surgeon. "Was it you last night who tried to break into my place?"

Her reaction didn't seem feigned; she looked truly surprised which was followed quickly with disdain. "What? Break into your place? Like I have nothing better to do?"

Now she was pissing me off. "Seriously? You went to Avery, while she was working, and demanded the codes, but you think I'm stretching by making the assumption you tried to gain access another way?"

A direct hit, calling bullshit on her nonchalance; the woman could technically be brought up on charges of harassment, maybe even stalking. And still she tossed out attitude. "I didn't come to your house last night."

"We're over. You know that. Why the hell did you go to Avery for the codes?"

Belligerent was the best way to describe her expression. "Because I thought if you found me in your bed, naked, and we fucked, you'd realize what a mistake you'd made."

"Is that the same reason you tried to fill her head with bullshit?"

"She told you that, did she? You have her trained well."

I could not believe I had ever found this woman attractive. "I'm going to be as clear on this as I can be. We're over. There is nothing you have that I want. And if you ever again bother Avery at work, or attempt to spew your brand of bullshit, we're going to have a serious fucking problem. A few words in the right ears and you'll be denied access to all the hot spots in town."

She paled even as temper sparked in her eyes. There was one thing she liked more than me and that was seeing and being seen. "Are you threatening me?"

"No, not a threat a warning."

"For her? I cannot believe you tossed me aside for that fat bitch."

I never had the urge to hurt a woman, but I had it now. Rage had my body going still, my hands fisting. "Be very careful Melody or I'll forget you're a woman."

Fear flashed in her eyes, but she tried to save face when she said, "You had all this and you're settling for her. Talk about trading down."

"And that is all this is about. You don't give a shit about me. You just can't stand that I ended it."

I had to leave because the urge to toss her over her balcony was becoming far too tempting. Reaching the door, I pulled it open. Looking over my shoulder, whatever I saw in her completely escaped me now.

"For the record, you're just a pretty cunt who gives great head. I didn't trade down. I hit the fucking jackpot."

I tried and failed to get some work done, too pissed with Melody to focus. She paid more attention to me now than she had when we were dating. The classic case of a spoiled child wanting what she couldn't have. And if my relationship with her wasn't case in point on how I'd been going through the motions. Hell, I hadn't even worked up the effort to break it off with her, a woman I didn't even really like. And I'd still be living like that had it not been for a feisty pastry chef riding into my life in her god-awful car. Speaking of which, she was home, her car had a distinct—in serious need of a tune-up—sound. I stepped outside to greet her. She looked tired, and it didn't help that I had kept her awake for most of the night. Not that I didn't intend to keep her awake tonight, but I was enough of a gentleman to feel badly about it. Watching her body move was like art in motion: graceful and alluring and completely unconsciously done.

As soon as she saw me, a smile spread over her face. "Hey." She said as she swung her bag over her shoulder.

Walking right into her, I yanked her close and kissed her, sweeping her mouth with my tongue because honestly, I was jonesing for a fix. With the way she kissed me back, I wasn't the only one. "How was your night?"

She didn't immediately answer as her tongue ran over her lower lip, licking my taste off.

"Keep doing that and we're missing dinner again."

I could tell she didn't have a problem with that. Her voice was husky when she finally answered. "I had an excellent evening, even more so after that kiss." Her eyes twinkled knowing what she was doing to me. She continued, "We tried something different, a chocolate tray paired with dessert wine. It was a huge success and Tina, my one sous chef, has mastered the art of tempering chocolate."

She cared, really cared about the people that worked with her. Some would feel threatened, even going so far as to hold back what they knew so the student didn't become the master, but not Avery. She not only led with her heart and went all in but from what I'd seen, that philosophy carried into every facet of her life. "They're lucky they have a boss like you."

She looked adorably confused. "Why?"

"You care."

"I do, that's true. It's easy, though, because they're great."

Humble too. "I've made some spaghetti and meatballs and a salad. Are you hungry?"

"Starving."

"It's done, so whenever you're ready."

"I'm ready now."

Taking her bag from her, I reached for her hand. "Then let's feed you."

Dropping her bag in the mudroom, I moved to the cabinets for the plates.

"There's wine in the rack if you want some."

"I'd love a glass."

"Get me one too?"

"Okay." She surveyed my wine, selecting a hearty burgundy before washing her hands and uncorking the bottle. While she poured the wine, I plated our food. Settling across the island from her, she held her glass up to me. "To dinner, finally."

She really was a goof. Her first mouthful of spaghetti had her eyes rolling into the back of her head. "You made this?"

"Yeah."

"I didn't know you could cook."

"I can only make a few things."

"Maybe so but you make them really freaking well."

It hadn't passed my notice that the woman didn't curse. Even when she was pissed, she refrained—another facet of her that I found adorable. "You don't curse."

"I try not to. Not that there aren't a few curse words that really say it all, but I do well enough without them. Nat, on the other, curses like a sailor."

"Does it bother you that I curse?"

"No." She twirled her spaghetti around her fork, her expression changing a bit. "What happened with the cops? Did they find anything?"

"No." Studying her, I couldn't decide what was causing the seriousness of her expression, concern or fear or a little of both.

I didn't wonder for long because when her head lifted, there was temper burning in her gaze. "It is such a violation. Do you think it was Melody?"

"I did, but I went to see her today and now I'm not so sure."

"What do you mean?"

"She's a bitch, but a terrible actress. Her surprise over someone trying to break in wasn't feigned."

"So if it wasn't her, then it's likely about your dad?"

"Probably."

"Should we be worried?"

"Smart, careful, watchful, but let me do the worrying."

"What do you think they're after?"

"I honestly don't know, but you're safe here Avery. The alarm system is state of the art."

"I know that." Concern still clouded her expression when she asked, "So what happened with Melody?"

"I told her if she didn't leave you alone, I'd make it so she was banned from all the social outlets she loves. I don't think she'll bother you again."

Incredulous was how she looked now. "Are you serious? That's all you had to do? She acts like you're her other half, but a threat against her social life and she's cured?"

"I'm not her other half, she's pissed I ended it not her. But she's a social being who needs to see and been seen. Threatening to take that away is hitting her where she lives."

"And you could do that, ban her?"

"Between Trace and Lucien, yeah."

She moved her spaghetti around her plate. "I think I'd like to see her denied access. To watch as her face turned all blotchy with temper."

"You're a bit cutthroat."

"When it comes to her, yes I am. Thinking about her is causing me to lose my appetite. What else did you do today?"

"Started sketching out a new project."

"Oh, yeah. For what?"

"It's for you, so I'm not sharing."

"Me?"

"Yep"

"But you won't tell me what you're making?"

"Nope."

"And there's nothing I could do to persuade you to share?"

"You can certainly try. I'd thoroughly enjoy your efforts. In fact, let's finish dinner so you can get started on that."

"Wicked man."

But she was grinning at me like the cat that just ate the canary.

Driving my fingers through her hair, protecting her head from the headboard, I slammed into her as my mouth sought her breast. The sexy sound that came from the back of her throat, when I twirled my tongue around her nipple, had my hips moving faster. Her nails scratched down my back, over my ass where they settled as her hips lifted, meeting me thrust for thrust. She was close; I felt her body begin to spasm around me, my cock driving even deeper. And then she screamed my name as she crested and it was the single sexiest sound I'd ever heard. She was still riding the orgasm, when I seated myself deep and felt the explosion of pleasure that had a growl burning up my throat. I pressed a kiss on her mouth before climbing from the bed to handle the condom. When I returned, Avery was fast asleep. Checking the house one more time, Loki followed me back to the bedroom and jumped up on the bed. Turning off the lights, I settled in next to Avery and pulled her close.

I was sliding headlong into love and that scared the shit out of me. I had learned early that life could change on a dime, people you love could up and leave. It was part of the reason why I lived as I did, keeping most people at a distance. But Avery had slipped through and I could be honest enough with myself to admit that her leaving would hurt in a way I'd likely never recover from. Reconciling the fact that I needed her like air while at the same time struggling with the reality that I had let her get that close, kept me up most of the night.

Sitting at a local café, sharing a meal with my dad, I needed to fill him in on the break in, wanted to know if anyone had approached him, but before doing so I asked, "Have you found a job?"

"Yeah, my parole officer helped me get work at a local garage. The owner is also an ex-con, so he doesn't have a problem with my past." He leaned up, placing his elbows on the table. "The Internet is fucking incredible, all that information right there for the picking. I know you've got a PI looking into the owner of the box Lucas wanted access to, Jeremy Paddington, but I've been doing some digging on my own and found out Jeremy worked for Morton Shipping."

"Josh learned that too, but it still doesn't give us much."

Dad looked odd, almost conflicted. "Morton shipping is owned by your mother's family."

Since I was unaccustomed to the idea of a mother, it took me a minute to understand his comment. I can't remember a time when we ever discussed her. But when I realized where his thoughts were going, anger replaced confusion. "My mother? You're thinking the robbery and your involvement wasn't a coincidence."

"Yeah."

"I got to tell ya, that really pisses me off. I don't know the woman, but what I know I'm not liking."

"There's more to the story, son."

"Maybe, but from my point of view, I find her seriously lacking."

Anger swept his face, anger directed at me. I was tempted to make an issue, but then had someone been talking shit about Avery I'd have slammed his fucking head into the bar. And that's when I realized my dad was still in love with her.

"You're still in love with her."

He didn't even attempt to deny it. "Yeah."

Feeling as I did for Avery, I got it. That didn't make it suck any less for him.

"Someone tried breaking into my place the other night. I had thought it was my ex, but after confronting her I know it wasn't."

"Shit. Are you serious?"

"Yeah and if it wasn't Melody, I'm guessing whoever it was it's related to you."

"Fuck. I'm sorry."

"We're family, your shit is my shit. I'm not telling you this because I want you to be sorry, but the more I know the better I can keep safe what's mine. What happened with Mom? Why do you think there could be a link?"

He rubbed a hand over his head; his gaze lowering but I caught the pain. Even now, all these years later, it still hurt. My own gut twisted.

"I met her through a mutual friend. We were really young, she was only sixteen, me seventeen, but it hit us both. Like getting struck by lightning. When we found out she was pregnant, I asked her to marry me. Her father, however, wasn't having that. He all but locked her up in a glass tower. The only time I was allowed to see her was the day he made her hand you over. It broke my fucking heart, the pain he put her through, but he said she either handed you to me or he'd make it so neither of us would ever see you. I tried to keep in touch, sent photos, but the mail was always returned. I didn't stop trying to reach out until I learned she was getting married. That was five years after you were born."

For a woman I didn't know, I felt gutted. What kind of monster was her father to force her to give up her child? And what kind of person had she become that she never sought me out? She'd be in her fifties now and still she stayed away. "You never saw her again?"

"No."

Sitting in that café, understanding dawned on why Dad had gone into that bank with a gun. "My school. You went into that bank so you had money for my school. Honoring what you knew would have been her wishes too."

"Yeah."

I battled regret and anger because what a fucking stupid thing he did to both of us. "Goddamn it, Dad. I would have preferred having the past twenty-five years with you."

"I didn't think, knew as I stood in that bank that I had made a mistake. I was surrendering, but Lucas killed the guard and my life went to Hell. I can't tell you how many times in the past twenty-five years I have regretted that decision, regretted losing my boy."

Another emotion moved through me, a much darker emotion. "I get it now, you not thinking it was a coincidence with Jeremy as the target and you getting selected for the job."

"Your mother, Alexandra, her father, Brynn Morton is a powerful prick. His anger over Alexandra getting pregnant was only because it threw a curveball in his plans for her. He had her life all planned out and then she gets knocked up from some no name blue-collared boy, which fucked up his plans. The man seems the type to hold a grudge, so I don't think it was coincidence at all. Especially since I'm convinced Lucas intended to turn me in from the beginning, the fuck was probably paid to do exactly what he had planned all along. Unfortunately for him, I beat him to it."

"So what happened to Lucas and Jackson?"

"No idea. But if they were paid to get something from that security box and came back empty-handed, maybe their employer wasn't pleased."

"What do you think Jeremy had in his box?"

"Something worth going to all that trouble to retrieve, it's got to be something that could cause someone a hell of a lot of grief if it got out."

"Which might explain why Jeremy died in a mugging shortly before his security box was broken into. Someone was cleaning house. Hell, the person who took out Jeremy could have taken out Lucas and Jackson, tying up loose ends."

"Yeah, puts suspicion on Brynn Morton." Dad wasn't wrong.

"It sure does." This information changed things; particularly since whoever was pulling the strings had dragged Avery and me into it when they attempted to break in to my place. Figuring out why just moved up on my list of things to do. I'd need to pay a visit to Josh, but for now I put it aside because Dad and I had been denied moments like this by these pricks for long enough. "Do you want to come to dinner?"

"I'd really like that, like it even more if Avery bakes the dessert."

"Like I could stop her." I signaled the waitress. "Would you have a problem if I have my PI look into Mom?"

"No. I asked some friends to look into her, but they kept hitting a wall."

"My guy's really good. Let's see what he can find out."

Watching Avery on the dance floor at Allegro, shaking it with Ember and Darcy, was seriously making me uncomfortable. The woman did not know the meaning of half measure. She tackled life with a care-free exuberance that was breath stealing to watch. Currently, she was jumping around in circles, shaking that ass and laughing like a loon, having the time of her life. Did nothing get to her? Her effervescence never seemed to dull.

"She isn't going to vanish." Trace said, humor lacing through his words.

Lucien had excused himself a little while ago to handle a problem and Kyle was using the excuse of dancing with the ladies to keep his fans from descending. His band had played earlier and as it so often happened, the women hunted him down after the show. It was just Trace and me at the table. And though his comment was harmless, there was more to it. "What?"

"You're staring at Avery like she's going to disappear."

"Just enjoying the show."

"Yep, that's what you're doing."

Shifting my focus from Avery, which annoyed me since I really was enjoying the show, I studied Trace. "Have you got something on your mind?"

"Only that I hope you appreciate what you've got there."

"Meaning?"

"Having been in your shoes, captivated by someone to the point of worship. I just hope you appreciate what you've found."

Oh I appreciated Avery, had been one lucky bastard the day she drove up my drive, but the more I thought on Dad and my conversation, the more I realized being with me put her in danger. And as much as I hated to admit it, even to myself, her being with me put me in danger—likely far greater than the threat I posed. "I know exactly what I've found, just not sure I can keep it."

Trace understood, better than anyone, the conflict I felt since he had felt similarly with Ember. "Not sure you have a choice, my friend."

There was always a choice.

Trace placed his bottle down, his focus still on me. "I get where your head is at. Trouble's brewing, you don't know all the players and so you can't guarantee her safety. Plus she's gotten under your skin and for guys like us, that's uncomfortable. I get it, but learn from my mistake. You fuck that up with her, you may not get a second chance. And I got to tell you, Rafe, Ember's the best fucking thing that ever happened to me. She and Faith, the fucking air I breathe."

Trace didn't say much, but when he did the man made a hell of a lot of sense. And he was right. A coward would run; I wasn't a fucking coward. "Thanks brother."

Satisfied that I'd heard his words, he reached for his beer and grinned. "And so it begins."

Before I could ask what the hell that meant, the women and Kyle returned; Avery's face was flushed, her eyes sparkled. I had never seen her looking more beautiful.

She settled next to me, reached for her beer and took a healthy pull, before she asked, "Are you getting out on the dance floor?"

"No."

"You don't dance?

"No."

"Why not? Kyle was dancing."

"Kyle's hiding."

Her brows furrowed, a line creasing the area between her eyes. I wanted to kiss her there. "Hiding from who?"

I jerked my head to the crowd standing behind our table, napkins and pens in hand, staring at Kyle like he was the second coming. "His adoring fans."

Twisting around to Kyle's fan club, she turned laughing eyes on him. "That's quite the following."

In response, Kyle blushed as his head lowered and he studied his beer as if it was the most fascinating beer in the world. "It can be a bit overwhelming."

Understanding moved over Avery's face. Her thoughts very transparent, not knowing if the women were interested in Kyle or the person he was on stage. Instead of whatever she had intended to say, she simply said. "I bet. I get the groupies though. Your band is incredible. You have such a grass root, organic sound and I love that you feature the acoustic guitar in most of your songs."

Kyle was now studying Avery like she was the most fascinating thing in the world and despite myself I actually got a bit annoyed. Stupid, Kyle was a friend, but it didn't matter.

Returning home, I let Loki out while Avery showered. I walked the perimeter of the yard, checked all the buildings for signs of forced entry. I was acting paranoid, but there was a threat and with Avery living here, any threat was unacceptable. I wanted to pack up her things and send her away for her own safety, but Trace had been right. Fucking things up with Avery wasn't something I was willing to risk.

My thoughts turned to what Dad had shared—the likely link between Mom's family and the robbery. What was that shit? The woman lost her kid and her man and then stood quietly by as her father took even more from us, likely being behind Dad going to prison and me into the system. How does a mother sit back and allow that to happen? Did she know? Why hadn't she made any attempt to warn Dad? Especially knowing how much of a prick her father was. Dad did his time and instead of getting his feet back under him, the past was coming back to knock him down again. Not if I could help it.

After the scan of my property, I waited for Avery in the kitchen, leaning against the counter drinking a beer. She'd be over after her shower; it was kind of an unspoken thing, her sleeping in my bed. Fucking loved waking up with her hair on my pillow and her scent on my sheets.

I should have realized my fate had been set seeing her in the market that day, swinging her celery and knocking tea boxes from the shelf. Instead of wondering what the hell I had gotten myself into, I had been congratulating myself on what I had gotten myself into.

"What's put that look on your face?"

So lost in the memory, I hadn't heard Avery enter the kitchen. "You."

"Me?" Surprise and pleasure weaved through that word.

"The day in the market with the celery."

There was a touch of embarrassment in her expression now, which surprised me since I'd tasted every inch of her body, knew her as intimately as a person could, and still she could feel embarrassed with me. I'd have to work on that, even while finding the flushing of her cheeks endearing. "I can only imagine what you thought of me."

"I thought you were adorable and sexy as hell."

"Right. Swatting tea boxes off the shelf with celery is really sexy."

Setting my beer on the counter, I pulled her to me. "When you do it, fuck yeah, it's sexy." Brushing my thumb over her cheek, I didn't like the dark circles under her eyes. "You're tired."

"I don't want to be, but I am."

My dick hardened, even knowing I wouldn't be enjoying her body tonight, the disappointment in her voice over that fact was like a fucking aphrodisiac. "There's always the morning."

"I like the way your mind works."

Placing my bottle in the sink, I took her hand and led her to the bedroom. Loki was already there, at the foot of the bed, snoring. She climbed under the covers as I stripped. Her gaze on me as I did, turned me rock hard. Knowing the effect she had on me, she smiled coyly. Joining her, I pulled her to me, her head coming to rest on my shoulder. She was sound asleep a few seconds later.

In the morning when I woke, Avery wasn't in bed, a fact I planned on rectifying. Detouring to the bathroom, I then went on the hunt.

Found her in the kitchen, sipping a cup of coffee as she looked outside. Hearing me, she turned in my direction as her lips curved into a welcoming smile.

"Morning."

"It'd be a better one if you were still in my bed."

"I had a thought for a recipe, wanted to write it down before I forgot. The smell of the coffee was too enticing."

She was too enticing, sitting there in her over-sized sleep shirt, her legs curled up under her, her hair down around her shoulders. Moving closer, I touched her chin to lift her lips to mine, catching her slight gasp of surprise, my tongue taking the advantage to sweep her mouth which tasted like coffee. The sexy purr that came from the back of her throat was all it took to turn the morning kiss into something more. Reaching for the mug, I set it on the table before lifting her into my arms. She giggled.

"I love that you can lift me like I weigh next to nothing."

"You do weigh next to nothing."

"Not with this ass I don't."

Tossing her on the bed, she laughed as I stripped out of my sweat pants and pounced. Her laughter died, desire replacing it.

"I love your ass. If you lose even one pound, I'll insist you gain it back."

Her eyes were glazing over, a sure sign that she had skipped ahead in her mind. Confirmed when she replied to my ridiculous comment with, "Okay."

Closing my mouth over hers, I savored her flavor, savored the feel of her breasts pressing against my chest, her hips moving into me, her delicate hands running over my back as if she was memorizing me. Moving her shirt up and over her head, my gaze moved to her breasts, her nipples were hard and awaiting my attention. Touching her with just the tip of my tongue, I felt her body jerk, watched as she arched her back like an offering. I played, teasing that tight bud, while watching her body writhe in pleasure. Her nails scored down my back, her legs spread wider, her pussy rubbing against my cock and already she was wet and ready. Pulling her breast deep, fucking loving how sweet she tasted, my fingers moved to between her legs, searching and finding her, pushing in and feeling as her body trembled. My mouth joined my fingers and as soon as my tongue pressed on her clit, she flew apart, my name ripping from her throat as the orgasm crashed over her. Reaching for the bedside table, I grabbed a condom, rolled it on before lifting her hips higher and slamming into her. She was still coming down from the last orgasm; she flew right back over again. Never had I had someone so responsive. Watching the place where we were connected, feeling her tight, wet body taking me deep, holding me...I blew like an adolescent as intense pleasure rolled through me.

Catching her eye, she grinned. "Again."

Rolling her so she sat astride me, I shifted my hips. "Give me a few minutes."

Pressing down on me, she lowered her mouth to mine. "Take all the time you need."

Round two commenced five minutes later.

chapter twenty-one

Avery

"ey, Mom. I'm on my way to work. Can I call you back during my dinner break?"

"Tell me that little trollop did not attempt to use you and your new job to get her baby shower at Clover." With all that was happening between Rafe and me, I had completely forgotten about Dad and that lunch.

"How did you hear about it?"

"Your father called, upset over the argument you had. When he explained why he went to see you, I think I turned him deaf with how loud I screamed. That oblivious man didn't even realize how what he was asking of you would hurt you. He knows now, not only did I give it to him but Harold gave him what for too."

"No, he didn't." Harold was a very laid-back man; he rarely got upset over anything. In fact in all the years I'd known him, I had never heard him raise his voice.

"He called your father a blind fool for not seeing the manipulation of his wife and her horrible treatment of you and Nat. I swear I kissed the man's face off while he was still on the phone with your father."

An involuntary shiver went through me even as a giggle burned up my throat. "We're getting dangerously close to you sharing too much information."

"Your father may have a mind for business, but his people skills suck."

"Truer words."

"Are you okay? I know how much that had to have hurt. And don't try and be brave. Tell me the truth."

"It hurt, it gutted. Why the man thinks he'll be any better the second time around when he failed so miserably the first time baffles me. How he could step all over my feelings. That he's unable to see how not only his request, but also the fact that he talks so blasé about having another kid would affect me. Yeah, I had a good cry, but then I went back to my awesome job and came home to a killer omelet made for me by my fantastic landlord. That helped a lot in soothing the hurt."

"I'm sorry, Avery."

"I'm okay, but I got to ask. What was it that attracted you to him because I honestly don't see it?"

Her exhale was loud enough for me to hear. "He was very charismatic, your father. And when he talked about his job, there was such passion and since we were talking about insurance, I assumed he was just a passionate man. After we'd been together for a while, the charisma faded and I discovered that his only passion was his work."

"That had to be lonely for you."

"I had you and Nat. I wasn't lonely at all. And now I have Harold whose passion *is* me. He knows how I take my coffee. I never told him, he's just so in tuned to me that he knows everything there is to know about me. We've been together for eleven years. Your father and I were together for twenty-three and that man doesn't even know what my favorite color is. Enough about me, tell me about this Rafe."

It was my turn to exhale on a sigh. "He's incredible. Hot, yes, but thoughtful, hardworking, funny. He wanted to know why I was here alone, where my friends were, where you were. I explained you and

Harold and Dad and how I never had many friends I'd be willing to help with burying the body. I told him I'd help him bury one, he said he'd help me too."

"Ah, bonding over a felony. That's adorable."

I laughed; my mom was a goof. I guess that's where I got it. The thought warmed me.

"I'm in love with him."

"I can tell." Mom's voice was very soft. "I want to meet him."

"I'd like that, but not yet. We've only just started and having you and Harold driving up in your RV would be weird."

"All right. We'll wait a little bit." Her voice turned questioning. "Are you really okay with the way things were left with your dad?"

"Yeah, I've finally reached my limit with him. He wants to be in my life, he needs to make the effort."

"Fair enough. We'll talk soon. Love you, Avery."

"Love you."

Stepping in the café near Clover, the line wasn't as crazy as usual. I understood why the place was always packed. The coffee was great, but it was the sandwiches that were inspired; my favorite, the roasted turkey, goat cheese, avocado and lime on twelve-grain bread. Yum.

Rafe's dad was coming to dinner tomorrow night, Rafe had called earlier asking if I'd join them. His first dinner with his father in his home was a big deal and he wanted to share it with me. I wouldn't miss it for anything.

While I stood in line, I noticed Melody just off to the side of it. I'm pretty sure I made some type of animal noise, since several people in the line were giving me strange looks. It wasn't a surprise to see her at this eatery—it was a very popular lunch spot—but the idea of interacting with her on any level was taking away my appetite.

It was while I stared at her wishing she'd vanish into thin air— where was that fairy godmother when you needed her—I noticed the man next to her. It was the manner in which he stood with her that gained my full attention. He was completely in her space and though she was very pretty and likely had people in her space often, she didn't look happy to have him there. Concerned, despite myself, I wondered if I should get closer to assess the situation.

As I debated on my course of action, I kept my focus on her on the off chance she'd see me and signal if she needed help. But as I watched, she never glanced over. I was beginning to think he was her new love interest, a thought I could wholeheartedly get behind, and she was just pulling her usual shenanigans when he grabbed her by the upper arm hard enough she not only winced in pain, but cried out. Several men in line started toward her because it was clear now, whatever was happening was happening without her consent. The man leaned in, said something that had her flinch, before he made his leave of her. When I got my first good look at him, my breath caught because despite being older, he was beautiful. He moved through the tables with grace; his suit exquisitely hung from his frame—a build that would make men twenty years younger jealous. And even as handsome as he was, his eyes were vacant. A chill went through me when he passed by me because he gave off some seriously dark energy.

Turning back to Melody, she was staring right at me, but instead of the malevolence I was usually treated to, she looked rattled.

Despite myself, I joined her. "Are you okay?"

"No." She wasn't just rattled; she was actually shaking.

"Who was that?"

"Not a good man."

"I could see that in the way he grabbed you. How do you know him?"

She didn't answer. Her silence not so much from fear now—she was bouncing back from the encounter—but intentional as she worked the angles. I shouldn't have gotten out of line.

"I need to talk to Rafe. He'll know what to do."

Despite the fact that I didn't like the woman, her scheming even less, that man hadn't been playing. Whether she knew it or not, she was in trouble.

"Melody, who was that man?"

Gone was the frightened woman, to be replaced with the bitch I had come to know. "It's none of your business. This is between Rafe and me."

Rafe? How the hell had that scene been about Rafe? It was pointless, me asking that, but I did anyway.

Her reply, "You're still here?"

I had never wanted to punch someone as badly as I wanted to punch her. Moving closer to her, there was no question what emotion fueled my next words. "Listen clearly you stupid bitch. I don't know what the hell kind of game you're playing, but I do know that man who just left gave off some seriously dangerous energy. You might not realize this because what you got in looks you seriously lack in brains, but that man meant business."

Maybe she wasn't as dumb as she looked because that got through. Fear shadowed her expression. Her next words did not at all clarify the situation. "I did something."

"What do you mean?"

"I didn't think it was a big deal, I was mad…"

Warning lit down my spine. "What wasn't a big deal?"

For a second I thought she was going to share, but instead she only further confused me. "That man is seriously unhinged. I need to warn Rafe."

"That man has an interest in Rafe?"

"Yeah."

Before I could press her for more, she walked around me. "I have to go."

And then she was gone. I just stood there like an idiot and watched her walk away because there was enough truth in what she said, and how she acted, that had me worried.

Reaching for my phone, I called Rafe.

"Hey babe, what's up?"

"I just saw Melody. Something is up with her. There was a man. He looked like a very bad man. He manhandled her, right in the café with plenty of witnesses. He didn't seem to care in the least. When I pressed her about it, she mentioned he was interested in you."

"Goddamn it."

"She's going to try to spin it, but whatever is going on, the man looked dangerous."

"I'll take care of it. Are you okay?"

"Yeah, just concerned for you."

His voice warmed, I hadn't realized how cold it had turned. "Don't worry about me, but I like that you are."

"What are you going to do?"

"Talk to her. If I'm going to be late, I'll call."

"Okay. Be careful."

"Later, babe."

Returning to work, my thoughts were on Rafe and how for the first time since I started my job, I wanted my shift over because I was worried…downright scared.

RAFE

Dialing Melody, I didn't even let her speak.

"Are you home yet?"

"Rafe, I'm so glad you called."

"Cut the shit. Are you home?"

"Almost."

"I'm on my way."

A half an hour later, Melody opened her door for me. A big smile on her face like this was a social call.

"Who was the man Avery saw you with?"

"Nice greeting."

Even now, she was still playing her games. I didn't hide my fury when I got right up into her face. "Who the fuck was the man?"

She pulled a hand through her hair. I had never seen her do that. She was nervous, or scared, under the makeup and practiced look she so carefully put together. Good.

"I was mad at you, wanted to hurt you like you had me."

"What did you do?"

"That man, he approached me a few weeks ago, knew about us—more to the point us breaking up—and asked me to help with providing him information on you."

I didn't like where this was going. "Come again?"

"I shared your schedule with him."

"My schedule?"

"Yeah, your schedule, that of Avery's and your alarm codes."

Rage, sharp and potent, slammed into me. Avery wasn't just on his radar; he'd likely been tracking her. "That's why you wanted the codes from Avery?"

"He wanted into your house. You have something he wants. My job was to tell him when you weren't home so his guy could get in."

Despite the fury at having my home invaded at the hand of someone I once cared for, apprehension straightened my spine too. "Are you telling me someone has been in my home?"

"Yeah, but only twice."

Even as rage had my hands curling into fists, my stomach dropped. Thank God Loki had taken to staying in the carriage house, but he'd have sensed them. He would have known someone was trespassing and wouldn't have been able to do a damn thing about it.

"Why did the man seek you out today?"

"You changed the alarm codes, he wanted the new codes and I wasn't getting them fast enough."

Son of a bitch. "What are they looking for?"

"A disc, like an old compact disc or something."

"And why the hell does this man think I have this disc?"

"It has something to do with your dad. He didn't go into detail."

Even suspecting this linked to Dad, it still rocked me. Someone was still interested in the robbery, enough that they were willing to commit a felony. Searching my place for something of Dad's made sense with him in prison, I'd be the one who had his stuff. A disc—that was likely what Lucas had been after. It certainly would fit in a security box, and compact discs were the popular storage method for electronic data in the early 90s—definitely not a coincidence.

"What's supposed to be on it?"

"I've no idea."

There was a sour taste in my mouth at how blinded I had been by a pretty face. "You invaded my privacy, put Avery and me at risk and all because you were pissed that I ended us and not you? And you claim to love me. You don't know shit about love."

It was likely just another of her games, but those words seemed to have hit home. Her eyes grew bright, but I didn't give a shit. "If these people are the same people I think they are, they have a tendency to kill those who come back empty-handed."

She paled; even under her makeup I saw that. At least her head was no longer up her ass. "You should be scared. Go to the police. Tell them what you know. I'll take you if you want."

"You would do that? Why?"

"Because people have died in whatever shit you've gotten yourself caught up in. And I might not like you, but I don't want to see you dead."

Her fear was easy to see now. She was playing with the big boys and had no idea just how dangerous a game she was playing. This afternoon gave her a taste and she clearly didn't like it. "I can't tell them much."

"Tell them what you told me, but we need to report it because these people have killed before. And since they haven't gotten what they seek, they're likely to do so again."

She visibly shook at that announcement. "Okay, I'll go."

"Let's do it now."

She wanted to object, but it seemed Melody was smarter than that. "Okay."

"And after, you might want to leave town for a while."

Yeah, she was definitely getting it because she didn't put up much of a fight. "That's probably a good idea."

Avery

Arriving home, Rafe was in the drive. Waiting.

"Is everything okay."

"Yeah."

"What happened?"

"Not now. I don't want to talk about it right now. There is shit we have to discuss, you need to be made aware, but not right now. Are you planning on taking a shower?"

My body hummed from the look in his eyes, he looked dangerous, in a really sexy way. "Yeah."

Lifting me into his arms, he carried me into the carriage house and right to the bathroom. Dropping me on my feet, he reached for the faucet before he turned into me. His fingertips brushed down my neck, along my shoulder burning a trail wherever he touched.

"Arms up."

I didn't hesitate; the look in his eyes captivated me because there was just so much going on behind them. After removing my shirt and bra, he lowered himself in front of me, gripping my pants and pulling them and my panties down my legs. He dropped the garments on the tile floor once I'd stepped out of them.

"My turn." But my hands were already moving over him, exploring his body over the soft cotton of his shirt. Lifting his shirt up, he bent his head so I could get it over. He was wearing those faded jeans I loved so much as I ran my hand over his hip and along his ass; the denim tenting from his erection. Moving my hand down that bulge and feeling what my touch did to him was heady. Unsnapping his jeans, I pulled them down his legs. Grabbing me, he pushed me into the shower, right up against the wall, as his mouth closed over mine. His tongue explored my mouth even as his hands did the same with my body. It was all so new and I loved this part of a relationship: the learning and discovering of the other person. I had never had a lasting relationship, but I suspected with a man like Rafe I'd love even more knowing him inside and out; knowing what made him tick— the familiarity and comfort of knowing him as well as I knew myself.

"You taste like cocoa." He muttered as he ran his tongue over my shoulder.

"I didn't use cocoa today."

"You always taste like cocoa."

"So that's what you like about me, I'm sweet."

His head lifted, lust and humor playing over his features. "You are sweet and a goof." He reached for the shampoo, squeezing a generous amount into his palm, before he started to wash my hair. I may have moaned.

Words were so not happening right now because I was trying really hard to keep my legs from buckling under me. And then he surprised me with what he said next.

"Trace is getting me some really good steaks for the dinner with my dad since he's always loved steak. I thought I'd do baked potatoes and a salad too."

Nervousness rang from his voice, slight but undeniable, but it was the fact that he wanted to talk about it with me, wanted to include me in the other parts of his life that had my heart feeling so full it didn't seem possible that it could be contained inside my chest. "Sounds delicious. I'll make dessert. Does your dad have a preference?"

"He always liked cheesecake."

"With a topping?"

"Usually plain."

"Okay, a cheesecake it is."

My fingers danced down his stomach, following the curves of his abs. He had a fantastic body and hands; I wanted to purr at how fabulous it felt having his strong fingers massaging my scalp. "You've wonderful hands."

Moving me under the spray, he washed the shampoo from my hair.

"Wonderful hands? How about now?"

His thumb pressed against my clit as his fingers moved into me, rubbing me on the inside. My breath caught, "Definitely now."

"Ride it, Avery, build it up." I felt his tongue on my nipple seconds before he pulled it deep into his mouth and the combination of his mouth and fingers; yeah, my hips had a mind of their own. Grinding into him—loving the feel of him inside me—I reached for him to give him pleasure, but he turned me and pressed me up against the shower wall.

"Tilt your ass back."

The fingers of his one hand were digging into my hip, moving me the way he wanted even as he sought my cooperation. I felt the tip of his cock on my lower back, felt as he ran it down the crack of my ass, before he reached my core that was already starting to quiver with mini orgasms. In the next breath, he buried himself deep.

"Oh, God." Mind numbing was how it felt having his bare cock moving inside me.

"I won't come in you, but I have to feel you."

"Don't stop, please don't stop." Arching my spine, his hips pumped, his cock pounding into me, his hand moved around my front and as soon as he pinched my clit, I came on a cry. His hips moved faster, his grip on my hips tightened and then he pulled out on a growl as he came on my back. Pressing into me, he wrapped his arms around my waist and dropped his forehead on my shoulder. "That was fucking fantastic."

The way he held me still, protectively, reverently touched something in me. No one had ever held me the way he was now, like I mattered, like I was the reason the sun rose and set.

Feeling deliriously happy, I teased, "You've ruined showers for me. I'll never take another one and not think about this."

"And that's bad, why?" He asked, as his lips brushed over my shoulder.

"I'm going to spend the rest of my life in the shower."

"Unless we make some memorable moments elsewhere in the house."

Turning into him, I wrapped my arms around his neck. "I like this plan. Any thoughts?"

"Fucking you on the kitchen counter, bent over the sofa in the living room, in my workshop."

My body started to throb. "I like all those ideas."

"Then we better get started, but first we need food."

"Agreed."

Lifting up on my tip toes, I ran my tongue along his lower lip before dipping into his mouth, his hand wrapped around my neck and pulled me closer as he took over the kiss, leaving me breathless when he ended it.

"I like being here, Rafe."

"I like you being here, Avery."

The following evening, while I set the table for dinner, I thought about last night. We'd christened several places in both the carriage house and here. It'd been fabulous. I'd asked him again about Melody, he alluded to the break in being connected to his dad, something we both suspected, but he asked if we could talk about it after his dad's visit. It was a big deal for Rafe, his father coming to dinner in his home. So, yeah, I was totally okay with waiting a day or two.

Liam had arrived a half an hour ago. The first stop on the tour was Rafe's workshop. I heard as they entered the house and moved to greet them. Seeing them together, it was uncanny how much they looked alike. Rafe saw me first; the smile that spread over his face was staggeringly beautiful.

"Avery."

"Rafe." Stepping up to his dad, I wasn't sure how to greet him so I settled for a kiss on his cheek. "How are you?"

"Better now." That was said in much the way I'd heard Rafe tease me. Like father, like son.

"Can I get you a drink?" Rafe asked us both. "Beer?"

"Sounds good to me."

"Yeah, me too." Liam added.

"While you show your dad around, I'll whip up a salad."

"Are you sure you don't want help?"

"Yep, I've got this."

"Okay." Rafe moved into me, pressing close, and kissed my neck. He whispered in my ear. "Thanks." Then turning to his dad, he said, "We can start in the living room."

Liam caught my eye as he walked out of the room, following his son. "Thank you, Avery."

And I knew he was thanking me for giving him some alone time with his son. I chopped the vegetables, their voices drifted to me from the living room.

"It's incredible. It doesn't look like the same place. You've brought it back to life."

"It's a slow process, but I'm finally getting to the point where I can see the light at the end of the tunnel. And you're right, it's like breathing life back into it."

"But you saw it. If I'd toured through the place looking as it did in those pictures, I'd have walked right back out again. You saw its potential. When did you know this was what you wanted to do?"

"Wood shop class in middle school. I loved every part of it."

"You can tell. And the furniture, you made that too?"

"Yeah."

"Beautiful."

"How's your job?"

"I'm working on cars, what I used to do. A bit different since now all the cars have onboard computers, but it's familiar which kind of helps me with adjusting."

"Have you ever built anything?"

"The occasional bookcase, but nothing like what you create."

"The business has taken off, I've got orders out the ass. I could always use another pair of hands. If you think it's something you'd enjoy, we can talk about it."

Tears filled my eyes just imagining Liam's reaction to that. His voice was a bit hoarse when he replied, "I'd really like that."

"Okay, you'll have to get trained on the tools, but I'd like that too. I'd like for you to be a part of what I've created here."

After I tossed the salad, I left it on the counter and stepped outside with Loki to give Rafe and his dad some privacy. And it was while I thought about the generous offer he had made his dad—walking around the place he had made a home—I realized I wanted to be a part of what he created here too. Who could have known by following my dreams I'd also lose my heart.

Rafe came searching for me a half an hour later. "You okay?"

"Yeah. How's it going?"

"Seeing my home through his eyes, it's an affirmation I never knew I needed. I asked him to work with me."

I smiled because I was seeing a different side to Rafe, the son: the proud son. "I heard, that's why I left you alone. I thought it was a moment that shouldn't be eavesdropped on. I think it's a wonderful idea."

He took a lock of my hair between his thumb and forefinger. "You were eavesdropping?"

"Well, you were speaking loud, but yeah. It's a big deal. Your dad is here, seeing your home through your eyes for the first time. Speaking of which, where is he?"

"He was sneaking some of the cheesecake you made for dessert." He reached for my hand. "Let's go fire up the grill." We had just reached the door when he stopped, his focus turning to me. "I meant it, Avery. I like having you here."

On second thought, I didn't lose my heart; I gave it away and happily.

RAFE

Dad and I were sitting in the living room; Avery had fallen asleep, curled up on the sofa, her head on my lap. It felt good, having Dad and Avery in my home. I had missed my dad, but I didn't appreciate just how much until I had him back. It was a hell of a feeling, showing him what I'd done here, the life I had carved out for myself. I wanted him to be a part of that, wanted to help him get to a place where he'd feel a bit of what I felt.

"Has your guy learned anything about your mom?"

"I haven't heard from him. I'll call him, set up a time for us to meet." Dad was across the room by the fireplace, his focus on the bottle in his hand, but his thoughts were miles away.

"You miss her."

His head lifted, the truth of my statement right there to see. "Yeah. Especially watching you with Avery. What Lexie and I had was very similar. We were so young but it was just right, the kind of right I knew I'd never grow tired of. Instead of building a life like you've done here, I lost her and then I lost you. It's amazing how quickly your life can shift. What you've found with her, hold onto to it, Rafe, because it comes around so rarely. She's good for you, keeps you on your toes and yet she can't stop staring at you anymore than you can with her."

He was right. What I'd found with Avery didn't come around every day. "We're that obvious?"

"Yeah, but it's good. That's what life is all about. It isn't about making money or getting the killer job or the fancy car. It's those everyday moments strung together that make up a life. I'd sell my soul to have the everyday moments I witnessed the two of you sharing tonight."

"It was like getting struck by lightning the day she walked into my life. Trace told me he'd hired a pastry chef, I expected a matronly woman, and then she appeared."

"This Trace, the one who dropped her in your lap, you owe him, son, a debt you'll never be able to repay."

"I'm just beginning to realize the truth of that statement."

"At least you see it. Some men have to lose it before they appreciate what they had."

"You're not talking about yourself."

"No. I appreciated, I was just too young to do anything about it."

"And what if you were to learn Mom was no longer married?"

"My gut reaction, seek her out and stake a claim, but she never once attempted to contact you. Me, I get, but her child? I don't know. She's a grown woman now, she can't still be under the thumb of her dad, so maybe the woman I thought she was isn't really who she is."

"I'm sorry, Dad." And I was, appreciated his situation all that much more after having met Avery. I couldn't imagine being denied the chance of exploring this wild and intense attraction we shared all because of someone's meddling.

"I'm not sorry, I got you."

My eyes stung, my chest felt tight hearing him say that. Realizing the effect he had on me and graciously changing the subject he added, "I think I'm going to take you up on your invite. It's late and I've had a few beers, best not to get pulled over for driving under the influence."

"Good idea. Avery insisted on making up the second bedroom, I think she might have even put a mint on your pillow."

He grinned. "She really is a goof, but definitely a keeper. Night, son."

"Night, Dad."

He had just reached the door when I called to him. "We lost a lot of time and I've got plenty of room. Think about moving in here."

And I knew he really meant to when he said, "Thanks, son, I will."

CHAPTER TWENTY – TWO

RAFE

A very recruited my dad to help with the gardens. I wasn't surprised he'd agreed; the woman was a dynamo. Unstoppable when she had her mind set. Currently she stood in my front yard, dressed in overalls. No shit, overalls, a flannel shirt and fucking straw hat. She had a can of neon orange spray paint that she was using to create the lines of the garden beds she wanted us to dig. She was having entirely too much fun with that can of paint. Loki, who was acting more like the puppy he had been—the big yard in lieu of our daily walks in the park bummed him out since now that Avery walked him everyday, he was more animated—was running around Avery barking. She was likely going to spray paint my dog and the sorry, besotted animal didn't seem to have a problem with that.

My dad wasn't any better. Grinning at Avery, which only encouraged her to be more of a goof. And who the hell was I kidding; I couldn't keep my eyes off her. She was like this brilliant ball of energy, mesmerizing to watch. I hadn't realized I was lonely until she drove into my life in that piece of shit car.

"Rafe, what do you think?" She called as she waved her arms wide to encompass the orange lines that now curved around the front of my house. "Why are you standing all the way back there?"

"I'm not interested in getting painted orange. It seems anything stationary for too long doesn't stand a chance."

Her hands on her hips were the precursor to her giving me lip. "I have only painted what I wanted painted, smart ass."

"So that's why your ass is orange and you've got a streak of it in your hair?"

"What?" She looked at my dad. "My hair isn't orange. Is it?"

"Just a little."

"A little? Come on, Dad. She is going to look in the mirror."

"Okay, maybe more than a little."

Most women of my acquaintance would, at this point, run screaming to the bathroom to ascertain the damage. Not Avery. Instead, she asked my dad, "Does it look good?"

"On you, yeah."

"Cool." And then those eyes landed on me again. "So are you coming over here or what?"

And it was while I stood in my front yard with my dad, looking at Avery doing a fair interpretation of a Beverly Hillbilly with orange paint, the color of a fucking traffic cone, streaking her hair that I realized I was in love with her. For the first time, I understood Trace and Lucien's intensity when it came to their wives. Like Lucien, I was whipped; a fucking goner and I so didn't care.

"Put the can of paint down and I'll come over."

Her nose wrinkled, she had a thought on that, but she did put the paint down. Reaching her side, I yanked her to me and kissed the scowl right off her face. She had an entirely different look about her when I took a step back.

"So are we digging this up or what?" I asked, knowing she was no longer thinking about garden beds.

Her eyes opened, but it took her a moment to find her balance, which pulled a grin from me. "You did that on purpose."

She was right; she knew she was right, I didn't need to confirm that for her.

Reaching for her shovel, I handed it to her. She smiled, and I knew exactly what she was thinking before she said, "I might be using this later, to bury not dig."

Fucking goof.

Four hours later we were all covered in dirt and mud. My back ached, my arms were sore and if I never saw another plant or shovel, I would die a happy man. But I couldn't lie; Avery's vision in reality was perfect. The curves of the garden bed and the foliage of the plants she selected softened the front of the house bringing visual interest to what had been seriously lacking.

Avery was walking back and forth, studying the garden from every angle. "It's perfect."

She wasn't wrong.

"God, I'm good. I can't wait to get started on the other beds."

"Let's give ourselves some time to enjoy this one."

She turned to me, a knowing smile on her face. "Backbreaking isn't it?"

And yet she didn't seem affected at all. "How are you not hurting right now?"

"I'm made of stronger stuff apparently."

In response my dad roared with laughter. "I can admit, I hurt like a mother, so I'm going to grab a shower and then a cold beer. Maybe we should call for pizza."

"Yeah, with avocado and bacon."

My dad and I both looked at Avery like she sprouted up from the ground. "On your pizza? That's sacrilege."

"It's delicious."

"Pepperoni, sausage and mushrooms."

"And onion." Dad added.

"Yeah and onion."

"Maybe I'll let you have some of mine after you taste it and realize what you've been missing your whole life."

She started for the carriage house and her ass in those overalls; I may have to rethink my feelings on them. "Avery."

"Yeah," she called from over her shoulder.

"Thank you. You're right, it is perfect."

She stopped walking, her head twisting around; the expression on her face rocked me. She looked a lot like how I felt. Her voice was soft, tenderness laced through the words. "You're welcome."

If my dad weren't here, she'd be naked, flat on her back and writhing under me. The idea was so appealing, I had to change the subject or else my dad would be getting a show. "Your choice of pizza toppings though is just fucking wrong."

I had the joy of watching her narrow her eyes, she even stuck her tongue out at me, before she turned on her heel and disappeared into the carriage house.

I was still grinning when the pizza arrived an hour later.

In my truck, after delivering a coffee table to a client, I kept seeing Avery in her overalls, the memory making me hard. Shifting my thoughts before I threw caution to the wind and kidnapped her from work, I pondered the shit with Melody. The cops hadn't laughed us out of the precinct, but just barely. They took down the little information Melody could provide and assured us the matter would be given the attention it deserved. I couldn't help thinking about that final scene in *Raiders of the Lost Ark* and how the ark was stored in that vast warehouse. I suspected her report would receive similar attention.

Melody had taken my advice and left town. The more I thought on the situation, the less sense it made. Someone thought I had something and attempted to break in. Not cool, definitely something that concerned me. But on the other hand, they had asked for Melody's help and were almost lazy in the way they were going about looking for whatever it was they wanted. I wasn't sure if the person behind this now was the same person who had sought the disc years before because they didn't seem like a threat, just a nuisance. I needed a sounding board. Hitting the Bluetooth button on the steering wheel, I heard Lucien's voice over my truck's speakers.

"Rafe, what's up?"

"Are you busy now?"

"No why?"

"You're not going to believe what I've learned. Can you call Josh and Trace? I'll get my dad so I can tell you all at once."

"It doesn't sound good."

"I don't know what the fuck it is."

"We'll be here." The line went dead.

The garage where Dad worked wasn't too far from my house and when I arrived, he was out front with a customer. He saw me and jerked his head in acknowledgment. I looked around as I climbed from my truck. The place did well, based on the number of cars in the parking lot.

Dad approached. "Hey, Rafe. What's up?"

"Have you had your lunch break yet?"

"Not yet."

"Will you come with me? You're going to meet my friends."

"Sure."

A half an hour later we were stepping into Allegro; Lucien and Josh were already there as was Trace.

Trace stepped up to Dad as soon as we entered. "Mr. McKenzie, Trace Montgomery."

"Trace, nice to meet you."

Lucien offered Dad his hand. "Lucien Black and this is Josh O'Donnell."

"So why are we here?" Trace asked without preamble.

I wondered if speaking the words out loud would make them any easier to believe, because honest to God the whole situation was fucked up. "After Melody and I split, she was approached by someone who wanted to know Avery's and my schedule so they could search my house. Feeling jilted, she shared."

Dad went rigid. "Are you fucking kidding me?"

Shaking my head, I continued, "After I changed the alarm codes, they got desperate and attempted to break in. They're looking for a disc of some kind. Melody doesn't know who's behind it and I convinced her to go to the cops, not that that did any good, but at least there's a report on file."

It was Dad who said what everyone else was thinking. "How much do you want to bet that's what Lucas had been looking for in Paddington's box?"

"I wouldn't take that bet." Trace said.

"Paddington worked for Morton Shipping, shines a light on them. Don't you think?" Josh said.

"Yeah, more so since Brynn Morton is my grandfather."

Josh was the only one not surprised by that news, but then he was looking into my mom so he already knew of the connection.

Dad answered. "Yeah, Lexie and I were getting married, her dad had a problem with that. I don't doubt for a minute that I had been targeted for the bank job and learning where Jeremy worked, I'd bet money Brynn was behind it. Especially knowing Lucas's MO was to rat out his recruit. Sending me to jail, yeah, Brynn would've arranged that without blinking."

"But why would he come after you? He'd already won, had gotten his daughter away from you." Josh asked.

"His pregnant daughter. That didn't work into his plans, I'm sure. Why wait ten years before exacting revenge? I don't know. The man's a ruthless prick, I don't put anything past him."

Josh started to pace. "So outside of being a dick and setting you up, why now? Why are they searching now for this disc and not when you were in jail?"

"My guess, because I'm not in jail. Lucas and Jackson were likely killed because they didn't have the disc. The only other person on the job was me. Whoever killed them thought I had it. But I was doing twenty-five years. They probably thought I'd handed the disc over as part of my surrender, likely waited on eggshells for the cops to show up at their door. When that didn't happen, the next logical place for me to hide it would be with my kid's stuff, but at nine, it'd be highly unlikely I'd share with him what I hid and where. Which meant it was just as secure in my hiding spot as it was in that deposit box. They got a reprieve for twenty-five years. Now that I'm out, they think I'm going to cash in. Searching Rafe's place makes sense, especially if they think they're running out of time."

"But why wait until you're out? Why not a year before you were released or two?" Josh asked.

It bothered me too; the timing didn't make sense, which was why I wasn't convinced it was the same person now as it had been to take out Lucas and Jackson. "I agree. And if they are keeping tabs, why did they wait until after I had the alarm system installed? I've been in that house for five years and up until a few months ago the place would have been easy pickings, so why'd they wait until it was like Fort Knox to break in?"

"Unless they only recently learned that what they wanted was at your place." Trace said.

That was a good point. "So who told them?" I asked.

"Good question." Josh added.

"And what's on that disc?" Lucien asked.

"And how real a threat is this? It seems like whoever is looking is only stirring the water lightly. They asked for Melody's help, so how serious can they possibly be in both finding the disc and wanting to keep what they find a secret? But on the other hand, the man Avery saw with Melody had not been gentle. A fact confirmed when I spoke to Melody, she was spooked, enough that she's left town for a while. The whole situation is very contradictory."

"If Avery saw the man, maybe she could sit with a sketch artist friend of mine. We get his name we'll understand better what we're dealing with." Josh said.

Case in point on how the cops hadn't taken Melody's report seriously. They never even suggested that. "I'll talk to her."

Looking at my watch, I stood. "Dad has to get back to work. I want that disc. I want to know what the hell this is all about, but I've torn that house apart in the remodel, I'm not sure it's there. If they were given a tip that I had it, I think the tipster is fucking with them."

Returning home, I was greeted to the sight of Avery attempting to hang a bird feeder from a tree using a chair. What was it with the woman and her staunch objection to ladders? She had pulled over one of the pair of chairs she had setup in front of the carriage house not too long after she moved in. I didn't really understand why she had them, since they faced the house and not the yard, but she often sat there with Loki. She had one foot up against the tree as she leaned dangerously far from where the chair sat to reach the branch she wanted. And though she was likely going to fall and break something, I had to say the view was fucking fantastic.

I waited until I was right behind her, so I could catch her if I startled her, before saying, "I need to buy you one of those helping hands."

"Funny."

"Seriously. There's a ladder behind the barn, I showed you."

"It's heavy."

"So you'd rather risk broken bones?"

"I do this all the time. The curse of being short."

"Would you like some help?"

"I got it."

And she did, though I wasn't sure why she was hanging a bird feeder when winter was coming. And thinking about birds had that conversation about eagles, when she first arrived, popping into my head. Fucking hilarious.

"Isn't it a bit late to be hanging a bird feeder? I think the eagles have migrated south already."

Her head twisted, her green eyes spearing me and though there was humor, I saw understanding too.

"You knew?"

"That you were lying your ass off? That the only birds you were viewing through those binoculars were Lucien and me? Hell yeah."

"I should be embarrassed, but I'm not."

"It was flattering."

"It was ridiculous and silly, but the view was lovely."

"Speaking of views, don't move I need a picture of this."

"Stop it."

Nimble the way she moved, climbing down from her perch effortlessly. She smiled up at me and my chest tightened at the sight, but I needed to fill her in. She needed to be careful and smart so I'd have the treat of that smile for a long time to come.

"I want to tell you about Melody."

Her smile instantly faded and I hated seeing concern clouding her expression, but at least she knew enough to be worried.

"That man you saw, he wanted her to tell him when we weren't home so he could have my house searched."

Worried shifted to anger. "Are you kidding me?"

"No."

"Why would she..." Understanding dawned, "She willingly shared that information with a stranger because she felt jilted?"

"Yeah."

"What a bitch."

Understatement.

"What were they looking for?"

"A disc, I'm guessing a CD-ROM."

She made the connection immediately. "This is related to your dad."

"Yeah."

"It was them, the night the alarm tripped."

"Yeah."

"That's a bit unsettling."

She looked vulnerable, scared, and the instinct to protect her by pushing her away was strong, instead I wrapped her in my arms. "I'm telling you this because I want you to be careful and aware of your surroundings. I'm not convinced we're in any danger, but it can't hurt to be cautious. Okay?"

"Yeah."

"Josh is looking into it, Melody filed a police report, not that I think that'll do anything, but you live here, you could become a target. And I'm not going to lie to you, Avery, I don't fucking like you anywhere near trouble, but I'd send you away if I thought it was serious."

Defiance entered her expression. "I'm not going anywhere."

"I agree, for now." She wanted to object, I didn't let her. "You saw the man. Would you sit with a sketch artist Josh knows? If we can figure out who's behind it, we'll figure out what the hell they're after."

"Absolutely."

chapter twenty—three

Avery

As I worked, whisking the eggs for the mousse, I thought about what Rafe had shared regarding Melody and the mystery man. I had to agree, the situation was irritating but not necessarily concerning. Still you had to wonder what could possibly still be of interest so many years later that someone would go to the trouble they had to find it.

Nat was coming for another visit, my irrational, crazy and brilliant sister and her boyfriend, Tyler. They'd be staying in the carriage house since I spent most nights at Rafe's; it seemed silly to let that space go unused. And as an added bonus, the place was like Fort Knox, so if there really was a threat, they'd be safe with us.

Rafe didn't want my rent money now that we were sleeping together. Just another reason for why I'd fallen for him and as sweet as that gesture was, the added income pushed up his timeline for the completion of his house. He didn't know, but I intended to stockpile the rent to give to him.

"Avery."

Looking up I was surprised to see Kyle and more the strain that twisted his expression.

"Kyle, what's wrong?"

"I just got a call from the hospital, Mount Sinai. They were trying to reach Rafe but his phone is going right into voicemail, so they called the other number programmed into the phone."

My heart dropped into my stomach. Liam. I had Clover's number as part of my voice mail message in case someone needed to get in touch with me while I worked. "Is he okay?"

"They didn't say only that there was some accident at work and he was being treated."

Trace walked in at the moment. "I'll take you. Kyle, you keep trying to get in touch with Rafe. Maybe he's with Lucien or Josh. Tina and Lee, this is all you tonight."

"Okay. Don't worry, Avery, we've got this." Lee assured me and I knew they did.

Pulling off my apron, my hands were shaking because the idea that Liam could be taken away from Rafe when they were finally finding their way back to each other was too horrible to contemplate.

Trace grabbed my purse and seeing that I was a bit out of it, touched my elbow and led me to the parking lot. Once we settled in his car, I called Rafe.

"Trace and I are on our way to Mount Sinai. Your dad had an accident at the garage. I don't know the details. As soon as I do, I'll call you."

I dropped my phone in my lap and looked out the window as tears burned my eyes. "I hate leaving him a message like that."

"He needs to know and it's better for him to hear it from you."

Entering the emergency room, we headed right for the front desk. Trace asked, "Liam McKenzie was just brought in. Can you tell us how he's doing?"

"Are you family?"

I answered. "No."

"I'm sorry, but I can't share patient information with you. If you have a seat, maybe the doctor will share more with you." That particular hospital policy sucked in my opinion.

Trace and I weren't seated for long when the doors opened and a woman entered. It took me a minute to place her, but she was the same woman who had called me out from the kitchen at Clover. Like then, she was dressed to the nines in some designer and she had an air about her that bespoke not only money but also power. Her eyes landed on me, recognition immediate, before she moved to the nurses' station. The conversation she had with the nurse was heated but after a few minutes the nurse called Trace and me over and shared what she wouldn't earlier.

"Mr. McKenzie was brought in for lacerations on his arms. Several were deep enough that he required stitches. The plastic surgeon was also called. The doctor will have more to share with you."

"But the wounds are not life threatening?"

"No."

"Thank God." Reaching for my phone, I left Rafe a message before turning my attention to the woman from Clover. "Thank you."

She nodded and at first I didn't know what to make of that. She had walked into the ER and cut through the bullshit and now she appeared almost aloof, until I saw the brightness of her eyes. She was holding back tears.

Suspicion replaced gratefulness because it wasn't a coincidence, her coming into Clover. Not with her being here now.

"Who are you?"

"Alexandra Titus, but my maiden name is Morton."

Trace knew what I didn't when he said, "You're Rafe's mom."

Shock hit first, Rafe's mom? But looking into her familiar hazel eyes, I couldn't believe I hadn't seen it.

"Yes, I'm his mother."

The fury came then, quick and fierce. Where the hell had she been? Rafe's father was taken from him at nine, he'd suffered through the foster system and all this time his mother had been close. What kind of woman treated her own flesh and blood that way? Before I could rip her a new one, she beat me to it.

"I know what you're thinking and you've every right to think it. I failed Rafe and his father."

"Why did you stay away? Rafe was in foster care, alone, young not understanding what was happening. He needed his mother then, why didn't you go to him, spare him all that unnecessary pain?"

"I didn't have a choice."

"There's always a choice."

"No, sometimes there isn't."

"Then why are you reaching out now?"

Her expression changed, a ruthlessness that was a surprise to see on someone so cultured and refined. "The game is changing."

I didn't understand what that meant, but she didn't let me pry her for information. "I won't ask you to keep this from Rafe, but please tell him that if I could have been with him, I would have been. And though I tried, I wished I could have done more."

She turned and walked out. Trace followed her. "I've a few questions for her. I'll be back." And then he too was gone.

And as much as I would like to be a fly on the wall for that conversation, my thoughts were on Rafe and Liam and how they were going to react when they learned that she had been here. I didn't have a long wait.

RAFE

Pushing through the doors of the emergency room, the moment my eyes landed on Avery, the wild thing that had been trying to claw out of my chest calmed. She was sitting with Trace, who looked about ready to break something. The last time he'd been here, it had been when Ember almost died. Her pregnancy had been a high-risk one; she nearly bled out and had landed in a coma for a few days. I understood how this place would not be his favorite and yet he was here, for me.

Avery saw me and immediately jumped up from her spot, walking to me even as I came to her. "He's okay. Complaining and bitching and flirting with the nurses."

I smiled, that sounded like Dad.

It wasn't even a conscious act when I pulled her to me. I needed to feel her, smell her and only then did the wild beast vanish completely.

"I want to see him." I said this as I stepped back from Avery in time to see worry move over her face. "Avery, what's wrong?"

"When we got here, the nurses wouldn't tell us anything because we weren't family."

Grinning, I tucked a lock of her hair that had fallen from her knot behind her ear. "Did you bat your lashes at the doctor?"

A sweet smile touched her lips but wasn't long lived. "No. A woman entered, the same woman who called me to her table at Clover."

It took me a minute to follow her story since she seemed to be jumping from subject to subject. "Small world, she's an administrator here?"

"No."

"I'm not following you, sweetheart."

Her face softened, for just a moment, and realizing it was my endearment that brought about that contented expression had me making a mental note to use endearments on her at least twenty times a day.

"Her name is Alexandra Morton-Titus."

And that quickly my mood changed as my body went numb with rage. "My mother was here?"

"Yes, she was the one to get the nurse to share with us what was going on. She told me she stayed away because she didn't have a choice, but now the game was changing and she wanted you to know that though she tried to be there for you, what little she did wasn't enough."

"Be there for me? When the fuck was she ever there for me?"

Trace closed in, knew he had done so because I rarely lost my temper but when I did it wasn't pretty. Thinking about the kid I had been, my father taken from me, ripped from my home, thrown in a place where life became a game of hiding from the bullies who took delight in rearranging my face on a weekly basis until I was old enough and strong enough to make them stop. My fury hit the danger zone because I had been left to fend for myself, had felt on more than one occasion the staggering sense that I was alone in the world. And she claimed she tried to be there for me? Bullshit.

Trace's focus had not left me. He placed himself in front of Avery, the idea that he thought he needed to protect her from me, had me seeing red even knowing he was right to do it. He braced, his legs parted, his hands at his sides, knew he was ready to take whatever I threw out. I honestly don't know what I would have done, but what happened next stopped me in my tracks. Avery moved, slipping between Trace and me even knowing the rage I felt could be seen on my face. There wasn't fear in her green eyes, only concern and tenderness, and then she touched her small hand to my cheek. It was the lightest of touches and yet in that moment I knew that all I'd been through, every tear, every bruise, and every broken bone had led me to this woman. My anger fled because I'd go through it all again just to see her looking at me as she was right now. The magnitude of that revelation had the words passing my lips without even a thought to hearing them back.

"I love you, Avery."

Her eyes widened, brightened before the first tear slipped down her cheek. Happiness shone on her face but so did relief. A hesitant, almost timid smile touched her lips as she unconsciously leaned into me. Her lips parted and in the softest voice she said, "It took you long enough."

For a moment there was dead silence as her words penetrated and then I laughed, the kind of laugh that breaks things loose inside, things you've held on to for far longer than you should have. And with that laugh the burden of my youth, that I hadn't even known I carried, slipped from my shoulders.

"Lexie was here?" And yet Dad didn't sound as surprised by that as I would have expected. He hadn't seen the woman in almost forty years and she shows up out of the blue. Had it been me, I'd be halfway down the hall on the prowl, looking for her. "Is she still here?"

"No, she left." Trace said before he added, "I had a word with her. She said it was a risk that she was even here at all, but she needed to know that you were okay."

Dad's face turned thunderous. "A risk? From whom, her fucking father?"

"She didn't go into detail."

"How did she even know Liam had been injured?" Avery asked, but it was Dad's expression that earned my full attention because he was looking anywhere, but at Avery. He knew something.

I wanted to press him for information, but I didn't want to put him on the spot. He wasn't volunteering the information, there was clearly a reason for that, so instead I answered Avery's question. "It would seem that she's been keeping tabs on him." I wasn't sure how I felt about that or taking that to the next logical place, her keeping tabs on me and yet still staying in the background. Was the cause of her distance the same reason it was a risk for her to come today?

Moving past that, I studied Dad's wrapped arm. "What happened?"

"I wasn't paying attention. It's not a big deal." And yet I had a feeling it was more of a big deal than he was letting on. A hunch confirmed when his gaze hit mine. He didn't want to discuss it now.

I acquiesced, but we'd be discussing this later. He understood when he exhaled before looking over at Avery. "Aren't you supposed to be working?"

"I was, but the hospital couldn't get in touch with Rafe so they called me since my number is in your phone."

"Jesus. I'm sorry, Avery."

"Stop it. You were injured. This is where I'm supposed to be."

A grin pulled at Dad's lips. "Now I'm starting to see some of that notorious red-headed temperament."

Avery's hands settled on her hips. "I'm as sweet as pie."

"I'm heading back. I'll arrange to have Avery's car returned to your house." Trace started from the room.

"Thanks, Trace."

He turned, his gaze moving from me to Avery, before his lips tipped up slightly. Dad asked as soon as Trace left, "What am I missing?"

Avery moved up next to me, pressing right up to my side. "Your son told me he loved me."

Dad's head jerked to me, his expression blank for a minute before he said, "It took you long enough."

She was sweet, Jesus her taste was like crack. Pushing my tongue into her mouth, I lifted her hips and moved deeper. Her arms held me close, her hips moved, the sounds coming from the back of her throat had me moving harder, my control slipping. Her mouth ripped from mine, her back arched as the orgasm moved through her, her body squeezing me bringing on my own release. And even just having her, it wasn't enough. I needed more, needed to possess her, wanted to claim her and when we'd burned ourselves out, I'd still want more. There was this warmth in my chest and I understood now that warmth was love. An emotion I never fully comprehended and never would have had had it not been for Avery. I never knew I'd been living only half a life because the best part of me was missing. And just when I thought I couldn't feel more for this woman.

"I love you, Rafe."

Pressing my mouth to hers, I ran my tongue along her lips, before pushing into her mouth. Threading my fingers into her hair, I held her steady as my mouth explored, tasted and devoured. Her hands on my chest lit a fire under my skin, the burn following her touch.

I tasted her tears and lifted my head; her eyes were overflowing. "What's this?"

Her cheeks flushed and her eyes lowered. "It's nothing."

Touching her chin, I forced her gaze back on me. "Avery?"

"I just never thought I'd be here. I never thought I'd find you, someone who knows all of my quirks and loves me because of them and not despite them."

And I did, I loved everything about her. I didn't need to tell her, she already knew, so instead I teased her. "I do, I love your ass."

"Now who's the goof?" Her smile faded a bit. "You seem to be handling the news about your mom in stride."

I wasn't handling it in stride; I just wasn't handling it. She gave birth to me, but she wasn't my mother. "I don't pretend to understand her life, but she isn't my mother. She made that choice. My only concern is Dad because despite everything, he still loves her. And whatever is happening now, I don't want to see him hurt again. Do I appreciate her stepping up? Sure, but it's too little too late for me."

"Maybe she had a good reason to stay away."

"Maybe. And maybe if I ever learn why, I'll feel differently, but I've lived my life without a mom. One small effort on her part doesn't change that."

"That's fair. I'd feel the same if my dad attempted to reach out now after being neglected for so long. But your mom, she had tears in her eyes, so I don't think it was just your dad carrying the torch. She said the game was changing. What do you think she meant by that?"

"I don't know."

"When she came into Clover, she'd been with a man that I didn't get the sense was her husband. I don't know why I got that vibe, but he seemed more guardian than husband. He got a call while I was at their table and they both hightailed it out of there. It was odd at the time, seems even stranger now. Knowing now who she is, do you think she knew of my connection to you?"

"Yes."

"The fact that she's there, that's she been watching, I think speaks volumes. And I get where you're coming from, but it's so sad that she was forced to be on the periphery of her family's lives. Your grandfather sounds like a real asshole."

Even angry she was adorable.

Rolling us so she was straddling my hips, I pulled her mouth to mine. "You're so fucking sweet."

"Shut up and kiss me."

"Yes ma'am."

chapter twenty—four

Avery

"Mom, aren't you heading to the West coast to see the Grand Canyon? That's always been a dream."

"Are you kidding? My daughter is in love. I want to meet this man."

"But Mom, seriously, it's like a bad sitcom. You can't show up here in your RV with your souvenir t-shits. It's mortifying."

"You're just going to need to deal, baby girl, because Harold and I are on our way. You tell that lovely Rafe we won't be any trouble."

"Right, except for the fact that he's going to have a small house parked in his driveway. Besides Nat's coming as is Jessica. Your visits are going to overlap and that's too many people for me to have parading around Rafe's home."

"It'll be fine, Harold and I can sleep in the RV. Oh, I can't wait to meet him in person."

I seriously needed to get her off the scent and so I threw my sister under the bus. "Have you heard about Nat and her new beau?"

"What? Nat has a beau?"

With luck she'd detour to Nat's first, which would give Rafe and me time to make our escape. "She does and he's wonderful. You really should meet him."

"I know what you're doing, Avery, and it isn't going to work. We're coming to see you first. You can expect us sometime early next week. How's the job?"

"Wonderful."

"That's what I want to hear." Her voice turned icy when she asked, "Have you heard from your father?"

"No."

"I just don't understand that man, not one bit."

"Nat wanted to buy me a new car when she was here. I wouldn't let her because I hadn't reached the place where she is, but I have reached that place. I understand why you and Dad aren't together, but we're his children. I don't understand how a man can treat his kids like that and even worse, have another child he'll end up ignoring. My heart goes out to that kid because Dolly will pay that child even less attention than Dad. It's not right."

"No, it's not."

"Anyway, I'll tell Nat you're coming and maybe we can stagger the visits a bit, but first I have to clear it all with Rafe."

"Good idea, but I'm sure he's as eager to meet us as we are to meet him."

I wasn't so sure that was true, but I didn't share my doubts with Mom. "Okay. I've got to get ready for work. I'll call you once I've spoken to Rafe and Nat."

"Can't wait to see you."

"Me too."

Returning home from work, my attention was immediately pulled to the back of the yard that, despite being dark, was lit up. Climbing from my car and grabbing my bag, I moved closer to see what Rafe was up to. There was a work light shining on the tree Loki and I often sat under, but it was the sight of Rafe tightening the bolt to the swing that had me feeling all gooey inside. Loki barked, which had Rafe turning in my direction.

He greeted me with a smile before he asked, "What do you think?"

"It's exquisite." And it was. It was a wooden porch swing that Rafe had stained a light cherry, but it was the design on the seat back that had my full attention—it was done in the shape of cupcakes.

"I know how much you and Loki like it back here, I thought this might be more comfortable than the bench."

"Cupcakes?"

He looked down, but not before I saw the grin that curved his lips. "It's for me too, I wanted a little piece of you outside."

I dropped my bag and launched myself at him. "I love it." Taking his face into my hands I added, "I love you."

He liked that based on how his mouth captured mine, showing me just how much he liked my words. Lust pitched his voice deeper. "Are you getting a shower now?"

Taking a shower with him? Absolutely. But first…"In a minute. First, I'd like to sit on this swing with you and then we'll get naked and wet."

"We?"

"As if I'll ever take another shower without you."

"As if I'd let you."

Settling on the swing, Loki dropped down next to us. "You're right, this is way more comfortable. This is the project you were working on for me, isn't it?"

"Yeah."

"It's perfect. And wait until the gardens are all done, we'll get to sit here and admire our work."

His arm came around my shoulders as I curled deeper into his side. I needed to tell him about my mom's visit, but instead I enjoyed the quiet of the evening with the man I loved. And it was because I was pressed up against his hard, muscular body, that contentment shifted to desire.

Jumping from the swing, I grabbed my bag and started for the carriage house, Loki on my heels. "Last one in the shower has to make dinner."

The words were barely out of my mouth when a strong arm wrapped around my waist and pulled me back against a hard chest. "I'll feed you, but let's work up an appetite first."

"I like the way your mind works."

Folding the chocolate into the whipped cream at work the following day, I thought about my meeting earlier with the sketch artist. He worked for the police department. We actually met at the station, before his shift started, and the experience was exactly like what I'd seen in movies. And when done, it was uncanny how accurately the artist had captured the man. Josh hadn't been able to join us, so the artist intended to fax the sketch to Josh after work. Hopefully the sketch would help with identifying the 'who' and the 'why' so this whole mess could be tied up before my family arrived.

And thinking of family had me thinking about the conversation I had had with Mom, specifically how I was ready to move on in regards to my dad. Harder to do than say, but I knew one way to help get the ball in motion. I needed a new car. I called Nat.

"If you tell me there's a fourth one, I swear to you I will plot your death for real."

"You're an idiot. No, I've decided it's time for a new car."

Her phone dropped; at least I'm pretty sure that's what caused the loud clanging noise in my ear. Once recovered, she asked, "Are you serious?"

"Yes, it's time."

"Shit, I have surgery in a half an hour."

"I'm working anyway."

"Oh no. We are striking while the iron is hot. Knowing you, you'll have a change of heart by the end of shift. I'll be on the road around three. You have a meal break, you're taking it at a car dealership."

"This can wait for a few days. We can do it during your visit."

"We are doing it today. And call Rafe. Another voice of reason to convince you out of purchasing the offspring of your sad-excuse for a car is wise."

"Calling you was a mistake."

"Mistake or not, it's done." Silence for a beat before she said, "I'm sorry you had to reach this point, but I'm glad I'll be there to help you through it."

Maybe this wasn't a mistake after all. "Love you, Nat."

"Love you. See you soon."

"That's flamboyant, I don't want that." As promised Nat showed up at Clover to steal me away to look at cars. When learning of our plans, Rafe immediately agreed to join us. Jessica was shopping with us too; Nat thought it couldn't hurt to have a third voice of reason, even though Jessica was not in person, but on the phone—parroting all of Nat's picks. Sometimes I wondered if they weren't the sisters.

"You can't go wrong with a Camaro, it's Bumblebee." Nat said, to which Jessica agreed fervently.

Rafe was clearly of a similarly mindset as Nat and Jess, but the car he had them bring around for me wasn't Bumblebee. A more fitting name would be Maleficent: all that power and beauty. A black, convertible Camaro with tan leather interior and all the bells and whistles pulled up and stopped just in front of me. It was ridiculously expensive and the most beautiful car I'd ever seen, but I wasn't spending that kind of money on a car. "I was thinking more along the lines of the Spark."

The disapproving groans were nearly in harmony, ruined when Jessica squawked through the phone. "What? The Spark. What is wrong with you? Are you inhaling the flour at work? You are, aren't you? Nat! Do not let her get the Spark."

Nat immediately chimed in, reiterating Jess practically word-for-word. Rafe, who'd been off to the side observing the dynamics, walked to me and draped his heavily muscled arm over my shoulders. I really liked his arm around my shoulders, liked that he was here, but more I liked that he didn't jump on the bandwagon, even knowing he felt the same about my car. Instead he was offering a silent sign of support. And then he said, "You've been driving around in, well, you know my feelings about your car. Live a little."

"Listen to Rafe, he's a very smart man." Jessica commented again, but she was practically licking her phone screen.

"You're just infatuated." I muttered.

"Doesn't take away from the fact that the man is right."

"You're teaming up on me." Walking to Nat, I handed her my phone. "I give up. You decide what I should get and come find me. I'm going in search of a cup of seven-hour old coffee. Maybe I'll land in the hospital."

I didn't get far; Rafe grabbed my hand and yanked me into his arms. Pulling his hands through my hair, he lifted it from my neck so he could press a kiss there. "What do you want? Whatever you want. I just want you happy."

Irritation dissolved, love replaced it. "I want to test drive the Spark."

Nat was not a gracious loser. "Fine, the Spark but that ride is not much better than your old car, I'm just saying."

"I've got to get Aidan down for a nap. See you next week. Hope your mom is still there when I get there. Bye!"

Oops, I hadn't shared the news with Rafe that mom was coming. "Your mom's coming?"

"In the RV and there is no stopping them. I tried, I truly did."

"I can't wait to meet her. Maybe we should hold off on the car and let her haggle the price."

I hadn't thought of that. "That's a good idea. She would love that."

"So are we test-driving the tin can?" Nat asked, still unwilling to concede defeat with style.

"Nay, there's time for a bite, let's go eat."

To which she replied, "This is a better plan."

Rafe didn't join us, he had to get back to finish up a dresser he was delivering in the morning. Before he left us though, he dragged me away from Nat so he could kiss me long and hard.

"I'll make you dinner. Do you have a preference?"

"Surprise me."

Naughty was the only word to describe the way his lips curved up. "Maybe in more ways than one."

And then he kissed me again; sweet and filled with promise before he waved to Nat. "See you next week."

"Later, handsome."

Rafe climbed into his truck, "She's almost as goofy as you. Have fun."

"Nat and me? Always."

Nat and I sat at the café just down the street from Clover. "He's crazy about you."

I got all warm and gooey inside. "He told me he loved me. I think I knew it already, but hearing those words from him. I found my Harold."

Her smile took up her whole face. "I know you have."

"What about you? How's Tyler?"

"Wonderful. He's so attentive and sweet. I think I've found my Harold too. And the body on that man makes me want to sin. My only complaint is he is so good about what he eats, I feel guilty when I'm shoveling a pint of ice cream into my face. I'd love it if he'd grab the spoon from me and indulge."

"You realize your only objection to your boyfriend is that he takes care of himself."

She flashed me a cheeky smile.

"He's still coming with you in a few days, right?"

"Yeah, he's looking forward to spending more time with you. Changing the subject, have you heard from Dad or the step monster since his attempt to squeeze a baby shower out of you?"

I snarled, didn't mean to, but couldn't help it. "Nope. Not one word. I imagine Dolly's pulling the injured party, the poor pregnant woman who isn't asking for much from Dad's selfish daughters. The really sad part, had she just asked me to my face I probably would have arranged it, but the way she went about it. No way."

"What I don't understand is how was the child conceived because I can't imagine Dad taking the time out of work to plant the seed."

"Oh my God, really Nat. You needed to put that image in my head."

"Yeah. Do you suppose she has a credit card reader on her..." Nat looked down at my lady parts. "...you know, payment before entry, like an amusement park ride? Canned moans too, like the pre-recorded ones for sitcoms. Oh yeah, baby; faster, harder, ride me, cowboy. Oh. Oh. Oh."

Putting my hands over my ears, I tried to hum the national anthem; I could still hear Nat imitating Dolly in orgasm. "I'm scarred, every time I use a credit card machine I'm going to think about Dolly's..."

"Her what?"

"Flower."

"Vagina."

"I need wine to numb my brain to this conversation, unfortunately I have to get back to work."

"It is so much fun teasing you."

"You better enjoy it, since you do it often enough."

She laughed out loud as she reached for the bill. "The perk of being the oldest and the one with the bigger brain."

My shift was over and I had just stepped outside when my cell rang. I couldn't help feeling disappointed seeing the unknown number because I had hoped it was Rafe. He'd been in my head all night, more particularly all the ways he intended to surprise me. My body throbbed at the thought; I had spent the night in a simmering state of arousal. Chocolate, cream, icing all took on new meaning when your body ached with a different kind of hunger. I was tempted to let the call go into voice mail—eager to get home so Rafe could do to me what he wanted—but found myself answering. Immediately a concerned voice came over the line.

"Avery? It's Tyler."

Exhaustion, and a lust-saturated brain, kept me from appreciating the oddity of Tyler calling me. "Hey, Tyler."

"Is Nat with you?"

I had been walking to my car, but that question stopped me in my tracks. "No, she left hours ago."

"She's not home and she's not answering her cell."

Dread, sharp and vicious, moved through me because Nat, for as scattered as she pretended, never took a detour without telling someone where she was going.

Tyler asked, "What time did she leave you?"

"Around five."

"She should have been back, even with hitting traffic."

"Her visiting me wasn't planned, maybe she needed to charge her car and…her cell died?" I didn't even believe my own words; Nat was religious about keeping her phone charged because she often was on-call at the hospital. "I'm getting in my car now. I'll backtrack. She likely took 9A."

"Okay. You're in Riverdale, right?"

"Yeah."

"I'll call the police, maybe they can send out a patrol car or get on the line with the State police."

"Good idea. She's fine, Tyler. Likely pissed as hell at her forgetfulness, so you'll want to have wine and ice cream at the ready."

He laughed, easing a bit of the tension in my gut. "Keep in touch, Avery."

"You too."

My hands shook as I pulled from Clover's parking lot, gripping the wheel I tried to calm down while wishing and hoping that I'd find Nat, in her car on the side of the road, yelling at herself for being so careless as to not charge her phone. I'd only gone a few miles on 9A, when I spotted her Tesla. Relief slammed into me as happy tears stung my eyes. Pulling over behind her, I hit the hazard lights and jumped from my car. She would not be living this down for a long time; I understood now why she loved ribbing me. It was a heady feeling. My smartass comment died on my lips because Nat wasn't in her car, but her phone and purse were. Everything sort of spun at that moment as I desperately tried to understand what my shocked brain was seeing. Had she left her car to seek out help? But why not take her phone?

"Nat!" Moving around the car, I walked along the road calling to her and with each step I took, the larger the hole became in my chest. I didn't know how much time passed when I returned to my car for my phone. There were several missed calls; I didn't look at any of them. I called Tyler.

"Anything?"

"I found her car."

"Oh, thank, God."

"Tyler, she isn't here, but her phone and purse are."

Dead silence for a several long beats. "Call 911. I'm on my way."

"Maybe you should stay there. We don't know what we're dealing with."

"Her purse and phone are in the car?" His voice broke a bit and knowing the kind of man he was, it had my own fear escalating because he was scared.

"We will get her back." I said as much for me as for him.

"Fucking yeah we will. I can't sit here. I'm coming to you."

I was glad for that. When we found Nat, she would want Tyler. "Do you have Rafe's address?"

"Yeah. Call the cops. I'll see you soon." He said and disconnected the call; I dialed 911.

chapter twenty—five

Avery

It had started to rain, my clothes were soaked to my skin and yet I stood on the side of the road watching the red and blue lights flashing, spinning around and around. Patriotic, police lights. I never noticed. The cops had asked me questions, standard questions like I'd heard on countless television shows. And I couldn't help feel as if I were in the middle of one as the unbelievable unfolded in front of me. They were processing Nat's car…Nat's car was being processed. The lump in my throat ached, but I refused to give in to the tears that demanded release because I knew once I started, I wouldn't be able to stop. There was damage to the bumpers on both the front and back of her car. The scenario the cops so callously painted was she'd been pinned, forced to stop and then taken from her car. They didn't go into detail on how she was taken—sparing me the gruesome—but it didn't take a genius to know she'd likely been held at gunpoint. Nat would never have unlocked her doors otherwise. And the idea of my sister having a gun aimed at her, my stomach squeezed, bile rose up my throat and I swallowed to keep it down.

Jax, the first cop to arrive on the scene, younger than his partner with kind brown eyes, held an umbrella over my head. He hadn't left my side since the detectives showed up and took over. "I'll take you home. My partner will drive your car."

I didn't object, couldn't image getting behind the wheel. "What happens now?"

"We try to get a match on the fingerprints we lifted."

"And if you can't?"

"There are cameras along the road." He said as he pointed to the small devices on the poles that lined the street. "We'll check those out, see if we get lucky. They took her and..."

My stomach squeezed again. "What?"

"She's not here."

"You mean her bod—" My voice broke on a sob.

"I'm sorry, I'm not trying to be insensitive, but they want her, which means you'll likely hear from them."

"Ransom?"

"Most likely." His voice turned even softer. "We'll find her."

And I knew he really meant it. Whether they did or didn't, his words comforted. "Let's get you home."

It wasn't until we were driving down Rafe's street that my shock-soaked brain realized I hadn't called Rafe. It was close to two in the morning, I should have been home hours ago. Those missed calls were likely from him and I hadn't called him back. Pulling along the curb, he was already coming down the drive—his long legs eating the distance between us.

He pulled me into his arms, his hold so tight it was almost painful. "Where the fuck have you been? I've been going out of my fucking mind."

"Someone took Nat." I whispered.

He's body jerked, like he'd just taken a blow. He pulled back, his face contorted with rage. "What?"

"Someone forced her to stop and took her from her car."

Rafe looked past me to Jax. "What's being done?"

"We're running the prints, we're checking the cameras. They took her, so they likely want something. The two detectives assigned to the case will be in touch." He shifted a bit before he added, "These two on the case, they'll want to rule everything else out before declaring it a kidnapping because once it's ruled a kidnapping, the Feds step in. They're hotshots, but they're good at their job."

"Kidnapping? You're thinking ransom?"

"Yeah."

Rafe put distance between us, and not just physically, and that felt like a knife to the heart. He started to pace, the dangerous energy rolling off him worried me that he'd act before he thought about the consequences.

"We have Avery's car." Jax said.

Rafe wordlessly moved to the gate and punched in the code before he returned to me and wrapped me in his arms.

And then those kind brown eyes were on me again. "We will find your sister." I couldn't respond because I feared the breakdown I was desperately trying to hold off. Understanding looked back at me as Jax waited for his partner to hand my keys to Rafe before they climbed into their patrol car and disappeared down the street.

"You're soaked." Rafe whispered as he pulled me closer to offer the heat of his body.

"They took her."

His body stiffened against mine and yet his voice was soft and reassuring when he said, "Let's get you warm."

I wanted to protest because Nat might not be warm; she might be soaked to the skin too, cold and terrified. But getting sick wasn't going to help my sister. A car pulled up to the curb and Tyler jumped out. Rafe's hold on me tightened.

Tyler didn't waste time on pleasantries; I didn't blame him. "Have they found her?" He looked awful; worry lines were etched over his face.

"No, not yet. Tyler this is Rafe, Rafe this is Nat's boyfriend, Tyler."

"I'm sorry, man." Rafe sounded as if it was his fault that Nat had been taken.

"What's being done?"

Rafe answered. "The cops are running the prints from the car and checking cameras along the stretch of road where Nat's car was found."

"I'm not leaving until we find her."

I agreed. "No, yeah, you should stay. Take the carriage house."

"Yeah, okay." He looked at his watch; I think he was in shock. "I should alert the hospital, get her surgeries canceled. And we have dinner reservations tomorrow…I guess it would be tonight now. I'll have to call the restaurant, dry cleaning, she actually got some clothes dry cleaned for her visit with you." And then he cracked. "Fucking hell, she's alone, she's scared and I'm not there."

I choked back the sob and pulled strength from way down deep. I wrapped my arms around him. "The cops believe we'll be getting a ransom call. They need her alive, so hold on to that Tyler. She's alive and we will find her. It's too late to do anything. We'll show you to the carriage house. Try to sleep."

He squeezed me before he stepped back. "I won't be able to sleep, but thanks for the place to crash."

"Avery, why don't you take Tyler the carriage house and I'll move his car." Tyler handed Rafe his keys before he followed me up the drive.

Once Tyler was settled, I found Rafe waiting for me outside.

"I'm sorry I didn't call. It was all…"

"Don't." The harshness of that one word cut. And though he held me tighter, I felt the distance between us growing. We said nothing else, not when we reached the bathroom and he started removing my clothes, when he turned on the shower, when he joined me—fully clothed—or when he dried me and wrapped me in his robe.

He led me to his bed and lowered the covers.

"I won't be able to sleep." And even as I said that, my eyes felt heavy as my body crashed, the magnitude of the evening hitting me in horrifying clarity.

He settled on the edge of the bed and though he didn't touch me, even as I ached to feel his strong arms around me, I still felt tremendously comforted. I fell asleep with him silently watching over me.

I didn't know what jarred me from sleep. Glancing at the clock it was almost seven in the morning. Climbing from bed, the hum of voices lured me toward the kitchen until I heard Rafe and my feet just stopped. He was beyond fury and rage, his voice so cold and detached.

"Even if I have to put a fucking gun to his head."

Another voice, his father. "That's not the answer."

"You didn't see Avery last night." His voice cracked, his next words a harsh whisper. "You didn't see her. They have her sister, they fucking took her sister."

"We don't know that. Did Avery sit with the sketch artist?"

"Yeah, Josh hasn't gotten the sketch yet, the guy got sidetracked. He's sending it over now. We need to talk to Morton. That fucking prick is behind this or knows who is."

My legs went weak, my hand reaching out to keep my balance. Shock had kept me from connecting the dots last night. My legs were unsteady as I made my way back to Rafe's room and reached for my phone.

I called Jax and didn't let him speak before asking, "Do you have anything new?"

"No. When we do, you'll be the first person I call. The detectives are running the scenarios. It hasn't been ruled a kidnapping yet, but they're leaning that way, which means they'll be camped out in your house until this is over. Hang in there, we will find her."

After updating me on what they were doing, he ended the call but not before promising to call with updates.

"Avery?"

Rafe stood in the doorway. He looked terrible; when he realized I was crying, he looked gutted.

"They took Nat for the disc?"

His jaw clenched, the battle he fought for control over his rage was very easy to see. "I think so."

"So they'll call."

"Yes."

"Why haven't they?"

"I don't know. I will get your sister back, Avery. I swear to God, I will get her back."

"This isn't your fault. You know that, right?"

Stricken was how he looked now because he didn't agree with me. "Rafe, you are not responsible for this."

He lost the battle, as his fury erupted like a geyser. "Your sister was taken, likely held at gunpoint, alone, terrified and with no idea what was happening or why and all because some fucks want something from me. And every time I think of yesterday and the banter between the two of you over a car, and someone took that moment and twisted it into a fucking nightmare. You were both pulled into Hell because of shit in my world. The fuck I am not responsible."

"You can't do that to yourself."

"You are the most vivacious, feisty, brilliant light I've ever known. Your energy and thirst for life damn near blinds a person and last night that light was gone. My shit did that to you." In a pained whisper, he added, "I'm so fucking sorry."

And then he was gone; the sound of the back door slamming closed followed shortly after. *I* followed after him, but was sidetracked seeing Tyler pacing the driveway, his phone to his ear. He saw me, held up a finger and finished his call. He disconnected as he walked over to me.

"All of Nat's surgeries have been canceled. I feel so fucking useless."

"There's nothing we can do. We just have to wait."

"The cops called me. Not even sure how they got my number, but they want me to look at some mugshots to see if anyone looks familiar, if I remember any of them around Nat. They're grabbing at straws, but at least I'm doing something."

I reached for Tyler's hand, his immediately closed tightly around mine. "We will get her back."

"She's a tough cookie, your sister, but she has got to be terrified. I can't stand the thought of her alone and afraid and I'm unable to go to her."

"You're here and when we get her back, you are the one she'll want comforting her."

"If something happens here, call me."

"I will and you do the same."

He nodded and walked to his car. He was determined to do what he could and I loved that. I also loved that he was here, that he dropped everything for the woman he loved.

Rafe stood on the other side of the living room. Shortly after his eruption, Trace and Lucien arrived along with Josh. They were strategizing and though I didn't know the details of their plan, they were at least forming one. Rafe hadn't spoken to me since that moment in his room. It broke my heart that he was carrying a burden he had no business carrying, but I also knew trying to talk reason into him when his temper was up would be completely pointless.

Having to tell Mom about Nat had been hard, but my mom didn't freak out. She asked questions, wanted to know what was happening, even demanded Jax's number so she could pepper him with questions. She and Harold would be arriving any minute.

Ember, Darcy and the gang arrived a short time ago. The counters in the kitchen were suddenly loaded with trays of food; those big coffeemakers ran along the one wall, paper cups, creamers and sugar next to them. Bizarre how in times of crisis people brought food. Logically, I understood the reasoning behind it, but eating was the last thing on my mind.

I could panic, felt a good attack coming on, but that wouldn't help Nat, so I sat there staring at the wall.

The sound of a familiar horn had the tears that were brimming my eyes, rolling down my cheeks. Mom was here. Jumping up from my spot, I ran out the door and down the drive just as they were parking. I reached her side; she jumped out and pulled me into a hug.

"She's going to be okay." And that was Mom, strong and solid.

Sobs that I had held in for hours, burst out of me now that my mom was here. She held me closer. Harold wrapped us both in his arms, and there we stayed for a long time. When we finally disengaged, Rafe was there. And if I thought he looked broken before, he was now shattered.

Mom being mom pulled him in and held him close. "I wish we were meeting under better circumstances, but it's wonderful to finally meet you."

Rafe's arms moved around her, his eyes closed and a single tear rolled down his cheek. "I'm so fucking sorry."

Seeing big, strong Rafe cry had a sob ripping from my throat even as Mom held him closer. But it was Harold who pulled us back from our emotional brink. "We don't know everything, but we know enough. This isn't your fault, son, and putting that on yourself is foolish and unproductive. We'll get her back and we'll do it together." Harold could always be counted on to be the voice of reason. "Let's get inside and then you can fill us in."

Introductions were made before Mom, Harold and I settled in the living room.

"Now tell us exactly what happened." Harold asked.

"I called Nat and mentioned I was thinking about getting a new car. She came right away, you know how long she's wanted me to do just that."

Both nodded, I continued.

"We went to the dealership and after, Nat and I went to lunch at a café just down the street from Clover." And it was while replaying the events from yesterday, that I remembered the odd sensation of being watched that day a few weeks back and in that same very café.

"Oh my God." My tears fell harder."

"What?" Mom asked.

"A couple weeks ago, I had the weird feeling that I was being watched while in that café. It freaked me out at the time, but I didn't experience it again so I forgot all about it. But I took Nat there. Maybe they saw us together, realized who she was. If we had gone somewhere else, maybe they wouldn't have taken her. It's my fault."

Rafe grabbed me, pulled me from the sofa, trapping me against his chest. "Don't you fucking put that on yourself. You didn't do anything. If they were watching even then, they already knew about your sister. I should have taken the threat more seriously. The blame falls solely on me, not you."

It was Mom who spoke and she sounded fierce, fiercer than I'd ever heard her sound. "And don't you put that shit on you, Rafe McKenzie. Do you understand? I will not have you blaming yourself for any of this."

God, I loved my mom. Rafe didn't let me go, but his muscles loosened, his expression conflicted when he said, "Yes, ma'am."

"Now, if I understand this correctly, you think Nat might have been taken because somebody wants something they think you have?" Mom asked.

"Yeah, that's exactly what I think."

"So why haven't they called to make their demand?" Mom asked exactly what I had.

Rafe replied to her as he had to me. "I don't know."

"Tyler's here too."

Mom's focus turned to me. "He is?"

"He's at the station. The cops wanted him to look at pictures."

"Whoever took Nat, it sounds as if they were not a part of Nat's world." Mom wasn't wrong.

"The cops are apparently working several angles."

Ember appeared. "Can I get you coffee?"

"I'll come with you, I need to keep busy." Before she followed Ember into the kitchen, she reached for Rafe's hand and squeezed it. Rafe released me, but it was how he did it, like he was letting me go, that had me grabbing his hand. "Mom's right."

"It was my job to keep you safe and by extension your sister. I failed."

He pulled from me and walked away.

"Come sit, Avery." Harold said and feeling nothing but numb, I did as he asked.

"He's hurting, kid. A man like that, something like this happening on his watch, he needs time."

"It isn't his fault."

"It is to him. You've got to respect how he feels and let him deal with it how he needs to."

I didn't agree with Rafe putting this on himself, but I respected and loved him, so I'd give him the time he needed. "Okay."

Harold pulled me closer and there we sat, waiting for the call I feared receiving and feared even more not receiving.

It was over an hour later, when the call finally came and on Rafe's house number. Any doubts that Nat's kidnapping was tied to the stuff with Liam evaporated. Unlike the detectives who were still running the scenarios, Josh played the odds and had set up a recording device on the line. Rafe put the call on speaker.

"I believe I have your attention."

Mom's hand grabbed mine hearing that sinister voice.

"Where's Natalie?" Rafe demanded.

"She's here. Unharmed. She'll stay that way if you bring me the disc. It is in that house and I want it."

"How do you know the disc is here?"

"A reliable source." Though he sounded even more ominous mentioning his reliable source. "You have twenty-four hours. Call me at this number when you've found it. I know you've involved the cops, but you come alone or she dies."

Josh whispered to Rafe. "We need proof of life. Get Natalie on the phone." Mom gasped, I held her hand tighter.

"I want to talk to Natalie."

"I thought you would."

Nat's voice came over the line. I had never heard her sound as she did. Mom's breath caught as her tears fell harder. "I'm okay. He too—

Natalie cried out as she was abruptly pulled off the line. I jumped up from my spot on the sofa. "You're going to die for this, you bastard."

"Ah, Avery." Chills moved through me hearing him say my name. "Use that anger and find me what I want. The clock is ticking."

The line went dead.

"What's the plan?" Mom demanded, which immediately had everyone talking at once. I left, walked out of the room and right outside. I couldn't get the sound of her voice out of my head. My wacky sister who feared nothing was terrified.

"I'll get her back."

Turning to Rafe, he stood just out of my reach—the distance intentional. And the warmth I had grown so accustomed to, no longer shone in his eyes. And even understanding why he was acting as he was, I resented him for pulling away from me when I needed him the most.

"What are you going to do?"

"I'm going to see my grandfather. Trace will stay here."

"Why? I'd rather him and the others having your back. If someone needs to stay let it be Josh. We need someone to liaise with the cops and Mom and I are not up to the task."

"Are you sure?"

"Yeah." I sensed he wanted to say more, but he didn't.

There was so much *I* wanted to say to him, but since no one else had penetrated his thick skull, I didn't hold out much hope I'd be any more successful. And I hated the distance that existed between us, but breaking down that wall wasn't going to happen until Nat's return.

"Be careful." I whispered.

He made a move toward me, but stopped himself. "I'll bring her home." And then he turned and walked away.

I walked inside shortly after Rafe; Harold was standing toe-to-toe with him. "I'm coming with you."

"Maybe you should stay here."

"No, that's my daughter. I'm coming."

My heart warmed, even as tears filled my eyes, hearing him say that because he was our father—the best one there was. I moved right into him and wrapped him in my arms. "I love you, Harold."

He held me tight. "We'll get her back."

"I know you will."

We watched as the men filed out of the room and hysteria edged my words. "We have to find that disc."

Ember spoke from the doorway. "I'll take the dining room."

"I've got the kitchen," Darcy said.

Josh pulled out his cell. "I'll call the detectives and then I'll take the living room."

Looking at Mom, she said, "We'll take the upstairs."

RAFE

"What's the plan?" Trace asked as we made our way into the building that housed the headquarters for Morton Shipping. And I was thankful for the question because thinking about Avery—the look of her last night and this morning, the heartache and despair—was like a knife to the heart. My shit had done that to her.

"What, punching the fucker in the face isn't an option?" Dad asked.

"Not if we need answers." Trace replied.

My cell went off, glancing at the screen it was Josh. "What do you have?"

"I just got the sketch and you aren't going to believe it. It's Nicholas Titus, your mom's husband."

I stopped walking and put the phone on speaker. "I'm listening."

"I've been looking into Morton Shipping and when it was formed there were three initial investors, Morton, Titus and a man by the name of Dominic Bennett. From what I've learned he was the one to persuade those in power to see things in the way that benefited Morton Shipping. In other words, he was the muscle, a real hothead.

Not long after the company started turning a profit, Dominic Bennett turned up dead."

"Shit."

"Yeah. Morton is retiring and before he does, he's taking the company public, which he stands to gain a load of money. As does Titus."

"What are you thinking?"

I think it was either Morton or Titus who took out Dominic and I would guess the idea of that leaking right when the company is about to bring in a shitload of money is making the killer very nervous. That disc, I'm guessing, points to the killer."

Fuck. And that killer, or one of his goons, now had Natalie.

"The house is swarming with cops, I have yet to share this with them since they'll go all in. I'm not getting the sense subtlety is big with the two detectives on point."

"Keep it to yourself a bit longer, at least until we're done with Morton."

He sounded almost jovial when he said, "Considering how late to the game these detectives are, stringing them along will be my pleasure."

Brynn Morton was not at all what I was expecting. The powerhouse I thought we'd be confronting was instead a man of average height and build. His dark hair had long ago gone gray and his hazel eyes had circles under them. He looked tired, jaundice and it was clear to me he was dying.

Dad was on point because he had waited a long time to come face-to-face with this man. And even with death knocking at his door, the man was still a prick.

"Liam McKenzie. I didn't expect to see you scratching at my door again."

Dad strolled into the man's office; dropping down in one of the leather chairs across from him and kicked his feet up on the antique walnut desk.

"You know, you will have to atone for your sins when you die and from the look of you, that's not far off."

Hatred stared back at Dad; he didn't even flinch.

"I heard you're taking the company public. Do you hear that, Rafe? Maybe you and your friends should grab a piece of that pie. Keep the company in the family, so to speak."

"Never." Brynn hissed, the action bringing on a coughing fit.

"Publicly traded, you don't really have a say." Lucien said and pulled out his phone. "I've got to get my guy on that."

"What the hell do you want?" Brynn snarled before he broke out into another coughing fit.

"Well, I want to hear from the horse's mouth why you set me up to go to prison but before we get to that, what do you know about Dominic Bennett?"

Fear flashed across the old man's face, quick but definite. "Nothing."

"Really, so the fact that he was your partner, you've forgotten that? He's dead, by the way. Has been for a really long time. What I didn't know, walking in here, was which of you killed him."

Brynn paled. Dad didn't even take a breath.

"Here's my theory. You're an arrogant son of a bitch who used your own daughter to form a relationship with Nicholas Titus, a financial genius. A man who, after marrying your daughter, has been heading up your financial interests. You brought on another man, to help pave the way for your company. His methods were likely illegal, which makes Dominic showing up dead not a real big surprise. You don't need those skeletons in your closet. One of you killed him and the other knew about it. Now the company is going public and having that kind of secret hanging over your head, especially when you stand to make a hell of a lot of money, would break a weaker man. Since you're dying, I'm guessing Titus killed Dominic. If you had, your secret would have gone with you to the grave. You were keeping Titus on a leash by holding the evidence of his crime over his head with that disc. So my question, what happened to the disc? How'd you fumble that so badly, holding all the power in your hands and letting it slip through your fingers? Your daughter is a hell of lot smarter than you gave her credit for."

Alexandra? Shit, yeah…that made sense. And by the way Brynn jerked, he knew it had been her too.

"You need to leave my office."

Dad stood and leaned over the desk, getting right into dear ole granddad's face. "Either way, you're going to be dead soon, but I want you to die with the knowledge that it was by your own daughter's hand that your company, you sacrificed everything for, slipped through your fingers. I hope like hell there is an ever after, so you can spend yours rolling in your grave you fucking motherfucker."

"I think we're done here." I said and started for the door. Waiting for Dad in the hall, I asked, "How'd that feel?"

"Really fucking good."

"So Alexandra took the disc."

"Yeah, it's the only thing that makes sense. Lexie steals the disc and sends it to you. That's fucking poetic justice. So where the hell is it?" Dad's voice turned hard, "And why the fuck didn't she give us a heads up? Even now, she has to know what's going on, so where the fuck is she?"

I'd been thinking that myself and I hated that Dad was seeing the woman he loved in a different light. But the truth was if she loved us at all, she wouldn't have put us in this situation. We were pawns to her, just like she'd been with her Dad. "I'm sorry, Dad."

"No, I'm sorry. I've had Lexie on a pedestal a long time, didn't want to believe she didn't deserve being there." I hated seeing the pain that moved over his face, followed quickly with profound disappointment. And then his focus fixed on me. "Don't push Avery away. She needs you to pull her in and hold her close."

"If something happens to Nat, she won't want me anywhere near her."

"If something happens to Nat, she'll need you right at her side. Don't be like me, a victim of circumstance. Fight for her, even if she's the one putting up the fight. There's love there and only a fool walks away from that. My son is no fool. Now let's go find that fucking disc."

Avery

We searched the entire house and nothing. Outside of ripping the wainscoting from the walls and tearing up the floors there was nowhere left to search. Sitting in the living room, my focus on the wall, my heart pounded in my chest because we were running out of time. The detectives had come and gone, two cops stayed back to handle any additional demands should they come. Jax had called; he was working another angle for the detectives. And the detectives, they were insistent on handling the drop, even though we didn't have what Nat's kidnapper wanted. They wanted to fake it, give him a phony disc. They wouldn't listen to reason, didn't heed the kidnapper when he'd said no cops. I wasn't risking Nat's life, so time wasn't my only enemy; I had to find the damn disc, and soon before the cops fumbled this. The two who remained were currently in the kitchen eating through the platters, their distraction worked in our favor.

"It has got to be here." Ember paced and bit her nails. "We've looked everywhere on this property though."

We had, every nook and nothing. My gaze settled on the clock, the perfect clock for a woodworker. The minutes ticking by, mocking me. And it was while I stared at the clock my focus shifted to the face. The whole clock was made of exotic wood in asymmetrical patterns, but the face was round with arts and craft style numbers: a nice round face that was roughly the size of a DVD. Rafe had mentioned his friend sent him that, a gift when he moved in. Standing up, I started across the room.

"The face on this clock, it's about the size of DVD wouldn't you say?"

"Yeah, why?" Mom asked clearly confused.

"Rafe said this was a gift. Sent to him when he moved in." I took the clock from the wall and turned it over. "I need a little Phillips head screwdriver."

Darcy started from the room, "On it."

My hands were shaking by the time Darcy returned with the screwdriver, so it took me a bit longer to unscrew the back, but when I pulled it off, staring back at me was a disc in a white sleeve.

"You found it! Holy shit." Ember whispered.

"We need to make a copy." Josh said.

"Can you?" I asked.

"Yeah, I have equipment at my office."

Ember asked, "Should we call the guys."

"There isn't time for that." I said as I handed the disc to Josh.

"The cops?" She added.

"You heard Nat's captor, no cops."

"Who do you suppose sent this?" Darcy asked.

"I don't know, but I'm making the call."

"I think Ember's right. We should wait for the guys or tell the cops, that's why they're here. I'm all for damsels doing the rescuing, no offense Josh, but you have no idea what you're walking into."

"Yeah, and he has my sister. I'm not waiting."

Reaching for my phone, I pulled up the number on Rafe's phone and dialed it. The man answered immediately "I hope for your sister's sake you have what I want."

Moving to the bedroom, I said, "I've got it."

Surprise edged his next words. "You do?"

"Yeah."

"Okay, meet me at Steeplechase pier by Coney Island in an hour. Do not bring the cops."

Cruel that the place I spent the best day of my life could be the place that turns into the worst of my life. "Make it two, I need to slip by the cops and it takes an hour to get there."

"Two hours. Don't be late."

My hands were shaking, the reality of what was happening finally hitting me. What the hell was I doing?

"Now what?" Darcy asked.

"I slip out the front door."

"We." Josh said at the same time Ember and Darcy did. And as much as I loved that Ember and Darcy wanted to help, there was no way they were coming.

"No. You have children and your husbands would hate me for life if something happened to you. I'll be fine."

"I'm coming with you."

"Mom, no."

"Avery, I'm not asking."

"I don't like this." Ember said.

"We're meeting at the Steeplechase pier. Tell the guys when they get here and they can come riding to the rescue, but I'm going to get my sister."

"He's going to be pissed, you do know that right?" Ember asked.

"I'm not waiting. Call Tyler." I jotted down his number. "He needs to know what's happening."

"Okay." Darcy said before she hugged me hard. "Come back with your sister and in one piece."

"I will."

Ember pulled me close. "Please don't be a hero."

"What car are you going to take? Yours is blocked in by the cop car." Darcy asked.

"The guys took the one we came over in." Ember added.

And Rafe's keys were in the kitchen with the cops.

"We'll take my ride." Mom said. "What? It's the only wheels we have."

"Damsels riding to the rescue in an RV, that's a first." Darcy said, and if I weren't sick with worry, I would have seriously found the situation hysterical.

RAFE

Pulling onto my street, the first thing I noticed was the RV was gone. "Where the fuck is the RV?"

"You don't think—"

I didn't let Lucien finish. "Yeah, I absolutely do think. Goddamn it."

Double parking in front of my drive, I jumped from the car...the back door slamming in my wake.

"Tell me she did not leave this house."

Ember and Darcy were in the kitchen looking nervous and worried. Two cops were with them looking frustrated and annoyed.

One of the cops said, "About an hour ago. These two aren't talking."

"Son of a bitch."

Trace spoke up from behind me. "Baby, did she find the disc?"

"She did, in the clock in the living room. Uncle Josh went with her, they stopped at his office to make a copy."

"Where are they meeting?" Trace pressed, she looked conflicted. "Ember, where are they going?"

"He said no cops."

"Ember."

"Tell him." Darcy encouraged. "Or I will."

"Steeplechase pier. They're meeting in..." Ember glanced at the clock on the stove, "forty minutes."

"Anna?" Harold asked.

"She went too."

"In the RV?" I asked for clarification, but bright side, it'd be easy to find them in the RV.

"Yeah."

I was already halfway down the drive by the time the others caught up.

Avery

"Thank you for coming." Josh sat at the table in the back of the RV, next to Mom as I drove.

"As if I'd let you go alone, especially since the disc is corrupt."

"How do you think this will work?" Mom asked Josh.

"Honestly, I think he's going to take the disc and then put a bullet in Avery's brain. I'm being blunt because you are walking into danger and candy coating that is only going to get you killed."

Crazy to think all that went into finding the disc and it's useless. "We have to try." I said.

"Yeah, but we have to be smart about it. As much as this thing is an attention getter, it may work in our favor."

"How?"

"He thinks you're coming alone. We can hide in here, you tell him the disc is in the RV. He's got to expect you'll be parking in the lot by the pier. It's late in the season; the park closes at six so there won't be many people around. If we can lure him over, we might be able to surprise him; maybe we get a few seconds to get his gun away, if nothing else we buy seconds for all of us to get away. Is there a back way out of here?"

"Yeah, the window in the bedroom's big enough to slip out of." Mom supplied.

"All right, let's get armed with anything we can use as a weapon."

I had never in my life been as afraid as I was while walking toward the pier. I knew Mom and Josh were close, believed Rafe was on his way, Tyler too, and yet as I walked to meet the unknown, I felt very much alone. And it was because I felt that staggering feeling of terror and isolation that I kept walking because my sister had to be petrified. And she'd been alone with her captor for hours.

It was cold, colder here near the pier. Nat had only been wearing a sweater when I'd last seen her. Was it really only just yesterday that she'd been teasing me; she had to be freezing. I hadn't even thought of that. I should have. What if Nat's captor wouldn't come with me to the parking lot? What if he killed Nat and me and searched the RV on his own? Now that I was here, I realized how stupid I had been because I was walking into the viper's den with nothing more than the clothes on my back and an excuse.

As I reached the pier, I saw Nat. She looked okay which immediately had the knot in my stomach easing. A man stood next to her and as I approached I recognized him. It was the man who had seen me home that one night at Allegro after I'd had too much to drink, Marco.

"You?" At first asked in disbelief, but as the reality finally sank in I said it again in a snarl. "You! It wasn't a coincidence us meeting at Allegro, was it? You were the one breaking into Rafe's house."

"Until the codes changed, then I needed a new way to gain access."

Another man stood in the shadows and yet somehow I knew he was the mastermind behind this. As soon as he stepped into the light, I recognized him too. He was the man at the café that day with Melody.

"Avery Collins. I'm Nicholas Titus. It's very nice to meet you. I've enjoyed my time with your sister, a delightful creature. I'd hate to have to put a bullet in her brain. Have you got the item?"

"Yeah, it's in my car."

Nicholas moved as gracefully as he had that day in the café, so the backhanded smack across my cheek completely took me by surprise as I stumbled backwards a few steps. "You're lying to me."

My cheek stung like it was on fire, but instead of feeling terror, anger stirred. Reaching for my phone, I pulled up the picture of the disc that Josh insisted I take. "Look! Proof. I have it."

He took my phone and studied it for a minute, before a creepy smile spread over his face. "Take me to it."

"Let Nat go and I will."

"You're making demands?"

"I'll take Nat's place. Let her go. She isn't a part of this."

"Why don't I just shoot you and your sister and retrieve it myself?"

"You don't know what car or where it's parked. Look, there are others coming for me. You think Rafe is seriously going to sit back while I walk into danger. Let her go and I'll take you to it. You'll be gone before they ever get here."

He seemed to study his options for a minute before he said, "Very well."

"No! Avery, don't go with them."

"I have to Nat." I pulled off the jacket I was wearing. "Can I give this to her?"

"Check it." Nicholas demanded of Marco.

Marco grabbed it from me. "It's clean."

Nicholas' head jerked and I didn't waste time moving to Nat to hug her hard. Whispering I said, "Mom is close, so it Tyler. Take my phone; call Rafe, tell him about Nicholas."

"Let's go." Nicholas was losing his patience. I released Nat. "Run. Get to safety. I'll see you soon, I promise."

God how I hoped that was a promise I could keep. Nat hesitated, conflicted with the idea of leaving me, but she needed to get to safety, needed to get in touch with Rafe. Seeming to understand that too, she ran. And as I watched her go, profound relief filled me because whatever happened now, Nat would be okay.

We'd started down the pier toward the parking lot; Marco walked close to the railing with me in front of him and his gun digging into my back. I tried to walk as slowly as I could to give Nat more time. Peering over the railing, the drop wasn't so bad. Maybe I could make a break for it and jump.

Marco's voice jarred me back. "Where did you find the disc?"

Couldn't hurt to share and talking might distract them so they wouldn't hear when Rafe and the others arrive. "Behind the face of the clock in the living room."

"Fuck me." Marco mumbled, but it was Nicholas's tone that sent a chill through me.

"And how is it that this woman finds the disc in just a few hours and you, a professional, had weeks collecting my money and came up empty-handed?"

Marco tensed, his gun easing at my back. "She had full access with no limitations, I had pockets of time in which to search. It's a big fucking house."

"And still." Marco was scary; Nicholas was downright terrifying. The man was as cold as ice. "The others who came back empty-handed got a bullet in the head for their efforts."

Marco picking up on the deadly undercurrent, stopped walking, yanking me in front of him, but he leveled his gun on Nicholas. "Are you threatening me?"

"I'm merely saying that when I pay for a service I expect results."

"Yeah, well maybe if you'd been smarter you wouldn't be scrambling at the last minute looking for the evidence that linked you to murder, charges they can pile onto the list the authorities already have."

Nicholas flinched. What the hell was Marco talking about?

"Yeah, I know about the pending arrest warrant, brought down and by your own wife too. Not too fucking smart, are you?"

Holy shit. Alexandra's comment at the hospital about the game changing made sense now. She was courageous, taking on Nicholas and winning. I hoped I lived through this to share that news with Rafe and Liam.

Under the cold façade, Nicholas was cracking; his eyes were all crazy. And as Nicholas and Marco had their standoff, I caught a movement further down the pier. People were coming, heading in our direction. Hope died as quickly as it flared because when I turned my attention back on Nicholas, he had a gun aimed at Marco. They were going to kill each other and me in the process and even as my survival instinct kicked in, Marco's hold was unyielding using me now as a shield.

"You're going to shoot me? I'll kill her and you'll never get your disc."

I heard a strange popping sound, the stirring of the air near my face, and in a terrifying moment of clarity I realized Nicholas had shot Marco. The pier railing was right behind us, and the momentum of the bullet caused Marco's body to fly backwards. Since he had a death grip on me, when he went over the side of the pier, I went with him.

I landed in a jarring heap, I may even have lost consciousness for a second or two, but I was alive. I tried to move, to get away, and then all hell broke loose.

RAFE

My phone rang, seeing it was Avery nearly had me crashing the car. "Avery!"

"It's Nat."

"Thank Christ. Where's Avery? Where are you?"

"The pier. Tyler found me. We're following Avery. They have her."

Fear, even with all the rage burning through me, the fucking fear nearly choked me "Who's they?"

"Some goon named Marco and his boss, Nicholas Titus."

Marco? Why the hell did that name sound familiar? "You've got eyes on her?"

"Yeah, Marco has her, a gun at her back. Wait, they've stopped; looks like Marco and Nicholas are exchanging heated words. Oh shit, you need to hurry."

"Did you call the police?"

But she didn't answer because the line went dead. We were just pulling up beside the RV.

"I'll check the RV." Lucien called as Trace went in search of Nat and Tyler, but I was already running to the pier. I didn't immediately take in the whole scene, since my focus was on Avery and the two gun-wielding assholes with her.

It happened so fast, a gunshot fired and one second Avery was standing on the pier and the next her body was being dragged over the side. More shots were fired, but I was running to Avery, didn't give a fuck if I got shot. Dropping at her side, I saw her eyes were open.

Relief hit me like a fucking punch in the gut. It wasn't that high of a fall, but she could have landed funny and cracked her neck. "Does it hurt?"

"Rafe. Where's Nat?"

Looking around I saw Nat and Tyler with Anna and Harold. The cops were swarming, setting up a barricade, not that they'd be able to hold the four of them for long. "She's fine. She's with your parents and Tyler. The cops are detaining them."

"Thank God." She looked past me to the pier. "I went over the side." And then she giggled. "Even with my ass."

She was clearly in shock. "What hurts?"

"My arm."

More sirens came from the parking lot.

Her eyes shifted to me and in them I saw heartbreak. "You pulled away from me. Why did you pull away from me?"

I answered honestly. "You lost your sparkle and I did that to you."

Her temper stirred and I preferred that to the haunted look she'd had a moment before. "No you didn't. None of this was your fault or your dad's and it's just stupid of you to think so."

"You're right."

She was getting ready to argue, but stopped; her bewildered expression was adorable. "I'm right?"

I couldn't wait another second to kiss her, taking her mouth as my tongue slipped between her lips to taste her. The kiss ended way sooner than either of us wanted when two paramedics dropped down next to us.

"Can you tell me what happened?" One of them asked me while the other splinted Avery's arm.

"She was pulled over the side of the pier."

It was only then that I looked over and saw the man who had dragged Avery over the side. He was lucky he was dead because I would have killed him.

"Did you lose consciousness?" The paramedic asked Avery.

"I don't know."

"Let me check your eyes." He flashed the light, a few times in each eye. "Equal and reactive. Anywhere else hurt besides your arm?"

"No."

"Any dizziness, shortness of breath, headache."

"No."

"I think you were very lucky, but we're going to take a ride to the ER and let the docs take a look at you."

Her free hand grabbed for mine. "Rafe, please don't leave me."

"I'm not going anywhere."

Three hours later, Avery still hadn't been checked out of the ER. Not long after we arrived, several other ambulances pulled up with accident victims. Since Avery's injuries were not life threatening, she had been made comfortable while the doctors took care of the critical patients.

Nat had privileges at the hospital so somehow arranged for several of us to be in the room with Avery. I hadn't left her side, her hand being held in mine.

She looked tired, but other than that you wouldn't know she'd just gone through the harrowing scene she had. "How are you feeling, sweetheart?"

There was that look again, fucking loved how soft her eyes went hearing that word. She was feeling feisty though when she answered, "I'm good considering my failed attempt at flying."

I was glad she could joke about it because I sure as hell didn't find anything funny about seeing her going over the side of that pier. That image wouldn't be fading for a long fucking time.

"What happened after I fell? Marco had mentioned that your mom gave up Nicholas, a warrant for his arrest was being issued from information supplied by her."

Dad answered since I hadn't a clue. My focus had been solely on her. "Lexie's security team, along with the cops, descended on the scene. Titus was outnumbered, his leverage gone, so he surrendered."

"How did she know where we were?" Avery asked and I knew Dad felt as I did on that account. Fucking furious.

"She was the one who sent me the disc, the puppet master pulling the strings. You mentioned the disc was in the clock?"

"Yeah."

"Fuck me." The 'A Friend' I'd been writing to for most of my life had been my mother. Too bad that act of kindness was completely negated when she knowingly pulled Avery and Nat into her drama.

"What don't we know?" Dad asked.

"I've been writing to her most of my life."

Dad's jaw clenched. "Too little too late."

Avery looked from Dad to me. "What do you mean puppet master?"

"She sent me that clock with the disc even knowing what it was and who was after it. She didn't give me a heads up or a warning and even after Nat was taken, where the hell was she?"

Avery's face paled even as anger turned her eyes bright. "Do you think she knew about Nat?"

"How else was she there at that pier?"

Avery's expression changed, sympathy coming off her now as she turned her attention to Dad. "I'm so sorry, Liam."

He didn't answer, only lowered his head, but I felt the weight of his pain from where I stood.

Nat, who had been wrapped in Tyler's arms, moved from her spot. "Avery, are you okay?"

She suddenly looked really pale. "Baby, what's wrong?"

"My head hurts."

"How long have you had a headache?"

"Not long. I just need to lie down, Nat."

I thought Avery was teasing, but she didn't look to be teasing. In fact, she looked confused. Nat said, "Sweetie, you are lying down."

Dark circles had formed under her eyes.

"Are you dizzy?" Nat asked.

"A little."

Nat looked over at me, worry coming off her in waves. "We need the doctor."

"I'll get him." Tyler said and hurried from the room.

"Nat, what's going on?"

"Blows to the head are tricky. It's this lucid period that throws people off because they think they're okay and then they crash."

"I think I left the stove on. Oh God, Loki's there. I have to go check on him." The words were barely out of her mouth before Avery started pulling at the needle in her arm.

Grabbing her hands, I held them in mine. "Avery, baby, Loki's fine."

She looked at me like she hadn't seen me in a while. A smile spread over her face and yet staring into her eyes, ice formed in my blood. Something was wrong. "Rafe. When did you get here?"

"Nat, what the hell is going on?"

"We need that doctor now." Running to the door, she practically bellowed at the nurses. "Possible epidural hematoma. The patient is crashing."

When Nat returned to Avery's side, she wasn't the sister, but the doctor. My next words were barely audible. "What does that mean, she's crashing?"

"We need at CT scan because her brain could be swelling and if we don't stop it, it could kill her."

Her words didn't immediately penetrate because Avery's fall hadn't seemed significant enough to cause that kind of trauma. How the hell could she be at risk of dying? She had been fine just ten minutes ago. But I couldn't deny she didn't look so good right now, she was fading.

"What time is it? I have work." Avery's words were slurred even as she grew agitated.

"You don't have work today, sweetie." Nat tried to soothe her, but it wasn't working because Avery was trying again to remove the needle from her arm.

I didn't want to hurt her, but I didn't want her hurting herself. I reached for her, and then she just stopped, her hands dropped, her eyes rolled into the back of her head and she fell back onto her pillow.

"What the fuck just happened?"

The doctor arrived, Nat was talking rapidly, nurses came running in and seconds later Avery was being wheeled out of the room.

"She's going to be okay." I heard Nat's voice, but it sounded as if it was coming from a very far distance. Her words meaningless because all I could think about was Avery and the thought of losing her. I never saw her coming and now I couldn't imagine life without her.

"I'm observing the surgery. She's going to be fine. I'll be out just as soon as I can." She touched my face. "She's going to be okay."

"If you hadn't been here." And that's what I couldn't get my head around. We were in the fucking hospital and yet if Nat hadn't kept a close eye on Avery, we could have lost her. "But I was. I'll be out just as soon as I can." She hugged Anna, Harold and Tyler and then hurried off down the hall.

Standing in that waiting room, I understood Trace's aversion to the place. How could you voluntarily enter a place that housed the very worst of your memories? And yet he was here.

A woman came running into the ER, a man and little boy just behind her.

"How's Avery?" Tears were streaming down her face.

Anna rushed to her. "Oh, Jessica. She's in surgery. We don't know anything just yet."

"She's going to be okay though, right?"

"Yes, honey. She's going to be okay." But Anna wasn't sure, not even Nat was sure. The brain was a delicate thing and even if Avery lived, she could have suffered brain damage.

I hadn't realized that Jessica had come to stand right in front of me until she spoke. "You're Rafe."

"Yeah."

She smiled, which I thought was extremely inappropriate for the moment. And then she said, "She got to you."

My words nearly got stuck in my throat because she really had. "Yes she did."

"You're in love with her."

"Yes, I am."

"And she's in love with you. I've never heard her as happy as she's been these past couple months." She then reached for my hand. "She'll get through this. Surely you know by now, Avery is tenacious."

And even during my lowest moment, thoughts of Avery made

me smile.

A little while later, Dad came to stand at my side. "You need anything."

"Just Avery."

"I'm not going to lie and tell you everything is going to be okay, because we don't know that. But I will say, whatever happens, we'll get through it. I'm here for you, son."

The reality of a world without Avery was crushing. I wasn't sure I wanted to get through it, if that meant a lifetime without her.

Ember and Trace approached, cups of coffee in their hands. I took one absently, didn't taste it when I took a sip.

"You want anything to eat?" Ember asked softly.

"No, thanks."

"She'll find her way back. She has a lot to live for."

And coming from someone who had, I believed her. "Thanks, Ember."

She moved away to check on Anna and Harold. Trace stayed where he was. "I know what you're going through, and I'm so fucking sorry you have to, but Avery's tougher than she looks. She'll beat this."

"How can you stand being here, being forced to remember?"

Trace looked over at Ember. "Because I do remember how close I came to losing her. I'm here for you brother. We all are."

And then a movement from the nurse's station caught my eye. It was Nat and she was crying but they were happy tears because she was smiling. Relief so profound nearly brought me to my knees. Closing the distance, Nat grabbed my hands, her smile growing even bigger. "She's fine, Rafe. She's awake."

Thank fucking God. "Is she talking?"

"Amazingly, she is. There may be motor function issues that she'll need therapy for, but her speech wasn't impaired from the surgery. Her first words…'she's buying the fucking Camaro. Life is too short.'"

My response was unconsciously done. I roared with laughter and realized the rest of the waiting room was too.

chapter twenty—six

Avery

Rafe walked into my room and I had never seen a sight more beautiful. "Hey."

He surprised me when he settled on the chair beside me and pressed his face in my stomach. Rafe McKenzie was crying, again.

"I'm fine, Rafe. Really. I mean I have a headache and I broke my damn arm which means not even celery is going to help me perform my work—"

I didn't get to finish because his mouth was on mine, his salty tears flavoring the kiss, his tongue plunging deep into my mouth—savoring.

His lips were still on mine when he said, "I love you."

Everything inside me went gooey. "I love you."

And then I remembered Titus, that bastard. "Where's Titus?"

"He's been arrested."

"And Marco?"

"Dead."

"Asshole pulled me over the side. I mean, in a way it's kind of cool that I was light enough to go over with him, but still."

Rafe's shoulders shook and I wasn't sure of the cause until his head lifted and laughing eyes looked down at me. "Even with your ass."

"What?"

"You said that, after, how easily you were dragged over, even with your ass."

I vaguely remembered that, but then I remembered what Nat said after the surgery and now I was getting pissed again. "They shaved part of my hair, I'm bald in the back."

"You could be completely bald and you'd still be beautiful."

"That's not going to work, Rafe. You love my hair."

He turned serious, the smile fading from his face. "I could have lost you. You're alive, Avery. I don't care if your hair ever grows back."

The high I'd been on crashed, the humor I used to hold back the reality of what had happened died as my body shook and tears burned my eyes. Rafe seeing the change somehow managed to climb into bed with me without messing up the tubes and wires. When he pulled me close, I sighed. "Don't let go." I whispered.

He held me tighter. "Never."

RAFE

Dad and I had been called down to the police station. The detectives were closing Nat's kidnapping case; Alexandra had been in with the detectives fine-tuning the case against her dad and Nicholas. She asked to talk to Dad and me, wanted to explain. Jax gave us one of the interrogation rooms. Dad stood by the door, his thoughts his own. I sat across from the woman who was my mother and felt nothing except fury that her shit almost cost me Avery, but unlike Dad, I had questions.

"Who was Jeremy Paddington?"

"He was the man my father hired to run a phone tap on Nicholas's phone. Dad wanted to get proof of Nicholas ordering the hit on Dominic Bennett, a partner in Morton Shipping who became a liability."

"And Nicholas Titus?"

"My father needed his money to get the company off the ground. Marrying me off to the man was his attempt at keeping a measure of control over him. Nicholas only agreed to the wedding because my father had put a large portion of his buy-in for the company in my name for tax purposes. Married to me, Nicholas had access to those shares."

"Jeremy ended up dead and I'm guessing that wasn't a coincidence."

"I wanted leverage, so I approached Jeremy sometime after he'd cut the deal with Dad. He was holding the disc in a security box, at the request of my father. I wanted it, so I paid him for it and he was all too happy to take my money. But then he quit, now floating on a sizable amount of money and since Dad had been holding the evidence over Nicholas' head, it didn't take much for Nicholas to put two and two together, especially after his source confirmed Jeremy had taken out the security box shortly before he quit his job. Nicholas had Jeremy killed and then he arranged the bank job."

"Lucas approaching Dad, who set that up?"

"Nicholas. He was trying to keep me in line by coming at both of you. After Liam was sent away, he told me he'd focus on you if I didn't toe the line. I tried to stay in touch, even got you into St. Agnes, but it was the most I dare do."

"When did you learn the disc had been corrupted?"

"After I paid Jeremy for it, I hired Prescott and his security firm to help me expose my father and husband, they were the ones to discover the disc was useless. No one but the team and me knew that, so I kept my silence. Lucas and Jackson ended up dead, Nicholas tying up loose ends. He intended to kill you too, but then you turned yourself in. With the disc missing and the only other person involved in jail, Nicholas thought he was in the clear."

"Then Dad gets out of jail and Nicholas resumes the search for the disc before Dad could use it against him."

"Nicholas is arrogant and believes he's invincible. I don't think he's even thought about that disc in years, however he learned recently that an arrest warrant was pending. My father is dying and for once in his life he's doing the right thing. He's a ruthless man but he loves his company and seeing it, year after year, pulling farther away from him, skirting and stepping over the lines of legal practices all pioneered by Nicholas, my father has agreed to testify against him. His motivation is selfish, because his ultimate goal is seeing the company publicly traded. I think he's being naïve to believe that will still happen, but he wants to try even knowing his testimony will shine guilt on him as well. Unlike Nicholas though, my father won't live to serve his sentence. Nicholas was scrambling to find the disc—why he took Natalie—so father's testimony regarding the murder would be hearsay. He doesn't realize the disc is useless. He really believes destroying the disc will save him from seeing the inside of a jail cell since he's convinced the other charges won't amount to anything. He's very wrong about that."

"What do you have on them?" I asked.

"Laundering, insider trading, a bevy of other white collar crimes. He's going away for a long time."

"Why did you send the disc to me, especially since it is useless?"

"It seemed the safest with you. Hindsight, I never would have sent it to you and placed you in the middle. I'm very sorry. I had thought to retrieve the disc, approached Avery that night at Clover with the intent of doing so, but I was afraid to draw more attention especially since we were getting so close to nailing Nicholas."

"And yet when Nat was taken, you still didn't step in. He was holding her at gunpoint and a call from you would have found us that disc sooner than later and yet you said nothing. I really need to understand why?"

She had the sense to look contrite and yet there was belligerence coming off her too. "I had lived in Hell for so long. I wanted them both to pay. And with the disc being useless, Prescott and his team had to build the cases against them. It took time and tons of resources, but we were so close to nailing them I didn't want to risk screwing that up."

My hands slamming down on the desk had her jumping back in her chair. "So you gambled with Nat's life so you could get payback."

"It wasn't like that—"

Dad's voice shook the room. "It was exactly like that, but even more disgusting is you were the one who led Nicholas to Rafe. You baited your husband by telling him exactly where that disc was, knowing it was out of his reach. You enjoyed making him squirm, and you put your son and his friends in harm's way. And who's next in line to take over the company with your dad and husband out of the picture?"

A sickening sensation soured my stomach that this woman, my mother, could be so calculating. "Is that true?"

Her non-answer was all the answer I needed. The apple didn't fall far from that tree. Bad enough, worse that my dad had to learn the truth about the woman he'd spent over half of his life loving.

His pain was masked behind rage when he continued, "I tried to make allowances for you, giving up your son, leaving me, staying away, but you are a grown-ass woman. Your father may have played you, your husband as well, but you're not stupid. They're both behind bars and you're sitting on top of an empire. So don't try selling either of us the bullshit that you didn't have a choice, that you feared for Rafe so you stayed with your husband. You had the choice; you made the wrong one. You wanted revenge more than you wanted your family. What little you did do for Rafe is totally canceled out by the harm you brought to Natalie and Avery." He moved closer to Alexandra, his hand fisting as he struggled to control his rage. "I sought you out, asked you what was going on and if Rafe was in any real danger. You assured me he wasn't. And you fucking knew it was lie, but it slid off your tongue with remarkable ease."

"What?"

"The accident at the garage. I was distracted because I was talking to your mother. Josh got me a number because knowing the link this had to her family, after the break in at your place, I called her and asked her if we needed to be concerned and she lied. It's a real kick in the ass to learn the woman you've spent your life in love with doesn't even exist. At least now, I can put you where you belong, in the past and move on with my life."

Dad's eyes shifted to me. "We've spent enough time in the sewer son, let's go home."

$\mathcal{A}$very

Mom was hovering and as much as I loved my mom, I really could do without the hovering. I was back at Rafe's, settled on the sofa. And like when Nat had been taken, the house was filled with people and food but unlike then, this was all about family and love and just exactly what we all needed. Well, all but Mom's hovering. I was to rest, the doctor said I should slowly introduce walking, but considering I had someone playing around in my head, the side effects from the surgery were minimal. And still Mom hovered.

"I'm fine, Mom."

"I know, but I need to do this. Need to be close until it sinks in that you are here and fine."

"I was lucky Nat had been in that room with me." And I had been because when I started to crash, it happened really fast. Had Nat not been watching me like a hawk, I wouldn't be sitting here with my mom doting on my every need.

Mom stopped fluffing pillows, teary eyes looked into mine. "I know."

I already knew the answer but I asked it anyway. "Did Dad come to the hospital?"

"No."

Mom looked about ready to level the house, she was furious. "Does he know?"

"I called him when you were in surgery, left a message since I couldn't get through."

"Nat was kidnapped, I had brain surgery. It's been over a week and the man hasn't visited or called?"

"The man is an asshole."

As hard as I tried to see more in him, there really wasn't more to him. He and Dolly deserved each other.

"Nat and I are lucky we have you and Harold."

"Family doesn't always have to be blood, sometimes the strongest bonds are forged from those not at all related to you."

Looking around the house, to the family we were lucky enough to be pulled into, she wasn't wrong.

"Where's Nat?"

"Walking Loki with Tyler."

"I like Tyler."

Mom smiled. "I like him too."

My cell buzzed and reaching for it, my heart leapt because it was my dad. "Hello."

"Avery."

"Dad."

"I heard you were in some kind of accident. Are you okay?" And though I was happy to hear from him, despite knowing better, he also sounded distracted like he was doing something else. Maybe I was being selfish, but when one of your daughters was kidnapped and the other needed brain surgery it deserved a father's undivided attention, even if that attention only lasted a few minutes.

"Are you busy?" I asked.

"I'm always busy and since I have to now arrange a baby shower, I'm even busier."

Oh my God, he did not just try to guilt me because I wasn't planning his wife's baby shower in the same call he was apparently showing concern for my 'little accident'. I couldn't make this shit up if I tried.

"I'm sorry, are you implying that I am somehow responsible for the fact that you have to plan the shower of the woman you got knocked up?"

"Avery, don't be rude."

"Do you realize that your one daughter was held against her will at gunpoint and your other daughter was tossed off a pier that result-ed in an epidural hematoma that would have killed me if Nat hadn't been there?"

"What the hell are you talking about? Nat was held at gunpoint? Your mom didn't mention that."

"Did she mention the hospital?"

"Yeah, but—"

I hadn't realized I was now shouting and had gained the attention of everyone; I was too flabbergasted by my father's callousness to even care. "I'm sorry, let me just make sure I have this right. Mom called you, even though she was experiencing the worst moment of her life, and because she didn't detail it out for you why I was in the hospital, the fact that I was in the hospital didn't warrant a visit or, dare I say, a phone call. I'm happy to hear that if you knew about the kidnapping that might have instigated a phone call, but it's been eight days since my surgery and you call, distracted with something else, and being very half-assed about your concern for me while laying guilt on me because I don't wish to be played by your social climbing, white-trash wife. Do I have this correct?"

He was mad now, but not at himself. "I don't like you speaking about my wife that way."

"And I don't like that you weren't here, didn't drop everything to be with your children in their time of need. I don't like your wife and I don't like you either. I have spent my life trying to get you to notice me, but Nat's right, I have to scrape you off because you will never notice me. I really do hope you get your head out of your ass for your new baby's sake because you suck as a father. Harold has been way more of a father to Nat and me than you ever were. Hell, even Liam has been more a father to me and I just met the man. Get your act together because your new kid isn't going to have the fabulous mother Nat and I did. Do it for that innocent baby who doesn't ever need to know that her father is worthless and selfish because you and me, Dad, we're done. Have a nice life, don't call again."

Disconnecting the call, I threw my phone across the room. Mom settled on one side of me, Nat the other. Rafe stood across the room and though I could see he wanted to come to me, he deferred to my family.

"You okay, honey?" Mom asked as she tucked my hair behind my ear.

"He's an asshole. A miserable, selfish asshole."

"Yes, he is." Nat said, which had my attention shifting to her. "You were right."

"I usually am."

And despite being angrier than I'd ever been, my goofy sister made me laugh.

Rafe and I were walking Loki. The house was filled with people and I loved having them there, but this now, just the two of us, I craved it. He was even more attentive now than he'd been, which I didn't think was possible. I understood. Nat and I had talked about the hospital and how I had just faded and fast. Rafe had witnessed that and putting myself in his shoes, I'd be acting exactly as he was now. It had been a month since the surgery and I had been very lucky. We'd resumed my walks with Loki just the other day and considering I had had brain surgery, my recover had been astounding. Due to the surgery, Jess and family postponed their trip and were coming later today. I couldn't wait to see her. I vaguely remembered her in the hospital. Mom and Harold hadn't left and Nat and Tyler were popping over all the time, it was like they had never left too.

My hand was being held in Rafe's strong one and if I moved too far from his side, he tugged me closer. Wishing to ease his mind, since I suspected his thoughts were on the scene in the hospital, I decided to tease him.

"I'm grateful for this walk, I need the exercise. I fear my ass may have grown in the past month." Even though I was teasing, there was a vein of truth in my words. I hadn't curtailed my sweets consumption, but I hadn't been moving around to help balance it out.

He grinned, that wickedly, naughty grin I adored. "Your ass is perfect."

It wasn't, but I loved that he thought so. My humor faded thinking about Alexandra. I'd gotten the cliff notes version and still I was livid that his mother had not only been complicit in what had happened but had set it all in motion. And even knowing that she meant nothing to Rafe, she had meant a great deal to Liam. How hard it had to be for him to realize the kind of person the woman he loved was.

"I'm sorry about Alexandra, that she turned out to be no better than her father."

"I never gave her much thought, but it came as a blow to Dad. I think he's dealing, probably better than I would in his shoes, but still. He's wasted a lot of energy on her."

"Do you really think her end goal was to get the company?"

"I do."

"Unbelievable, but on the bright side, it's something else we have in common?"

His head dipped, his eyes finding mine. "How so?"

"We each have one kick-ass parent and one really awful parent."

He stopped walking and turned into me. Cradling my face in his hands, he just looked his fill. "Are you ever going to wear your hair down?"

"Not while I'm bald in back."

"You aren't bald. It's the smallest area."

"My scalp is visible, I'm bald."

"Goof." But as I watched, his easy smile vanished, his eyes looked haunted. "Seeing you in the hospital, watching as you slowly lost consciousness, the fear that I'd have a lifetime ahead of me learning to live without you." He caressed my cheek with his thumb, "I love you, Avery. I think I might need to say that often for the next few months until the knot in my stomach eases and reality settles that you're here and you're fine."

Tears stung my eyes, happy tears because I had never felt as cherished as I did in that moment. He wiped away the one that rolled down my cheek. "Hearing you tell me you love me, repeatedly, yeah, let me work up an objection."

The memory had a smile touching his lips even as they lowered to brush over mine. "Cocoa. I love the way you smell. When we get the house back, I've still to make good on my promise."

I wasn't following him because I was still caught in the magic of the moment. "What promise?"

"We haven't made love in the barn, or the garage. The dryer, when it's on, could be fun."

Now I was feeling an entirely different kind of warmth. "I like this plan."

"It's getting late. Let's go home and I'll make you an omelet."

That memory brought a smile to my face. "Sounds perfect."

"I had planned to do more with you, Jessica. I'm sorry I'm not much fun."

"Are you serious?" Jessica looked over at my sister as we swung on the swing Rafe had made me. "Did the doc take out part of her brain?"

"I told him it wouldn't make a difference, but he kept it intact."

"Nice." I muttered even as I chuckled.

Jess reached for my hand, "I shouldn't joke. It isn't funny."

"It's a little funny." I said.

"How are you both? It all seems so unbelievable, terrifying and yet you look oddly calm."

"It was terrifying, all of it. I'll be haunted for a good long time, but it's over and everyone made it out okay." Eventually the night-mares and the panic that came over me out of nowhere would stop, but Rafe didn't let me deal alone, held me until I calmed. Made love to me when I woke in terror. I'd find my way with him.

Nat rested her head on my shoulder. "We never had this kind of excitement at home."

"How's Rafe?" Jess asked.

"I think he's okay. He doesn't talk about it, outside of the danger I put myself in. I think he's still trying to get his head around all of it—my downward spiral that nearly took me from him, Alexandra and how the reality of her is a huge disappointment for his dad."

"I really hoped for the happily-ever-after for them." That surprised me because Nat wasn't really a happily-ever-after kind of gal. She knew what I was thinking when she added, "Well, it would have been sweet. Rafe gets his mom, Liam gets the woman he loves."

"You're right, it would have been, but she's nowhere near good enough for Liam or Rafe."

Rafe appeared, strolling from his barn with Tyler.

"I seriously get why you sit here." Nat said. "What a view."

"Yes it is."

Rafe's gaze caught mine, like he knew we were talking about him, and the look he gave me was similar to the one I'd seen Kit give Jess—unequivocal love. My heart was pounding so hard it really should have beat right out of my chest.

"Damn, that is a great look." Jess whispered. "Must be nice to have that look directed at you."

Her comment was so ridiculous my head jerked to her. "Are you serious? Do you know how many times I've watched Kit give you a similar look?"

She did know; her smile conveyed both humor and sincerity. "I know. I'm just happy you have someone looking at you like that."

And then the gates opened. "Are you expecting someone?" Nat asked.

"No."

A heartbeat later, Maleficent rolled up the drive with a big red bow on her.

"Are you seeing this?" I asked, just to be sure my eyes weren't playing tricks on me.

"Boy gets serious points for that." Nat said, then added, "No Spark. Thank Christ."

I elbowed her in the ribs.

The man that drove Maleficent climbed out and strolled to me dangling the keys from his fingers. "Avery Collins?"

"Yes."

"Congratulations."

It was unconsciously done, my hand raising to take them. My attention turned to Rafe who appeared at my side, his hands in the front pocket of his jeans, his focus on the car. "Did you buy me this car?"

"I did."

Just when I thought I couldn't love the man more. I loved the car; never had I received such a gift, made even more fabulous because Rafe gave it to me. And still it was a moral imperative that I give the man a hard time. "I was getting the basic model."

"And I wanted you to have this one. Don't worry, I took your mom and she haggled a good price."

I tried to put my hands on my hips but with the cast, it didn't look as effective. "Rafe McKenzie."

"Avery Collins. You love this car; you know that you do. I love you. I bought you the car. So shut up, kiss me and get in."

Nat and Jessica both howled—yes howled—with laughter. "Let's go check on our boys, Jess." Nat said, still laughing at me as she and Jessica headed inside.

My feet wouldn't move because even knowing Rafe loved me, having heard him say it repeatedly since the ordeal, it still hit me right in the chest that all that was Rafe McKenzie loved me.

Seeming to understand my temporary case of paralysis, he swept me into his arms. "Because of the cast, I'll drive."

"Okay."

"Are you going to give me more grief about the car?"

"No, I love it, more so because you bought it for me."

"Good."

He settled me into the passenger seat, clicked on my belt, and then kissed me, long and hard. Once he folded himself behind the wheel, I had to admit he looked damn fine in this car. "You look good in this car."

The pad of his thumb brushed my lower lip, I nipped it with my teeth, and his eyes went from emerald to forest green in a heartbeat. "Not sure you're ready to christen your car, but you keep looking at me like that and you're going to have to be ready."

Oh my God, the thought of sex in this car with Rafe. I'd probably pull every muscle and dislocate a few things and yet that was now on the top of my to-do list.

"Once everyone leaves, we are so having sex in this car, on this car, near this car."

"Fuck, now I'm hard."

"I need a shower and I can't get my cast wet. After our ride, you could always help me." I offered as I wiggled my eyebrows.

Rafe growled. "Deal. Now let's see what this baby can do."

Rafe was baking me a cake because I was craving something sweet. I offered to help; he said I needed to rest. Mom and Nat joined him as the three of them banged around in Rafe's kitchen. Jessica sat with me while Kit and Aidan played catch with Harold and Tyler.

I was getting restless, hated being idle. "I wish I could work, I hate not being able to get my hands dirty."

"Give yourself time, you've been through a lot. I'm sure your boss agrees."

"He does, Trace has been wonderful and my sous chefs are fantastic, handling things until I get back. I'm still going in for staff meetings and to set the menu but then my team makes it happen. Hopefully not too well that everyone will realize I'm not necessary."

"Nonsense. I like Rafe."

"You've mentioned that, repeatedly."

"No, I mean, I really like him for you. Seeing him in the hospital that day, the look on his face when he thought you might be taken from him. I don't think I'll ever get that look out of my head."

My heart hurt even as tears burned the back of my eyes. "I'm glad I didn't see that look."

Jess strived to lighten the mood when she added, "And you complement each other, plus the man adores you because even now he's attempting to bake you a cake because you're jonesing for one. Most men would just run to the store."

I had taken stock of how lucky I was and I was lucky—a very, very lucky girl. "Not only did I find my dream job, I found my dream guy. It's like having my cake and eating it too."

"I just knew this adventure was going to lead you to everything you always wanted. I'm so happy for you."

Resting my head on her shoulder, I wiped at my eyes. "I'm so glad you're here."

Rafe appeared then, Mom and Nat right behind him; both had bright eyes and were looking at me like their brains had dripped from their ears again. Rafe was carrying a plate with a chocolate cupcake on it, the white icing swirling up about two inches from the cake. It looked delicious.

"That looks amazing. You made that?"

He didn't say anything just approached and hunched down, holding the plate out in front of him. He looked adorable, flour and chocolate on his tee and jeans. I wanted to eat him, almost said as much but not with my mom looking on. So I shifted my focus to the cupcake and I immediately forgot how to breathe as my eyes landed on the diamond ring settled in the icing. And scrolled in raspberry sauce around the cupcake were the words. "Marry me."

Tears rolled down my cheeks, his eyes looked a little bright too. There were so many things I wanted to say and yet when I opened my mouth only one word came out. "Yes."

He took the ring from the cupcake and handed the plate to Jessica and then he put my ring in his mouth; yes, he licked off the icing before slipping the ring on my finger. Lacing his fingers through my hair, he lowered his head and touched his lips to mine—a light brushing before he took the kiss deeper, his tongue stroking my own; the sweetness of the icing still on his tongue.

Lying in bed, I studied the brilliant cut stone Rafe had placed on my finger. It was exquisite, three carats at least. I couldn't stop looking at it because I couldn't quite believe I was engaged to Rafe. He entered the room, wearing only his jeans—a sight I had dreamed about seeing—Loki at his side. He'd been locking up the house. In his hand he held the cupcake that I never ate because I had been too excited.

"Thought you might want this now."

"We can share."

He handed me the cupcake before he stripped from his jeans. The cupcake was completely forgotten having all of that magnificence in my sights. Climbing into the bed he took the cupcake from me, dipped his finger into the icing and held it up to my mouth. Eating all the sugary goodness from Rafe's finger was decadent, hell, being with Rafe felt decadent—indulgent and addictive.

Swiping a dollop of icing, I held my finger to his lips; he sucked it into his mouth, his tongue swirling around the tip.

"Avery McKenzie, I like the sound of that." I said, my eyes on his mouth.

He moved, forcing me to my back as he settled between my legs. "Not as much I do." He took the cupcake and pressed it, icing side down, on my clavicle, running it lower to between my breasts, leaving a sweet, sugary trail in its wake. Then he held it to my mouth and I took a bite.

"We'll eat this cupcake." He said, holding the cupcake to my lips again. "And then I'll eat you."

"This is a good plan."

A softness came into his expression, a sort of reverence. Love looked back at me as did tenderness and awe. "Mine."

My heart really should have split it was so full.

And then he kissed me, so sweetly. Yep, being with Rafe was decadent so beautifully decadent.

EPILOGUE

RAFE

The far back of my property twinkled in white fairy lights; that's what Avery called them when she had strung them up last week. She'd used a ladder; one I had built for her that was sturdy but light-weight so she had no excuse to risk broken limbs to hang anything. Of course she'd have me now and just the thought of her being mine settled very comfortably in my chest.

"You ready?" Trace asked as he, Dad, Lucien and I stood near the carriage house, also lit in fairy lights. It was my wedding day. Six weeks from the day I had asked her to marry me. The woman didn't want to wait. I was happy for that because I didn't want to wait either. I wanted my other ring on her finger, wanted her last name to be my last name. I would have had guilt depriving her of a big wedding, but I would have, so it was lucky all the way around that she was as eager as me to make it official.

"I think I was ready for this moment the second I stepped out of the barn and saw Avery hugging my dog."

Trace placed his hand on my shoulder. "I'm happy for you."

"Is she taking it easy at work?"

She had gotten the all clear from the docs to return to work. I wanted her home, wanted her to rest some more, but she was itchy and I got that. I don't think I'd have handled being unable to work for almost three months as well as she had. Even so, I didn't want her to overdo it.

"You know Avery. She goes all in, but Lee and Tina are handling it well, doing more of the work because she does get tired more easily these days."

"I've noticed that."

Trace grinned. Lucien said, "You know there is a reason why women get tired, sleep more, eat more."

It hit me like a sledgehammer, more the reality that I really wanted *that* to be the reason she was tired all the time. "She would have told me."

"She might not know. Avery's adorable, you know I love her, son, but she's a bit spacey."

A grin pulled at my mouth because my sweet Avery was spacey. "I call it goofy."

"That works too."

"Pregnant. I'll have to sneak out later for one of those tests."

Trace added, "If she is, once you've done your celebrating, Ember and Darcy are going to be all over that. Anna is going to have her hands full with everyone jumping in to help."

Dad laughed, "And she'll love every second."

The thought that Avery was carrying my child, I almost wanted the day over so we could do our own celebrating. But thinking of the parade of women that had made my home theirs in the past few months continuing for the next several would likely turn me batshit crazy. "I've already had every female relation in this house. Just when I think I'm going to have Avery all to myself, they descend to talk about flowers, gowns even wedding colors. I never knew a wedding actually had official colors. And the cake, they had to sample the cake...all of them. My head's spinning." But the cake was a work of art. Avery had outdone herself with the five-tiered confection, draped in gum paste flowers and the cake itself was lemon chiffon with a whipped lemon curd filling. Fucking delicious.

"Ember could have worn sweats, as long as she said I do, I didn't give a damn. But remembering her on our wedding day, yeah it was worth the time apart."

"He's right. Darcy and my wedding was simple like this, but trust me, brother, when you see her coming toward you, all of that shit will have been worth it."

Standing there I appreciated the irony of a man who had grown up as a quasi-orphan and had learned to prefer solitude and now I couldn't imagine a day passing where I didn't hear Avery laughing or complaining about the plight of the short person. Or seeing my dad, a man who I'd lost for so long and now he lived in the carriage house and worked alongside me crafting memories through wood. Or the parade of women that came through my home, led by Nat and Anna. I wouldn't change one thing.

The music started, the small procession came from the house, Ember and Faith, Darcy and Emily, Jessica, Nat and Loki, with a pillow on his back holding the rings. And then Avery appeared with Harold and Anna and my breath stilled. She literally took my breath away. Her white gown looked like one of her confections, full with a hint of sparkle. Her hair, which had grown part of the way back, was pulled back from her face with flowers tucked in it. In her hands were white roses, with pink tips. But it was the smile; the serene smile directed only at me, that had my chest growing tight as love and possession filled me. She reached my side; the urge to pull her to me almost had me doing so.

Harold lifted her veil and kissed her cheek, her mom kissed the other, before he placed Avery's hand in mine. The magnitude of the moment, the significance of that act I'd seen done at countless weddings, was staggering. They were giving her into my care, but I knew as I stood there with her small hand in mine, that it was I being given into her care. She had stolen my heart. Her fingers curled around my hand and I did pull her close, right up against me.

"You look exquisite." I whispered.

"So do you."

"Are you ready?"

"So ready."

They were the last words I remembered, the rest of the night went by in a blur, a really fucking fantastic blur.

That night, I leaned up against the wall while Avery was in the bathroom. She called through the closed door. "I can't believe I didn't even think of that."

As soon as everyone left, I ran out for a pregnancy test. When I had mentioned it to Avery earlier, her expression was priceless and goofy. She hadn't a clue.

"I just assumed it was a side effect of the brain surgery."

I hated when she mentioned that, hated thinking about how close we had come; I supposed in a sense it was good to remember so I'd never take her for granted. Not that I ever would.

"So?" She had been in there longer than the three minutes.

"I can't pee with an audience."

Lowering my head, I grinned. Adorable.

Another minute or two past, before the door opened. She looked disappointed and the disappointment I felt at the false alarm actually had my eyes burning a bit. I didn't realize how much I had wanted to see her growing with my child, but now I intended to exhaust countless hours making that wish a reality.

"We'll just have to work really hard to get you pregnant. Long hours, late nights, and early mornings. We can do this, Avery, but you're going to have to go all in."

She laughed, the sound just washing over me. She held up the stick. "I am pregnant, goof."

It took me a minute to process those words and when I had, I lifted her over my shoulder and tossed her on the bed. Before she could catch her breath, I pounced.

"You tease."

Her smile softened, as her palm cupped my cheek. "We're going to have a baby."

"I hope it's a girl."

"I hope it's a boy."

"Thank you."

Her brow furrowed. "For what?"

"Finding me. Showing me I was going through the motions but I wasn't living. Thank you for turning my house into a home."

Her eyes grew soft, a tear slid down her cheek that I wiped away with my thumb. "How'd I do that?" she asked.

"By just being you."

She was trying really hard not to cry. Her breath hitched before she whispered, "You're my home too."

"One kid is great, but I want more than one so we should practice so we're ready for when it counts."

"And you call me the goof."

"I wasn't kidding, long hours Avery, day and night."

"Stop talking and get on with it."

And so I did, I made love to my pregnant wife—all night and well into the morning.

Nine months later Rafe and Avery both got their wish when Natalie Ann and Cael Liam McKenzie entered the world.

Recipes

Avery's Cheesecake

2.5 lbs. of cream cheese at room temperature
1 ¾ cups sugar
3 tablespoons of all-purpose flour
Zest of 1 lemon
Zest of 1 orange
¼ teaspoon vanilla extract
4 jumbo eggs
2 jumbo egg yolks
¼ cup whipping cream
9-inch springform pan, bottom lined generously with butter and patted with graham cracker crumbs

Heat oven to 500°F. Prepare springform pan. With an electric mixer, beat cream cheese, sugar, flour, orange and lemon zests and vanilla until smooth. Add the eggs and yokes, beating in one at a time, and finally the cream.

Pour the mixture into the prepared springform pan and bake for 10 minutes. Reduce oven temperature to 200-225°F and bake for one hour longer.

Turn oven off and allow cake to cool in oven with door open for about 20 minutes. Take cake out and allow to cool completely. Refrigerate overnight.

Avery's Oil Olives Lavender Cake with Citrus Glaze

For cake...
2 cups all-purpose flour
1 ¾ cups sugar
1 ½ teaspoons kosher salt
½ teaspoon baking soda
½ teaspoon baking powder
1 ¼ cups extra-virgin olive oil
1 ¼ cups whole milk
3 large eggs
1 ½ tablespoons culinary-grade lavender

Preheat oven to 350° F. Butter and flour a deep (2 inches at least) 9-inch pan. Parchment paper bottom.

Using a spice grinder, pulse the lavender until ground. Add to sugar, blending until combined.

In a bowl, combine the flour, lavender-sugar, salt, baking soda and powder. Using an electric mixer with the whisk attachment, whisk the olive oil, milk and eggs. Add the dry ingredients to wet and whisk until combined.

Pour batter into the prepared pan and bake for 1 hour, until the top is golden and inserting a toothpick comes out clean. Transfer to a rack and let cool for 30 minutes.

Run knife around edges and turn cake onto cooling rack.

Citrus Glaze
1 ¼ cups powdered sugar
½ teaspoon finely grated lemon zest
½ teaspoon finely grated orange zest
1 ½ tablespoons fresh orange juice
1 ½ tablespoons fresh lemon juice

Whisk together ingredients and drizzle over top of cooled cake.

Rafe's Spaghetti and Meatballs

Enough to serve Trace, Ember, Lucien and Darcy too.

For sauce...

4-28 ounce cans of whole/peeled tomatoes
1 large onion
1 pack pork ribs
½ cup hearty red wine
3 tablespoons tomato paste
3 tablespoons of garlic
Generous dashes of red pepper flakes, parsley, basil and oregano
Lots of black pepper

For the meatballs...

2.5 lbs ground beef
4 slices of white bread, crust removed, for every 1 pound of ground beef
¼ to ½ cup of buttermilk

½ cup grated Parmesan cheese
1 large onion finely minced
1 tablespoon minced garlic
Generous dashes of red pepper flakes, parsley, basil and oregano
Lots of black pepper

To prepare the meatballs... (**Note:** Make ahead and refrigerate so the meatballs set and won't break apart when you fry them.)

Cube the white bread. In a large bowl add buttermilk and spices to bread. Add the black pepper, enough that your wrist hurts from all the cracking. Add the garlic, onion, cheese and mix until all ingredients are incorporated. Add ground beef and mix until thoroughly blended. Roll out the meatballs, ¼ cup of mixture per meatball. In a preheated Dutch oven, add olive oil and brown the meatballs, 3-4 minutes on one side before flipping over and frying other side for an additional 3-4 minutes. Set meatballs aside.

To prepare sauce...

Remove fat, from meatballs, from Dutch oven. Add oil olive and brown ribs, 2 minutes each side on all four sides. Set ribs aside. Separate whole tomatoes from juice and put juice in a pot over low heat. Add spices and garlic and reduce down by half. Remove seeds from tomatoes and place on a baking sheet, drizzle with olive oil and roast in a 400°F oven for twenty minutes or until edges start turning dark. In a Dutch oven, add minced onions and salt evenly. Sauté onions, scraping bits of meat from bottom of Dutch oven. Add tomato paste to onion and cook until paste turns brownish. Add wine, two tablespoons at first to deglaze pan, meaning to remove any remaining meat pieces from bottom of pan. Add rest of wine and reduce until mixture is thick. Add roasted tomatoes to juice that is reducing, use an immersion blender to break up the large pieces of tomato to make sauce thicker. Add tomatoes to onion/wine mixture and stir well. Add meat to sauce and let simmer. Boil up pasta, toss together and serve.

ACKNOWLEDGEMENTS

Thank you to my beta readers, Ana Kristina, Kimmy, Meredith, Lauren, Michelle, Amber, Helen, Lynnette, Sue, Alyse, Cass, Ailyn, Sarah, Donna, Beth, Markella, Dawn, Andie, Raj and Audrey for taking the time to read and give feedback on Rafe and Avery's story. I love interacting with you and love that you are all over the world and still we've been brought together by the love of books. Thank you!

To my friend, Ben Cornelius, thank you for the carriage house sketches. They add the perfect touch this story.

Melissa Stevens, the Illustrated Author, you rock. The formatting of the paperback is awesome and the typeset graphics are perfect, again. Thank you!

Trish Bacher, Editor in Heels, your attention to the fine detail is incredible. Thank you for your copy editing expertise, as always, you're amazing.

Murphy Rae of Indie Solutions, I adore the cover.

Amber Russell, you totally nailed the title. Thank you.

About the Author

The Beautifully series…
Beautifully Damaged
Beautifully Forgotten
Beautifully Decadent
The Harrington Maine series
Waiting for the One
Just Me
Standalones
His Light in the Dark
A Glimpse of the Dream
Always and Forever
Collecting the Pieces coming November 2016

To learn more about what's coming, follow L.A. Fiore…
https://www.facebook.com/l.a.fiore.publishing
https://www.facebook.com/groups/lafemmefabulousreaders
https://twitter.com/lafioreauthor
https://www.instagram.com/lafiore.publishing

Send her an email at: lafiore.publishing@gmail.com

Or check out her website: www.lafiorepublishing.com